REBEL FEVER

A NOVEL BY

DAVID HEALEY

PublishAmerica
Baltimore

ISBN: 1-4137-0005-5
PUBLISHED BY PUBLISHAMERICA, LLLP
www.publishamerica.com
Baltimore

Printed in the United States of America

To Joanne, for all her love and support

Bearing the bandages, water and sponge,
Straight and swift to my wounded I go,
Where they lie on the ground after the battle brought in,
Where their priceless blood reddens the grass the ground. ...

– Walt Whitman, *The Wound-Dresser*

---

fever ... 1b: any of various diseases of which fever is a prominent symptom ... 2a: a state of heightened or intense emotion or activity b: a contagious usually transient enthusiasm: CRAZE

– Webster's New Collegiate Dictionary

Note to Readers

In the 1860s, even the best-educated doctors could only guess at how disease was spread. Some blamed "vapors" or "miasma of the air" for causing diseases such as yellow fever, cholera and even bubonic plague. Others believed that exposure to the clothing or bedding of the sick was enough to spread disease.

REBEL FEVER was inspired by an actual incident that took place in 1864 when a Confederate physician plotted to start an epidemic in Northern cities using blankets from yellow fever victims.

It was by no means history's first attempt at biological warfare. That distinction probably goes to the Tartars, who catapulted the bodies of bubonic plague victims over the city walls to infect their enemies during the siege of Kaffa in 1346. History says the plague swept the besieged city, which fell to the invaders.

The plague is one of mankind's most ancient and devastating diseases. Huge epidemics of plague have struck three times in history, first in the Roman Empire during the Plague of Justinian in A.D. 542, then in the "Black Death" that swept Europe from 1347 to 1350 and killed 20 million people (roughly one-third of the population), and finally in the 1890s when an epidemic that began in Asia spread around the globe as far as San Francisco, where from 1900 to 1907 there were 288 cases of plague resulting in 207 deaths.

Plague is spread primarily from infected rats to people through the bite of a flea. Scholars speculate that plague came to Europe in 1347 in infected fleas aboard merchant ships arriving from Asia. Once humans are infected, they can develop pneumonic plague, a highly contagious form spread through the air by coughing and sneezing. It's this version of plague that strikes residents of the Irish shantytown Swampoodle in the novel.

With a little imagination, it's possible to see how Jefferson Verville's plot might actually have succeeded, though purely by accident. Fleas can survive for months without feeding and would certainly have been populous in the crates of contaminated clothing and bedding the Russian ship carried from a plague epidemic in China.

Although the plot of this novel is pure fiction, the details of Civil War-era Washington, espionage and military life in the 1860s are drawn from real life. Several of the characters are based on actual persons. There are many excellent accounts of the dismal Washington hospitals that have been helpful in writing this novel, especially Walt Whitman's *Specimen Days*. The National Museum of Civil War Medicine in Frederick, Md., also has a wealth of information about hospital life, 1860s medical treatment, and the doctors and nurses who served the wounded.

Probably what stands out the most when studying Civil War medicine is that medical knowledge was so archaic in the 1860s, while the technology of warfare was extremely modern. Inventions such as the telegraph, submarine, and even the machine gun were employed during the Civil War, but doctors still believed that simply wiping off surgical instruments between operations was enough to prevent disease and infection. Practices such as this resulted in many needless deaths.

Medical knowledge slowly began to catch up. In Scotland as early as 1865, Joseph Lister was experimenting with antiseptic surgery through use of his carbolic solution. In 1874, French scientist Louis Pasteur recommended the boiling of surgical instruments to sterilize them. In 1890, rubber gloves were first used during surgery at Johns Hopkins Hospital in Baltimore. By 1900, when scientists were coming to realize that diseases like yellow fever and bubonic plague were caused by bacteria spread to humans by mosquitoes and fleas, antiseptic methods of surgery were widely in use.

One can't help but wonder how much agony might have been spared Civil War soldiers if the discovery of improved methods of surgery and disease control had only been made by the 1860s. Some historians estimate that of the 600,000 Civil War dead, at least 300,000 died from disease. Conditions and treatment were equally bad in the North and South despite the best efforts of competent real-life doctors on whom the character of Major William Caldwell is based.

As portrayed in this novel, wounded Confederate and Union soldiers often found themselves side by side in the same hospital, comrades in suffering despite being enemies on the battlefield. That fact was not lost on Jonathan Letterman, medical director for the United States Army during the Civil War, who noted at the time, "History teaches us that a wounded and prostrate foe is not then our enemy."

DAVID HEALEY
dfh@delanet.com

Chapter 1

SHARPSBURG, MARYLAND, SEPTEMBER 1862

All Captain William Caldwell could see was blood.

His eyes felt gritty from exhaustion and he closed them, feeling the lids scrape down, refusing to open again.

God, he was tired.

For the past thirty hours he had been sawing bones and sewing up flesh, stopping only to gulp a mug of coffee laced with whiskey. His surgeon's apron was crimson with blood, even his boots were soaked through so that he left bloody footprints whenever he stepped away from his makeshift operating table.

And still the wounded kept coming.

They carpeted the ground in moaning heaps all around the barn that now served as the regimental field hospital. Most of the wounded wore blue, but there were a few gray Confederate uniforms mixed in. The majority of the wounded suffered in silence, although the humid September evening was filled with sobs and cries for water.

Many had died before Caldwell could get to them, and hospital orderlies moved among the wounded, prodding the still bodies to make certain they were dead. Those no longer among the living were carried away and laid in a trench. There were too many dead to dig individual graves.

"Captain?"

The voice sounded distant, like something heard in a dream. It took Caldwell a moment to register that his orderly was speaking to him, and he wondered if he had fallen asleep on his feet. He felt himself swaying and realized his eyes were still shut.

"Can I get you some coffee, sir?" the corporal asked, tugging Caldwell's sleep-starved mind back to the living nightmare inside the barn.

"Yes," Caldwell said, not wanting to open his eyes but knowing he must, praying that the blood would be gone when he did. Even with his eyes closed, he could smell the blood with its coppery stink, like a wet penny. The hard-packed dirt floor of the barn was slippery with it.

"They're bringing more wounded in!" someone called.

Caldwell opened his eyes.

Blood.

The first thing he saw were the three oak planks that served as his operating table, still red from the last operation. The blood was already thickening, turning gummy, like grease in a cooling skillet.

"Wash this table down," he snapped.

"Yes, sir."

A bucket of creek water was produced, and his assistant splashed it across the boards. For a blessed instant, the blood was gone, the gore sloshing off the boards to create a slick, pink-tinged mud under his boots.

The barnyard was a perfect scene from hell, all the result of two huge armies clawing and smashing at each other for two days. Forces under Union General George B. McClellan and Confederate General Robert E. Lee had fought bitterly in the woods and cornfields around the Maryland town of Sharpsburg. Already, the newspapers in New York and Washington City and Richmond were saying that 27,000 men had been killed or wounded. It was an astonishing number of casualties. Whole companies, even entire regiments, had been wiped out and the bodies now lay in the fields like rows of cornstalks felled by a scythe, waiting for the burial details. Surgeons like Caldwell had been left to deal with the men who had been lucky – or unlucky enough – to survive.

Men lay on blankets, staring up at the roughhewn beams overhead, bloody bandages swathing the stumps that had once been their arms and legs. Maggots crawled in some of the open wounds and the soldiers stared in helpless horror as the vermin devoured their flesh. A Catholic priest was bending over a dying Irishman, muttering some holy gibberish in Latin as the man slowly bled to death from the wound in his belly. A dying boy kept pleading, "Mama, Mama, Mama," over and over again and nobody had the courage to tell him to be quiet. Another soldier stared with glassy eyes as an orderly tried to stuff the man's blue entrails back into his abdominal cavity. Caldwell saw it and growled at the orderly to let the soldier die in peace. Everywhere was a smell of unwashed bodies and excrement.

Outside the barn, many more wounded waited for their turn under the surgeon's knife.

"Next!" Caldwell shouted.

Two orderlies slung a wounded soldier onto the table with all the care they might have given a slab of beef. The soldier moaned with pain from a leg wound. He was just a boy, Caldwell noticed, no more than sixteen or seventeen years old, not so much as a whisker on his face. Caldwell blinked rapidly to clear his bleary eyes and force himself awake. He quickly examined the leg, peeling off a rough bandage that was now as hard as tree bark with dried blood.

The wound was bad. A miniè bullet had struck the boy's leg just below the knee, shattering the bones and shredding his flesh. Nearly two days in Maryland's warm fall weather had hastened infection, and as Caldwell surveyed the wound he caught a foul whiff of rotting meat. Gangrene.

"Don't take my leg," the boy pleaded. His eyes were feverish and liquid in the lantern light. "Please don't take my leg."

"Chloroform," Caldwell said, ignoring the boy.

An orderly put a cone of cloth soaked in chloroform over the boy's face and Caldwell had a glimpse of the eyes watching him. Fearful. It was the same look a wounded deer might have before its throat was cut.

"It's only a leg, son," Caldwell managed to mutter. He was thinking of all the bodies out in that trench just beyond the barn. Flies feasting on the eyes. Open mouths that would soon fill with maggots. If the boy didn't join them, he could count himself lucky. "You can live with just one leg."

You might never run again, or ride a horse, or walk behind a plow, thought Caldwell. *But you'll be alive.* He paused for a moment, trying to tally the number of amputations he had performed in this barn. Too many. He closed his eyes, felt the lids rivet shut. His mind began to drift. God, what he would do for a few minutes of sleep–

"Captain?" the orderly again. The corporal had reappeared at his side with a steaming tin mug. Good lad. Despite the two stripes on his sleeve, he was no older than the soldier on the operating table. "Here's your coffee, sir."

"Keep it coming." Caldwell gulped down half the mug of coffee, ignoring the fact that it was scalding hot. He hoped it would keep his senses sharp. The world had taken on a muddled, dream-like quality and Caldwell knew this was the closest he might ever come to operating in his sleep.

His assistant was already cutting away the filthy wool fabric of the soldier's trouser leg. He wrinkled his nose in disgust. "Goddamn! That leg stinks. The whole thing is rotten."

"Hurry up," Caldwell said. This assistant was damn near useless, but camp fever had killed off two of his best men just a week before the battle. "Get the tourniquet on and be quick about it."

As the assistant finished cutting away the trousers and began slipping the leather strap that served as a tourniquet around the wounded boy's thigh, Caldwell took a bottle from another plank nearby that served as his workbench and poured a generous amount of whiskey into his coffee. Whiskey and coffee. It was the only thing getting him through this hell. He drank deeply.

"He's senseless, sir," the assistant with the chloroform said.

"Let's begin, then." Caldwell realized he was dizzy from the effects of exhaustion and whiskey, and he shook his head to clear it. He had no business operating, considering he could barely see straight, but Caldwell knew damn well that he was the only hope for the wounded boys spread all around the barnyard. Better an exhausted surgeon than none at all.

He selected a long, double-edged knife from his surgeon's tools and wiped it quickly on his blood-caked apron. Because the wound had already begun to rot, it was necessary to amputate the leg above the knee. If the boy was lucky, the gangrene had not yet spread that high.

His long, practiced fingers took hold of the top of the boy's thigh and squeezed hard, bunching the muscle up in his hand and pulling it away from the bone. Then he plunged the knife into the gathered flesh and pushed until the tip struck bone. Expertly, he guided the blade up and over the bone, then forced the knife all the way through the leg until the point came out with a spurt of blood on the other side. Caldwell cut up and out until the blade was free. Despite the tourniquet, blood ran in rivers from the butchered leg and the orderly, jumping in to help, swiped at it with a rag already sopping with blood to clear enough of it away so the surgeon could see. Caldwell repeated the process, this time cutting down when the knife tip encountered bone.

"All right," Caldwell said.

The assistant slipped his already blood-caked fingers into the slits Caldwell had cut and grunted with the effort of separating the flesh. It made a damp, peeling sound, like a hunk of rare beef being carved off a roast. Caldwell sliced at a few stubborn tissues until the flaps of thigh muscle peeled apart. When the assistant was done, the thigh was now divided by a V-shaped cut, with the heavy thigh bone at the juncture of the V.

Caldwell put the knife down and selected a bone saw. The tiny teeth were still clogged with damp bits of bone from the last operation, so Caldwell tapped the saw on the edge of the operating table. The white chips fell down and mixed with the mud under his feet.

"Hold him," Caldwell ordered. He began to saw. The blade skidded on the wet, bloody bone and Caldwell blinked and squinted in the dim light. He tried again, and this time the teeth caught and held the bone. Quickly, he sawed through the thigh bone and smoothed the edges of the rough cut with a pair of gnawing forceps. The severed leg was tossed atop a nearby pile of human limbs: hands, feet, arms and legs. It could have been the bloody leavings of a charnel house.

The newly cut flesh was bleeding profusely, so Caldwell put aside the saw and reached for his hooked tenaculum. This instrument was pointed and sharp like a fishhook, and he used it to snag the arteries in the bloody stump and draw them out so he could tie them off. Finished, he deftly joined the two edges of the V flap together with widely spaced sutures.

Just five minutes had passed from the administration of the chloroform to the knotting of the final suture.

"Loosen the tourniquet," he said. He waited a moment as his assistant obeyed and the blood supply, previously cut off, rushed into the stump. There was some bleeding, but not the telltale spurting of blood that showed he had missed tying off an artery. Not bad, he thought, for a surgeon nearly asleep on his feet.

Caldwell nodded, and two orderlies carried the now one-legged boy away. Briefly, the surgeon wondered if the boy would live. Amputations above the knee had a significantly higher chance of fatal infection – sepsis – but with the leg so far gone with gangrene, Caldwell hadn't had a choice.

There wasn't time to dwell on it. From the field hospital, the boy would be taken by ambulance to one of the military hospitals in Washington City. Caldwell supposed that if sepsis didn't kill the boy, the long, jolting ride over Maryland's country roads would finish what the Rebels had started. He had done what he could for the young soldier.

The assistant sloshed another bucket of water over the makeshift table, rinsing away the blood from the operation. Caldwell took a sip from his mug of whiskey and coffee, wiped the double-edged knife on his apron to clean off the gore, and called out in a weary voice, "Next!"

Chapter 2

General Orders No. 142
War Department
Washington

October 18, 1862

Effective immediately, Captain William T. Caldwell, currently regimental surgeon to the 116th Pennsylvania Infantry, 2nd Corps, is promoted to the rank of Major. Major Caldwell will henceforward assume all duties of chief surgeon to the 2nd Corps.

By order of Lt. Alfred Foster
Adjutant

Brig. Gen. Howard W. Frederick
Commanding

General Orders No. 76
Headquarters
Department of the Army
Washington

November 15, 1862

Major William T. Caldwell, currently assigned as surgeon in the 116th Pennsylvania Volunteer Infantry, 2nd Corps, will assume duty immediately as director of Armory Square Hospital, Washington. He will report to the office of the Army medical director upon his arrival in Washington to accept such post and receive further orders.

By order of Jonathan Letterman
Army medical director

James Claiborne
Lt & A.A.

Chapter 3

BALTIMORE, DECEMBER 1862

The clipper ship *Caroline* was anchored in Baltimore harbor, set apart from the other ships because of the yellow flag that flew from her topmost mast. That flag was known as the "Yellow Jack" and it was a sign that the ship was under quarantine. She carried sickness and fever after a voyage to the Orient, and all the other merchantmen in the harbor would stay clear until the disease had run its course. Those on board who still lived in a few weeks would help unload her cargo of tea and raw silk.

Jefferson Verville was interested in something other than the ship's cargo. He had been waiting for some time for a ship involved in the China trade to arrive in Baltimore under a Yellow Jack. He had made some inquiries around the waterfront and from the symptoms he had heard described, Verville knew this was just the ship he wanted.

"I ain't goin' aboard with you," said the man working the oars of the skiff. He was one of the waterfront riffraff who earned a few coins ferrying passengers to ships in the harbor. "I hear they got the fever bad aboard that ship."

"I've already told you," said Verville, huddled in the bow of the skiff, his dark cloak drawn tightly about him to keep off the December chill. "You're not to come aboard. You just tie up and wait for me."

"How do I know you won't have the fever?" the oarsman asked.

"I'll sit in the bow on the trip back," Verve said. "You won't have to come near me."

"You're a fool to come out here," the oarsman said. He spat tobacco juice to emphasize his point. "What do you want with a ship like that, full of fever and worse?"

"I'm a doctor." Verville tried to keep his voice level. He did not like being called a fool, but this was not the time to make an issue of it. If things went according to plan, this man would never make it back to shore. Verville could have no witnesses. "The crew aboard that ship needs assistance."

"Like I done said. You're a fool. You're going to end up with the fever, too."

16

"Just row the boat," Verville said in a menacing voice that forced the other man into a sullen silence.

A nighttime hush had fallen over the city piers. Sounds from shore drifted across the water. Verville heard a whore's drunken laughter, arguing voices, strains of fiddle music from a tavern. The stench from the wharves mingled with the salt air. Dampness clung to Verville's clothes and face. Most of the crews were ashore, enjoying a whore's bed or cheap rum. On the water, the silence was broken only by the creaking of the tarred anchor lines and the suck of the tide at the wooden bellies of the ships.

Verville was dressed all in black, with a cloak over his old-fashioned, high-collared suit and tight-fitting leather gloves. He looked more like an undertaker than a doctor, but the truth was he did not want one square inch of exposed flesh once he went below decks where the pestilence reigned.

The skiff carried them toward the *Caroline* and bumped against the bow.

"Hello the *Caroline*!" Verville called up to the dark gunwales and rigging that towered overhead. A lantern appeared over the side of the ship and a face peered down toward the skiff.

"We have fever here," the man warned. "You had best push off."

"Let's go," the oarsman whispered nervously. "They don't want us here."

"Be quiet!" Verville snapped. He raised his voice to the man on deck. "I am a doctor. I have been sent by the harbormaster to determine the health of this ship."

The sailor hesitated. "It's late," he said. "Come back in the morning."

"The harbormaster was very insistent."

"Come aboard, then, if you must."

A rope ladder thudded down and hit the water with a splash. Verville turned to the oarsman. "Wait for me."

"I don't know," the man said nervously. "They got the fever bad here."

"I'll pay you double when we get back to shore."

A greedy light came into the oarsman's eyes. "Triple."

"Very well."

Verville climbed the shaky ladder and reached the deck of the ship.

"I'm Shelton," the man with the lantern said. "First mate."

"Show me to your sick men," Verville said.

"There's only two left alive," Shelton said. "Three others died. We've got them below, separate from the rest of the crew. Everyone else is sleeping on deck."

"In this weather?" Verville asked incredulously. For a southern state, Maryland could be bitterly cold in winter, especially on the water.

The first mate snorted. "I'd rather be cold than sick with whatever they

17

have," he said. "You'll see."

"What sort of fever is it?" Verville asked, even though he already knew.

"Nobody knows for certain," Shelton said hesitantly, and Verville had the impression that the man knew full well what his comrades suffered. He crossed himself. "It come over them off the Carolinas. Some crates broke open in rough seas and they were sent into the hold to set things right. Two days later they took sick. If it had happened earlier in the voyage, we would all be dead. At least here in port we can keep them separate. It's the worst damn sickness I ever seen."

Verville nodded. "I'll have to see for myself."

"Take the lantern," the mate said, handing it to him. "No way in hell I'm going near those men."

"All right," Verville said. "Let's get on with it."

The mate led him to a hatch, threw it open. "Don't come looking for me when you're done," the mate said. "You'll understand why once you see them. Just get over the side. You can call up to me then."

Verville nodded, then slipped into the hatch.

Below, the ship was still, dark and cold. He could hear water gurgling on the ship's hull. There was a distant sound, too, that might have been a man moaning. The smell of death was thick, as if bodies were decomposing somewhere in the belly of the ship.

Verville moved in the direction of the moaning. He paused to take a silk scarf from his pocket and tied it over his face so that his eyes were the only part of his body exposed. He tucked the loose edges of the scarf into the cravat at his neck. Doctors had no special immunity to disease.

He found them in a small room deep within the ship, still in their bunks. Even through the scarf, the smell was rank. Verville raised the lantern high and caught a glimpse of black flesh and open sores. Somehow, impossibly, one of the diseased things moved. Verville gasped and fled.

In the passageway, he realized he was shaking. The disease was truly horrible. He had read descriptions, of course, but they fell short of the real thing. He remembered the sight of that blackened flesh and shuddered. Verville moved farther away until he felt calm, then started deeper into the ship, using the lantern to light the way.

From time to time he passed a dead rat. Another sign of the disease. He was counting on some of the rats not being sick yet, or maybe on new rats climbing aboard by the anchor lines. Baltimore Harbor was full of rats.

He made it all the way to the hold, the dampest, darkest part of the ship. The feeble lantern light illuminated the bales of raw silk that would be unloaded as soon as the quarantine was lifted.

Something scurried between the bales, running from the light.

Rats.

He opened the large doctor's bag he had brought. Inside was a flat sheet of metal screening with four hinged sides. At the top of each side was a metal ring, and a length of cord was tied to each one. The cords then joined together at the base of a much longer cord, which Verville tossed up over a beam. He laid the metal screening flat on the floor of the hold, with the four strings fastened to each hinged side resting loosely on top. At the center of the screen he placed a chunk of hard, yellow cheese.

Verville had set his rat trap.

He didn't wait long. After such a long voyage, the creatures were starving. Soon, a rat nosed at the trap. The creature's hunger overcame its caution, and it began nibbling at the cheese. Another rat came out of the shadows. Then another.

Verville gave a quick tug on the cord and the four sides of the trap sprang shut. The weight of the rats kept the sides closed tight. He tied off the end of the string and the rat trap dangled in the air, the squealing rats casting weird shadows that danced on the crates of Oriental tea. Verville slipped his bag around the trap, closed the top, and cut the string, leaving the rats sealed inside.

Verville didn't have time to trap more rats. The first mate would become curious if Verville stayed below much longer.

He started his ascent through the eerily dark ship. Somewhere in the bowels of the *Caroline* he could hear one of the sick men moaning. Verville made certain he did not go in that direction.

He reached the deck and snatched the scarf off his face, glad to breathe the fresh, cold air of the harbor. Below, the atmosphere was stale and still as death itself.

"Well?" the first mate called from the far side of the ship. Verville could make out several other faces watching him curiously. "How are the poor bastards?"

"I've made them as comfortable as I could," Verville said. "Don't go near them, unless you want the same to happen to you."

"We'll leave them alone," the mate said. "You can be damn sure of that."

Verville made his way to the ladder and was almost surprised to see that his oarsman had waited for him. It was impossible to climb the ladder with the heavy bag in his arms, so he lowered it to the skiff. Then Verville climbed down.

"Keep to the bow," the oarsman said, shrinking from Verville. "You'll be downwind of me on the trip back."

"As you wish," Verville said, and took his place in the bow, settling on a hard, wooden seat and keeping the medical bag at his feet.

They followed the same route back through the anchored ships riding the harbor swell. Once they were out of sight of the *Caroline*, Verville put his hand inside his pocket and drew a derringer. The double-barreled pistol was so small that it resembled a child's toy, but it was deadly enough at close range.

Verville aimed the pistol at the man working the oars.

"What are you doing?" the oarsman asked in disbelief, his eyes growing wide. He stopped rowing in mid-stroke and the oars hung over the water. The night was so quiet that Verville could hear them dripping. *Plink, plink.*

Verville fired.

The other man gasped as the bullet struck him in the belly. Verville moved forward and tipped him into the harbor. The water closed over the oarsman's head and one hand flailed weakly at the skiff. Then the black water was still.

Verville took up the oars. It was risky, firing a shot from the derringer. Not that anyone would be too curious. Pistol shots on Baltimore's rugged waterfront were common enough. It had been necessary to shoot the man because Verville did not want any witnesses to his visit tonight aboard the Caroline. The crew was one thing – he couldn't very well dispose of them, and the sickness might do that, anyhow. But the oarsman was another matter.

He leaned into the oars, being careful to avoid getting too close to any of the ships. He pulled toward the docks, heading toward a spot far from where he and the oarsman had left, in case the man had any curious friends lurking about.

Verville laughed to himself and looked at the black bulk of the doctor's bag, which stirred slightly from the movement within.

He knew just the place to begin his experiment. After all, his plan so far was based only upon a medical theory. Tomorrow night, he would put his theory to the test. He would have to wait for the Russian ship to arrive before his plan could be fully enacted. However, the rats were a start, a glimmer of things to come. Verville knew just the place to set them loose.

He had learned that his old Army colleague, William Caldwell, had been given charge of Armory Square Hospital in Washington City. Caldwell. The man had ruined Verville's military career, and it would now be Verville's chance to repay the favor. Some might say he had already taken his revenge against Caldwell, terrible revenge. But Verville would never be satisfied until he had achieved the man's ruin.

Verville patted his leather bag.

This was the beginning. With what he had taken from that ship tonight, he could both settle an old score and begin to bring about the destruction of the Union.

Chapter 4

WASHINGTON CITY

"They say there's going to be a big fight down in Virginia," Caldwell said, making his final rounds of the night at Armory Square Hospital. "It's to be at Fredericksburg on the Rappahannock River."

"Do you think we'll get many of the wounded?" asked Louisa Webster, the hospital's chief nurse, who was hurrying to keep up.

"You can be sure of it."

"I don't know where we're going to put them," she said.

"We'll make room," he said. "Even if we have to put them two to a cot."

They walked between the neatly arranged rows of iron cots placed side by side for what seemed as far as the eye could see. There was just enough space between the cots for the nurses and doctors to move. Every wounded soldier had a thin mattress stuffed with straw, a pillow, and a single blanket to keep off the cold. The hospital was filled with the wreckage of war, young men missing arms and legs, blinded, ravaged by diseases like typhoid and dysentery. In spite of their suffering, not one soldier moaned or complained – at least, not the ones who weren't out of their heads with fever.

Caldwell moved in a kind of pleasant, warm blur. He had been helping himself all evening to his favorite drink of coffee laced with whiskey, and the liquor was beginning to have an effect.

Not that he was drunk. Caldwell was in control of himself as he made his final rounds. He was an inch over six feet tall, lean, and his prematurely gray hair was cropped close to his skull, like a Roman centurion. He wore a faded blue uniform over which was a clean, white apron. Caldwell did not wear his major's insignia and his best uniform had not been out of his trunk in months. As a doctor, he didn't have much use for rank or ceremony. This was his hospital, and that was all that mattered.

Once, just a few days after he had started his duties at the hospital, Louisa had asked him why he never wore his officer's shoulder straps.

"You know why they promoted me, don't you?" he said. "That's the Army's way of dealing with officers it no longer knows what to do with. That goes for medical officers, too."

22

"Don't be so eager to pity yourself," Louisa had said sternly. "You're an excellent doctor and the Army is lucky to have you. The wounded here need you."

She had turned on her heel and walked away. But the words had their effect. He began to snap out of his lethargy. He even drank less. It was as if some fog had lifted, and he had Louisa to thank for that.

Since coming to the hospital just a few weeks ago, he had barely had a moment's rest. The Washington hospitals were so short of staff that Caldwell could not sit in an office all day while he let younger or less competent surgeons do the work. Despite what Louisa said, he knew well enough the promotion to major had simply been to get him out of the field before he went to pieces. He had come to the brink of a kind of mental unraveling in the weeks after Antietam.

At the age of thirty-eight he was nearly a broken man, in charge of this hospital, no longer able to stomach being in the field. He had been with the Army since the Mexican War and had cared for the wounded of Chapultepec, then served in various godforsaken frontier posts. None of that mattered now. After the war, the Army would have little use for a surgeon who didn't have what it took to deal with the carnage of a battlefield.

However, as long as the war still left men broken and maimed the Army would keep him.

"How's the leg, Sergeant?" Caldwell asked, stopping at a cot where a young man was propped up, trying to puzzle out the pages of *Harper's Weekly* in the dim lantern light.

"Tolerable, sir." The sergeant smiled. "I'll be dancing in a week."

Caldwell grunted. "That would be a miracle, because you couldn't dance worth a damn before you were wounded."

That brought laughter from the sergeant and the soldiers in the cots nearby. Even the ever-serious Nurse Webster allowed herself a rare smile as she followed along behind Caldwell, listening carefully to his instructions. At the age of twenty-eight, Louisa was considered a spinster, too old for marriage, but pretty enough that several soldiers watched longingly as she glided past. If she noticed, she ignored the glances.

"Plenty of beef tea for this one," Caldwell said, continuing on and stopping at the cot of a perilously thin soldier. The boy was asleep. His face looked hollow, cheekbones protruding, his eyes sunk deep in their sockets.

"Yes, Doctor Caldwell," the nurse said, making a mental note.

Caldwell went down the long rows, prescribing laudanum for one man, alum salts for another. For some, there was no hope, and the doctor merely tried to ease their pain until death came for them. Many of these terminal cases had been wounded weeks or even months before, and their deaths were slow and agonizing. Sometimes, Caldwell thought it would have been better to put down the badly wounded ones in the field, just like the cavalry did with injured horses. A single pistol shot to the temple would be more humane than dying far from home in some goddamn iron cot, Caldwell thought bitterly. Some might have been surprised to know a doctor thought this way, but Caldwell had always been a practical man.

"Morphine every two hours, Miss Webster," he said, standing over the bed of a young man who writhed in his blankets, nearly senseless with pain. He lifted the soldier's wrist and checked his pulse, then confided quietly to the nurse, "This one will be gone by morning."

The doctor moved on and Nurse Webster followed.

Their rounds sometimes seemed endless and the sight of so many mangled young men was depressing. What made it worse was that Caldwell knew his hospital was just one of many in Washington City. The sheer number of wounded was astounding. There were fifty-one thousand soldiers lying in twenty-one hospitals within sight of the Capitol dome. That meant the population of wounded alone was larger than the whole population of the Union capital had been at the outset of the war.

Almost every public building had been converted into a hospital at some time or another, and the white-washed walls of hastily erected hospitals had sprung up in the vacant lands around the city. Armory Square was one of these, built near the mall on land that had been used for a pasture.

Caldwell reached the end of the ward, where a young man, the ward master, sat with his boots on a battered table, reading a copy of *The Washington Star*. "You might read that aloud to some of the men, Sergeant," Caldwell said. "That is, if you really can read."

"Yes, sir." The sergeant hid a smile. He had been ward master long enough to get used to the doctor's sarcastic sense of humor.

As the sergeant carried his chair closer to the cots, Caldwell turned to survey the room. Just a whiff of the smell of the place came to his nostrils, because he was almost immune to it by now: stale blood, chamber pots, a faint odor of rotting meat. He sighed. This, really, was war, these endless rows of cots and stinking air, not bright blue uniforms with gold braid and flags flapping in the breeze and men dying neatly and bravely on lush green fields like in some painting.

War was a bad business altogether, Caldwell knew, and doctors like himself were left to clean up the mess the generals made.

"Coffee?" asked Louisa, handing him a tin cup. No whiskey in it, of course.

"Thank you." Their eyes met for just a moment, and Louisa looked away, embarrassed.

Caldwell sipped his coffee. He wasn't so old yet or so weary that he hadn't noticed Louisa's interest in him. But he had ignored her so far, shrinking away from recognizing her as anything more than a trusted nurse. After Julia's death, he had sworn off women. That was enough pain for one lifetime.

He realized he was clenching the mug of coffee in his hand and the hot tin was close to burning him. Quickly, he switched it to his other hand.

"I'll take the first shift," he said to Louisa. "You get some rest."

"Well, there's a pot of beef tea in the kitchen for whoever needs it," she said, efficient as always. Her voice took on a stern note. "You might try that for a change, instead of whiskey. Good night."

The comment about his drinking stabbed at him. He liked to think he stayed sober enough on duty, when his patients needed him. Did his drinking show that much? Whiskey had been his only consolation since Antietam. Every man had his vices, he thought. At least his was whiskey and not opium, which had ensnared so many doctors and patients alike. Already opium addiction had a nickname in the Army: "Old Soldier's Disease."

"Good night, Louisa," he said as she turned away, but too softly for her to hear.

* * *

"Rats?" Sally Pemberton was on the verge of laughter, staring at Verville as if he were insane. "We're going to defeat the Union with rats?"

"Not just any rats, my dear Sally," Verville said, forcing himself to smile. He had just returned from Baltimore, and his patience was worn thin after an exhausting night. "These rats are carrying bubonic plague from the Orient."

"This is the most ridiculous thing I've ever heard," Sally said. "I can understand plans to assassinate President Lincoln, blow up the White House, steal secret orders. But rats?"

"Not that you would share this plan with anyone," Verville said, an icy note of warning in his voice. "You will keep it to yourself."

"Of course."

He and his conspirators were meeting in Sally's parlor. Just himself, Sally and the newspaper reporter, Charles Wilson. It was the first time the three of them had met together. Wilson and Sally already knew one another. In fact, it was Sally who had recruited Wilson for their plan. Verville's impression of Wilson was that he was dependable enough. Like most journalists, his clothes were a bit threadbare and he ate as if Sally's pastries were the only substantial food he had seen in days, but he was obviously clever and devoted to the Confederacy.

There was a fourth conspirator, too, but Verville would never reveal that man's identity to Sally or Wilson. Too much was at stake, and a careless word from either of them could ruin all Verville's plans. It was no secret that the Union had eyes everywhere. He had even gone so far as to avoid speaking with the fourth conspirator for several weeks. When the time came, that man could be useful in the same way as a hidden pistol or an ace up his sleeve. Everything might depend on him. No, he wouldn't breathe a word about him to either of the others.

"Well, these rats are a start, at least," Wilson said. "What are you going to do with them?"

"I'll set them loose in Armory Square Hospital. With any luck, the disease will spread to the patients."

"Why there?"

Verville smiled. "An old friend of mine from Virginia is the chief surgeon there. He turned his back on his home to serve the Union. His hospital would be a good place for an epidemic to start."

"As good a place as any," Sally agreed.

"Oh, it's a better place than most, believe me," Verville said. "The name of the surgeon there is Caldwell. He's a traitor. He deserves every ounce of misery I can put on his head."

Both Sally and Wilson were staring at him. He realized he was clenching his teeth and fists. Well, he thought, old grudges die hard.

Relaxing, he helped himself to what was left of the pastry Sally had served with the tea.

"I thought Wilson and I were supposed to do something for the Cause. Right now, it sounds like you're doing everything."

"Oh, you'll help. Both of you." He smiled and began to explain. "First of all, once these rats make a few of the patients in Caldwell's hospital sick, Mr. Wilson here is going to write an article for his newspaper telling how the whole epidemic was, in fact, Doctor Caldwell's idea because he's a loyal Southerner. He's a Virginia man, after all."

"You mean, make the story up?" Wilson asked. He sounded astonished.

"Come now, Mr. Wilson. Newspaper reporters do that all the time. Believe me, Caldwell won't be in any position to deny it, and even if he does, no one is going to believe him. At any rate, the War Department will then turn its full attention on him and leave us free to do what we must."

"I still don't see how this is helping the war effort," Sally said.

26

"But it is," Verville said happily. "You see, I have a plan."

"What do those rats have to do with it?" Sally asked.

"That's just a taste of what's to come," he said. "Our plan really begins once our Russian friend Captain Khobotov arrives with our cargo."

"More rats?" Sally wondered.

He shook his head. "No, but there will be plague aboard, all the same. We have some friends in China who have packed crates for us with the clothing and bedding of plague victims, mainly Europeans there for purposes of trade. Once the crates arrive, we'll distribute the clothing to second-hand shops all over the city and in other cities as well. It won't be long before the plague is raging all across the North."

"My God," Sally said. "It's just crazy enough that we might pull if off."

"Oh, we will," Verville said. "The best part is that there will even be a valise filled with new, custom-made shirts exposed to the plague. We shall make a special gift of these to the tyrant himself, Abraham Lincoln."

Wilson and Sally nodded at him, spellbound.

Finally, Sally walked over to the sideboard and poured them each a brandy.

"To the South," she said.

They raised their glasses in a toast and drank to victory.

Chapter 5

Thomas Flynn stopped in a shop on Pennsylvania Avenue and bought a cigar. After his long trip from Richmond, dodging Yankee patrols nearly every step of the way, he felt he deserved a good smoke. Still, he was shocked at the price.

"Goddamn expensive," he grumbled, glaring at the shopkeeper.

"Don't blame me, mister," the shopkeeper said nervously. "It's the war."

Gloomily, Flynn reflected that the merchants in Richmond made the same excuse. He had been in the Confederate capital just three days ago, before slipping across the Potomac River.

The truth was, Flynn would have preferred a drink over a cigar, but resisted the temptation. One drink could easily lead to two or three, and there was work to be done.

Flynn paused on the wooden sidewalk to light his cigar. A pair of convalescent soldiers hobbled past on crutches. One soldier was missing a foot; the other man's leg was gone below the knee. Poor bastards.

He sucked on the cigar and made a face. In spite of its steep price, the cigar was a foul thing compared to what was available in Richmond, but good tobacco was becoming scarce north of the Potomac.

His mood wasn't helped by the fact that he had never cared much for Washington City. Although it was largely a Southern city – the natives pronounced it "Washtone" – the place had an unfinished air about it, a sense of uneasiness. There was nothing comfortable about Washington. Its inhabitants only planned on staying long enough to fulfill the duties of their military or political offices, so nothing felt permanent here. The streets were a muddy mess, and over it all loomed the unfinished dome of the Capitol, covered in scaffolding. Washington was a city under construction, awkward and uneasy, like a boy with gangly arms and legs.

Somewhere in all this sprawling mess he was also supposed to find a Confederate traitor named Jefferson Verville, who was plotting something the Confederate Secret Service didn't approve of, and Flynn's orders were to stop him. Flynn guessed that meant he would probably have to kill Verville. After all, that was why they had sent him and not somebody else.

There was a Yankee doctor who was supposed to help him find Verville, although the doctor didn't know it yet. The trick might be finding this doctor, considering the number of hospitals in Washington City. Richmond also had its share of wounded, but not on the scale of the Union capital.

He walked on to the corner of Pennsylvania Avenue and 16th Street, near the Willard Hotel. He would have liked to stay there, but the funds allotted him by the Confederate Secret Service would only go so far. The Willard was for rich men, not one of the Confederacy's errand boys. Tonight he would pay for a room in one of the less expensive hotels or maybe even a boarding house.

Flynn stood there, smoking his cigar, and waited.

Several minutes passed before he noticed a well-dressed gentleman sharing the sidewalk, also enjoying a cigar. The man's fine clothes made Flynn feel shabby in his own suit and overcoat, although they were the best that could be found in Richmond, where the Union blockade was already having a telling effect on goods such as clothing and medicine.

The man moved closer to Flynn, but did not look at him.

"Do you whistle Dixie?" the gentleman asked, keeping his eyes fixed on the houses across the street.

"When I must," Flynn replied, answering with the code words he had been given in Richmond. His voice still held a trace of his boyhood Irish brogue, which he worked hard to hide, unless it suited his purposes.

He turned to look carefully at Thomas Nelson Conrad, one of Richmond's chief spies in Washington. Flynn knew Conrad only by reputation. In Washington, from his home at the old Van Ness mansion located just a stone's throw from the White House and practically next door to the United States War Department, Conrad ran a network of Confederate spies. Unlike openly rebellious spies such as Rose Greenhow, he was a very careful man. So far, he had managed to elude any attention from the Yankee spycatchers.

"That's a horrid cigar," Conrad said. He spoke with an elegant Southern planter's accent. A gold watch chain stretched across his ample belly. "It smells quite stale."

"Well...." Flynn wondered what his cigar had to do with anything.

"Try one of these," Conrad said. He turned to look at Flynn with eyes as big and blue as robin's eggs. He gave Flynn a cigar, around which was wrapped a small bit of brown paper which almost blended with the leaf wrapping of the cigar. Anyone watching on the street wouldn't have noticed.

"Thank you," Flynn said.

"You're quite welcome," Conrad replied. "I'm afraid that under the circumstances, I can't give you more than one cigar."

Flynn was confused. Conrad was obviously talking in code, as if he thought they were being watched or overheard. "How can I contact you?" Flynn blurted. "In case I need more cigars."

"Don't," Conrad said sternly. "The one is all you get. I consider my obligations met." He gave Flynn a polite smile, and moved off toward the crowd in front of the Willard.

Flynn put the cigar in the inside pocket of his overcoat and walked on. Conrad's paranoia was contagious, and he waited until he was sure he was not being followed, then stopped to unwrap the cigar. The brown slip of paper contained a message written in a tiny, cramped hand that read:

Major Caldwell may be found at Armory Square Hospital. No word on the whereabouts of our mutual enemy.

Flynn twisted the paper together and used the end of his cigar to ignite it, letting it burn down to the tips of his fingers before dropping it to the muddy street. No sense taking chances. The Union spycatchers were good at their job, and there would be no trial for any spies caught, just a cold cell at the Old Capital prison, a nasty interrogation, and perhaps a bullet or a rope.

It was getting dark. Flynn would eat, and then he would visit this doctor at Armory Square Hospital.

* * *

Caldwell felt a chill.

"Shut the goddamn door!" he shouted to the ward master at the far end of the hospital.

"I don't know who opened it," the young man complained, slapping down his newspaper and hurrying to close the door against the winter night. Although several stoves had been set up around the hospital ward, they barely kept the patients warm enough. The wounded had suffered through the August heat, panting like dogs in the airless hospitals – yet it still managed to get plenty cold every winter. Heat was too precious a commodity to leave the door open.

Caldwell had already seen too many soldiers contract pneumonia because of the drafty hospital. Each man's death was like an affront to his medical skill, and Caldwell kept two former slaves – "contrabands," the Army called them – working around the clock to stoke the stoves. He paid them each forty cents a day out of his own pocket to keep the soldiers warm. Caldwell also paid a former soldier three dollars a week to make sure the contrabands did their work.

He looked up from his patient. A tall figure in black caught his eye as it swept through the rows of patients near the rear of the hospital.

"Who the hell is that?" Caldwell wondered aloud. It was 10 p.m. and too late for casual visitors. He started toward the dark back reaches of the hospital ward.

There was something oddly familiar about the man in the black cape. Caldwell sensed he had seen him before. But where? He hoped for another glimpse of the intruder, but there was nothing but shadows. For a moment, he felt uneasy. Had he glimpsed some otherworldly apparition? Knowing how many had died there in agony, it wouldn't have surprised him if the hospital was stalked by the uneasy ghosts of the dead.

"Doctor, come quick! He's bleeding!"

The call came from the opposite end of the ward, and Caldwell quickly forgot about the man in black. As he rushed that way, Nurse Webster following in his wake, Caldwell ran down a mental list of the soldiers at that end of the ward and their wounds. There were several seriously injured.

"It's Henderson, sir!" a patient in a neighboring cot cried out.

At once, Caldwell remembered. He kept a mental catalog of his patients: Henderson … Henderson … twenty-five years old … from Ohio … minié ball entered anterior to left angle of lower jaw, fracturing the bone–

"He's dying, sir! Do something!"

Blood.

A red fountain gushed from the soldier's mouth and also from the exit wound the minié ball had left in his throat. Quickly, Caldwell recalled that after hitting the boy in the left side of the face, the ball had blasted through the floor of his mouth, then passed out the neck. The blood was bright red, arterial, and already it stained the wool blanket and dripped to the floor.

So much blood was rushing from the soldier that the boy had only minutes to live. Caldwell knew he would have to move fast.

"It's the sublingual artery," Caldwell announced. "Bullet must have nicked it."

"What do you want me to do?" Louisa asked, instantly at his side. She was a better assistant than most of the junior surgeons.

"We've got to ligate the carotid," Caldwell said. "Hold him."

"He can't lie down," Louisa said frantically. "He'll choke on his own blood."

A crimson flood escaped the soldier's lips. He was gagging on blood, trying to breathe, the whites of his eyes showing in terror.

"Prop him up and hold him." He turned to a strapping farmboy nearby with a minor wound. "You there – help the nurse."

Another nurse came running up with a bucket of water and a handful of bandages. "You'll be needin' these," said Mae O'Keefe, a stout, middle-aged Irishwoman who had come to the hospital to care for her husband and hadn't gone home after he died. "Mother Mae," the boys called her. She pinned the patient with powerful arms.

Caldwell took a small medical kit from his pocket and flipped it open to reveal several devilish-looking instruments held in place with leather straps against a background of red velvet. He withdrew a scalpel.

"What about chloroform?" Louisa asked.

"No time."

Caldwell cut. Then he reached for his pocket kit again and took out a small spool of silk thread. With deft fingers, he tied a loop of thread around the carotid artery just above the omo-hyoid muscle. The hemorrhage stopped instantly.

Louisa swiped blood from Henderson's mouth with her finger. He was gagging on the stuff. With the hemorrhage stopped and his mouth cleared, the boy gasped in a deep breath, like a drowning man coming up for air.

"Easy, son," Caldwell said. "You'll be all right now."

Caldwell instructed Louisa to press a bandage to the incision he had made above the carotid artery. Briefly, Louisa's eyes met his own. To his surprise, they were shining with admiration. This time, it was Caldwell who looked away in embarrassment.

"Hold that there until the bleeding stops," he muttered, then returned his scalpel and thread to his portable medical kit. "After that I want you to pack the neck wound with persulphate of iron. That should help keep this from happening again."

As Louisa hurried to get the persulphate powder, Mae helped prop the boy up and smoothed his tousled hair. "There now, lad," she said in her thick Irish brogue. "You'll only get better from here on out. You're in good hands with this doctor."

Caldwell waited until Louisa returned and set to work on the wound, then he walked away between the cots, his pristine apron now spotted with blood.

He was aware of the eyes watching him. Several men smiled. It wasn't the first time their surgeon had saved a life after some hasty operation performed in a field hospital had not held up. They were so used to the utter incompetence of Army surgeons. Their major was different, and their pride in him showed in their faces.

Caldwell didn't feel so proud. In fact, he felt like a charlatan. It was easy to work miracles – at least what looked to be miracles in the eyes of these young soldiers – here at a hospital in Washington City. He thought of all the field surgery he had done. Butchery, really, considering he was sometimes so exhausted he saw double as he sliced at tissue or sewed up a wound. He saw enough of the same kind of sloppy work arriving in Washington, much of it due to inexperience. The Army was overwhelmed by a need for doctors, and not all of them were qualified. Whoever had worked on Henderson had missed the damaged artery, an oversight which had almost completed the work of the Confederate bullet.

Something snapped him out of his reverie. What? There. At the back of the hospital, Caldwell spotted the tall stranger in black once again.

"You there!" he called.

The man glanced up, but in the dim lantern light Caldwell couldn't make out the face shadowed by the brim of a top hat. Still, something familiar there.... Then the man was gone, rushing for the backdoor of the hospital.

All Caldwell could think was that the man was a thief. Why else would he run out? The soldiers here in the hospital had little enough, but there was some money and a few personal items of value. The idea that someone would steal from his helpless patients enraged him. The adrenaline that had pumped through him minutes before as he performed the emergency surgery found an outlet as he started after the man.

Mae O'Keefe had seen the intruder, too, and she called out a warning. "Let him go, Major. You've no business chasing the likes of him, especially at night."

Caldwell ignored her and ran out the back door into the dark, wintry streets of the Union capital.

Up ahead, he could see the dark figure turn into an alley. He charged after him. There was a small fire in the alley, warming a group of what were known as "wild boys" – deserters and former soldiers who lived on the streets as best they could. They tried to stop the running man ahead, but there was a flash of steel as he slashed at them with a knife. And then he was gone.

Caldwell ran right into the middle of the angry crowd of rough men. This time, they were ready.

"Hold him, Johnny!" someone shouted, and suddenly Caldwell felt hands grabbing at him in the darkness. He wheeled and tried to twist away, but more hands gripped him. A fist slammed against his temple, and the dark night was filled with stars that swam before his eyes.

"Wait– " he gasped, still breathless from the chase, but the outraged men in the alley weren't interested in listening. He tried to fight back, swinging wildly at the dark forms spinning around him. His fists swished harmlessly through the air. Someone punched him from behind, low, in the kidneys, and

Caldwell doubled over in pain. Something hard hit him over the head and he was suddenly sprawled in the filthy floor of the alley, being kicked by his attackers.

"You bastards done cut Josh real bad!" someone shouted. Dimly, Caldwell realized he could hear an injured man howling just beyond the circle of attackers. "You gonna pay!"

"It wasn't me," he tried to explain, knowing whoever he was pursuing must have injured the man. "I was chasing–"

"Shut up!" For his trouble, someone kicked Caldwell in the head. He saw more stars and his head rang like a bell. He knew he had made a terrible mistake coming after the thief. The city's alleys were dangerous, deadly places.

The men threw more trash on the fire so that they could see their victim.

"A Yankee soldier boy," someone said.

"You an officer?" demanded a former Rebel with a thick Southern accent, a wild beard, and breath that stank of onions and whiskey. "Always wanted to kill me a Yankee officer, boys."

His attackers moved toward him. Then stopped.

An uneasy hush fell over the group. Caldwell rolled over and saw that someone else had arrived in the alley. He was a big, brutal looking man with a heavy brow under a shock of thick, black hair. Caldwell assumed the man was another one of the wild boys, and the man's cold smile made the hair on the back of Caldwell's neck stand on end.

"It's another one of the bastards," one of the men said.

"The fun's over." The big man held his fists loosely at his sides. "Let the man go."

"Go to hell," said one of the wild boys. With a shout, he launched himself at the man.

The big man waited for him. At the last instant, he brushed aside the Rebel's punch, cocked his fist, and slammed it low into the Reb's belly with such force that the man's feet lifted off the ground. The Reb collapsed into the shadows.

The haggard band of men hesitated. They circled like a pack of wolves – mangy ones, at that.

"You ought to mind your own business," one of the Rebels said.

"This is my business, lads." He nodded at Caldwell on the dirty floor of the alley. "Now, let me take this poor fellow home and we'll call it even."

"Go to hell."

All at once they went at the big man. The first one to reach him got a clip on the jaw that cleanly knocked him out. Then the big man was fighting like a wildcat as fists and kicks came at him from all directions.

But the big man held his own. He was quick and strong, no stranger to using his fists. Caldwell watched as one of the attackers ducked a punch, only to be felled by a fist to the groin that left him writhing on the ground. That was hardly fighting fair.

It was over in seconds, with Caldwell's attackers fleeing down the alley. Two or three of them were on their hands and knees around Caldwell, moaning, and one fellow who had pulled a knife was limping away, sobbing and holding his wrist as it flapped at an odd angle.

The big man reached down and pulled Caldwell to his feet. "Let's get out of here, Doctor, before the bastards come back. We got lucky this time around."

"I was chasing a thief," he tried to explain.

"Well, if those bastards didn't stop him, we won't. He's long gone by now, anyhow."

He draped Caldwell's arm across his broad shoulders and half-carried, half-dragged the doctor through the alleys back toward the hospital.

"It's a good thing you came along," Caldwell managed to say. His mouth was filled with the salty taste of blood. He spat.

"I never met a doctor who could fight worth a damn. Guess you're all on the wrong side of the business."

"How do you know who I am?" Caldwell was puzzled. He wondered how the man had found him in the alley.

"You're Dr. William Caldwell, aren't you?"

"Yes."

"My name is Thomas Flynn. I've been looking for you."

Caldwell shook his head to clear it. "Why would you be looking for me?"

"First, let's let the good nurses fix you up, Doctor. We can talk later."

They returned to the hospital and Flynn helped the doctor through the back door.

Louisa gasped when she saw Caldwell. She rushed toward him. "What happened to you? Oh, Major."

"You ought to see the other fellow," Caldwell said, attempting a joke, although his injuries were really beginning to pain him.

"I tried to tell you that you were a damn fool to go chasing after some thief," Mae said. "It's a good thing I told this big fellow here which way you went."

Louisa gave Flynn a curious look, but not an altogether friendly one, as if he might somehow be to blame for the doctor's injuries.

"Hmmph," was Louisa's only reply.

Now that she was over her initial shock at seeing the battered condition of the doctor, Louisa set to work. She brought a bowl of water and wet a clean cloth in it, then tenderly washed the cuts and scrapes on Caldwell's face. None of the wounds were very deep, and nothing was broken. Caldwell's pride was the main casualty.

"If there hadn't been so damn many of them, I might have had a chance," Caldwell grumped. He winced as Louisa touched the beginnings of a bruise.

Flynn noticed that the nurse's attentions went beyond mere professional courtesy, even though Caldwell himself appeared oblivious to the fuss the nurse was making over him.

"Listen to you!" Flynn laughed. "You're a surgeon, Major Caldwell. You're supposed to fix people up, not injure them. You leave fighting to the likes of me."

"Who the hell are you?"

"Well, Major, I'm here to help you catch that thief you were chasing."

Caldwell was beginning to be annoyed. Although the fight in the alley had left him shaken, he was starting to recover his ornery disposition. He jerked his head away from Louisa's washcloth. "Enough of that, Miss Webster. Thank you." He turned his attention to Flynn. "Now, what's this nonsense about being here to help me catch a thief? You weren't just happening by. I don't know you, and I have precious few friends, anyhow."

"Do you know who you were chasing, Major?"

"No, just a thief. He looked familiar, but I can't think of anyone who would come at night to steal from the patients."

"He wasn't here to steal," Mae O'Keefe announced. The group turned her way in surprise. "He was setting rats loose."

"Rats?" They all turned to stare at Mae. Caldwell couldn't believe his ears.

"The boys saw him, Doctor," Mae said. "He had a bag filled with rats, and he let them go in here. A couple o' the boys an' I tried to ketch 'em, but they was too fast fer us. One o' the wee vermin bit a boy. One o' the Rebel lads, it was."

"Who in hell would let rats loose in a hospital?" Caldwell sounded as if he thought they were all mad.

"Well, Major sir, it wasn't a thief you were chasing, after all," Flynn said. "You might know him, as a matter of fact. His name is Jefferson Verville."

"Verville." Caldwell's bruised lips formed around the name as if he could taste it. His face raced through a variety of emotions before he settled on anger. "That bastard."

"You do know him, then?" Flynn asked, although he had already been told that much.

"Oh, I know him, all right."

"I've come to catch him," Flynn said. "I need your help, sir. It will be like catching one of those rats he set loose."

"Verville isn't even the equal of a rat."

"What's he doing setting rats loose in the hospital?" Flynn asked, puzzled.

"Who the hell knows?" Caldwell said. "Verville never did do anything that made sense. But you can be sure of one thing. Whatever he's up to, it's no damn good."

Chapter 6

"You'll have to let me buy you supper, Mr. Flynn," Caldwell said. "It's the least I owe you for saving my life."

"Normally, Major, I'd let you buy me a drink and leave it at that," Flynn said. He thought it was good that Caldwell felt beholden to him, considering he would need the doctor's help to catch this madman Verville. "But I'm just about famished, and we have some business to discuss, besides."

Caldwell left the hospital under the charge of a younger doctor and they set out for Pennsylvania Avenue – "The Avenue," as it was called, considering there weren't any other thoroughfares in Washington to rival it.

"I wouldn't leave if Miss Webster weren't there," Caldwell said. He had a gruff, direct way of speaking, Flynn noticed. "Most of the surgeons I've got barely know the difference between a bandage and a bucket."

"She seems capable," Flynn said.

"I inherited Miss Webster when I took over the hospital," Caldwell explained. "She's really the one who keeps the place running from day to day. To be frank, I couldn't do it without her."

"Not a bad-looking woman, either," Flynn added, hoping to prompt the doctor. Caldwell only grunted in reply.

They walked toward where the cheaper taverns were located on Pennsylvania Avenue. The war was changing the face of the city, and many eateries had sprung up to profit from the crowds of hungry men the war had brought to Washington.

"You'll have to forgive me, Mr. Flynn," Caldwell said as they walked past the entrance to the Willard Hotel, one of the city's finest. Several well-dressed men stood near the entrance, smoking cigars, and pointedly ignoring the Army doctor in his faded blue uniform and his companion in rumpled clothes. "I'm afraid I don't dine often at the Willard."

"The Army doesn't pay well, I take it?"

Caldwell laughed. "Most nights, I just eat whatever soup happens to be heating in the kitchen. It's good and healthy, mind you. We give the patients decent food, but it's not fancy."

They settled on a rather disreputable-looking tavern that was nonetheless filled with diners – always a good sign. Caldwell ordered oysters and ale for them. They sat at a table by a frost-limned window, surrounded by other officers who were not independently wealthy. Conversation buzzed between them about a huge battle that had taken place at Fredericksburg, Virginia. Telegraph messages had carried word of a terrible Union defeat.

Several civilians were dining there, too, oblivious to the war news, men whose well-worn suits made it clear that they hadn't yet caught the wave of prosperity the war had brought to the city. Outside, they could see the gaslit, frozen expanse of The Avenue. The crisp winter air rang with the clop of horses' hooves and jangling harness.

"It's a man after my own heart who loves an oyster," Flynn said, fairly diving into a platter of raw oysters on the half shell. The oysters were harvested in prodigious quantities from the nearby Chesapeake Bay and shipped as far north as New York City. Flynn washed them down with plenty of ale.

He watched as Caldwell ate methodically, in a manner that suited a surgeon, carefully slipping a knife along the smooth interior of the shell to fully separate the oyster, then gently tipping the quivering gray mass into his mouth. Flynn, meanwhile, was noisily sucking down the oysters and tossing the empty shells into a pile.

"That was close, there in the alley," Caldwell said. "I have to thank you again, Mr. Flynn. You saved my life."

"Like I said, I never met a doctor who could fight worth a damn."

Caldwell was curious. "You seem to know a bit about fighting."

"Well, it's how I used to earn my daily bread, Doctor. Bare knuckle fights to all comers. Toughest man wins."

"And you were the toughest," Caldwell said. It wasn't a question.

"A man's got to eat," Flynn explained. "There was one or two who got lucky, but I made a point of catching up to them later, just to prove who was the better man."

Caldwell cast a sideways glance at Flynn, then grunted again as he delicately freed an oyster from its shell.

"You're not a prizefighter anymore, I take it?"

"I found work that pays better than being punched," Flynn answered.

"Now comes my real question," Caldwell said. "Why the hell are you looking for me? I hope it's not because I amputated your brother's leg on some battlefield, and you want to get even with me."

Flynn laughed. "If that was the case, then I suppose I would have let those rascals in the alley finish you off." He slurped down an oyster. "I think we ought to finish our supper first, Major, and then we can talk business."

"Very well, Mr. Flynn."

They ate the oysters and washed them down with the ale brewed right on the tavern premises. When they finished eating, Caldwell had a bottle of whiskey and two fresh glasses brought to their table.

"This is horrible whiskey," Caldwell said as he poured a glass full and held it up to the light to examine the amber liquid. "Of course, if we were dining at the Willard Hotel we could get real Southern bourbon, not this busthead that they've pawned off on us poorer sort. You will notice that this is clear corn liquor colored with molasses. At least it will take the ache out of my bones, if nothing else."

Flynn was taken aback as he watched Caldwell gulp his whiskey and then smack his lips in satisfaction. They had already drank a great deal of ale with their supper, and as a rule Flynn knew it was better not to mix ale with hard liquor – and oysters, too, no less. Flynn did not fill his glass as full as the doctor had, and he only took a sip. The burn of it hit the back of his throat and reached all the way to his belly, where it settled atop the oysters and ale like a scratchy wool blanket. It was rotgut whiskey, all right.

"Now we can talk business," Caldwell said. "Tell me why you were looking for me – and for Verville."

Flynn wondered how much he should tell. He decided to gamble on the truth, because Caldwell by all appearances was a straightforward man. "Well, Major, the first thing you should know is that I was sent by certain authorities in Richmond."

"So, you're some kind of Confederate agent? A spy?"

"For Christ's sake, Major." Flynn could see that the doctor was already more than a little drunk. "Why don't you just stand on a chair and announce it to the room?"

"You'd be hanged, wouldn't you?"

"That is a possibility," Flynn acknowledged.

"And you expect me to help you? Why? I don't want to get mixed up playing spy. I'm a doctor."

"I've been told you know Verville, or, at least, you knew him," Flynn said. "He's the real reason I came here."

"What does Verville have to do with anything?"

"He's also a spy," Flynn said. "Only he's got it in his mind to do things his own way. Bad things."

"What's he going to do?"

"That's what I was hoping you could tell me."

"I don't have any goddamn idea what Jefferson Verville is doing." Caldwell took another gulp of whiskey. "All I know is that he's a bastard."

"He did have those rats. The ones he set loose in your hospital."

"He did." Caldwell looked puzzled. "Why rats, do you think? You would think he'd try to assassinate Abraham Lincoln or burn down the capital."

"The British already did that in 1814, Major."

"And a lot of good it did them," Caldwell pointed out. "They still lost that war."

"I wouldn't underestimate the English," Flynn said. "They lost that war because they hardly knew they were fighting it."

"Well, the same can't be said of the South," Caldwell said. "Your Confederacy fights damn hard. It doesn't need Verville."

"The South can't win this war, Major," Flynn said. "We both know it. You're from Virginia, too. The North has more supplies, more soldiers – you'll simply wear our side down. A lot of people in Richmond know that, and they're more than willing to use any means they can to change the odds."

"I don't see how one man, even one like Verville, can make much difference. He's not going to win the war all by himself."

"Maybe not, but he's going to try."

"By setting rats loose in the hospital?" Caldwell shook his head, gulped more of the cheap liquor. "It doesn't make sense."

"You did say something about the rats being vermin, spreading disease."

Caldwell shrugged his shoulders dismissively. He reached for the bottle to refill his glass and spilled some of the liquor. Flynn finished pouring for him. "Well, there's no clear scientific evidence, but you could make a case that rats do contribute to some diseases."

"How do diseases start?" Flynn asked.

"No one really knows," Caldwell said. He spread his hands, palms out, and Flynn saw that the doctor's hands were well-scrubbed, the fingers long and sinewy, blunt-tipped. "There are many theories: miasma of the air, foul conditions. Rats would seem to fit in with that. Anyhow, I'm just an Army sawbones, Flynn, not a scientist."

"It does seem odd he was letting rats loose in your hospital," Flynn said. "Why the hell would he do that?"

"If he's out to destroy the Union as you said, Flynn, he's not going to do it with rats."

Flynn wasn't so sure. He had seen a few rat fights back in Richmond, had even won and lost more than his share of money at them. There was a saying the gamblers had. *Never underestimate a rat.* Or a madman like Verville, he thought. "Tell me about Verville," Flynn said.

"The man is a bastard." Caldwell's voice was bitter. He took another deep drink of whiskey.

"You served in the Army together."

"Yes. We were in Texas, at a frontier post. We were the two surgeons at the fort. Spent most of our time digging stone arrowheads out of backsides, if you want to know the truth. I was his superior – hell, Flynn, I've been in the Army since the War with Mexico. I was at Chapultepec; now, that was some battle. That bastard Verville always resented me for that, because he was too young for Mexico. It meant because I had seniority that I would always get the promotions and the better posts. Also, I had seen battle, and he hadn't. He was still a virgin, in terms of that experience."

"You're both from Virginia."

"The Army always favored Virginia men, at least before the war. General Winfield Scott was one himself. Scott was in Mexico, too, you know, and the War of 1812, for that matter."

"When this war came, though, you sided with the Union."

Caldwell nodded. "It wasn't easy, going against my state. My homeland, really. But the Union, Mr. Flynn, the United States – that's something worth fighting for. Of course, I'm sure you disagree. You're a Confederate agent, after all."

"If I had been living in Boston when the war broke out, it's likely I would be a Union man. But let's get back to Verville. He didn't think the Union was worth fighting for. He went back to Virginia."

"Verville would rather suck a hog's teats than salute the Union flag," Caldwell admitted. His voice was strained, and Flynn sensed a great deal of rage there. It surprised him. Caldwell struck him as a man on an even keel, even if he had a taste for the drink. Caldwell continued, "Verville was even that way back in Texas. When it became clear that there was going to be war, he resigned from the Army and went to Richmond. That's the last I heard of him – until now."

Flynn could feel the anger radiating off the doctor like heat off a stove. There was something else about Verville that Caldwell wasn't telling him. Caldwell was studying the amber whiskey in his glass, which he had refilled several times. Flynn was still working on his first drink of whiskey. Whatever this doctor's link was to Verville, Flynn's superiors at the Confederate Secret Service back in Richmond thought it would be enough to convince the doctor to help stop Verville. Flynn waited until the doctor had sipped a little more liquor before he asked his next question.

"Major, I can tell you hate Verville. Why?"

Caldwell was a long time answering. He drank more of the whiskey. Flynn decided that if the man had any more to drink, he would have to carry him home.

"I used to be married," Caldwell finally said.

Flynn could only imagine that Verville had stolen the man's wife. He asked his next question carefully, "What happened?"

"Verville killed her."

"Dear God."

"Verville hated me," Caldwell said, his eyes glassy from the liquor. "I almost managed to get him dismissed from the Army, which is no easy thing. One day I rode out on patrol, he stayed behind. He never went on one damn patrol, the son of a bitch. I should have sent him and stayed put but the truth was he wasn't much of a surgeon and the boys would need help if they ran into trouble."

"How did you almost get him dismissed from the Army?"

"There was an Indian boy Verville had living with him at the fort. It was a little unusual. Then one day I found out what he was doing with the boy." Caldwell shook his head. "I put a stop to it."

It took a moment for what the doctor had said to register. "The bastard's a sodomite!" Flynn exclaimed.

"He's evil, Flynn, that's what he is. Not long after that, I was away on that patrol. I left Verville there, although by rights I could have sent him out with the patrol while I stayed behind, but the man wasn't any damn good in the field. While I was gone, Julia took sick with fever."

Flynn wasn't sure he wanted to hear more. "Go on," he managed to say.

"Verville bled her to get the fever out. It's an old-fashioned remedy, Flynn. You see, it doesn't do any good. Why do men die when a bullet hits an artery? Because they bleed to death. The idea is to keep blood in the body, not expel it. Verville knew that. But he still bled her, filling up bowls with her blood. Bowls and bowls of blood, Flynn. Imagine it. He murdered my wife out of revenge, one drop of blood at a time, and he did it under the guise of treating her for fever."

"Jesus, Mary and Joseph," Flynn said. He made the sign of the cross. "I would have killed him."

Caldwell slumped as if Flynn had struck him. "I know, I know," he said, looking tortured. "I ... I couldn't. I wanted to, believe me, to avenge my wife, but I couldn't do it. I'm a doctor, after all. Much as I hated Verville, I couldn't take his life. I suppose I could have challenged him to a duel, but what would be the point? I'd almost have preferred if he had killed me."

"Surely there was an inquiry...."

Caldwell shook his head. "There was no proof, you see. There are still fools who believe bleeding can cure a fever. It is an accepted remedy by some. And people still die because of it, like my Julia did."

"I'm sorry." Flynn felt for the man. He wished now he had never tracked him down. Caldwell had enough troubles of his own.

"I'll help you catch him, Flynn," Caldwell said. He looked up. His eyes were glassy from the liquor. "Then you can kill him for me."

"I've been sent to keep him from doing whatever it is he's planning to do," Flynn said, wearing a nasty smile. "I guess killing him would be a good way to stop him."

They prepared to leave. The bottle of corn liquor was mostly gone, and Caldwell insisted on paying the bill for supper, even though his fingers were so thick and wooden that he could barely get the money out of his pocket. He started for the door and stumbled into a table filled with merchants hunched over their ale. They were a rough bunch and they cursed at Caldwell, but shut up when Flynn gave them a look as he put an arm around the drunken doctor's shoulders to guide him out.

The cold night air sobered Caldwell up enough to walk, as long as Flynn supported him. Some men might have been disgusted with the doctor's behavior, but Flynn had seen drink get the better of worse men than the doctor. Besides, he knew that sometimes it did a man good to get drunk and forget his troubles.

Flynn got him back to Armory Square. The doctor's living quarters were in the rear of the hospital. Although Flynn tried to be quiet, he ended up tripping over a chair in the dark and made one hell of a racket. He put the doctor down on his bed, struck a match, and lit the oil lantern. He turned just in time to meet Louisa Webster face to face as she came through the door. The nurse took one look at the semi-conscious doctor, then turned to glare at Flynn.

"You got him drunk," she said angrily.

"No, Miss Webster, he got himself drunk. Stinking drunk, I might add."

Louisa was not amused. She scowled at him. It was clear to Flynn that the chief nurse was someone to be reckoned with when she was angry. "This isn't the first time he's been like this," she finally said.

"Got a problem with the bottle, does he?"

"Only when fools like you come along," she said in an accusing tone.

Flynn wasn't about to be cowed by Miss Webster, no matter how outraged she might look. Besides, he hadn't come to Washington to argue with a nurse – and a pretty one at that. "He's a grown man," he finally said. "And an officer. I think he decided to get drunk on his own. I didn't pour it down his throat, you know."

Louisa ignored him. She knelt and unlaced Caldwell's ankle boots. "You can at least help me get him undressed," she snapped.

"Yes, ma'am," he said sarcastically. Flynn would have been happy to dump the doctor into bed and let him sleep it off, but he did as Louisa told him. Flynn raised his eyebrows as she unbuttoned Caldwell's uniform coat and began take it off him.

"It's nothing I haven't seen before, Mr. Flynn," she said. "I've been a nurse too long to be a prude."

"What's a woman like you doing working in this hospital?" Flynn asked.

"Is it too much to believe that a woman would want to help her country the best way she can, considering I can't shoulder a musket – at least, I'm not supposed to do that."

Louisa's fierce eyes dared him to say something about hospital work being too rough for her. He didn't take the bait. Besides, from what he had seen of Miss Webster so far, she appeared to be a match for just about anything – or anyone.

"The major has nothing but good things to say about you," Flynn said.

"Really?" She sounded surprised.

"From what I've seen so far of the doctor, I think he tends to keep compliments to himself. But he told me he couldn't run the place without you."

"It's about time he said something that made sense," Louisa said. "Even if he was drunk."

They finished getting the major into bed. Louisa hung his uniform on a hook behind the door to keep it from becoming wrinkled, then made a quick circuit of Caldwell's room.

"What are you looking for?" he asked.

"When he wakes up, the first thing he'll want is another drink to take the edge off his hangover. He has a lot of work to do in the morning. I think he should be sober."

"He may be sober, but his head is going to hurt like hell."

"That's his own fault."

Louisa made a quick search of the room. Nearly hidden behind a stack of paperwork she found a half-empty bottle of whiskey. "I'll take this," she said. "We could use a little more whiskey in the ward, anyhow."

"For medicinal purposes," Flynn said.

"Of course."

Louisa extinguished the lantern and they left the room. Caldwell was already snoring deeply on his narrow bed.

"He's a good man," Flynn said out in the hallway. "I like him."

"He thinks he's a failure," Louisa said, sadness dulling her brown eyes. "In the field, after a battle – he just couldn't take it anymore. Especially after

Antietam. That's why he's here."

"There's no shame in that," Flynn said, being honest. He had never found battlefields or soldiering to his own taste. Only a fool marched into a cannon. "A man can only take so much."

"I'm glad we agree," she said. She paused a moment, studying his face. "Who are you, Mr. Flynn, and what do you want with the doctor?"

Flynn hesitated, then decided there was no harm in telling the truth. "I'm a Confederate agent and I've been sent to stop the man who set the rats loose in your hospital. He's planning something much worse than rats to hurt the Union, believe me. Your Major Caldwell may be able to help because he knew this other doctor from before the war."

"I see," said Louisa. She nodded slowly. "You're a spy. Well, if there's anyone who can help you, it's Major Caldwell. I just don't want to see him hurt."

"I understand."

She hesitated, as if she had more to say, then thought better of it. "Good night, Mr. Flynn."

"Good night." Alone in the hallway, Flynn shook his head, thinking that it was no wonder Caldwell didn't mind leaving the hospital in Miss Webster's hands. Exhaustion suddenly washed over him, and he went in search of a spare cot in the orderlies' room.

Chapter 7

Caldwell woke up Sunday morning with a splitting headache and a mouth that felt like it was packed with sawdust. He lay there for a moment, blinking his eyes against the pain brought on by the early morning light through the windows. The pale winter morning did little to cheer him up.

God, when would he learn? Almost every morning since Julia died had been the same, filled with aching, the stale aftertaste of whiskey, and regret. With the hangover, that empty feeling inside, that black pit, always returned. Damn Verville.

"What I need is a drink," he said aloud to the empty room, and managed to swing first one leg, and then the other onto the floor. His bruised body hurt from the fight in the alley last night. The room seemed to lurch, and he reached out and touched his hand to the wall to steady himself. The boards under his bare feet were cold, damn cold, the goddamn hospital was always freezing in wintertime, but the crisp air helped clear his head.

With a twinge of embarrassment, he foggily recalled how he had told Flynn the story of his wife's death at Verville's hands. It was such a painful thing that he thought he was better off keeping the story to himself. Louisa was the only other person he had told – in similar drunken fashion.

Already, the happy times in Texas and before were so long ago, another lifetime really. Long before the war. If he thought about it, he could see now that he had begun unraveling then, after Julia's death, well before those horrible days at Antietam. This war was ripping out the final stitches of a wound that wouldn't heal.

He stumbled across the room, only to discover that the whiskey bottle was gone from his desk.

"Louisa," he said, smiling to himself. Vaguely he remembered her helping him to bed. The big fellow, Flynn, had been there, too. Was Flynn really a Confederate spy? Caldwell wondered what he was getting himself into, and Louisa, too, for that matter.

Louisa was a good woman, but fast becoming a spinster, using what youth she had left ministering to the soldiers – and to him, he thought wryly. For some odd reason she was attracted to him. He had felt it, ignored it, turned his back on her. He didn't need a woman in his life. Not anymore. He had been married once, and the memory of his wife's death at Verville's hands was like acid on his brain.

Verville.

At the mere thought of Verville, bile from Caldwell's sour stomach rose up and filled his throat until he gagged and choked it back down. Whatever Verville was planning to do in Washington City could not be good.

Caldwell went to the old sea chest where he kept his extra clothes, opened the lid, and took out a bottle of whiskey. Louisa didn't know all his secrets.

Caldwell pulled out the cork and sniffed. His stomach heaved again at the smell of liquor after last night's binge, but another drink was always the best remedy for a hangover.

Something stopped him, however. He realized what it was. He was sober, and he liked the clear-headedness that came with it. He was tired of the whiskey-induced haze that made the nights pass in a blur and brought humiliation. The drinking had not helped his career, and when he came right down to it, the whiskey had never really dulled the pain of Julia's death. Only time would do that.

Resolutely, he put the cork back in the bottle without taking so much as a sip. He tucked the bottle back in the bottom of the old sea chest. He was done with drinking – at least, for now.

There was a knock at the door.

"Hold on, goddamnit."

Quickly, he pulled on his trousers over his woolen longjohns, letting the suspenders hang down. He pulled the door open and found Louisa standing there with a tray.

"I brought you some breakfast," she said. "I thought you could use it after last night."

"Yes. Well," he tried to explain himself, "I had a bit too much to drink."

"It's not the first time," Louisa said disapprovingly.

She carried the tray in and waited as Caldwell cleared a space for it on the cluttered desk. There was a large tin mug of coffee, good and black and so strong it could take the rust off nails, a basket of hot biscuits, butter and jam, and smoked ham.

Caldwell felt a welcome pang. Hunger. When was the last time he had actually felt hungry? God, that food looked good.

"Where in the world did you find ham?"

"One of the ladies with the aid society brought three hams yesterday for the soldiers. I saved you some."

"The men deserve it more than I do."

"There was plenty."

Caldwell smiled as he surveyed the tray of food. She had prepared a feast. "Won't you join me, Louisa?"

He was painfully aware it was one of the few times he hadn't called her "Miss Webster." Her name had rolled naturally off his tongue. Maybe if he could just keep from drinking so much, his working relationship with Louisa might become something more. He was surprised to find that he welcomed the idea.

"I only brought one cup–"

"Ah!" He snatched a tin cup from his desk and blew off the dust. "This one suits me. You take the one you brought."

He settled on the edge of his cot while Louisa made use of the chair at the desk. The only sound came from the legs of the chair scraping on the wooden floorboards, but they were accustomed to each other's silences, like husband and wife. They ate heartily, and Caldwell took a deep drink of coffee. He looked at Louisa over the rim and smiled. The coffee was making him feel much better, even without any whiskey to go with it. It had always been one of his favorite combinations, whiskey and coffee. Being a wide-awake drunk had its benefits, especially if you were an Army surgeon.

"There's news this morning of a battle in Virginia," Louisa said. "The men in the hospital have been talking about it."

"Then we had best prepare for more wounded," he said.

"Yes." By now, they were both all too familiar with the caravan of ambulances that would arrive in the city.

"How is Henderson doing?" he asked. Henderson was the young soldier Caldwell had done emergency surgery on when Verville first appeared in the hospital last night.

"Much better this morning. If the wound in his neck heals quickly enough, he might be able to return to duty in time for the spring campaigns."

Caldwell grunted. "I'm sure that will cheer him up."

Louisa laughed. "You're such a cynical man."

"If I weren't cynical, I'd be wearing a gray uniform by now, not a blue one."

"Some might say that you're patriotic, not cynical."

"I might have been patriotic once, when I was young and foolish. I just believe that the South is wrong. It's a bad cause. There's no honor in fighting to preserve slavery. Cut a man open and we're all the same inside, regardless of our color."

"For a medical man, William, you haven't forgotten what it means to follow your heart."

49

So, William, was it? She had never used his first name. He wondered why they had taken so long to getting around to using each other's first names. He realized how embarrassed they acted at times with each other. *What are we,* he wondered, *schoolchildren with a crush on each other?*

Louisa was a mystery to him. He did not know much at all about her life before the one in Armory Square Hospital. At the same time, he realized that he had never asked.

She was smart and educated; obviously, Louisa had spent her youth in one of those fancy schools for young ladies from good families. He realized he knew very little about Louisa's life before the war. The odd hours when she was not working in the hospital, he knew that she read books. He had even seen her with a volume of poetry by that man Whitman who came around the hospital, giving small presents to the wounded and trying cheer them up. *Leaves of Grass*, he believed Whitman's book was called. Caldwell himself had never been one to read much beyond medical texts and practical books; he thought poetry and novels were a waste of a man's time. He decided not to share that opinion with Louisa.

There was no doubt that Louisa was intelligent, well-read, and an extremely capable nurse. However, he couldn't help wonder why she had traded whatever previous life she had to come work in the hospitals. Why take on such hardships – the poor food, the danger of catching one of the many illnesses that raged, the poor pay – without a good reason? Caldwell wondered if Louisa was running from her past. Or maybe the soft, middle-class life of a woman rapidly approaching spinsterhood had simply lost its appeal and she had traded it for something for meaningful. He couldn't understand why someone would waste their time with novels and poetry, but he could see how they would not want to waste their lives doing, well, nothing in particular. He realized he had a lot to learn about Louisa Webster.

"You could have been killed last night," Louisa said, frowning at his bruises. "That man Flynn told me who he is and why he's here. I know you'll help him. You'll feel duty-bound to do it. But I don't want you getting hurt."

"I'll be all right," he said.

"Just don't forget that he's a spy and you're a doctor," she said. "There is a difference, you know."

"I'll keep that in mind," he said.

They sipped their coffee and Louisa brought up the safer topic of hospital business. "We're short of blankets," she said. "We've had to put coats over some of the men to keep them warm enough."

"I'll talk to those fools at the sanitary commission and see what they can get us. I won't have the cold finish the work that the battlefield began."

Caldwell remembered that he had once eaten breakfast with Julia like this, talking over the problems of the day ahead. It had been a good thing, being married. Maybe he was wrong to think he never wanted a woman in his life again. He looked toward the rough table alongside his bed. On it was a daguerreotype of his wife. The image was dark and murky, although it didn't matter because Caldwell knew well every angle of her face. He would never forget Julia, no matter what.

"What's wrong?" Louisa suddenly asked. She noticed he was looking at the daguerreotype. "You miss her, don't you?"

Silently, he nodded. Caldwell felt his throat tightening, and he took a gulp of coffee and swallowed hard. "Good God, Louisa, what's to become of us all with this war?" he asked. He sighed and stared down into the blackness of his coffee. *Damn hangover has made my nerves soft.*

Quietly, Louisa reached across and put a hand on top of his own. It was the sort of natural, comforting move that a nurse would make. Caldwell surprised himself by gripping her hand hard, bringing it to his lips, kissing it.

"William," she said, startled, but she made no effort to take her hand away.

"Louisa. You are too kind to me."

There was a knock at the door. Caldwell gave Louisa's hand one final squeeze and stood up.

"What is it?" he snapped impatiently, then threw the door open to find an orderly standing there. The young man's eyes darted to Nurse Webster, then back to Caldwell's face. If he guessed anything by the sight of her in Caldwell's room, he kept his face neutral.

"Sir, you're wanted in the hospital. Mrs. O'Keefe said to come straight to you and tell no one else, sir."

"Well, what's so damn important? Out with it, Corporal!"

"It's the Rebel soldier who was bitten by the rat, sir. He's taken sick."

51

Chapter 8

In her day, the *Rynda* had been a truly grand warship, a vessel that the Dutch, the Germans and even the British treated with respect. She was still a fine ship, strongly built of oak from the ancient forests near the Ural Mountains and manned by a well-trained crew of seasoned Russian seamen and officers. Most of the men aboard the frigate were, like Captain Vladimir Khobotov, veterans of the sea battles of the Crimean War.

However, as he stood on the quarter-deck Sunday afternoon, Khobotov was thinking that the glory days of his ship were over. In fact, she was already badly outdated, relying on the wind in her sails and the resilience of that Russian oak in a new era of steam and iron. In these days of steam-powered ironclads, the *Rynda* had become obsolete. Even with two dozen thirty-two pound guns, her broadsides would bounce harmlessly off an American ironclad, a fact which made Khobotov uneasy. They couldn't even hope to outrun a steam vessel. He looked up into the rigging, at the tarred lines crusted with ice from the freezing winter fogs they had encountered along the American coast. No, he thought, his ship wouldn't be outsailing any steam vessels in this weather.

These Americans were always one step ahead of their European betters, it seemed, and Khobotov did not think this was a good state of affairs. It went against the natural order. Men, and nations, did well to remember their place, he thought.

Lieutenant Nikolay Sergeyevna interrupted his thoughts. "The horizon is clear, Captain," reported Sergeyevna, who stood beside Khobotov on the quarter-deck and was busy using a pair of field glasses to scan the hazy boundary where the watery winter sky met the equally gray sea. "Not a vessel in sight."

"Excellent," Khobotov said. "Make certain the helmsman knows to change course if any other vessels approach. I want no contact with the Americans – Union or Confederate."

"Yes, Captain," Sergeyevna said without enthusiasm. He went off to see that the captain's orders were relayed to the helmsman.

Khobotov frowned. It was obvious that Sergeyevna did not approve of this sneaking about the coast. Sergeyevna was becoming a problem of late because he did not agree with Khobotov's view that being a ship's captain entitled him to use the czar's ship for his own financial gain. The captain shook his shaggy head and sighed. Sergeyevna was a good officer and would never disobey orders, but at the same time, he was naïve about the ways of the world. It was a fault that was forgivable enough in an earnest young man. Khobotov planned on curing Nikolay of his youthful idealism by giving him a share of the money he would receive upon delivering the cargo of opium.

Khobotov would be glad to put to shore. The American capital at Washington was a poor substitute for the great cities of Europe, but it still offered drink and women, and that was all that really mattered to any sailor, no matter what nation he was from.

It had been a long and troubling voyage. In China, the plague was loose in the port cities, so he had kept his crew confined to the ship, an action that did not make him popular with the men.

Then there was the voyage itself. Aside from the irritation of having an idealistic young first mate, they had passed through terrible storms and made a harrowing passage of Cape Horn. Now, they were finally nearing the American coast. Khobotov would have liked to put into port sooner rather than later, but he ordered the ship to sail well off the coast. He did not want to be mistaken for some blockade runner and put himself at the mercy of a Union ironclad's guns. No, that would be too embarrassing, hardly good for the morale of the crew. He would not bow to some American navy vessel. Russian sailors were the best in the world!

Then, too, Khobotov had other reasons for wanting to avoid the Americans. After all, his hold was filled with a substantial quantity of raw opium, which would be smuggled into the Confederacy to be turned into medicines such as laudanum. It wasn't as if he were hauling guns and munitions for the South; this was medicine, after all. But the least contact he had with the Union navy until the cargo was out of his hold, the better.

The opium was one thing – Khobotov didn't mind that – but the other cargo in the hold disturbed him. When the crates were put aboard, a Chinese man who spoke broken English went with them into the hold to watch over the cargo. Khobotov thought that arrangement was highly unusual, and he became wary of the cargo when that man died of plague. He had ordered the blackened, bloated corpse tossed overboard by men wearing gloves and scarves over their faces to protect them from that disease. He then set one of his own crew to watching over the cargo out of fear that Jefferson Verville wouldn't pay him if something went wrong.

The sailor he assigned to the task was something of a simpleton, of no great use to the ship. Still, when that man died a week later, his corpse also black and bloated with the rotten flesh nearly falling off the bones, Khobotov refused to lose another man. Young Sergeyevna had been adamant that they dump the entire cargo into the sea to prevent the whole crew from being killed off. Khobotov would not allow it. Instead, he had the hold sealed up, and that was how it would remain until the ship arrived in Washington City.

Khobotov would be paid, the cargo unloaded, and then he would have no further dealings with Verville, profit be damned. He wanted no part in whatever Verville was planning. In fact, with any luck, they would be back on the high seas by then, considerably richer.

"You like these Americans we are going to spend the winter with?" Khobotov asked Sergeyevna as he arrived back on the quarter-deck.

"Yes, I do," Sergeyevna replied, his gaze steadily on the blue vastness of sea. He would not look at Khobotov. "They are a people who love ideas and principles. Their very nation is built on an idea."

"Ha! They are fighting a war over their principles," Khobotov said. "Ask a dead soldier or sailor what ideas he has in his head."

"A man might be better off dead if he has no principles, Captain."

Khobotov sometimes wondered if Sergeyevna had something more dangerous than youthful idealism in his head. "You think too much, my young friend," Khobotov said. "That is a dangerous quality in a Russian. Russia is not a democracy."

"Forgive me for saying so, Captain, but this idea of democracy is the very reason I like America so much."

"Democracy is for fools," Khobotov said with finality. He was thinking of the terrible cargo in the hold of his ship, of what sort of horror it would unleash. What sort of democracy was that? If it wasn't for the promise of Verville's money, he might have dumped it overboard. "Look at the war it has caused these Americans to fight. Brother killing brother! What foolishness. You will see. Dead men have no ideas, other than that they would rather be alive. That is true even in America."

* * *

Verville woke in Sally's bed, dry-mouthed and shaky in the first light of dawn, hung over from his nightly dose of opium. His head ached, although not as badly as it might have after a binge on red wine or whiskey. Trembling, he managed to light the lantern and sipped more laudanum from his tiny blue bottle. He had told Sally it was to ease the pain from an old war wound.

54

Just a sip, although he could easily drink the rest of it down. In fact, he wanted nothing more than to find the opium's sweet oblivion again, but it would have to wait. He had work to do this day.

Sally was asleep beside him. To his surprise, he found he didn't regret giving in to his urges. It was true she might try to gain some advantage over him because they were lovers, but he would not be manipulated. When the time came, he would deal with Sally.

He got out of bed, used the chamberpot, washed his face and hands using the pitcher and basin. Then he combed his long ringlets and added a fresh, scented pomade until his hair shone. Some of the remaining drug-induced fog lifted from his brain. His suit was wrinkled from having been thrown carelessly over a chair – foolish, he chastised himself – but his fresh clothes were back in his hotel room so he was forced with some loathing to wear his linen for a second day straight. With his hat in one hand and cane in the other, he went in search of clean linen and breakfast. Sally had nothing in the house worth eating that he could see, besides tea and toast.

Briefly, he debated whether or not to leave her a note, but decided against it. As a Confederate agent, he knew that the less put in writing, the better, even if it was something seemingly as harmless as a note to a lover. Sally knew he would return, and besides that, he had already given her an assignment for the day. There was some information he needed, and she was the perfect one to gather it.

He walked to his hotel, put on fresh clothes, and descended to the dining room. The place was hardly well-appointed, but the coffee was black and strong. He wasn't hungry, really, but decided he should eat anyhow to help steady the trembling in his hands. Opium and an empty stomach caused that. He ordered beefsteak and fried potatoes, greasier than he would have liked, but he ate it all. He had another cup of coffee and felt enormously better.

Beef and real coffee. Poor as the quality of the food might have been, it was better than what they would be having for breakfast this morning in Richmond. The war had transformed the simplest of foods into rarities in the Southern capital.

"Excuse me, sir, do you have the time?" asked a gentleman at a nearby table. Curiously, the man was wearing a suit just as fine as Verville's. He had an eye for such things. The gentleman's presence struck him as odd. Verville was dining in this rather shabby hotel by choice. He didn't know why anyone who could afford better would be there.

Verville could not ignore the man without being rude. "Half past eight," he said.

"Thank you," the gentleman said. Verville felt the man's keen eyes studying him. "My watch is broken and I've an appointment I don't want to miss. It's so important to be punctual, don't you agree?"

"Yes." Verville attempted a smile, but his face felt cold and rubbery. He wasn't sure if his stiff expression came from the effects of last night's opium or from some misgivings about the gentleman with the broken watch. Verville tried to reassure himself that his fellow diner was only a businessman. However, there was something unsettling about the man's eyes. They were hard and calculating. He turned back to his coffee, hoping the man would realize Verville wasn't interested in making conversation. Thankfully, he was not disturbed again, and he finished his coffee, nodded at the gentleman, and left the dining room. Now that he was properly washed and fed, he could attend to the business of the day.

The December morning was crisp but dismally overcast, the air tinged with the smells of wood smoke, horses, and an unpleasant undertone of garbage and urine that came from the wet slurry at the edges of the street. A trio of pigs trotted by, squealing, chased by a little dog that was in turn being chased by a duo of boys. Verville shook his head. The streets of Washington City would never be confused with those of Paris or London – or even New York.

Washington was a city that desperately wanted to live up to expectations – it was the Union capital, after all – but there was still a backwoods, frontier flavor about the place. On the muddy streets, a finely appointed carriage was quickly followed by a threadbare farmer with a battered wagon, in from the country for the day to hawk firewood. Two or three richly dressed staff officers rode past on good horses, only to be followed by a barefoot, decrepit black man leading a mule.

There were some well-dressed blacks, too, and Verville eyed them malevolently. Next thing you knew, the Yankees would have them marrying their daughters.

If the sight of prosperous blacks on the street wasn't enough reason to hate Washington, Verville also despised the city because it was the center of Union power. In a few days, however, death would begin to come for fine officers and uppity blacks and firewood salesmen alike. The streets would be deserted, or perhaps filled with citizens on the verge of panic as they carried their household possessions to the countryside in wagons. In time, the bodies would be stacked in the streets like cordwood.

Verville made a game of it as he walked, looking into the faces he passed and wondering who would live and who would die. Some of the faces were children's, but it didn't matter to Verville. It was out of his hands. The Yankees had brought this upon themselves.

God would be the ultimate judge. Verville was merely his servant.

He walked on to the waterfront, the tip of his cane making a rhythmic tapping on the wooden sidewalk. It was a long distance from the hotel, but the fresh air did him good, reinvigorating him. The streets became more tawdry as he neared the Potomac. Gone were the carriages and officers in tailored uniforms. In their place were immigrants in rags and tumble-down buildings.

It was just such a building that was Verville's destination. He had never been there, but sources in Richmond had given him directions. Other Confederate spies had relied on the MacCrae brothers in the past to help smuggle supplies into the Confederacy. He would need their help once the Russians arrived.

He found the tavern easily enough. It looked just as it had been described. The door opened to a small common room, a squalid place with damp boards underfoot that smelled of stale beer. The place reeked of cigar smoke and whiskey. Even at this hour of the morning two men stood by the bar, while a third, large man in a worn suit coat poured their liquor. The three men ignored him.

"I'm looking for James MacCrae," Verville announced.

"He's not here," the bartender said, leaning his bulk on the bar. The two customers had stopped drinking and watched the exchange expectantly.

"I know he's here. Now get him. I have business."

The big man behind the bar straightened up. He was as tall as Verville, but much heavier. His face had the battered, lumpen look that longtime prizefighters get. "Look you, I don't take orders from nobody. Now, either buy something to drink or get the hell out."

Verville stood his ground. "Tell MacCrae I'm here."

The big fellow glanced at the two other men, as if seeking sympathy for how badly his patience was being tried. Then he sighed, came out from behind the bar, and started toward Verville with all the confidence of a man used to hurling unruly patrons out the door.

"All right, I warned you, you fancy son of a bitch."

Verville waited for him to come, his cane ready in his hands. Just as the man started to reach for him, Verville grasped the boar's head knob in his right hand while holding the body of the cane in his left, and tugged hard. He pulled free a slender sword blade sheathed inside the cane and whipped it toward the man. The razor sharp tip pressed gently into the soft flesh of the man's throat, not hard enough to cut him, but sufficient to stop him in his tracks.

"I said I want to see Mr. MacCrae," Verville hissed. All Verville had to do was flick his wrist, and the other man's bright blood would splash on the dingy floor once the blade sliced his jugular vein. Maybe he would do it anyway, he thought, and he increased the pressure on the man's throat. The big fellow gasped.

"That's enough. Put that pig-sticker away," said one of the men at the bar, whom Verville had forgotten all about. "I'm MacCrae."

Verville glanced at him. MacCrae was a short, lean man, wearing clothes that might have been elegant once, but were now showing signs of hard use and hard living. His face was narrow as a hatchet, with a permanent ruddiness that might have come from alcohol – or frequent exposure to the winter winds of the Potomac aboard a smuggler's boat. He held a revolver in his hand, pointed at Verville's belly.

"How do I know you really are MacCrae?"

The man laughed. "You'll just have to take my word for it. But you should know that a gun beats a sword any day, so you'd best do as you're told."

Slowly, Verville lowered the sword blade, then slipped it back into its sheath inside the cane. The bartender attempted a shrug to show he hadn't been afraid, but his pale face indicated otherwise. Verville could smell the fear on him, a scent like sour onions. The man glared at him.

"Let it go, Harry," MacCrae said. His voice held just a trace of a Scottish burr. Reluctantly, the bartender backed away.

"Right nice little sword," the man at MacCrae's elbow said admiringly. "I can see it comes in handy."

"My brother, Angus," MacCrae said, nodding at his brother by way of introduction. The revolver never wavered. As Verville stared into the black muzzle, it occurred to him that MacCrae might be thinking what he himself had thought just moments ago as he held the sword to the man's throat – why not just let the blood run?

"Pour the man a drink, Harry," MacCrae said to the bartender. He plunked the revolver down on the bar, within reach, but he had evidently decided that Verville was no longer an immediate threat.

Verville sipped the amber liquid. The whiskey was surprisingly good. He raised his eyebrows.

"Fine stuff, eh?" MacCrae said. "I can get you all you want, two dollars a bottle."

"I'm not in the market for whiskey, Mr. MacCrae."

"How is it you know my name and we haven't even been introduced?"

"We have mutual friends, Mr. MacCrae. Friends in Richmond."

"That's all well and good, but who the hell are you?"

"Jefferson Verville."

MacCrae stood a moment, letting the name roll around his head. "You didn't even make that one up, if you are who you say you are. I seem to remember your name being mentioned. You're a doctor, ain't you?"

"Yes."

"I got this ache in my knee," MacCrae said. "Maybe you could make me up a poultice for it."

"I'm afraid I no longer practice medicine, Mr. MacCrae. Because of the war, I have moved on to other pursuits."

"What might those be?"

"I'm in need of a skiff or two to transport some cargo, some men to unload it, and a wagon to carry it to my destination," Verville explained.

"You're a smuggler then," MacCrae said. He sipped his whiskey. "Smuggling is dangerous work, Doc. It can get a man put in prison. It can even get him killed."

"My friends tell me you might know something about how to avoid all that."

MacCrae shrugged. "Like I said, it's dangerous work."

"What you're saying is that it's going to cost me," Verville said. "Rest assured that money is no object."

MacCrae raised one of the bushy eyebrows on his ruddy face, then glanced at his brother and Harry the bartender. He laughed – one harsh, derisive snort. "Money is always an object. At least, it is for us."

"I haven't come to haggle over a price," Verville said. "I'll pay you a thousand dollars for one night's work."

All three men stared at him.

"What the hell are you smuggling?" MacCrae demanded. "Diamonds and rubies?"

"Nothing like that at all, as a matter of fact. I can't tell you what the cargo is. It must be kept secret."

MacCrae shook his head. "We don't move anything unless we know what it is we're moving."

"You're moving cargo, Mr. MacCrae. That's all you need to know. Cargo worth a thousand dollars to you."

MacCrae was frowning. He finished his whiskey and nodded at the bottle. Harry poured him more. The other MacCrae brother, Angus, hardly spoke at all. He was a small man, wiry and compact, and he stood quietly to one side, his eyes roaming all over the room, all over Verville. At first, Verville thought Angus MacCrae was nervous, but then he realized that the man was sizing him up the entire time, the way a prizefighter would survey his opponent, looking for the weaknesses. He decided that if things ever went wrong with the MacCrae brothers, it was this one he would have to watch out for. James MacCrae might have the brains and bluster, but this other brother was a killer.

"I'll be honest, Doc. I don't like this kind of situation. Tell me what you can, because we'll need to plan. There are things we need to know. Will we be moving crates or barrels – or people?"

"Crates," Verville said. "There will be several smaller ones that can be carried by a single man. There will be two larger ones that will require maybe four men to lift and carry."

"Will these larger crates fit in a skiff?"

"The crates will be about four feet wide and six feet long. I don't see why they wouldn't fit."

MacCrae scratched his chin. "Sounds like we'll need some extra men."

Verville guessed what he was angling at. "For a thousand dollars, Mr. MacCrae,you should be able to arrange for the Spanish Armada if you think we'll need it."

"Hmm." MacCrae scratched his chin again. "It ain't as simple as you think, Doc, smuggling cargo ashore. The navy patrols on the Potomac are as thick as a flock of ducks, and they do raise a quack. Where do we pick up this cargo – off a blockade runner?"

Since the beginning of the war, the Union had operated an ever-tightening blockade to cut off the South's trade. Still, many ships filled with smuggled goods made it through.

"Off a vessel," Verville said, not wanting to reveal more than was necessary.

"I know that," MacCrae snapped. "But what kind, man? And where do we meet her?"

The truth was, Verville had not worked out these details.

"I can't tell you that."

MacCrae snorted again. "Why the hell not? We'll need to know, Doc!"

"I will tell you once we're on the water."

"I don't like this, Doc, let me tell you. So we're to meet a ship on Chesapeake Bay in the dead of winter in the middle of the night, I reckon. Any other surprises we should know about?"

Verville hesitated, then decided it would be better if MacCrae got used to the idea: "The vessel we'll be getting the cargo off is a Russian warship."

MacCrae sputtered as he drank his whiskey. "What the hell are you getting us into?"

"Never mind any of that," Verville said. "None of it concerns you. Now that you know some of the details, do you still want to make that thousand dollars or not?"

MacCrae hesitated. His brother and the bartender were watching him, waiting for his decision. Verville wasn't sure if the man had genuine concerns about what was expected, or if he was only bluffing, trying to drive the price of the smugglers up. He glanced at his brother, then at Harry. "All right, but it sounds like a goddamn mess, if you ask me. The first sign of trouble from the goddamn navy and that cargo goes over the side, and maybe you with it. None of us wants to get put in some prison to rot."

"Don't threaten me, MacCrae. If I'm paying you, then you're working for me. Understood?"

MacCrae bristled. His brother, the quiet one, was smiling – not that it was a pleasant expression on his ferret-like face.

"We'll need to talk some more, to make the arrangements," MacCrae finally said. "Come back tomorrow, and bring half the money."

"I'll see you then," Verville said. "Until tomorrow, gentlemen."

Verville moved toward the door, being careful not to turn his back on the MacCrae brothers. With a final nod at the three men inside the small tavern, he shut the door behind him and headed back to his hotel.

* * *

Inside the tavern, MacCrae snorted again. "Goddamn stuck-up fancy pants doctor! Reminds me of one of the goddamn lairds back home. What's he about?"

"Don't know, but we'd best find out," his brother said.

MacCrae grunted, then turned to call into a back room, "Billy! Get your arse out here, lad."

As quickly and quietly as a bird flitting through the air, a boy entered the room from a door behind the bar. He was about twelve years old, dark-haired, dressed in the ragged clothes that marked him as one of the city's newsboys who hawked newspapers on the street corners. "Yes, sir?"

"You been listening, I reckon?"

The boy looked at the floor, but he wore a sly grin on his face. MacCrae cuffed him on the ear.

"One day you'll hear something you shouldn't, lad. Now follow that rooster of a doctor, and find out where he roosts and what he's about today."

The boy moved toward the door.

"And Billy, lad, don't let him see you and for Christ's sake don't get caught. He's a bad fellow. Don't let his clothes and manners all nice-like fool you. That man wouldn't think twice about cutting your throat with that sword he keeps in his cane."

Billy nodded and slipped out, working the latch and closing the door without a sound.

"Let's have another drink, lads, and figure out what we've gotten ourselves into," MacCrae said, waiting for Harry to refill his glass. "If Verville is willing to give us a thousand dollars to smuggle this cargo of his to shore, we just might have to claim it for ourselves once it's off that Russian ship."

Chapter 9

"What do you mean, the Rebel's taken sick?" Caldwell demanded, wondering what in the world the orderly was talking about. "That Confederate soldier was doing fine yesterday. His wounds were healing."

"It's not the Rebel's wounds, sir," the orderly explained. He glanced past Caldwell to Louisa, took in the remains of breakfast in the room. "Sorry to interrupt your breakfast, Major."

"To hell with breakfast," Caldwell said. "Tell me what's wrong with this sick soldier."

"He's got a fever," the orderly said, then hesitated, as if there was something he didn't want to tell Caldwell.

"What is it?" Caldwell demanded.

"Something ain't right, sir. His skin is turning black. Ain't nobody seen the likes of it before."

Louisa was at his shoulder, listening to the orderly, and Caldwell turned to her. "We had better go take a look."

They rushed out, leaving their dishes and half-empty mugs of coffee behind. Once they were in the hallway, Caldwell realized again that he had come to trust Louisa's judgment in all matters at the hospital. In fact, she was probably the most competent person on the staff.

They hurried toward the ward. As soon as they entered the cavernous room filled with wounded, faces turned toward them expectantly, and Caldwell knew with a growing sense of unease that something just wasn't right. There was a tang of fear in the air, almost like a bitterness he could taste, and now he understood why the orderly had been reluctant to say anything other than that the Rebel soldier in the ward was sick.

The Rebel was at the back of the ward, in a chill corner where the best efforts of the tin stoves barely kept the winter at bay. Not that he was being relegated to the cold because he was a Rebel – several Union wounded nearby also struggled to stay warm despite the extra blankets they had been given. A handful of Confederate wounded were mixed in throughout the hospital. The Union and Confederate soldiers who had once been enemies intent on shooting and bayoneting each other got along well enough now that they were gathered under one roof at the hospital. For the wounded, the war was over.

"Over here, Major," said Mae O'Keefe, standing by the Rebel's cot and looking down with pity at the boy there. She made the sign of the cross, which annoyed Caldwell. Religion was only so much hocus pocus to him. Besides, by crossing herself that way she might as well have announced to the ward that the boy was dying.

Caldwell hurried over. One look at the boy, and he could understand Mae's reaction. The soldier was shivering, his face was pale and waxy, and there was an unhealthy black undertone to the skin, like a potato that was beginning to rot. At first glance, he could not tell what was causing the sickness. He, too, had never seen anything like it before. "When did this start?" he asked Mae.

"Early this mornin'. He looked fine last night, that he did, even after all that excitement."

"He's definitely feverish," Louisa said, touching the boy's brow.

"Where did the rat bite him?" he asked Mae.

"On the ankle. He was sittin' on the side of the cot when the rats come along. Why do you think that man in the cape set rats loose in our hospital?" Mae asked.

"He's a lunatic, that's why," Caldwell said. Louisa flashed him a glance – he realized something in his voice must have hinted that he knew more about their mysterious visitor than he had let on.

He turned back the blankets covering the Rebel soldier and rolled up the soldier's trouser leg to examine the bite. The rat's teeth had left two small punctures in the snow white flesh of the soldier's ankle. However, the wound appeared to be healing nicely. There was none of the angry redness that would indicate the bite had become infected.

Louisa must have been reading his thoughts. "I don't understand," she said, peering at the bite mark. "It looks fine."

Caldwell, too, was puzzled. If anything, he would have expected some infection of the rat bite to be responsible for the boy's illness.

"A doctor always looks for the obvious first," he explained to Louisa. "It's a matter of simple cause and effect. If a man falls down and complains that his arm hurts, you look for broken bones. If a rat bites a man, you look for infection."

"But if the rat bite didn't make him sick," Louisa asked, "then what did?"

"I'm afraid I don't know," he said.

Something was nagging at him, an uneasy feeling, that sense of intuition that all good doctors have. "It's not typhoid or cholera. Still, I don't like the looks of it."

Mae touched the soldier's forehead. "Whatever it is, the lad is burnin' up with fever," she said in her brogue. The old Irishwoman had brought a bowl of water and a rag, which she took and wrung out with her rough, calloused hands. Gently, almost lovingly, she mopped the boy's face with the cool cloth.

Caldwell ran his hands along the body, probing for some clue as to the cause of the fever. He noticed that the lymph nodes in the soldier's groin were swollen to the size of a hen's egg. When he touched them, the soldier flinched in pain even though he was barely conscious.

Strange, Caldwell thought.

"I want him moved," he said to the orderly. Maybe he was overreacting, but the rat bite, the black cast of the youth's flesh, and above all, Verville's hand in it – none of it was right and it made him uneasy. "Put him in the annex."

The "annex" was a sort of shed at the back of the hospital. It was where they put the terminal cases of contagious diseases. The room was whitewashed to a cheerful brightness and the tin stove kept it comfortably warm. In Caldwell's estimation, it was the least any dying man deserved.

"Sir?" asked the orderly.

"You heard me, Corporal," he snapped with too much sharpness. "I want him out of the main ward."

"Yes, sir."

"I'll help you," Louisa said, moving to assist the orderly.

"No," Caldwell said hastily, then added, "I need you here in the hospital. You too, Mae. One of the other orderlies can help."

Louisa gave him a long, questioning look, and Caldwell scowled at her in return. As the orderly went off to get help, she said in a low voice, "You don't want us to catch it, whatever it is. That's what you're thinking."

Caldwell was irritated. The idea that Louisa knew him well enough to read his thoughts made him uncomfortable. He shrugged. "Something isn't right," he said. "People don't die from rat bites. Something isn't right at all."

"Sir?" It was the orderly again.

"What is it?"

"We found both of the rats just now, sir. Both of them dead in the corners."

"Take them out and bury them. Make sure you don't touch them with your hands. Use a shovel."

"Yes, sir."

When the orderly had gone, Louisa asked in a nervous voice, "William, what's happening?"

"I wish I knew," he said. "By God, Louisa, I wish I knew."

* * *

Caldwell made some vague excuse about having work to do and disappeared into his office. Louisa knew well enough that he would spend the next several hours poring over his medical books, looking for some clue as to what fever had afflicted the wounded Rebel.

She moved off through the ward, straightening things as she went in the same way a fussy mother might. She tucked a blanket around the shoulders of a soldier who was shivering with the cold and he smiled up at her gratefully. At another cot she picked up a copy of *Harper's Weekly* that had fallen to the floor after the soldier reading it had fallen asleep. A patient called out for water and Louisa brought him a metal cup and supported his head while he drank his fill.

Just over one year ago, Louisa Webster never would have imagined herself as a nurse in a Washington City hospital. Even now, after endless months tending to the wounded, it was sometimes hard to believe this was her new life. Most mornings, she still experienced a swirling sense of bewilderment and confusion as she came awake in her narrow camp cot in a back room. She would forget that she was no longer in her bedroom in Weathersfield, Connecticut, that the window did not overlook a well-tended yard and the village green, beyond which lay a view of the Connecticut River. She would lie there, her head dizzy even on the pillow, until the sounds beyond the door – a clattering tray, the murmur of wounded men like a church congregation all mumbling their prayers – reminded her that she was in a hospital, that she was now Nurse Webster, and Miss Louisa the spinster was just a memory like the muffled rooms of her family's stately home, just down the street from the house where George Washington, Le Marquis de Lafayette and Le Comte de Rochambeau had planned the sacking of Yorktown.

Needless to say, her parents had not been pleased with her decision to go to Washington City. But considering that she was 28 years old, there was little they could say or do to stop her. The truth was, Louisa was tired of her dull, yet comfortable spinster's life. The young men had stopped calling at the Webster house years ago, and those who came infrequently now were paunchy, bald and thoroughly uninteresting. As a young woman, Louisa had not been given to coy giggling and witty conversation, and her somewhat haughty air and plain looks assured her a spinster's life. She had been content

66

until the war came and she had watched the men march off to have adventures. She found herself wanting to go with them; life in her parents' home was suddenly unbearably dull, and she began writing letters until she secured herself a nurse's position.

Now, when she thought of home, she remembered quiet rooms and dust floating in the sunlight, the stale smell of her father's cigars and the swishing of her mother's hoopskirts with all their crinoline. Hoopskirts – they had been the first casualty of life as a nurse, because there was no room for them in the narrow aisles of a hospital ward. Compared to her comfortable feather bed in Connecticut, she would gladly choose her Spartan cot by the stove. Each day was filled with more events than had happened in a month back home. Here, at least, she was needed. Here, she did something important.

Of course, she would have been dishonest with herself to deny that it had been hard at first. She would never forget that first night the wounded had come after a battle in Virginia. She had been roused in the early morning darkness. An autumn chill was in the air. All she had wanted to do was wrap herself more deeply in her blankets. But the other nurses were already up and busy, so Louisa, confused and with bleary eyes, had forced herself out of bed.

The streets outside the hospital were filled with what to her inexperienced eyes looked like market carts. They were, in fact, ambulances, lined up down the street and out of sight, having carried the wounded many miles over rough and rutted roads.

Many of the wounded were beyond help and they were left outside on the ground to die. To Louisa, that seemed terribly cruel. Nurses were detailed to give these dying men water and blankets to make their last hours comfortable. Many of the badly wounded were members of an Irish regiment and a Catholic priest moved among the soldiers in his somber cassock, giving them last rites. Louisa had never thought of the Irish as anything but servants all annoyingly named Bridget or Mary or else drunken laborers, and to see so many of them dying now for the Union made her realize how wrong she had been. They were all brave men.

Coldly, heartlessly, the surgeons had judged each case arriving – this one could be helped, that one could not. They were playing God with men's lives.

"We have to wash 'em, Miss," Mae O'Keefe had said, handing her a bowl of water, a rag, and a thick cake of vile, yellow soap. Mae was resilient. She had come near the beginning of the war to help her dying husband, and as a widow had stayed on. She showed deference to the refined Nurse Webster. "Come, Miss, get to washin' 'em as fast as you can, if you please. Tell 'em to take off shoes, socks, coats and shirts. Do it for the lads if they can't do it themselves. Scrub 'em well now, put clean shirts and socks on 'em, and the orderlies will finish 'em off as to what's below the waist and lay them in their beds."

Appalled, Louisa took the basin, the soap and the rag. She had never seen a man's naked torso, much less scrubbed one down. Tentatively, fearfully, she set to work. The men were all so dirty and bloody; some wore filthy bandages made from rags that had been in place for days, the dried blood making them stiff as old leather.

The first man she came to was an old Irishman with a bad head wound, his curly gray hair poking from beneath the bandages. As she bent to untie his muddy boots, he made a sound of dismay and said in a thick brogue, "Ugh! Don't go touchin' them dirty boots, Miss. It wouldn't be right to see them pretty hands used so."

Before she could protest, the man managed to sit up and unlace his boots. The effort exhausted him, and Louisa helped him lie down again. Then she set to work with the soap.

"May your bed above be aisy, darlin', for the day's work ye are doin'! Aye, it's hard tellin' which is the dirtiest, the foot or the shoe."

The other soldiers nearby laughed, and Louisa felt easier. She scrubbed the Irishman down, got him into a clean shirt, then moved on to the next man. Some leaned their heads against her like sleepy children as she scrubbed, while others turned red in embarrassment. She worked for hours, leaving soap suds and clean soldiers in her wake.

At first, Louisa was repulsed by the horrible injuries of the soldiers. Some were missing arms and legs, crudely hacked off at some field hospital. There were soldiers without ears, some without eyes. Louisa could hardly look at them. Her stomach heaved with nausea, but she managed to keep from being sick. Until coming to Washington, the bloodiest thing she had seen was the weekly butchering of a chicken for Sunday dinner.

Later, once Caldwell had come to the hospital, he watched her carry out this washing of the wounded and nodded his approval. "You do good work," he had said matter-of-factly. "Come along with me. Let's see how you are at dressing wounds."

"All right," she had said. The former chief surgeon hadn't trusted any of the women with more than the most menial tasks.

"Most of the ones we get here will live," Caldwell explained as he worked, unwrapping a dirty bandage to peer at the raw stump of an amputated arm. "At least, their wounds alone won't kill them if they've made it this far. There's still infection to worry about, and disease, but the bullets themselves have already done their worst."

"It's horrible," Louisa said, afraid she was about to lose the contents of her stomach at any moment.

"You'll get used to it," Caldwell said. She noticed that while his tired face was craggy and stern, his eyes were kind. Not a bad-looking man, either, she thought. Something stirred in her, feelings she had thought were permanently dormant. It was silly. She was a spinster!

As she watched, he flipped open a small leather medical case he carried to reveal several instruments strapped against the red velvet lining inside. "See if you can thread the needle in there for me. I'm afraid my hands are all covered with blood."

Louisa took out the needle and had the silk thread through the eye on the first try. To her surprise, her hands weren't shaking at all.

Caldwell was smiling at her. "Looks like we'll make a nurse of you yet, Miss Webster," he said.

* * *

Civilians were frequent visitors to the hospital. At the beginning of the war, many of the visitors had simply been curious. By now, the sight of a soldier, let alone a wounded one, was far from a rarity in Washington.

The visitors who came now had a purpose. Some were looking for their relatives, while others came to bring some small comfort to the sick and wounded soldiers. One such frequent visitor was a shaggy bear of a man with sad brown eyes. Louisa knew he had some clerical job for the government and also that he wrote poetry. In fact, she had read Walt Whitman's most recent book.

"Good morning, Miss Webster," he would say, and give her a kind smile. He gave the soldiers small gifts of writing paper, candy, newspapers, even money. It was amazing how much a few sheets of paper could mean to a man when he was confined to a cot, penniless, and eager to write home. The poet would even write the letters for them if they wanted.

The visitor to the hospital that afternoon was quite different from Mr. Whitman. She was well-dressed, with red hair neatly pulled back under a snood. She was attractive, too, and the soldiers who weren't too sick or weak to care grinned as they watched her wander the rows of cots.

"Are you looking for someone?" Louisa asked. Since last night, when their strange visitor had come with the rats, all the hospital staff had been paying more attention than usual to who came and went in the ward.

"Oh, no, not anyone in particular," the woman said. She seemed flustered by Louisa's sudden appearance, blocking her path. Something about the woman wasn't right. Louisa's first instinct was that the woman was some kind of harlot, even though she obviously wasn't the kind to be found on the street corner. "I just wanted to thank our poor boys for doing so much for our country."

"I see," Louisa said doubtfully.

"Actually, I came here this morning because I heard these young men were especially bad off," the woman said, smiling sweetly. "Something about an unusual fever."

Louisa stiffened. "Where did you hear that?"

"Oh, on the street. You know how rumors are. I've been talking with some of the soldiers here, too. They told me some of the strangest stories."

"Yes," Louisa said. She tried to keep her voice steady, but knew some of the color was draining from her face. Did talk really spread that quickly, even in this city that thrived on it? "Well, those are only … rumors. Everyone here is just fine, except for the usual ills, of course."

Still smiling, the woman pushed past Louisa and distributed a few small gifts to the soldiers in a perfunctory fashion. It was as if the woman couldn't wait to leave.

Louisa watched her for a moment, then busied herself adjusting the blanket of a soldier shivering with fever. After all, she had more important things to worry about than some do-gooder at the hospital. Still, there was something odd about the woman, something not quite sincere.

When Louisa looked around again a few moments later, the woman was already gone. Louisa shrugged and walked on.

* * *

The young Rebel who had taken sick was dead by the next morning. His flesh had turned black and his limbs were swollen to the point that they threatened to burst through the clothes still on the body. Caldwell ordered that the body be buried immediately.

"I've never seen anything like it," he admitted to Louisa, making certain that no one else in the hospital overhead. "Bodies turn black and bloated like that if they lie on the battlefield under the hot sun – but that boy rotted from within."

"Septicemia?" she asked. She tried to think of what else could have caused such horrible symptoms. "Gangrene?"

He shook his head. "There's no wound to fester. Not unless there was some internal injury I overlooked. Even then, it doesn't make sense. He was doing fine."

"Until the rat bit him," she pointed out.

Flynn walked up. He had been making himself useful around the hospital, fetching and carrying, even reading out loud to the wounded. Louisa was surprised at how well he read in a strong, clear voice. She would not have expected it. But then, she had the impression that Flynn was a man full of surprises.

She also kept forgetting Flynn's impressive size. The doctor was six feet tall with a lean build. Flynn was a hulk beside him. His shoulders were round and heavy as sacks of grain.

"Why the long faces?" Flynn asked.

Caldwell told him about the young Rebel's manner of death. "I don't like it," he concluded. "I see Verville's hand in this. There's something unusual going on here."

Louisa nodded. Caldwell had told her about Verville, about what he had done to the doctor's family, about chasing him through the city after Verville appeared mysteriously in the hospital with his rats. He had not told her that Flynn was actually a Rebel spy. Flynn had sworn him to secrecy for the time being.

"You think Verville had something to do with the boy's illness?" Flynn asked.

"Well, the rat must have, and Verville is the one who set it loose." Caldwell looked troubled; obviously, there was something else he wasn't telling them.

"What is it?" Flynn asked.

Caldwell waved his hand. "Nothing. It's just – never mind. I just had a thought as to what the illness might be, but I must be wrong. At least, I hope I am." Still, Caldwell looked unhappy. "By the way, Flynn, I want to apologize for my behavior–"

"Trying to drink the city dry, you were," Flynn said. He laughed. "It's nothing. You had the kind of night that ended best with a few drinks in you."

Louisa was giving them both the disapproving look of a New England puritan.

"Well, there's really no excuse," Caldwell said.

Flynn hid a smile. He was sure the doctor was trying to appease Louisa as much as anything.

"I visited several other hospitals today," Flynn said. "Nothing like this has happened anywhere else. Your hospital is the only one Verville has visited with his rats."

"My God," Caldwell said, his eyes going wide. There was a flash of fear in them. "It's all beginning to make sense now. You told me Verville came

71

to Washington City to launch some sort of plot against the Union."

Louisa looked from Caldwell to Flynn, then back again. "What on earth are you talking about? What plot?"

Before Caldwell could explain, an orderly came running up. He looked plainly frightened. "Major, two more have taken sick with that same fever the Rebel had."

All eyes turned to Caldwell. He sent the orderly away, then looked to Louisa and Flynn. "God help us," he said, shaking his head. "What I was saying before about the kind of illness this is … unless I'm mistaken, and I pray to God that I am, Verville has set bubonic plague loose in Washington."

Chapter 10

They sealed off the hospital.

No visitors were allowed in, and none of the patients or staff were allowed to leave. It wasn't an easy decision to make, considering they knew the wounded from Fredericksburg would soon be flooding the city and every available hospital cot would be needed.

Caldwell ordered the two most recent cases of plague carried to the annex where the first victim had died. An orderly volunteered to care for the men and he was locked in with them.

"Anyone else showing symptoms of the disease is to be put into the annex," Caldwell ordered. "The disease must be contained."

"How badly do you think it has spread?" Louisa asked.

Caldwell shrugged. "It's hard to say. After the Rebel soldier became ill, I pored over my medical books, trying to find an illness that matched his symptoms. I've never seen anything like it. There were several possibilities. Of course, I didn't want to believe he had bubonic plague, although I suspected it as soon as I saw the swelling in his lymph nodes and the black coloring of his skin. This is a disease that spreads very rapidly and kills quickly. There are accounts of people feeling fine at breakfast and being dead of the plague by sunset."

"Jesus," Flynn said. He gave a low whistle. "I thought cholera and typhoid and smallpox were bad enough."

"They are bad, Flynn, but they're nothing compared to the plague. This is the disease that killed a quarter of Europe's population when it first struck in the 1300s. More than 25 million people died in three years."

"The 1300s? That was a long time ago," Louisa said. "These are modern times. Why would such an illness show up here, and now?"

"That's easy," Flynn said. "Verville."

"He's a madman," Caldwell said. "Only the devil himself would set plague loose."

"What about us?" Louisa asked. "What about Mae O'Keefe and the orderlies? The whole hospital may have been exposed."

"I wish I knew the answer to that," he said. "All I know is that if we make it to tomorrow morning without coming down with this, we'll probably be all right."

The others nodded as if they understood, although there were worried expressions on their faces. Caldwell turned away, wishing he felt as confident as he sounded. By this time tomorrow, he knew that every soul in the hospital might be dead or dying. If that happened, the entire city of Washington might be next.

"What can we do?" Louisa asked helplessly.

"Pray," Caldwell said with a sigh. "All we can do is pray."

* * *

"I can hardly believe it," Sally said, "but it seems that your rats did their work."

"Are you certain?" Verville asked.

"The nurse there wouldn't come out and say it, but she turned white as a sheet when I mentioned that I'd heard they had some unusual sickness there."

They were sitting in Sally's parlor. Despite the fire in the grate, the room was cold. Sally had drawn the heavy curtains to stop the drafts of cold air washing in around the windows, but it was so windy outside that the fabric still fluttered slightly from the breeze seeping in. Unfortunately, the curtains had also blocked out the winter sunshine and whatever warmth it contained. The only light besides the fire came from the gas lights burning in their sconces along the walls.

Verville sipped his tea and looked at Sally with an admiring smile. She smiled back. Women had always told him he was handsome, that he had the dark good looks of a Don Juan. The truth was that Verville didn't always find himself drawn to women. There had been something to Caldwell's accusations about the Indian boy back in Texas, although it had been none of his damn business. But with someone like Sally, he had to be very careful. She had a certain power over men, he had to admit, and he could not fall victim to it. His service to the Cause would not allow it. Still, he was not made of stone. He was a man. He had been tempted and given in to the temptation.

"How many at the hospital are sick?" he asked.

"With the bubonic plague?" Sally shook her head. "None that I saw."

"Damn."

"But as I said, that nurse was terribly nervous when I asked. Something must be wrong. She was hiding something."

"Well, even if the rats had no effect, the rest of the cargo I need will be here any day now. This was just a trial. I wanted the epidemic to start in that hospital."

"They locked the doors, you know," Sally said.

"When?"

"This morning. They weren't letting anyone in, or anyone out, either."

"Then it must be the plague. Why didn't you tell me sooner?"

"Well, now you know."

Verville struggled to control himself. He needed Sally Pemberton, at least for a little while longer. He knew he had precious few friends in Washington as it was. The MacCrae brothers he was working with were poison, plain and simple. They would betray him at the slightest opportunity. He knew he could count on Sally and the journalist, Charles Wilson. They were loyal secessionists, loyal to the Cause.

"You've done well," Verville said.

A strand of her red hair had worked itself loose and Sally twisted it absently, winding it around one finger. For some reason, he found it strangely seductive, which was just what Sally intended. And he thought, just this one night, what does it matter? We might all be dead of the plague ourselves by the end of the week, or as good as dead, locked up in prison by the Yankees.

"How can you ever repay me?" she asked, smiling playfully.

"I think I know how," he said.

* * *

"Well done, Billy," MacCrae said, tossing the boy a coin. "Good lad."

The boy quickly told James MacCrae what he had learned. He had followed Jefferson Verville back to his hotel without being seen. Later, Verville had gone out again. He didn't go anyplace in particular, but seemed content to stroll the city's streets. After a while, the boy had grown tired of waiting for something to happen and returned to the MacCraes. But he had learned enough to satisfy the brothers.

"I don't trust Verville," MacCrae announced, once he had sent the boy on his way.

His brother laughed. "When have we ever trusted anyone? We haven't stayed in business this long by being fools."

James grunted and reached for the bottle of whiskey to pour himself another drink. It was true that his brother didn't say much, but when he did speak, his words usually made good sense. Of course, there was always an edge to whatever his brother said. Angus MacCrae had been born with a mean streak a mile wide, and James was always wary of it, brothers or not.

"You've had quite a bit of that rotgut already today, James." Angus' voice was stern.

"It's nothing I can't handle."

"You need to keep a clear head," Angus said. "We have business tonight – another prizefight."

"Aye," James said. He pushed his glass aside without refilling it. The truth was that he would have preferred to drink steadily through the afternoon, but Angus' words had a note of warning in them, and even he didn't dare argue with his brother when he was using that tone – especially when, deep down, he knew Angus was right. "Who are you putting your own money on tonight?"

Angus grinned. Although the MacCraes staged the prizefights, making money selling bottles of whiskey to the crowd and from a percentage of the wagers, they also bet on the fighters. Often enough, the brothers even bet against each other. Contrary to what some might think, the fights were not fixed. The more bloody the fight, the more the crowd bet, and fixed fights with their pulled punches were never as brutal as the real thing.

"The Kraut," Angus finally said. "That big German can fight."

James had planned to put a few dollars on the German's rival, Ned Smith. Smith was an English brawler who had come over last year to make some money in America. When he wasn't in a prizefight, Smith was employed by the MacCraes, doing jobs whenever muscle and quick fists were required.

The German fought for another small-time crime boss. Still, that didn't stop Angus from betting on him.

James snorted. "Your Kraut can barely speak English."

"He don't need to speak the language to beat the hell out of Ned," Angus said.

"He'll need to know enough to beg Ned to quit hurting him," James said. The brothers looked at each other and laughed; some topics could be safely disagreed upon, and the talents of particular fighters was one of those. James had to admit, though, that his brother always had a good eye for a fighter. "Now, getting back to Verville. Like I said before, I don't trust the bastard. I'll keep Billy watching him from time to time. "We'll take his money, and when the time comes we'll take this valuable cargo of his, too, and send this fancy Verville to the bottom of the Chesapeake. I never could stand a gentleman, a goddamn fancy pants."

"Aye." Angus nodded. "What do you think the cargo might be?"

"It's just a few crates, so it's opium, most likely, for medicine. Or maybe guns. You heard Verville's accent. He's a Reb, probably working for Richmond or dabbling in the black market, thinking he's going to get rich."

"If he's working for the Confederates, they might not be happy with us killing their agent and stealing their cargo."

"That shouldn't be a problem, Angus. The man is working alone – if he had any friends in Washington City he wouldn't be coming to us for help. Nobody in Richmond will ever know what happened to Verville – or to the merchandise. At least, they'll never trace anything back to us."

"True enough," Angus agreed.

"Now, let's see to that prizefight. I have Harry down at the warehouse setting things up." MacCrae smiled. "And if you're putting your money on the Kraut, to hell if I'll bet on Ned Smith. I may be the businessman in the family, Angus, but you've never been wrong about a fighter."

"Come now, James. How about two-to-one odds?" Angus' voice was tinged with mock innocence. "I can't always pick a fighter."

"Like hell you can't."

Both men laughed.

* * *

Louisa went about her duties at the hospital, trying not to think of the fact that this might be her last day alive. She had heard of the Black Death, of course, and knew that it ravaged Europe. Still, that all was so long ago; she didn't know how it was possible that such an ancient sickness had come to stalk them in modern times. It was bad enough that there was a war going on, but then, disease and war had always walked hand in hand.

Caldwell had disappeared again into his office with his medical books. She knew he would be poring over them, searching for any clues as to how they might fight the plague. She suspected, however, that there was little they could do.

"Nurse, may I have some water?" a soldier asked as she went past. Louisa smiled and brought him a drink in a tin cup.

"I hear there's some sickness going around the hospital," he said, after he had taken a long drink. His voice had a Midwestern twang. "What is it?"

"Nothing much to worry about," she answered, surprising herself by how smoothly she lied. She was aware that several men on the cots nearby were listening closely. "It's just a fever going around. You get that this time of year."

"It ain't the same fever that Rebel had, is it? He up and died, didn't he?"

"He had a weak constitution," she said. "It's a common problem with Southerners because of their poor diet. It's all that cornpone and salt pork they eat. He took sick and couldn't fight it off."

"Some of the boys are calling it Rebel Fever," the wounded soldier said. "You reckon it only kills Confederates?"

"You have nothing to worry about," Louisa reassured him. She patted his shoulder and moved on. She felt a twinge of guilt about lying to the man, but she didn't have much choice. After all, she couldn't tell him that the Black Death was loose in the hospital ward. That might cause a panic.

She was sure he would have been angry with her if he knew the truth. Or would he? If there was one thing she had learned as a nurse, it was that the wounded liked to be reassured above all else. The truth was often too painful for a man to bear.

She crossed paths with Mae O'Keefe, who was hurrying past with a tray loaded with tin mugs of beef tea. Mae made huge batches of the hearty and nutritious broth, simmering bones and scraps of meat in a huge kettle, then straining the resultant broth through cheesecloth to create the clarified "tea."

"You look tired, Miss Louisa," Mae said, then she caught herself. "Not that you look sick, mind you. Not at all."

"It's all right, Mae," Louisa said, forcing a smile. "I know what you mean. And I'm not feeling sick, not at all."

Mae hurried on with her tray of beef tea. As Louisa watched her go, she thought: the problem was that she *did* feel tired. She couldn't remember the last time she had managed to get a full night's sleep. Probably not since she started at the hospital. She noted with some bitterness that Mae never looked tired. In fact, she was energetic enough to notice Louisa's appearance. Well, that was the Irish for you. They worked like dogs and had the constitution of draft horses. Louisa supposed it came from not expecting much out of life but hard work and misery. The Irish met suffering with a smile, both the wounded soldiers and women like Mae.

Somewhere nearby, a soldier was coughing. She looked over and saw the man on his cot, his shoulders shaking with a deep, phlegmy hacking. *My God,* she wondered, *has he got the plague?* As Louisa stood, transfixed, she saw Mae O'Keefe hurry over and give the soldier beef tea. He drank it down and the coughing fit subsided.

I should have done that myself. What's wrong with me? Louisa realized her heart was racing, and she took a deep breath. Each cough, each fever in the hospital ward had become a portent of more horror to come. It was ridiculous, she knew, to worry about every little cough in the ward or hint of sickness. This was a hospital, after all. But she knew that if the plague did spread, the whole hospital might be wiped out by tomorrow night. It was not a comforting thought.

For the first time since that night that now seemed so long ago, when the ambulance convoy of wounded roused her from her sleep and initiated her into being a nurse, Louisa regretted ever leaving Connecticut. But it was too late now for regrets. The hospital doors were locked, the wounded needed tending, and only time would tell if the Rebel Fever would kill them all.

* * *

Flynn went looking for Caldwell and found the doctor at work in his shabby office.

"This is a bad business, Major," Flynn said.

"That it is," Caldwell said, looking up from his books.

"You studying up on the plague?"

"Yes." Caldwell sighed, pushed away from his desk, rubbed his eyes. "Unfortunately, I'm afraid I don't know much more about it than when I started. Nothing I've read so far explains its causes, and nothing explains how to cure it. There's been no shortage of descriptions in these books about its effects."

"I don't know much about the plague," Flynn said. "Just that it's something I'd rather not get."

"I have learned that there are at least two kinds of plague," Caldwell continued. "The kind we've discovered here in the hospital matches the typical descriptions of plague. We can thank our good luck that we haven't been struck by pneumonic plague, which is far more contagious."

"What's the difference?" Flynn asked.

"Well, the pneumonic version can develop from the primary form of plague. It attacks the lungs, and it is always fatal."

Flynn shook his head. "What the hell is Verville trying to do?"

"Look at this," Caldwell said, moving aside so that Flynn could see the illustration on the page. The drawing showed a figure in a long, hooded cloak that swept the top of his shoes. The man wore a wide-brimmed hat and a strange, bird-like beak and face mask with eye holes covered with glass. The mask was tucked into the tightly drawn hood, so that no part of the face was exposed. His fingers were encased in claw-like gloves and he held some sort of stick or wand in his hand. The writing around the illustration was in an old-fashioned script that was hard to decipher, but Flynn could pick out the words "*Pestarzt in einer Schubfleidung.*" In the background was a smaller picture of the strangely dressed man with a group of children running away from him toward a town.

"Looks like the Angel of Death," Flynn said. "Or the Cuckoo Bird of Death."

Caldwell laughed. "Believe it or not, he's a German plague physician from 1656. That beak he's wearing is filled with perfumed cloths to protect him against the 'bad air' that carried plague."

"Be glad you weren't a doctor then," Flynn said. "This poor fellow probably lasted about a day on the job before he took sick himself. And with that outfit, I'd say he scared to death any patients the plague missed. Look at those children in the background running away from him. Can you imagine seeing someone dressed like that at your bedside? It wouldn't be encouraging, now would it?"

"There's nothing here about how effective his clothing was. But you're right, Flynn. I doubt very much that a beak filled with perfume actually kept him from catching the plague, although there's nothing in the text about whether or not the good doctor, thus garbed, survived the epidemic."

"Why was this doctor going around like this in 1656? I thought you said the Black Death ravaged Europe in the 1300s?"

"It did, Flynn, starting in 1347, and it swept through whole cities like wildfire, leaving 20 million dead in three years. It says here that the Black Death can be traced to China and was likely brought to Europe aboard merchant ships."

"China seems awfully far away," Flynn said. "I wonder how it got here this time?"

"Who knows? But that plague that struck in the 1300s never really disappeared or went away for centuries. Plague bounced around Europe in limited outbreaks until 1800, and then it faded away. It still reappears every now and then, but mainly in the Orient."

"And in Washington City."

"That's what diseases do, Flynn. They lie dormant, and then for no apparent reason they rise up and become epidemics. After all, the Black Death wasn't the first time plague struck Europe. According to these books, the 'Plague of Justinian' took place in Roman times around 542 A.D. and helped bring about the fall of the Roman Empire."

"This is wonderful news you're telling me, Doctor," Flynn said. "We have a plague loose in this hospital that devastated Europe and brought the Roman Empire to its knees. If it spreads, the whole city, hell, the whole United States and the Confederate States as we know it could be destroyed."

"That's why I've put this hospital under quarantine," Caldwell said. "No one in and no one out. The good news is that according to what I've read, this disease doesn't linger. If there are no new cases within a day or two, I think we'll be all right."

"Until Verville comes back," Flynn pointed out. "For all we know, he's turning the plague loose all over Washington, like setting brush fires."

Caldwell nodded. "That's why we have to get help, Flynn. We have to get in to see the secretary of war and let him know what's going on."

"Stanton?" Flynn stared. "You can go see him. He would have me strung up if he knew who I was. I'm a Confederate spy, remember?"

"You'll be all right."

"Easy for you to say," Flynn said. "You're not the one who might not walk back out again."

"We'll go together, Flynn," Caldwell said, clapping him on the shoulder. "From now on, you're Doctor Thomas Flynn."

"That's just wonderful," Flynn said. "But I have a feeling I would rather catch the plague than walk into the United States War Department."

Caldwell turned back to the pages of his book. "If the plague spreads through the hospital, Flynn, we won't have to worry about much of anything. None of us will live to see sunset tomorrow night."

Chapter 11

On the morning after his meeting with the MacCraes, Verville breakfasted once again at his hotel. Although the dining room was hardly opulent, he rather liked the steak and eggs, as well as the fact that there was plenty of real coffee to wash them down. His mood had improved since yesterday morning because he had been sparing of his dose of laudanum the night before. Sally had occupied him in other ways. He had taken just enough to soothe his nerves and help him sleep, and the night had been filled with dreams, not the opium-induced visions that left him feeling exhausted with the dawn.

To his surprise, the well-dressed gentleman he had seen in the dining room yesterday was there again, tucking into his own heavily laden plate of steak and eggs, with a mountain of biscuits beside it. He looked over at Verville and smiled affably as he chewed.

"I see you've discovered the house specialty," the gentleman said.

"It's quite good," Verville agreed.

"You really ought to come back for dinner," the man said. "The chicken and dumplings are pretty good."

"I'm sure they are," Verville said, turning back to his plate. He had no desire to be caught up in conversation with anyone. Talking meant questions, questions meant lies, lies meant trouble.

"Do you like oysters?" his fellow diner asked, not ready to let him go yet.

"As long as they're cooked," Verville said. "I can't abide the raw ones that are so popular here."

The man made a *tsk, tsk* sound of regret. "They're damn tasty on the half shell."

"Perhaps it's the fact that I'm a physician by trade," Verville said. He thought there was no harm in revealing that much. "Forgive me for saying so, but raw oysters remind me of nothing so much as, well, innards."

The gentleman laughed. Between bites of steak and eggs, he explained that he was in Washington City on business. "I'm staying at the Metropolitan Hotel because I'm not very adventurous when it comes to bed bugs and physical comforts. However, I am adventurous when it comes to food, which is why I found this place. And you, sir? Are you in Washington on business as well?"

"Oh, yes," Verville said.

"Doctoring, I suppose?" the other man asked.

"Tending to the sick."

"Where?"

"In the hospitals," Verville said vaguely, hoping the other man would take the hint that he didn't wish to talk about it.

"I see." The fellow speared a gobbet of steak on his fork, smiled at Verville, then went on eating, returning his attention to a copy of the *Washington Star* spread on the table beside him.

Verville finished his own breakfast, then went out. He did not notice the gentleman look up from his newspaper to watch him go. Once Verville was outside, a man standing near the hotel doorway slipped into step behind him like a shadow, hanging back a few feet as Verville strode along, the heavy tip of his cane beating a rhythm on the wooden sidewalk. A second man fell into step behind them from another doorway, so that Verville was being followed by a pair of spies.

Verville found himself without much to do until the Russian ship arrived. Now that he had made contact with the MacCrae brothers, it would only be necessary to work out a few details of the arrangement with them. Still, Verville would be wary. He didn't trust the MacCraes. They were smugglers, after all, so by their very natures they were not to be trusted.

Not that James McCrae worried him too much. It was the quiet brother, Angus, that Verville knew he would have to keep an eye on. Angus MacCrae reminded Verville of a certain type he had known down South, the plantation overseer. Like many of the overseers, the Scotsman obviously resented his betters and sought every advantage over them. If there was a vacuum of power, a man like MacCrae would fill it, make it his own. Yes, Verville warned himself, if there was trouble with the MacCraes it would come from Angus.

Behind him, the spies trailed him through the streets.

Verville did not notice.

* * *

Caldwell slept fitfully and awoke with gritty eyes that felt as if handfuls of sand had been poured into them. He had turned in after midnight, leaving orders that he be awakened at the first sign that anyone else was coming down with the plague. He thought every sound outside the door was the orderly coming to tell him that someone had taken sick and the epidemic was spreading. The orderly did knock once around three a.m. – to inform him that the two sick soldiers in the hospital annex had died of the plague. Caldwell ordered their bodies taken out and buried at once, demanding that the two contrabands doing the work should wear gloves and scarves to protect themselves against the disease. At four a.m. he gave up trying to sleep, pulled his boots and coat back on, and went out to the main hospital ward.

Louisa was already there, wandering between the long rows of cots, giving out a drink of water where needed, or stopping to sponge the brow of a wounded soldier burning up with fever. Even without the plague, there was no shortage of sickness at the hospital. She saw him in the dim lantern light and walked over. Most women would have considered her dress to be incredibly plain. The dress had no hoops and was made from a somber but practical gray plaid. Caldwell thought she looked lovely in it.

"Are you just starting for the day or didn't you ever quit?" he asked.

"I couldn't sleep," she said.

"In other words, you never went to bed."

"I suppose not."

Caldwell felt a stab of exasperation, and realized it was because he was worried about her. "You have to keep your strength up, Louisa. It's going to be a long day, especially if we have any more cases of plague. Why don't you lie down for a while?"

"Why don't you?"

He shook his head. "It's no good. I can't sleep."

"What good are you going to be to anybody?" Louisa asked.

"You know, after Antietam, it's as if I don't need sleep anymore. I don't think it's possible for me ever to be that tired again." He didn't tell her that there was no way he could survive another experience like Antietam. Operating for days straight on the wounded whose mangled limbs were already putrid with gangrene, fueled by coffee and whiskey; it had been inhuman, a living hell for both the medical staff and their patients. Although Louisa hadn't been there, she was sympathetic about what he had experienced.

"Well, you look tired, Doctor, even if you don't feel it."

Caldwell smirked at his head nurse. "Your bedside manner leaves something to be desired, Nurse Webster. You certainly know how to give a patient confidence."

"I just thought I would give you a dose of concern, Doctor. You looked as if you could use it."

Caldwell smiled, but the grin faded as he thought of the two patients who

84

had already died of the plague. "Damn Verville," he said out loud. "Doesn't the fool know that if bubonic plague got loose in the city that it could kill thousands? The man has no decency."

"I doubt it's decency he's after," Louisa said. "You said Dr. Verville served with you in the Army out West, before the war. But when the Confederate states declared themselves to be independent, Verville went home to join the South."

"Yes, that's just what he did. He sided with Virginia, his home state."

"But you didn't."

"No," he said, shaking his head. "There were a lot of men in the Army who felt that sense of loyalty – Virginia, right or wrong. I was never one of those. Maybe it's because I was in the Army so many years and away from home. In any case, it seems to me that the Union – the United States of America – is far more worthy of loyalties than the Confederacy."

"The Union stands for freedom," Louisa said. "We're setting the slaves free. It's a rare Virginian who is an abolitionist at heart."

Caldwell smiled. He had the sense that Louisa was teasing him now. She had a dry sense of humor, sharp as a scalpel, and he liked that in a woman. He nodded toward a black man who was busy stoking a coal stove against the pre-dawn winter chill. "How could anyone fight to keep a man like that in chains?" he asked. "Who's to say the African race is any less human than the white race?"

"Your questions are entirely rhetorical, Doctor."

"Yes, Louisa, they are. But it breaks my heart to think of so many good Virginians fighting for a cause that has such evil at its core."

"The war isn't all about slavery," Louisa pointed out.

"No," Caldwell said. "It's not. But the North can claim it is fighting to free the slaves. What can the South claim?"

"You're saying that the South has no moral basis for the war?"

"There never has been a good moral basis for any war," Caldwell said. "There's not much that's worth young men spilling their blood for. What I am saying is that the North needs to win this war, Louisa. It's the only hope for the future of the United States."

"I doubt that's what your fellow Virginians are saying," Louisa said. "They don't want to be part of that future."

He nodded. "You're right, Louisa. Verville might even be trying to win the war with those damn rats of his. He's willing to spread bubonic plague to do it. Like a lot of Southerners, he wants victory at any price."

"He's willing to start an epidemic? That's reprehensible. It goes against the laws of mankind," she said. "Besides that, where is he going to get enough rats?"

Caldwell shrugged. "Who knows? But knowing Verville, he'll find a way."

He looked at her tenderly. Louisa had been a nurse for some time now, but maybe not long enough if she still believed that there were any basic laws of mankind. He reflected that he was no longer surprised by what one man was capable of doing to another. In the West, he had seen the brutality of white men against the Indians, and also the other way around. All through the early months of the war, he had seen worse in the field hospitals than they would ever witness here in Washington.

"War is reprehensible no matter what rules it's fought by," he said to Louisa. "Look at what we do all day long, trying to patch men – boys, I should say – together again. You've seen what a minié bullet does to flesh and bone. That's horrible, no matter what rules are being followed. Verville is just making new rules, using new weapons, and we have to stop him."

Caldwell began to make his morning rounds, and Louisa accompanied him. It was much earlier than usual. He generally waited until the men had their breakfast. But the men in real agony were already awake, sleep being an elusive commodity for them. The sleeping men they left alone. Sleep was the best tonic there was for the wounded.

"How is that leg doing?" he asked a soldier named Barnes, who was propped up on his cot, straining to read *Harper's Weekly* in the dim light.

"I reckon it's all right, Doctor," Barnes stated in a country drawl.

"You'll ruin your eyes trying to read in this light, Corporal Barnes."

"If that's the only part of me that's ruined, Doctor, I'll count myself a lucky man."

With deft hands, Caldwell peeled back the bandage to reveal his wound. Barnes had been hit in the thigh by a bullet, but he was lucky; the bullet had missed the bone entirely, which meant he had a chance of keeping his leg. Still, the bullet had torn the flesh cruelly and left a jagged exit wound. The scabbed surface was streaked with pockets of white pus that resembled the marbled fat in a rich steak.

"There's some laudable pus, which is a good sign," Caldwell said, using the medical term for what doctors called "healthy" pus. "A wound won't heal without pus."

"I don't care about the pus, I just wish it wouldn't hurt so damn much," Barnes said, then nodded sheepishly at Louisa. "I'm sorry, ma'am. I don't mean to cuss. My mama didn't raise me like that, but it's the Army life that does it."

Caldwell took a lancet and poked at some of the larger veins of pus in order to get them to drain. Turning to Louisa, he ordered that the wound be dressed with persulphate of iron and a fresh bandage. They moved on.

Flynn found them making the rounds, roaming from aisle to aisle, and they moved to an area where they could talk without being overheard by the soldiers in the cots. Flynn did not look well-rested, but neither did any of them. It had been a long, largely sleepless night for all of them, considering that the seeds for one of the deadliest epidemics in human history lurked under their roof. Flynn was drinking a huge tin mug filled to the brim with coffee.

"Well, we're all still alive," he remarked as he took a gulp of coffee. "Any sign that the plague has spread?"

"The two other soldiers with the plague died during the night," Caldwell said.

"But no one else is sick?"

"No one else is sick."

"That's good, isn't it?"

"We're not entirely safe yet, Flynn, but at least the plague doesn't seem to be spreading throughout the hospital."

"Thank God," he said.

Louisa interrupted. "I can finish the rounds with one of the assistant surgeons, Doctor," she said. "I think you and Mr. Flynn should get ready to see the secretary of war to let him know there's a Confederate madman trying to set the Black Death loose in Washington."

Flynn looked hard at Caldwell. "As I said before, I'm not so sure I like this idea."

"If what you've told me about Verville is true, we need to let the authorities know. They can help us find him, and if he's trying to start an epidemic, the government can help us stop it before it gets started."

"All right," he said. "I suppose we don't have much choice."

"Good," Caldwell said. "Now let's see if we can't find you something decent to wear, like maybe a blue uniform."

Appalled, Flynn choked as he took a big swallow of his scalding hot coffee.

* * *

The two men following Verville were among the best.

Martin Goodman and Joshua Sandford had been employed by the United States Secret Service in this kind of work since early in the war. They were so successful mainly because they were almost completely nondescript.

In his late forties, Goodman was too old to be a soldier. He was of medium height with a large belly. His round face was hidden behind a dark beard flecked with gray, and the truth was that he resembled half the men on the streets of Washington – the half that weren't in uniform.

Sandford was tall and gangly, an awkward sort of man no one would bother to look at twice. However, his eyes, shaded by the brim of his hat, were quick and searching, darting from one spot to the next like a bird's.

At first, Verville was remarkably easy to follow. Verville strolled down the sidewalk and Goodman bobbed along in his wake. Child's play, really, for two men who had followed everyone from experienced Confederate agents to Union officers suspected of disloyalty. They worked for the man in the restaurant, whose name was Lafayette Baker, chief of the United States Secret Service.

All that Sandford or Goodman knew about Verville was that he was a frequent visitor to the home of a known Confederate sympathizer named Sally Pemberton. Her house was under constant surveillance, although the foolish woman didn't know it. Verville's visits to her house made him suspicious, and Baker had ordered him watched. Verville was obviously a Southerner himself, so anything he did was automatically under scrutiny.

"There's something special about this one," Baker had said. "Let's see where he takes us."

The first sign of trouble came when Verville paused to light a cigar and cast a furtive look behind him as he cupped his hand around the match to guard it from the winter wind. Goodman managed to stop as well and buy a copy of the *Washington Star* off a newsboy. By the time he had the paper in hand, Verville had walked on and Goodman hurried for several yards to keep him in sight.

Not that Verville was hard to miss in the press of people on the sidewalk. He was very tall and well-built, and he wore a dark cloak that made the doctor look even larger as the wool fabric fluttered in the wind. It was a bitterly cold day and they were walking into the teeth of the wind. Goodman flipped up his own coat collar to protect his cheeks and ears.

Verville had an evil look about him and Goodman decided he was glad they weren't following this fellow through the empty streets of the night-time city, when anything might happen if the doctor realized he was being followed. Goodman carried a pistol in his coat pocket for just such situations, but he doubted Verville would be a danger in broad daylight.

Still, Verville was an uncanny bastard. As the sidewalk became more crowded in the neighborhood of the Willard Hotel and treasury building, Goodman quickened his pace to keep up with Verville. The doctor suddenly stopped and turned, studying the faces of the crowd behind him. Goodman had no choice but to keep his eyes straight ahead and continue walking right past Verville.

It was all up to Sandford now. He had been hanging far back, and Verville turned around again and continued walking. He could see Goodman's squat figure down the street ahead of Verville, but there was no chance Goodman could get back in the game now. The doctor would certainly become suspicious.

Verville swung off the more crowded wooden sidewalk and started down a side street. Sandford followed, keeping a great distance behind. However, Verville appeared to be satisfied that he wasn't being followed. Evidently, his maneuver back on the sidewalk had convinced him he was alone.

Tricky bastard, Sandford thought. Anyone less experienced following him would have been smoked out.

He followed Verville down 14th Street and then Independence Avenue and Sixth Street. The wind grew more bitter, and for good reason; it was a straight walk down Sixth Street to the wharves, and the wide expanse of the Potomac River was just ahead. Then Verville reached the waterfront and the wind was like a gale. Sandford clapped his hand more tightly on his hat and walked on. Verville came to a seedy little tavern and ducked inside. Sandford waited outside for half an hour, lurking in doorways and stamping his feet against the cold, but Verville did not reappear.

Now we'll see what you're about, Sandford thought with satisfaction, then he turned back toward Pennsylvania Avenue.

Chapter 12

In the end, Flynn's gray civilian suit had to do.

The trip from Richmond and the fight in the alley had left it dirty and rumpled. But they could not find an officer's uniform large enough to fit him. His wide shoulders would have split Caldwell's spare coat in an instant.

Mae O'Keefe had busied herself with needle and thread to repair the worst rents in his suit, then brushed it down.

"You look like the village bachelor on his way to Mass," Mae said, trying to tug Flynn's lapels into respectability. "He'd be wearing the good suit he found in the corner where he tossed it the Sunday before."

Flynn's voice slipped easily into a brogue. "Och, woman, I'm not so entirely helpless as that."

"I've never met a man who isn't helpless when it comes to clothes," Mae said with motherly exasperation. "Look at you – your hands are so big you can barely get your buttons buttoned."

"Do the best you can with it, Mae dear, because if things don't go well at the secretary of war's office this may be the suit I'm hanged and buried in."

"Don't say such things! It's bad luck to speak of them. Just keep your mouth shut and let Doctor Caldwell do the talking. You'll be all right then. The doctor has been in the Army a long time, and he knows all the right things to say. He's an educated man."

A few doors away, Caldwell was dressing more solemnly, alone in his quarters. It was a rare occasion when he put on his dress uniform. Especially now in Washington, he just wore his old coat most of the time with an apron over it. These were his working clothes and they served him well.

However, the faded uniform wouldn't suffice for visiting Edwin M. Stanton, the secretary of war.

From deep in his sea chest, Caldwell took out his dark blue trousers and good boots. The boots could do with a shine, and he gave one of the boys who worked in the kitchen a coin to black them. He took out his coat and brushed it down, then went at the brass buttons, polishing them until they gleamed. He took out a neatly folded clean shirt, boiled to a blinding white, and put it on. Then he slipped on his uniform and retrieved the boots the boy had left outside the door.

It was strange how different it made him feel to put the uniform on. There was so much tradition behind it, so much authority, and suddenly he felt stronger and more sure of himself than he had in months. He was proud of this uniform and of being an officer in the United States Army. Never for one moment since the war had broken out had he regretted his decision not to resign his commission and serve Old Virginia instead. Some might call him a traitor to his home and family, but Caldwell never felt that way. As he had told Louisa, there were some things more important than loyalty to your home state, and the Union was one of them.

He wound his silk sash around his waist. It was green, a color that denoted a medical officer. On his shoulders were epaulettes, the gold faces had "M.S." – medical service – engraved on them in script. The last item to come out of his chest was a cavalry saber. Most medical man merely wore decorative swords, but Caldwell had been given this one by a lieutenant after saving his life on the frontier. It was a heavy and savage thing with a long, wicked blade. He had seen a few saber wounds in his career and knew the blades sliced through flesh and bone like a butcher's cleaver. Fortunately, saber wounds were rare. Caldwell had never bothered to sharpen the blade. He buckled the sword on. The weight felt reassuring on his hip, even if it was purely ceremonial.

"I hardly recognize you."

He spun at the sound of the voice. Louisa stood in the doorway, smiling as she watched him. The haggard look she had worn earlier that morning was gone.

"What are you doing there?"

"The door was open."

So it was; he had forgotten to close it all the way after fetching his boots. Still, he felt embarrassed to be caught trying to get his sword to hang just so.

"It's a ridiculous thing, this full uniform."

"You look very handsome in it, Major Caldwell."

He blinked, shocked that Louisa had said something so direct. She appeared to have surprised herself by speaking her thoughts out loud. Her face flushed crimson.

"Thank you, Louisa," he said quietly. He managed a small smile. "It's been some time since I've worn it."

"The secretary of war will be impressed."

"Impressed or not, I just hope he listens. None of the other patients have displayed any symptoms of the plague?"

"The men in the ward are calling it Rebel Fever because that poor

Confederate boy was the first to come down with it," she said. "Fortunately, there's no more sign of it. This morning there's a new case of pneumonia and one of flu, but nothing worse."

"Thank God," Caldwell said. "If this so-called Rebel Fever hasn't spread by now, I don't think it's going to. I'll give the order that the workers who have been quarantined here can go home."

"They'll be glad to hear it."

"How does Flynn look?"

"Like he slept in his suit, but it can't be helped. Nothing else will fit him."

"He's a big man."

"You don't think you'll get him in trouble, taking him to the War Department?"

Caldwell shrugged, jangling the fringe on his epaulettes. "I think he'll be all right, just so long as he doesn't come right out and admit he's a Southern agent. If he does that, they'll lock him up in the Old Capitol Prison, or hang him."

"My God," Louisa said.

"It's a serious business, this spying," Caldwell remarked. "I'll be glad to let wiser minds take it on from here and decide what needs to be done. Doctoring is what I'm good at, Louisa, not intrigue."

She smiled, reached for his hand. "You're a good man, William. A brave man."

He smiled back. "We'll see what the secretary of war has to say about that."

* * *

He felt so weak.

Jack O'Grady had once been a big strapping fellow whose ability to knock a head or carry a load as the occasion demanded was much the pride of his friends and especially of his red-haired wife, Maureen.

No one would have known that now by watching O'Grady make his way home just after dawn through the muddy streets that crisscrossed the Irish slum of Swampoodle at the city's edge. He walked with a limp and his shoulders were stooped.

The war and soldiering had done that to him. He had taken a Confederate bullet in the leg at First Bull Run. Not that a hot chunk of Rebel lead had been enough to stop the likes of Jack O'Grady. He fought on, brave as the Celtic hero Cuchulainn, until an exploding shell smashed his shoulder.

His moment of glory on the battlefield resulted in months in the hospital and weeks more recuperating under Maureen's care. O'Grady survived, but the strong man's spirit had died on the battlefield. He worked nights now in Armory Square Hospital, making sure the coal stoves were stoked properly by the contrabands, scrubbing pots in the kitchen when needed, and using what remained of his strength to help lift the wounded so that the nurses could change the sheets. Dr. Caldwell paid him four dollars a week. It wasn't much, considering skilled tradesmen made ten dollars or more per week, but it put food on the table.

"I'm feeling damned tired," O'Grady muttered to himself. He wiped the back of his hand across his forehead, and felt a feverish heat there, in spite of the cold air. *What's this? Coming down sick?* Not that he was surprised. There was a whole host of sicknesses flitting about that hospital including typhoid, influenza, and whatever horrible illness had killed that sick Confederate and turned his flesh black. They were calling it Rebel Fever. O'Grady reflected that it was a wonder he wasn't dead yet, working in a place as pestilential as that damned hospital.

"Och, O'Grady, drunk again, are you, man?" called one of his neighbors, a bony scarecrow of a fellow heading to work as a laborer on the new Capitol building project.

"Shut yer gob, Joseph Cavanaugh," O'Grady growled with some of the authority he'd once had. He realized he was, in fact, staggering. "I've got a touch o' fever, workin' in the hospital."

He coughed, reaching to keep his balance, and Cavanaugh caught him by the shoulder to keep him from toppling over.

"Aye, O'Grady, after Maureen gets through with yer drunken arse you will be feelin' under the weather, indeed."

Laughing, Cavanaugh walked on, and O'Grady reflected that his neighbor would never have dared speak to him that way in the old days. He would have knocked him senseless. He searched for some parting insult to hurl at Cavanaugh's back, but didn't have the energy. His mind was feverish and full of cobwebs.

He reached the door of a shabby clapboard hovel badly in need of paint and stumbled inside. Maureen was at the table, drinking weak tea, and looked up crossly as he lurched through the door. Two of the children were there, too, pale underfed things that stared up at their father with big, hungry eyes.

"Jack O'Grady, if you're drunk again—"

"No, woman, I've taken sick."

Her look of anger changed to one of alarm and she jumped up from the table. "Mother of God, Jack, look at you! We must get you into bed."

"I don't understand," he said. "I was fine when I left the hospital. It come over me on the walk home."

"Well, yer not fine now. Let's get you into bed and then I'll bring you a nice cup of tea."

For a poor man like O'Grady, sickness meant disaster. If he couldn't work, he wouldn't be paid, and there would be no money to buy food or pay the rent. Only charity had kept them from starving while Jack was in the hospital after Bull Run.

O'Grady felt dizzy. He held on to the walls with both hands as he made his way upstairs and into the bedroom. He wondered that he should feel so weak for someone who had once been the strongman of Swampoodle. Maureen helped him off with his shoes and clothes. His legs felt heavy as logs; she had to help hoist them into bed. The children were underfoot and she shooed them out of the room.

"Don't you worry, Jack, we'll have you right in time for work tonight."

"Aye, Maureen," O'Grady said, and he closed his eyes. It was like the lid on a hot stove slamming shut. He coughed and his lungs sounded as if they were filled with fluid.

Maureen studied his fevered face with a worried look. Although his wounds in this damned rich man's war had sapped his strength, her husband had always been a healthy man – otherwise he wouldn't have survived the hurts that would have killed other men. It wasn't like him to be sick. She sent one of the children to wet a rag.

Briefly, she couldn't help but consider what she would do if Jack ever died and left her alone with the children. It had been a close thing after Bull Run, left to rely on the charity of her pinch-faced sisters-in-law and Jack's drunken brothers. The church was of no help – although she had heard from Mrs. Mullins, who did the cooking, that the priests could afford wine every night with dinner and whiskey, too. What would she and the children eat? A woman could only make so much taking in mending.

"There, there, Jack, you'll be right in no time," Maureen said, caressing his forehead with the damp rag. She could feel the heat rising off him. "Just a little fever you've got."

O'Grady didn't hear. There was a curious gray-black pallor under his pale skin that Maureen didn't like the looks of. No telling what a man could catch in that hospital. Deep down, she began to be afraid, and just under her breath she started to mutter the only words that had been any consolation to Maureen O'Grady in her difficult and unhappy life: *Hail Mary, full of grace, the Lord is with thee. ...*

* * *

Flynn would just as soon have entered hell itself than the United States War Department.

A sense of uneasiness settled in his belly like a cold stone as he climbed the marble steps with all the enthusiasm of a man ascending the scaffolding for his own hanging. This was the lair of the enemy, a den of blue-coated lions. The place even smelled bad: damp wool, stale cigar smoke, a hint of urine in the air. Gas lamps burned night and day in the dim corridors, but Flynn felt as if no amount of light would ever reach some of the rooms and dark corners.

He realized he had made a terrible mistake in accompanying Major Caldwell to this pit of Yankee vipers. Like the dreaded Old Capitol prison, this was the sort of place a man might enter and never leave, especially if he was a Confederate.

"Are you sure you can't do this by yourself?" Flynn whispered to Caldwell as they were whisked along by a very well-dressed young aide. He was a slim young man with a mustache that was entirely too large for his thin face. The effect was the same as if he had been wearing his father's overcoat. However, it was clear from the youthful captain's haughty manner that he considered Flynn and Caldwell to be unimportant.

"If Stanton wants proof, you're the closest thing to it I have," Caldwell said. "I can't bring him a corpse to look at, so you'll have to do."

"Why, thank you," Flynn muttered bitterly.

"What I mean, Flynn, is that you're a genuine Confederate agent. If he hears the plot from you, he'll know it's the truth."

"You mean he'll know to hang me and clap you in irons for meddling in affairs that are over your head."

"Just let me do the talking," Caldwell snapped.

Caldwell was convinced that coming to the War Department was the right thing to do. Where he sensed that Flynn was a man who had an innate distrust of institutions, preferring to depend upon his own wits – and fists, if need be – Caldwell was a career military man. As such, he had a great faith in authority that bordered on the religious. That was what a good soldier did, after all, when he so much as came to a fork in the road: he asked his superior officer which direction to take. To Major Caldwell, seeking out orders in a situation like the one he now faced was as natural as breathing. The difference was that he had come right to the top, to one of the highest authorities in Washington short of President Abraham Lincoln. Caldwell would settle for nothing less than a meeting with the secretary of war.

The sight of the crowded reception room at the War Department was not encouraging. Edwin M. Stanton conducted business differently from everyone else in the city. There were no appointments or private meetings. If you had business with the secretary of war, you brought it to the reception room in the morning – along with everyone else.

By the time Flynn and Caldwell arrived, the room was already overflowing with cashiered officers and favor-seeking politicians and civilians, all of whom waited in line for a chance to state their business to Stanton while everyone else in the reception hall listened. There was no chance at graft, no deals to be made in smoke-filled back rooms. All business was conducted in the open, in full view of the reception room, with Stanton making his decrees with an unsmiling face and dry voice. This was a thoroughly democratic process that was almost entirely alien to Washington City. It also made Stanton one of the most hated men in the capital.

Flynn took a long look at the United States Secretary of War. His appearance was hardly impressive. Stanton stood behind a tall writing desk that reached to his chest, surrounded by various aides and clerks. He was short and had a round body that reminded Flynn of a giant egg with legs. He wore steel-rimmed spectacles that made his eyes appear larger than they were as he stared intently at a white-haired officer who had his ear at the moment. His face was covered by a thick beard, although his upper lip was shaved bare, making it look as if he wore a false beard that had been tied behind his large ears.

"We need to see Mr. Stanton," Caldwell announced to the captain who had brought them in.

"You'll have to get in line with everybody else, Major," the captain said. "These other people have been waiting since first thing this morning."

"It's important," Caldwell insisted. "He'll want to hear this. He needs to hear what I have to say."

"Sorry, sir, but you'll have to wait your turn," said the captain in a less patient tone.

Caldwell began to surge forward through the line of waiting supplicants. A murmur rose up as people turned to see what the commotion was about. "I haven't come this far to–"

The captain started purposely toward Caldwell, but Flynn stepped forward and neatly blocked him with his back. He took the major's arm as images of a dark Yankee prison swirled up to fill his head. "Come now, Major, this won't do. We'll wait our turn like everyone else."

The captain dodged around Flynn. He was an annoyingly persistent fellow. "Major, you'll have to leave, sir."

"Everything's fine now," Flynn said.

"Sir, I'm afraid I must insist–" The captain might have tried to force

96

Caldwell to leave, but Flynn stared him down. The young officer, who was more used to bullying bureaucrats and the grieving wives of imprisoned Southern sympathizers, quickly retreated to his post by the door.

"You there, what's all this ruckus?" Stanton had seen the commotion and waved them toward his desk. "Step up, step up. I haven't got all day."

"We needed to see you right away, sir," Caldwell said.

"What's your complaint this morning, Major?" Stanton asked, taking in Caldwell's medical service uniform with a quick glance before his weirdly magnified eyes roved to settle suspiciously on Flynn. "You surgeons are always complaining about the state of the hospitals. Nothing is ever good enough for you, but that we spend and spend and spend."

"No, sir, no complaints. But there are dire circumstances I must relay to you."

"Which hospital do you work in?" Stanton asked. He looked around until he had spotted the annoying captain. "Wilkerson! Be sure to take notes."

"Yes, sir," Captain Wilkerson said, poising his pencil above a blank sheet of paper.

"Now, Major, where do you work?" Stanton asked again.

"Armory Square Hospital, sir. My name is Caldwell. I'm the chief surgeon there."

"Did you know, Major, that in 1860 the United States had exactly one official infirmary with forty beds?" Stanton looked to be a man whose head was filled with such facts.

"I am aware of that, sir. I was in the Army long before the war."

"Do you know how many hospitals we now have, Major?"

"I have no idea, sir."

"There are exactly one hundred and eighty-seven hospitals, with one hundred and eighty-one thousand beds."

"Yes, sir."

"I tell you this to put things in their proper perspective. Armory Square is just one of the sixteen hospitals here in Washington City, an important fact to keep in mind no matter what problems you may have there."

"That's true, sir, but we may be the only hospital with an outbreak of a particular illness, which is why I came here this morning."

"And what disease might that be?" Stanton asked, his eyelids drooping.

"Bubonic plague, sir."

The others in the room had been listening intently to the exchange between Stanton and the doctor. At the mention of bubonic plague, the whispered conversations in the reception room would not have ended more abruptly if an artillery shell had exploded in their midst. Several people took a step back from Stanton's desk. Captain Wilkerson brushed nervously at the sleeves of his uniform, as if the doctor might have carried the disease in with him.

"My God," Stanton said, his mottled face blanching where it wasn't covered by the gray beard. Sweat appeared on his rubbery upper lip. "The Black Death?"

"One and the same, sir. All the symptoms match. There's no doubt in my mind that we have the plague in our hospital, although we've managed to contain it. Three men have died, one Confederate patient and two of our own soldiers, although there haven't been any new cases."

"That is interesting, Doctor, and a matter for concern, but I'm sure you are better qualified to handle an outbreak of this contagion than I. Is that why you've come here this morning?"

"No, sir."

"I was afraid not," Stanton said wearily. "What matter, then, is so urgent?"

"This outbreak of bubonic plague did not come to my hospital by chance. It was brought by a Southern agent. He intends to spread the disease through the city."

"A plot to bring the North to its knees?" Stanton actually smiled, although on his serious face the pale lips looked disturbingly frosty. "Not another one of those!"

"But sir—"

Stanton waved him to silence. "And this silent, rather menacing fellow at your side is undoubtedly also an agent of some kind, come to verify your plot?"

"Sir, the plague—"

"You've already said you've done what you must to contain the outbreak," Stanton said. "The plot has begun and ended."

"This agent has rats—"

"Rats, too?" Stanton was chuckling, but he busied himself by shuffling some papers on the high desktop in front of him. He was showing Caldwell that he was done with him. "Thank you, Major. Now, I have many people to see today."

"The rats are being used to spread the plague—"

When Stanton looked up again, his gaze went beyond Caldwell to the next person in line. It was as if Caldwell wasn't there at all. Captain Wilkerson appeared at Caldwell's side, artfully placing himself between the doctor and the secretary of war, as effective as a door closing on the interview.

Caldwell, though, was stubborn. He started to protest, to tell Stanton he

98

was wrong, that the threat of a Southern plot was very real, that thousands could die. Stanton was being a fool. Seeing that the doctor was working himself up, Flynn stepped in and took him forcibly by the arm. They had tempted the lion's den and lived; if the Yankees thought the doctor's theory on a Rebel plot was crackpot, then that was their own damn fault.

"Come on," Flynn said, and together with the aide he propelled Caldwell out a side door, even though the doctor was still sputtering in protest. Once they were in the hallway, the aide left them and disappeared back into the reception room.

"He actually laughed at me," Caldwell said in disbelief. "I go to him to report this plot to destroy the city and he laughs at me."

"He's a fool, Doctor. He wouldn't believe you unless Jefferson Verville had the whole damn city dying, and even then I'm not so sure."

"I don't know who else to go to," Caldwell said. "I started at the top, right with Stanton himself. If he won't believe me, then I might as well give up."

"No, Doctor. We're not giving up. We're just getting started. We know what Verville is trying to do, and it's up to us to stop him. Us, and no one else."

Caldwell nodded. "I suppose you're right. But how do we start?"

"First, we have to find him," Flynn said. "That's the first step."

"But how do we track him down in this city? He could be anywhere."

"I have some ideas," Flynn said. "But it's going to take some time."

They reached the frozen, wintry street and went out. After the dark confines of the War Department building, Flynn thought he had never smelled such sweet air. He realized the place had the same oppressive atmosphere as the headquarters of the Confederate Secret Service in Richmond. Beside him, Caldwell walked with stooped shoulders under the weight of Stanton's ridicule.

Neither man noticed Captain Wilkerson slip out after them and follow behind as they walked back to the hospital.

* * *

In the ramshackle house in Swampoodle, Jack O'Grady was slipping closer to death. His breathing was shallow and labored, and he had barely stirred since getting into bed that morning. The sickness moved with amazing swiftness, Maureen thought.

She watched with resignation. It was a skill the Irish Catholics of Swampoodle had mastered during a lifetime of hardship. Even so, Maureen silently cursed the war that had robbed her husband of his legendary strength.

The old Jack O'Grady would never be sick in bed with fever. She blamed it on the rich man's war – to free the darkies, of all things, so they said – that had ruined so many men like her husband. He had never been the same after his wounding at Bull Run. Now here he was, once the strongest man in Swampoodle, about to be carried off by some fever.

He woke around three o'clock to ask for water. "It's the Rebel Fever," he said, after he had taken a sip with parched lips. "The Rebel Fever has done me, Maureen."

"Hush now, and save your strength, Jack O'Grady."

That was the last her husband said that made any sense. An hour later he was muttering gibberish in Irish, a language he hadn't spoken since he was a boy. At four o'clock Maureen summoned the children, seven of them, to gather around their father's bed. She sent the oldest for the priest, although the damn greedy man would want a dollar for giving Jack his last rites. There was nothing to be done about that, however; a man needed that final sacrament to ease his entry into heaven.

He died a little after sunset, just as they were lighting the lamps. Father Larkin arrived too late in his black robes, but he took his dollar anyhow and anointed Jack's head with oil and holy water. Somehow, Maureen was managing to get through all of it, thinking ahead already to the wake and funeral. The wake might have to be shorter than the usual three days, she decided, taking a look at Jack's face, which was turning black like an old potato peel left to rot. A cruel disease indeed to do that to a man.

The youngest one, dear little Catherine, interrupted her thoughts. "Ma," she said, looking up at Maureen with feverish eyes. "I don't feel good."

Chapter 13

"Major, we caught a spy!"

Caldwell finished applying iron persulfate to a wound that was refusing to heal and walked toward one of the Invalid Corps soldiers who served as an orderly at the hospital. He had recently put the man on sentry duty. "What do you mean, 'a spy'?" he demanded.

"He's a spy all right, sir," the guard said happily.

Because they were short on help, Caldwell had been reluctant to assign men to guard the hospital. But since Verville's appearance, Caldwell didn't think they had much choice but to post the guards.

"What makes you so sure he's a spy?"

"We found him lurking about. When we asked his business, he demanded to see you."

"Me? I'm not expecting any visitors, spies or otherwise." He looked around for Flynn and spotted him on the other side of the ward, playing cards with some of the patients. "Mr. Flynn! Come here, would you?"

"This better be important," Flynn yelled back. "I'm about to win a fortune off these boys."

They followed the guard outside. The man limped badly. Caldwell observed that one leg was shorter than the other, and he guessed it must be a result of the suppuration of the tibia after a bullet wound.

The alleged spy had his back pressed tightly against the clapboard wall of the hospital building. The man looked extremely nervous and pale, although Caldwell wasn't sure if that was because he had been found out as a spy or due to the fact that the guard, wearing the sky blue uniform of the Invalid Corps, had the bayonet on the end of his Springfield rifle held just inches from the fellow's chest.

Flynn pushed the bayonet away. "Easy now," he said to the excited guard. "Don't stick him before we can talk to him."

"Do you recognize this man, Flynn?" asked Caldwell, who had seen the young officer's face just that morning.

"Sure," Flynn said as a grin spread over his face. "This is the snotty little bastard from the War Department. Did Mr. Stanton send you, lad?"

"Nobody sent me," the young aide stammered, trying to regain some of his composure after being held at bayonet point. It was clear his indignation was quickly returning, although he had as much dignity as a flustered chicken. "I came on my own. I believe what you said about this Confederate plot, and I want to help."

"We had better go inside and talk," Caldwell said, casting a sideways glance at the guards. He knew the soldiers' penchant for gossip and that the story of the aide's capture and mention of a "Confederate plot" would be all over the Invalid Corps by morning, much less the hospital.

"Good job, lads," Flynn said to the soldiers. "That's just how you want to do it – don't stick lurkers with the bayonet until we can question them. Bayonet wounds just make extra work for the doctor."

Flynn sent the War Department aide through the door with a mighty shove, then he and Caldwell followed. They took him to Caldwell's office and sat him in a straight-backed chair. Flynn stood in the doorway, blocking it with his bulk.

"This isn't some game, lad," Flynn began. "We're not playing at spy."

"I know that."

"I'm not sure you do. A boot-licker like yourself will only get his uniform dirty to have fun."

"I didn't come here to be interrogated," the aide sniffed.

"Interrogated!" Flynn barked. "If this was a goddamn interrogation I'd be beating you bloody right about now. I might still do that just for fun. Now, why don't you start by telling us your name?"

"Captain C.J. Wilkerson."

"You're awful young to be a captain, Wilkerson. You must have a rich daddy."

"My grandfather was a congressman."

"Ah, that's a good lad, volunteering information. So tell me and the doctor here why you came to the hospital."

"I followed you right out of the War Department. I was curious, and I wanted to know if you were who you claimed to be."

"Did Mr. Stanton send you?"

"No, I already told you I came here on my own. I followed you here this morning. I had to return to the War Department, and then I came back after I was finished for the day."

"You're not much of a spy, Wilkerson," Flynn said. "Hell, we told you where you could find us. There was no need to go sneaking about."

"Who knew if you really were who you said you were? I wanted to make sure."

"You mean that Stanton wanted to make sure."

Wilkerson shook his head. "Mr. Stanton isn't interested in intrigue. He's a bureaucrat, not a spycatcher. He leaves that sort of business to the likes of Lafayette Baker."

Lafayette Baker's name was the stuff of nightmares for Confederate agents, but Flynn ignored that uneasy thought and continued to press the captain. "The real question, Wilkerson, is why did you come looking for us?"

Wilkerson stared at Flynn as if he were an idiot. "The War Department knows all about this plot with the bubonic plague, Mr. Flynn," Wilkerson said. "The entire plan was explained in a letter from the Confederate Secret Service."

Both Flynn and Caldwell stared at the young captain. "What?"

"Well, I didn't actually read the letter myself. But I heard its contents from one of the other clerks. That's how I know you're telling the truth."

"Of course it's the truth," Caldwell said. "Why would I make it up?"

"Like I said, Stanton doesn't believe there is a plot. At least, he doesn't want to waste his time with it. But I believed every word you said. That's why I'm here, to see if I can help. This Doctor Verville is a madman, and he must be stopped."

* * *

Washington was a city still under construction.

Above the muddy avenues and weedy vacant lots rose the unfinished dome of the United States Capitol. The architect of the city, a Frenchman named Pierre L'Enfant, had intended the building to anchor one end of Pennsylvania Avenue. One mile to the west, the White House would anchor the other. There was supposed to be an unbroken vista between the executive mansion and the Capitol so that the president and Congress could keep an uneasy watch on each other.

However, the newly constructed Treasury Department building jutted slightly into the avenue, blocking the view. It was somehow appropriate that the treasury interrupted the sight line, considering that money was the root of so many disagreements between the executive and legislative branches of government.

The cornerstone of the new Capitol building had been laid by Millard Fillmore on the Fourth of July in 1851, but construction had languished under the Buchanan administration. Even now, jumbled blocks of marble lay about the grounds like giants' toys. Work on another nearby edifice, the Washington Monument, had stopped in 1855 due to a lack of funds.

The national street between the Capitol and executive mansion that Major L'Enfant intended when he carved the city out of swampland along the Potomac River was not well traveled in Washington's early years. Even until the late 1850s, weeds and small trees sprouted in the middle reaches of Pennsylvania Avenue as the swamp threatened to reclaim the little-used street.

The war changed all that. Now Pennsylvania Avenue bustled with traffic and the vacant lots along it and other streets were beginning to fill up as newcomers built shops and houses.

President Lincoln had urged the completion of the Capitol building despite the war, and the dome was beginning to rise proudly above the city. Scaffolding encircled the building and a host of workers swarmed over it for ten hours a day or more. After all, the Capitol had become a symbol of determination and optimism; the war could not stop it, and a nation that wasn't confident in its own eventual victory would not be busy building a Capitol fit for ruling a continent.

None of this mattered to Joseph Cavanaugh, whose mind was rarely inclined to dwell on much beyond his next meal. Even that thought had no appeal because he felt too ungodly sick to move. He was sitting on a spare chunk of marble and holding his head in his hands.

"Cavanaugh!" barked the foreman, spotting him at once. "What the hell are you doing?"

"I just need to get off me feet," he said. "I feel weak all of a sudden."

Not for the first time, the foreman wished it wasn't against the law to whip Irishmen. They were all lazy bastards. "Maybe my boot in your backside would help you overcome your weakness, Cavanaugh. Now get back to work, unless you're too drunk, that is."

Cavanaugh lurched to his feet and stood there swaying. He remembered how he had accused Jack O'Grady of being drunk this morning in Swampoodle when the man claimed to be coming down sick. *Och,* he thought. *The Good Lord is punishing me for that now.* He wondered if he was coming down with whatever O'Grady had. If that was the case, it was catching damn fast.

"I'll get back to work in a minute," he told the foreman.

"You'll get back to work now!"

Cavanaugh nodded, cursing the day he had ever come to America. It had been nearly twenty years since he had left Cobh Harbor, long enough to forget Ireland's horrors. Besides, he was just a boy then.

He shuffled over to join a line of men clearing away a pile of rubble. For a minute or two he thought he would be all right, and then as he bent to pick up another piece of rubble between his leather-like hands, Cavanaugh abruptly fell over and lay there moaning, his forehead hot as an iron skillet awaiting an egg.

"Cavanaugh!" the foreman shouted furiously. He could hear the man as if from a great distance. Dimly, he was aware of a circle of faces staring down at him. Many were neighbors, fellow Irish laborers from Swampoodle, and they were more sympathetic than the foreman.

"Sick as a dog," he heard someone remark. "Best take him home to his wife."

And so three kind-hearted Irishmen missed an hour's pay to bring him home to Swampoodle, exposing themselves all the while to Cavanaugh's sickness.

* * *

Flynn, Caldwell, Louisa and Wilkerson were gathered in the doctor's office. It was an uneasy group. None of them knew Wilkerson, but by necessity he was now one of them after appearing that evening at the hospital. Still, he made the other three uncomfortable as the fit of a new shoe, a stranger among friends. For his own part, the young War Department officer had the good sense to keep his mouth shut.

Things weren't all bad, however. None of the other patients in the hospital had come down with the Rebel Fever, as even Caldwell had begun to call it. Still, they knew now that Verville wouldn't be satisfied until the fever was running rampant through Washington City. That couldn't be allowed to happen. Once caught, bubonic plague was a deadly thing. None of the three victims had survived, and their black, putrefying flesh as they lay in their cots was a horrible sight.

Caldwell began, "We know Verville has a plan. Captain Wilkerson here has confirmed it. The question is, how do we stop it?"

"First, we have to find Verville," Flynn said.

"How do you propose to do that?"

"I have my sources, although I can't share them with any of you," Flynn said, then turned to Wilkerson. "And if you know what's good for you, Wilkerson, you won't go following me around. If I catch you at it, I promise to beat the hell out of you, lad. You still work for the War Department, and I won't have you putting the finger on any of these people."

"I can help," Wilkerson said, not bothering to deny that he had considered following Flynn.

"The best way you can help is to go back to the War Department and keep your ears open. When the times comes, we may have enough evidence for you to present to Stanton. At least he'll probably listen to you."

"Maybe," Wilkerson said. It was well-known that Stanton didn't play favorites, even with the officers on his staff. The man was dour as a priest and his religion was the War Department.

"Meanwhile, the good doctor here and Nurse Webster should stick close to the hospital. I've never met Verville, but from what I hear he's the kind of man who will be back once he learns his rats didn't kill all of you dead with the plague. He wants revenge against the doctor, and he'll either return to try his rats again – or something else."

"I'll make sure the guard is posted at all times," Caldwell said, glancing at Louisa. Her face had blanched, but she was a strong woman. Still, Flynn's talk of Verville's need for revenge had unsettled her. She was a nurse; Caldwell knew all this was more than she had bargained for. "Louisa, you could always transfer temporarily to a hospital in another city – Baltimore or Philadelphia. Or you could go home, at least until all this business is finished."

"No," she blurted. "I would rather stay here with you." Her pale face flushed. "What I mean is that my duty is here. Mr. Flynn will catch this Dr. Verville and put him in prison."

Flynn looked grim. "I'm glad you have such confidence in me," he said. "But the truth is that it's not going to be at all easy to catch Verville."

* * *

Flynn lingered all day near the entrance to the Willard Hotel. He knew who he was looking for, but not where to find him. Pennsylvania Avenue in front of the Willard seemed as good a place as any. After all, it was where he had met Thomas Nelson Conrad when he first came to Washington City a few days ago, when Conrad had supplied him with a decent cigar and the whereabouts of Dr. William Caldwell. It seemed likely that Conrad would make another appearance at the Willard, although it had never been agreed that the two of them would meet again. He wasn't sure how Conrad would react, but it was a chance he would simply have to take if there was to be any hope of finding Verville. Conrad might at least know where to look.

Flynn reflected that his chances of seeing Jefferson Verville here were also good. Unfortunately, he had no idea what the Confederate madman looked like. No one seemed to have a daguerreotype of Verville, or even so much as a sketch. Of course, it was possible Flynn would know him when he saw him. He had a good sixth sense when it came to people; it was a talent

106

that helped keep a man alive in Flynn's trade.

This sense of people was one reason why he didn't entirely trust Captain C.J. Wilkerson. It was understandable that a young man like Wilkerson, who had all the energy and excitement of a puppy, would jump at the chance of playing spy in a game of political and military intrigue. Still, there was something not quite right about Wilkerson. Flynn couldn't put his finger on it. But they would have to take whatever help they could get.

Flynn watched carriages whisk up in front of the Willard Hotel, either to deposit well-dressed people at the hotel door or to pick them up. This was no poor man's establishment, and Flynn felt shabby in his ill-used suit, like some malingerer who at any moment would be found out and asked to leave. He also felt very much like an Irish immigrant, out of place in this aristocratic American society.

The Willard was the place where everyone who was anyone stayed while in Washington City. Built in 1850 by Henry Willard, the hotel had hosted every president from Franklin Pierce in 1853 to Abraham Lincoln at his inauguration in 1861. It was a place that served exquisite and expensive food in its dining room, and everyone from generals to congressmen rubbed elbows in the hotel's famous bar. The Willard also must have held an attraction for Thomas Conrad, because not an hour had gone by when Flynn saw him descend from a carriage and start toward the hotel entrance.

Flynn managed to slip through the crowds of men smoking cigars out front and reach the doors first. Conrad blinked with surprise when Flynn materialized before him, blocking his path into the hotel.

"We need to talk," Flynn said.

"Yes, of course," Conrad said, still stunned, but with enough of his wits still about him to know how dangerous it was for them to be seen together. Flynn knew it, too. Eyes were surely watching the hotel entrance and ears in the crowd were listening, for the Union Secret Service had spies everywhere. "Let's go to my carriage, shall we?"

Fortunately, the vehicle had not yet left the street in front of the hotel, and the man waved a gloved hand to attract the coachman's attention so that he would not drive off.

They climbed inside the well-appointed carriage and Conrad tapped on the roof with his cane. In a moment, the carriage started off down the street. Despite Conrad's cool actions, he was obviously quite angry. One eyelid had developed a tic which did not stop until he had expressed himself: "That, sir, was very foolish. A meeting in broad daylight in front of the Willard Hotel? Idiotic! There are spies everywhere, on all sides, and not just those of the United States. If my position were compromised, well – and you, sir, might

107

find yourself at the end of a rope."

Flynn had considered all this, and he hadn't come to be lectured. "We all have to risk something once in a while if we want to gain something."

"What is it you want?"

"Some information," Flynn said. "I need to find Jefferson Verville. Tell me where he's staying."

Conrad blinked. He had the aristocratic bearing of a true Southern gentleman, but there was an intensity that bubbled just beneath his calm demeanor. The man was neither a fop nor a fool.

Espionage was an extremely sticky web, and Flynn knew he was just a minor player, if a player at all. His specialty in the service of the Confederate spy network was being handy with his fists; he had never made any claims to being cunning. There were all sorts of strange alliances Flynn didn't understand, and intuition told him that the gentleman here had received wind of Verville's plot. There was a chance, however, that Conrad could be in support of the madness Verville proposed. For all Flynn knew, Conrad might even be helping him.

"Give me Verville and I will put you in contact with a highly placed officer in the War Department. Just a captain, but he works at Stanton's side."

"Intriguing," he said. "Where do this captain's sympathies lie?"

Flynn smiled. "With gold, sir. Purely with gold. He's a greedy bastard, but there's nothing he won't do for money."

"How do you know him?" Conrad asked.

"As luck would have it, he's an acquaintance of this Yankee doctor who is helping me."

It was all a lie, of course. He was using that puppy Wilkerson for bait, and if it came to it, he was sure he could get Wilkerson to bluff it out long enough that he would be done with this business about Verville. Still, it was a dangerous gamble. Who knew how much the man on the carriage seat opposite him knew about the War Department? It might also get Wilkerson locked up in the Old Capitol – not that the young captain meant anything to Flynn. It was all risky, but as he had just told Conrad, nothing risked, nothing gained.

"These highly placed junior officers often know more than they should be trusted to know," Conrad said, as if thinking out loud. "In any case, I am interested."

"Where can I find Verville?" Flynn asked again. He did not bother to point out that just a short time ago the man had denied any knowledge of Verville. It was all part of the game.

"He is staying at the Metropolitan Hotel," Conrad said. He smiled. "As a matter of fact, it's just down the street."

"Who does he have helping him?"

Conrad hesitated. "I don't know–"

"What's the harm in it? A man at Stanton's elbow ought to be worth it."

"All right," Conrad said reluctantly. "Verville has gone to the MacCrae brothers on the waterfront."

Flynn nodded. That information alone was golden. Still, something didn't seem quite right. "How do you know this? Whose side are you on, anyhow?"

Conrad laughed. "Come now, Mr. Flynn. Some of Verville's friends and supporters in Richmond are also friends of mine. In fact, Verville even came to me for money, nearly a year ago. Not that I gave him any. I don't agree with his methods, and I take my orders from the Confederate Secret Service, not from zealots."

Flynn struggled to keep his anger in check. "Then why didn't you tell me Verville's whereabouts before, the day you told me where to find Caldwell."

"The truth is, I didn't know then."

"You know now. If you don't agree with what he's doing, then why don't you try to stop him?"

"I deal in information, not action. That would be your jurisdiction, Mr. Flynn. Now, tell me the name of this captain you know at the War Department."

"His name is C.J. Wilkerson," Flynn said. He smiled. Wouldn't Wilkerson be surprised? The lad was going to get more than he bargained for by sticking his nose into this business. "He'll be more than happy to help."

Conrad knocked his cane at the ceiling once more, and the carriage rolled to a halt. Flynn swung open the door; to his surprise they were already in the northern quarter of the city. He had been so engrossed in his conversation with the spy opposite him that he had forgotten to look out the window.

"Good day to you, sir," Flynn said, making an attempt at refinement, although even to his ears it sounded false and mocking. He got out.

"Do me the favor, Mr. Flynn, of not being seen in my company again," Conrad said, a steely tone coming into his voice. "You'll get us both killed."

At that, the carriage door slammed shut and the vehicle rolled off.

Flynn turned and started on the long walk back toward Armory Square Hospital to gather the doctor and maybe two or three of the Invalid Corps guards who were still sturdy enough to help. With luck, they would have Verville by nightfall.

* * *

Verville wasn't one to dawdle.

Even when he walked without any particular destination in mind, Verville strode with real purpose in his step. His black cape fluttered in the winter wind and his cane never touched the sidewalk; he kept his left hand clenched tightly around it. The wind was bitterly cold, and he stopped suddenly and turned in the opposite direction – no point in fighting the wind when he was merely out for a stroll.

A smallish man in a brown coat nearly collided with him, then continued down the sidewalk in the direction Verville had been taking until a moment ago. Something was vaguely familiar about the man, but there must have been fifty others just like him on the street. Ahead of Verville there was now a thin man of medium height in another nondescript coat. Strange. In the back of his mind it registered vaguely that he had not passed the fellow in the opposite direction.

All at once, Verville's blood ran even colder in the December air. *Bastards.* They were following him. He remembered now: the smaller one with the brown coat had been right behind him yesterday when he turned suddenly on the street.

Verville struggled to control the sudden rage bubbling in him. He was angry at himself, too. How stupid he had been not to see them sooner. With a momentary sense of panic, he wondered how long the men had been trailing him. If they had been with him these last two days, it was disastrous. He would have been followed to the MacCraes' and to his hotel. Everything was known.

He glanced over his shoulder. About one hundred feet back the man in the brown coat was looking in a shop window. Up ahead, the thin man threw an occasional backwards glance in Verville's direction. Nothing you would notice if you weren't looking for it. Now that he realized he was being followed, spotting the fools trailing him was easy. As far as he could tell, there were only the two.

A stream of questions flooded his mind. Who were they? Who had sent them? He pushed those thoughts aside to settle them later. The only question that mattered now was what to do about them.

There was no point in giving them the slip. They already knew where he was staying and what his business of the last few days had been. Verville found himself growing angry at the two men.

He would not be their fool.

The hunted would become the hunter.

Chapter 14

"We want him alive," Flynn warned the two hospital sentries he had pressed into service. They were eager to help, glad for a chance at action instead of guarding the hospital grounds.

"Yes, sir," both men said. One was named Blevins, the other Hicks. Flynn had sent a message to Wilkerson, but he was too busy at the War Department to get away. Secretary Stanton made a habit of working until he fell asleep at his desk long after midnight and he expected his staff to be on hand.

"Just be sure you don't shoot him unless he's about to shoot you," he warned the sentries. He turned to Caldwell. "You had better take along your pistol."

"I don't want a gun." Caldwell shook his head. "Besides, I don't even have any ammunition for that thing."

"What?"

"It's purely ceremonial, something I strap on with my uniform. It's ancient, too, made sometime around the Mexican War."

"I can borrow a pistol off one of the officers here in the hospital," Flynn said.

"No, thank you. I'm not interested in shooting Verville. If I were, I would have done it a long time ago out West."

"He won't hesitate to shoot you, Doctor. You have to protect yourself."

Louisa arrived in time to hear them arguing. "Listen to him, William," she pleaded. "At least carry it with you even if you don't plan to use it."

"I don't want it."

In the short time he had known Caldwell, Flynn had seen how stubborn the man could be. Knowing better than to waste his breath, he shrugged and slipped the pistol into his own coat pocket. "Suit yourself."

"If you're not going to take the pistol, William, then stay here," Louisa said. "You don't have to go."

"I'm going, Miss Webster, and that's the end of that," Caldwell said gruffly.

Louisa gave Caldwell a withering look, then turned and walked out of the doctor's office.

"You've done it now," Flynn said. "I reckon you'll have to buy her something pretty on your way home from catching Verville."

The two soldiers in the office grinned. They were married men and understood just what Flynn was saying.

Caldwell reddened. "I can assure you, Mr. Flynn, that Nurse Caldwell and I merely have a working relationship–"

"So it's not just your pistol that stays in its holster?"

The two soldiers, unable to contain themselves, doubled over with laughter.

"Goddamnit, Flynn!" Caldwell's face was the color of a boiled beet. "You have no right, no right at all, damn you–"

Flynn was laughing, too. "Calm down, Doctor. Calm down. I apologize. You know I think the world of Miss Webster."

"You do?"

"She's a good woman," Flynn said. "She has real mettle. Obviously, she's from a good family, rich family, I'd guess, and she came down here to Washington City to help the sick and wounded. Now, what kind of woman would do that?"

"Yes," Caldwell said, as if talking to himself.

Flynn knew he had gone too far in joking with Caldwell, but he couldn't help himself. He was suffering from the old jitters he used to get before a prizefight, or before his one and only time going into battle. A man needed a good laugh to forget them. Snatching up Verville wasn't going to be easy.

He took out his LeMat revolver one last time, checked the loads, and swung the cylinder shut again.

"All right," he said. "Let's get going."

* * *

Verville forced himself to walk at a normal pace, although it wasn't easy knowing there were two men watching his every move. He was angry at himself for not noticing them sooner, but that could not be helped. What mattered now was how he would deal with them.

He paused outside a shop to examine the window. Christmas was coming, and many of the shops were decorated for the season. There were boughs of greenery, sprigs of holly and mistletoe, ribbons and candles. He ducked inside.

Verville had no intention of shopping. Fortunately, the shopkeeper was busy with a customer, so it was easy enough to slip past him and into the back room. Boxes were stacked neatly from floor to ceiling, and there were piles of goods on the shelves. Although he really wasn't in a state of mind to notice such things, he was a little awed. He doubted there was a single shop in Richmond filled with so many goods, and this, after all, was just a tiny shop.

He found the back door, but the thing was locked with an elaborate latch. That made sense. You didn't want thieves sneaking in at the back. At the front of the store he heard the sleighbells hung on it ring as the door to the street opened. Was that the customer going out or one of his pursuers coming in? Either way, it was taking him too long to work the latch. He struck at the thing in frustration with the heavy silver knob of his cane and the latch came undone. He shoved through the door into the alley.

It was no more than ten feet wide. Directly opposite him were the ugly backsides of more shops. A couple of swaybacked horses were tied up there, stamping to keep warm in this cold, sunless spot.

Someone was moving down the alley and to Verville's consternation he realized it was the thin watcher. Damn him. These two thought of everything. He had only been in the shop for perhaps two minutes, but it had been enough time for one of them to slip between two buildings into the alley to watch the back door.

His heart was pounding and he took a deep breath to calm himself. This was not how he had planned it – he had hoped to set some sort of trap, a snare for both of his pursuers. Well, it was clear now that wasn't going to happen.

Already, the thin man had seen him. The man busied himself with some crates by an entrance, stacking them up, and Verville had to admit he wouldn't have given the man a second look if he didn't know he was being followed. There was no cover in the alley, nothing to interrupt the view down the whole block, so Verville moved to put the horses between himself and his pursuer. The derelict beasts shielded most of his movements and he stepped into one of the narrow, two-foot wide spaces that separated some of the buildings.

Then he drew his double-barreled derringer and waited. He steadied the small pistol with two hands and kept it pointed toward the alley.

He didn't have to wait long. Already he could hear the man moving through the alley, the soft whinny of the horses as he approached. Then he was opposite Verville, looking down the gap between two buildings on the other side. He did not appear especially cautious. He would have expected Verville to be cutting through to the street on the other side. He turned and crossed the alley and Verville hunkered further into the damp space. Verville was sure the men had not been sent to do him harm but to watch him. Still,

113

it was likely the man was armed.

A face appeared, peering into the gloom. Verville took a step forward out of the shadows and saw his pursuer's look of surprise. Then Verville shot him in the face.

Verville stepped out from between the buildings. Some detached, clinical part of his mind registered that the .32 caliber bullet had entered just below the eye, where it would have traveled directly into the brain. A bloody pool was forming beneath the head and he knew the slug had shattered the cranium upon exiting the skull. He bent and quickly searched the man's pockets. No papers or personal items of any kind. Very professional. He found a few coins in the coat pocket and took them, leaving the pockets turned out, vaguely hoping to make the killing look like a robbery. In the other pocket he found a Colt pistol, which he transferred to his own pocket.

Most men at that point would have counted themselves lucky and fled. However, Verville didn't like being played for a fool. He quickly returned to the door at the back of the store and waited beside it.

* * *

Where the hell was Verville?

Martin Goodman lingered outside the store for several minutes, waiting for Verville to come out. Sandford had headed into the alley behind the row of stores just in case Verville tried to give them the slip. Not that Goodman thought that would happen. Verville had shown no sign of realizing he was being followed.

Still, Verville was an awfully cautious man. Ever since they had begun watching him, Verville acted as if he expected to be watched. He just hadn't spotted his followers yet. Goodman smiled. After all, he and Sandford were some of the best.

They never took chances, never gave anything away. That was exactly why Sandford had gone to watch the alley – just in case. Verville was just slippery enough to try sneaking out the back door.

Several minutes had passed, and Goodman was beginning to wonder what was going on. What struck him as suspicious was that Verville had never gone into any of the other shops in the city, except for the apothecary, which was to be expected, considering the man was a doctor, after all. They had inquired later to see what Verville bought. Laudanum. Goodman thought the man must be drinking it himself. He wouldn't be the first soldier who had a taste for liquid opium.

But why had Verville settled on this shop? Did it have something to do with his business in the city? Was the shopkeeper actually some secret Rebel contact or had Verville spotted his pursuers? When another few minutes passed and there was no sign of his partner or Verville, Goodman decided to risk entering the store. It was a rich man's shop, not for the likes of Goodman, and the clerk gave him a disdainful look before turning back to a well-dressed customer. Verville was nowhere to be seen in the small shop. Puzzled, Goodman went to look for the back door. He found it, and it was unlatched. Well, there was his answer. Verville had run out the back and Sandford must have gone trailing him down the alley. Goodman cursed under his breath. If he hurried, he might be able to catch up. He reached for the latch.

* * *

The door swung open and the second watcher emerged. The sight of Verville standing there startled him. Martin Goodman gawked in surprise as he stared into the muzzle of the derringer.

"Come all the way out and the shut the door," Verville hissed.

Goodman did as he was told. "Where's the other fellow?" he asked, glancing around the alley.

"Dead." Verville smiled maliciously at the look on the man's face. "Unless you want to end up just like him, you had better tell me who you are and why you're following me."

"I can't do that," Goodman said.

Verville waved the derringer. "I believe you can."

As the man nervously licked his lips, Verville reflected that it was not surprising he hadn't noticed him before. The man was short, fat, with a bland face and nondescript clothes. Nothing remarkable or memorable about him. You could pass this man a dozen times on the street and pay no attention to him. Verville felt the anger wash over him in a wave. He had been tricked, duped by these Yankees. They were all snakes, vermin, ungentlemanly.

"We were paid to watch you and report back," Goodman said.

"Who paid you?"

"He never told us his name."

"I don't believe you."

Something rattled at the door – the shopkeeper, coming to check where those sudden drafts had come from, pulled the door snug from the inside then latched it again. Verville glanced at the door. Goodman ducked under the pistol and ran.

"Stop, damn you!"

115

There was just one shot left in the derringer and Verville aimed carefully. The small gun was useless at any sort of distance but the man was no more than ten feet away when Verville pulled the trigger. The derringer's sharp crack filled the alley.

Verville's aim was true. The man's arms flailed wildly as he stumbled and fell to lie gasping in a pool of muddy water. Verville walked up to him, passing the horses, which were spooked now and tugging at their tethers, ears laid back flat as he walked past to stand over the wounded man.

"Bastard," he moaned up at Verville, struggling to keep his face out of the puddle.

"Who sent you to follow me?" Verville demanded.

"Go to hell."

Verville stepped on the man's head, pushing his face down into the dirty water.

He relented, let the man come up for air, gasping and sputtering.

"This is your last chance," Verville said, letting the man feel the pressure of the foot on the back on his head. "Who sent you?"

"Colonel Baker!" the man said through a nose and mouth clotted with mud.

"Baker?" Verville felt a chill. "He's chief of the Union's Secret Service."

"I've told you the truth. Now, for the love of God, have mercy."

Verville's boot pressed the man's face into the puddle again. His arms flailed weakly, but the man didn't have the strength to free himself.

A door opened onto the alley and a voice called, "Hey! What the hell is going on?"

"Thieves," Verville replied. Two men had come out into the alley. Shopkeepers. "They attacked me."

"Let him up or you'll kill him!"

Verville reached down and yanked the man out of the puddle roughly by the hair.

Then Verville fled down the alley.

* * *

Flynn would have preferred making the raid on Verville's hotel room with more than four men. He knew the worst mistake you could make was to underestimate a man, and so far Verville had shown himself to be anything but an easy mark.

Flynn led the group to the street outside the hotel. They waited until dark, when it was likely Verville would be in his room. It was a four-story frame

116

building that looked anything but inviting, although it fell short of being seedy – the sort of hotel where a thrifty country lawyer would stay on a business trip to the city.

"Dismal place," Caldwell remarked. "I would have thought Verville would do better than this."

"He's on a mission, not a pleasure trip," Flynn said. "Actually, we couldn't have asked for a better place. There aren't any porches or balconies for him to go out the windows, so as long as he's upstairs we've got him like a treed raccoon."

"How do we know he's in his room?"

"Go to the desk and inquire if he's in – if you would, please, Doctor," Flynn said. He turned to one of the hospital guards. "Blevins, I want you to go around back and make sure there aren't any porches there, either. We don't want him climbing out."

"Yes, sir." The guard scurried off, his hobnailed shoes clacking in the quiet street. A few of the hotel's guests straggled in, men in clean but unfashionable clothes who looked as if they had been ill-used most of their lives. They also looked like men who could use a hot meal, a large drink of whiskey, and a clean bed.

The guard came back. "Nothing there, sir. No way he could get out a window."

"Good. We won't watch the back, then."

"He's here," Caldwell said, coming out of the hotel. He gave Flynn the room number on the third floor. "He didn't use his real name, but when I described him they knew exactly who I was talking about. They saw him go up about an hour ago."

"All right," Flynn said. "Here's what we do. Doctor, you and Blevins wait in the lobby. If he gets past us, I want you to stop him. Shoot him if you have to, Blevins. Private Hicks and I will go upstairs to his room"

They went inside. The lobby was small, but no one paid much attention to two men in uniform standing by the foot of the stairs. After all, half the men in the city now wore uniforms. Flynn and the guard started up the stairs.

"Take out your gun, lad," Flynn said, reaching for the LeMat revolver in his own pocket. It was a deadly weapon, an ugly hunk of iron that fired six shots from its revolving chamber. A second trigger fired a lower barrel loaded with buckshot. It was like being armed with both a revolver and a shotgun.

They met no one else on the stairs. When they reached the third floor, Flynn turned left and started down the hall, which was dimly lit by gaslights in sconces along the wall.

117

The door to the room was closed. Flynn pointed to a spot along the wall near the door and Hicks moved into position, his revolver at the ready. Flynn reached for the doorknob, careful to stand to one side in case Verville began shooting.

He turned the knob. Opened the door.

Empty.

Not just empty of Verville, but of any clothes or personal items. He had left in a hurry – the bed was neatly made as if it hadn't been slept in, but several drawers in the room's chest were pulled out and empty – it was clear that Verville was gone.

"Damn," Flynn said. "The bastard's given us the slip. Hicks, go down and fetch the doctor."

In a moment, Caldwell came bounding up the stairs and joined Flynn inside the room. "They said downstairs that he never checked out. His bill was paid in advance."

"He might have slipped out while they weren't watching."

They rummaged through the room, but all that they managed to find was a small bottle Flynn discovered under a chair.

"What's this?" he asked, holding it up for the doctor to see. "Looks like a medicine bottle."

"It is," Caldwell said. "Laudanum."

"You mean that medicine made with opium? Is he sick or something?"

Caldwell nodded. "He has what's known as Old Soldier's Disease. A lot of doctors get it, in fact."

"Old Soldier's Disease? What in God's name is that?" Flynn asked.

"Our friend Verville is an opium addict," Caldwell said. "He's been one as long as I've known him. Just like some men take to drink, he's taken to opium."

"Well, it doesn't make him any easier to catch."

"No," Caldwell said. "But it does show he's as human as the rest of us. He has weaknesses."

"Where would he get this?"

Caldwell shrugged. "Just about any apothecary sells it."

"That won't help much in finding him," Flynn said. "There must be scores of apothecary shops in the city."

"Damn him," Caldwell said. "He must have known we were coming."

"Yes, but how? He didn't spot us out the window. If that had been the case, he would have had to leave something behind."

"How did you know he was here?" Caldwell asked.

Flynn hesitated. "I really can't tell you that. I had my sources, that's all."

"Maybe whoever told you, told him," Caldwell pointed out.

"I don't know," Flynn said. "I just don't know. Now we'll need another way to find the bastard, and we probably haven't got much time."

* * *

From the shelter of a doorway across the street from the hotel, Verville watched Caldwell arrive.

At first, in the darkness, he hadn't been able to tell it was him. However, he knew at once that the men were soldiers. They had that bearing about them, and then he had glimpsed Caldwell and the two others in uniform. He didn't recognize the fourth man, the big fellow who seemed to be in charge.

He waited until they had gone into the hotel, then walked on. No point in taking any more risks.

Really, he was quite surprised. He hadn't expected Caldwell at all. It wasn't like the doctor to come chasing after him – someone else had put him up to it. That big man? Who was he? One of Lafayette Baker's men? He doubted it, because the Union spycatcher would have sent better men than Caldwell and a couple of broken-down hospital guards to catch him. Was Caldwell trying to catch him himself? The idea was laughable.

Verville walked on. He had been staying at Sally's house the past few nights, and was only using the hotel room to change his clothes. As far as he knew, no one had yet followed him there, so the house remained a safe haven. Damn Caldwell and his meddling.

Verville consoled himself that the Russians would arrive soon with his cargo. Certainly he could hide out until then.

Once the plague was unleashed there would be no more hiding. Not for him. Not for anyone.

Chapter 15

Flynn turned up his collar and walked into the freezing rain that blew in sheets across the city. Ice was coating the tree limbs so that they crackled in the wind. From time to time, whole limbs snapped under the weight with a sharp crack. It was a cruel sound, like bones breaking.

Few people were braving the storm in the waterfront district, but Flynn still managed to ask his way to the MacCraes' place of business. He found the tavern, and it was packed full on account of the ice storm. There was no work to be done outdoors on such a day, so laborers and watermen filled the tables in the smoke-filled room. The men had nothing to do but drink. Flynn had wondered if Verville might be at the tavern, but it didn't seem likely that Verville would feel at home with the tavern's clientele.

The tavern's patrons were a rough and rowdy bunch, and wild laughter was thick as the tobacco smoke. Someone was trying to get a tune out of a reluctant fiddle. Several eyes turned his way when he walked in, but Flynn looked unremarkable enough. Just another refugee from the storm. He found an empty place at the bar.

"Whiskey?" the bartender asked, although it really wasn't a question. Whiskey was all that was served. Flynn saw at once the man was an old fighter. Cuts around the eyes. Broken nose. He was already reaching for a glass and bottle.

"I'm looking for MacCrae," Flynn said.

"Which one?" the bartender asked.

"The one that hires prizefighters."

One fighter could always tell another. "Wait here a minute," he said, and recruited one of the regulars at the bar to continue serving whiskey. He growled a warning at the man, "Give any drinks away and I'll break your goddamn arms."

He motioned to Flynn, who followed him behind the bar, then through a door at the back of the tavern. It opened onto another room, just as large, still thick with smoke, but not nearly as crowded. Flynn had been in a score of rooms like it before, and had hoped never to enter one again.

"What is it, Harry?" asked one of the men, pausing with his whiskey glass halfway to his lips.

"This man says he wants to be a prizefighter, Mr. MacCrae."

"Does he now?"

MacCrae stood. Judging from his slight burr, he had begun life in Scotland. He wore a suit as fine as any Flynn had seen in Washington and a thick gold watch chain across his waist. MacCrae was not a big man, but he looked to be handy with his own fists. He had the eyes of a cat as they flicked over Flynn, judging him. His face was flushed red as if he'd had more than a little whiskey to drink.

Flynn stood with his hat in his big hands, water from his coat making a puddle on the floor.

Laughing, MacCrae stood and almost in the same motion threw a punch at Flynn.

Flynn saw it coming. He moved his chin a fraction of an inch so that the hard knuckles just brushed his skin like a puff of wind. The force of MacCrae's swing threw him off balance, and Flynn quickly hooked one foot behind MacCrae's leg and bumped him with his hip. MacCrae flew across the room and landed with a crash among some empty chairs. Flynn hurried to help the man up, wondering if maybe he had already broken the bones of his potential employer, but MacCrae was laughing as he took Flynn's outstretched hand. Flynn pulled him to his feet, watching for tricks.

"You fight dirty," MacCrae said. "I like that. Comes in handy both in and out of the ring, don't it?"

The men at the table laughed in agreement.

"Aye," Flynn said, determined to sound as Irish as possible in his new role.

"You're a Mick," MacCrae said. "That's good. An Irishman knows how to fight. It's in his blood. From the looks of you, you've spent some time in the ring."

"But he's no match for the Kraut!" someone at the table sang out.

"The Kraut?"

"There's an uncommon good German boxer who recently knocked out our own fellow in the ring. Maybe you've heard of Ned Smith, the English prizefighter?"

"Aye." In truth, Flynn had never heard of him.

"The late Ned Smith, I should say. The Kraut killed him in the ring. Fortunately, my brother bet on the Kraut, so we didn't lose too much money." MacCrae turned to a man at the table who bore a slight family resemblance, only this man was thinner, a hard-looking sort whose expression lacked any of the humor evident in his brother's face. "What do you say, Angus? Can he beat the Kraut?"

Angus shrugged, as if the question didn't matter to him, but his sharp eyes looked Flynn over. "That depends," said Angus MacCrae. "Can he beat Harry?"

His brother slapped his hands together. "Can he? Why, that's just the thing we need on a rainy day to pass the time, a fight between Harry and this fellow here. What did you say your name was?"

"Tom Mullins," Flynn lied.

"We need a fight between Harry and Mr. Mullins here. What do you say to that, Mr. Mullins? If you win, we'll take you on as a fighter."

Flynn shrugged. "Fine by me."

"Harry, do you think you can take this Irishman's measure?"

Harry gave Flynn a nasty smile. "With pleasure, Mr. MacCrae."

"Good, good. Billy, run and tell everyone in the bar that there's to be a fight," MacCrae ordered, and an urchin of a boy dashed into the next room. "Give Mr. Mullins here a drink."

"No drink," Flynn said. He saw Angus MacCrae nod his approval. "A fighter needs a clear head."

"So it can get knocked clear off, eh?" MacCrae laughed. "Harry might just do it for you. The man used to fight for us all the time until he was promoted to run the bar here."

Flynn grunted and began taking off his overcoat. He threw it in a wet heap on a chair, then added his hat, suitcoat and shirt until he stood in his long underwear top. All around him the room was being set up, chairs and tables cleared away, lanterns being hung by nails along the walls. The drunken workers from the tavern itself began pouring in to form a rough circle about twelve feet across. Most of them worked for the MacCraes on the docks and they loved nothing better than a fight. It was the perfect entertainment for a stormy day.

Flynn flexed his arms, stretching them over his head and wondering how he had ever managed to get himself in this mess. A prizefight again. He thought he had left that part of his past behind him for good.

Still, deep down, Flynn looked forward to the fight. The last few days had been frustrating, trying to track down Verville and being thwarted at every step, not sure if they were making progress or not as the epidemic threatened Washington. Here in the ring, everything was so much more clear. Either you won or you didn't, everything settled with fists.

The little urchin named Billy used a piece of chalk to draw a line on the floor in the middle of the ring. Flynn toed it with real anticipation as all around him the bets were being made. Most of the money appeared to be going on Harry, the local favorite.

MacCrae stood on a chair to make an announcement. "Look here, boys!" he shouted, holding his right hand high. In his fingertips a twenty-dollar gold piece glittered dully. "We have Harry, everybody knows Harry–" a roar went up from the crowd of drunks "–and a newcomer, this Irishman, Tom Mullins." There was a chorus of booing, but MacCrae raised his voice above the din. "Whichever man wins the fight gets twenty dollars in gold!"

Harry stepped into the ring, also stripped down to his longjohn top. He was smaller than Flynn, past his prime as a fighter, loose-fleshed and with a gut on him. But his upper arms still bulged and there was a cruel smile on his face, as if he thought he was about to teach Flynn a lesson.

Flynn decided Harry would come after him fast, just wade right in as if he were settling another bar brawl.

"You won't last a minute with me, Mick," Harry said, once the two men were face to face.

"Aye," Flynn said. "Not a minute."

There was no bell. MacCrae stood on a chair and brayed above the din, "Fight!"

Harry plowed in with both fists swinging. He hit Flynn with a left and a right, a left and a right, pounding away. Flynn kept his own fists up to protect his face as the blows landed thump, thump along his ribs. When Flynn didn't go down in the first few seconds, Harry stepped back and circled.

Flynn didn't want this fight to last long – he knew he had to make a good show for the MacCraes.

"Show 'em, Harry!"

"Kill the Paddy!"

Flynn slipped a punch under Harry's guard and split his lip. Harry spit a ropy stream of blood on the wooden floor and came at Flynn again. A fist slipped past and stung Flynn's jaw. He was keeping his reflexes slow, just a second behind, to make Harry overconfident. Another punch shot in and struck his eye. Flynn kept his hands up and blocked the punches just enough to take the sting out of them. The crowd saw Harry closing in and shouted wildly. Greenbacks waved as more of the bar's patrons placed bets. For just an instant, Harry acknowledged the ring of spectators, gave them a smile as he went in for the kill, to knock out the Irishman.

"Good ol' Harry!" someone shouted.

Flynn hit him with a quick left that sent him staggering. Before Harry could recover, Flynn planted his feet and swung with the full weight of his body behind it. His fist struck with the power of a cannonball. The blow caught his opponent under the chin and lifted him bodily off the floor. Harry went down with all the grace of a side of beef, knocked out cold. He lay sprawled on the wooden floor, the crowd pressing around him, trying not to step on him.

At first the men in the room were stunned. Their favorite was unconscious on the floor, drooling blood and spit, with the Irishman standing over him. And then they cheered wildly. In the ring, a man went from being a hero or a loser in an instant, all on the luck of a punch.

MacCrae waded through the crowd. If he was angry at Flynn for knocking out his bartender, he didn't show it. He jerked his chin at Harry. "Throw some water on him." MacCrae turned to Flynn. "You're a tricky fighter, Flynn. I like that. You gave ol' Harry just enough rope to hang himself."

"Aye. He's a strong one, though."

"Oh, Harry can fight, all right. I've seen him take on and beat all comers. He just ain't as young as he used to be."

Angus MacCrae approached through the crowd. Flynn noticed that unlike his brother, no one dared clap Angus on the shoulder. Men stepped quickly out of his way. There was an air of danger about the man, even though he had a slight build, hardly bigger than that of a twelve-year-old boy.

"You did good," Angus said, fixing Flynn with his dead cold eyes. Flynn was reminded of a fish – a shark, something predatory.

"He dropped his guard."

"Not many men have knocked Harry down, let alone out."

Someone was slapping Harry's face to bring him around, while another dumped a tankard of beer on his head.

"What if I had lost?"

"Then we would have thrown your arse out in the street to freeze. The whores would have stolen all your clothes."

Flynn believed him.

James MacCrae surged through the crowd and managed to reach Flynn and his brother. He had a fistful of banknotes, which he flashed at his brother before stuffing them into a pocket. "Not bad for a few minutes' work, I'd say."

"What about that twenty-dollar gold piece?" Flynn said. It wasn't that he wanted or needed the money, but any hard fighter on the waterfront would make a point of asking about it.

MacCrae looked sly. "That was just for show, to talk things up. You couldn't really have expected me to give you twenty dollars for knocking Harry out."

"Aye, so I did," Flynn said. "I'd be grateful if you handed it over like you promised."

MacCrae's happy expression quickly gave way to anger. He was a mercurial man. "Listen to me, Mick, nobody tells me what to do. I never promised you any money–"

"Give him the twenty dollars, James," Angus said. "He's worth it."

"Keep out of it, Angus–"

"Go on, give it to him," Angus said, not taking his eyes off Flynn. "We need someone who can fight the Kraut, and Mullins here might very well be the one. If nothing else, it will be a good fight."

Fuming, James MacCrae reached into his coat pocket, withdrew the twenty-dollar piece, and slapped it into Flynn's hand.

"My brother is always right about a fighter," he snarled. "But I'll tell you this, Irish, the first fight you lose, you'll give me back that twenty dollars or I'll make sure you end up at the bottom of the Potomac."

Flynn clenched the coin tightly in his fist and considered whether or not to smash MacCrae in the face. MacCrae read his eyes, and what he saw there made him even angrier. "Do it, lad, and you'll not walk out of here alive."

Angus took Flynn by the arm. "Maybe it's best you leave. I'll walk you out."

"Aye."

Angus brought Flynn deeper into the MacCraes' waterfront complex. They quickly left the crowd behind.

"My brother's a hothead," Angus said. "You've got no call to taunt him. You might be handy in the ring, but my brother don't box, he kills. Of course, I always side with my brother in a fight, if not in an argument."

"I see your meaning, Mr. MacCrae."

"I thought you would, Mullins. Now tell me, why haven't I heard of you before? That's not the first time you've been in the ring."

"Well, back home in Ireland–"

"Don't give me that, Mullins. You weren't born in Ireland. Leastways, you didn't stay there long. You don't have the brogue for it."

"I'm from down South," he admitted. It made Flynn nervous that Angus MacCrae had already seen through part of his story, but then, the truth would be in his fists. "I've been prizefighting since I was a lad, mostly in Richmond."

"What are you doing up here? In case you haven't noticed, Mullins, there's a war on."

"That's exactly why I came North. There's no money to be made in the Confederacy. The war has ruined everything. Besides, if I stayed there I might end up in the Army, and I ain't interested in carrying a rifle through the mud all over Virginia."

Angus brought him to a side door. It did not fit snugly, and the winter wind from outside whistled in the cracks. A gust of freezing rain buffeted the building. Night was coming on, and Flynn knew it was going to be a cruel, wintry one for all the soldiers on both sides who were unfortunate enough to be outside in this ice storm.

"Come back tomorrow, and we'll have a little something for you to do until we can organize a fight."

"Work?"

Angus shrugged. "Call it what you want. Not that you'll be hauling boxes and sacks down at the docks. But we can't have our new fighter starving on us. That twenty dollars you won tonight won't get you far in this city. The cost of everything has gone up on account of the war."

"Thank you, Mr. MacCrae," Flynn said. "I'll be back tomorrow."

He went out the door into the storm. It hadn't let up any. The whole city now appeared to be glazed with ice.

He expected to be followed, because men like the MacCraes didn't succeed without being careful. Sure enough, the door that he'd come through opened again, spilling pale light into the winter dusk. He wouldn't have noticed if he hadn't been watching for it. Out slipped the boy, Billy, who melted into the shadows.

Flynn walked on. He imagined he could feel the weight of the gold coin in his pocket, not that twenty dollars was much, but it felt like money he had truly earned.

He was glad for the wind and the stinging, cold rain because it dulled the pain he was beginning to feel after the fight. Even though he had come out of the ring relatively unscathed, nobody was hit in the body and face by a man Harry's size without feeling it.

He hoped it was all worth the chance to get closer to Verville, and now that the MacCraes had taken him on, it was only a matter of time until they led Flynn to him.

Flynn felt sorry for the boy trailing him, out on such a stormy winter twilight, so he didn't lead him too far. He found a likely looking boarding house and went inside. The woman who owned it was a bit put out that he had walked through the door unannounced and his battered appearance after the fight didn't help.

Not that he wanted a room, anyway. He decided the boy would watch the house for five minutes, ten if he was especially diligent, before seeking shelter from the ice storm. Flynn pretended to be interested in a room, then announced he would return later after he had thought about it. The woman who ran the boarding house looked as if she wanted to take a broom to him, and Flynn left by the back door. There was no sign of the boy, and he headed back to Armory Square, keeping an eye on the streets behind him.

Chapter 16

"What the hell happened to you?" Caldwell demanded. He was busy stitching closed a suppurating wound that had reopened on a soldier's arm.

It was the morning after the fight, and Flynn's face bloomed with bruises. "I'm signed on with the smugglers who are going to help Verville," he said.

"Looks like you had quite an argument with them."

"Actually, Doctor, they've taken me on as a prizefighter."

"Have you gone out of your head?" Caldwell demanded. He tugged the stitching with such force that the soldier howled. The doctor ignored him and went on sewing. "Prizefighting is for barbarians. To subject yourself to such a beating with bare fists is idiotic, and to deliver it to another man is cruel."

"It's the only way I can think of to find Verville again, after he gave us the slip from that hotel."

"Stupid, stupid, stupid," Caldwell muttered, sewing the man's arm furiously. The poor soldier's face was a ghastly white. "Well, don't expect me to fix you up if you get the hell beaten out of you. Look at your face!"

"I've been sent here to find Verville, and I will do that no matter what it takes. I really don't have any choice. The sooner I find this bastard, the sooner I get to go home."

Caldwell wasn't listening. "Look at this wound," he said, studying the soldier's injured arm and pointedly ignoring Flynn's explanation. "It's a curiosity. Tell Mr. Flynn here what happened to you, son."

"I was stabbed with a bayonet."

"In all my years in the Army I've only treated a handful of bayonet wounds," Caldwell observed. "Strange, considering they're such a fearsome sight when you see a regiment waiting to advance with fixed bayonets."

"Doctor, I will find Verville."

Caldwell wouldn't look at him. "Do what you must."

Mae O'Keefe was at his elbow. "Come now, Tom, let me have a look at that face." She sniffed. "If the good doctor is too busy, then I'll see to it."

"Thank you, Mae."

He let the old Irishwoman lead him away. Mae was certainly a motherly sort. She sat him on a cot near a lantern on a table. Although it was daylight, the pale winter light beyond the small hospital windows did little to lift the gloom in the ward. She washed his face with a cloth and touched up the cuts with ointment. Her hands moved deftly, well used to this kind of work. Unlike so many of the younger nurses, she had no fear of men, but sat knee to knee with Flynn so that she could better see what she was doing.

"Don't mind the doctor," she said. "He gets into such pious moods."

"Well, he's the best doctor I've ever seen, moods or not."

"Sure, that's true. Some of these Army doctors ain't much better than butchers. Drunk half the time. You ought to see the messes we get to clean up when we get the wounded from the field hospitals."

"The doctor is mad at me for prizefighting, Mae. It's something I'm doing for another reason, not for the fighting or the money. I've been a prizefighter before and I've no real desire to go back to it."

"The doctor sees too many men hurt by stupidity. That's war for you – and prizefighting."

"I'll try not to hurt myself too much."

Mae laughed. "No need to worry about that. It's the other fellow the doctor is worried about."

"If I knew another way, Mae, I'd try it. But we need to find this doctor we're after, the one who set the rats loose in the hospital. These men I'm fighting for can lead me to him."

"No need to explain anything to old Mae," she said, still dabbing at the cuts on his face. "Our Dr. Caldwell is something of a gentleman, and he doesn't always understand the ways of the world. A gentleman don't like to get his hands dirty."

Flynn would never have put Caldwell in the same category as the idle gentlemen he had known down South, but he could see Mae's point. As gruff as Caldwell could be at times, his job was to repair the damage men did to each other. It was no wonder he took a dim view of violence.

"I see what you mean, Mae," he said, and studied his skinned knuckles. "Looks like I'll have to get my hands dirty enough for both of us."

* * *

"Mother of God."

Father Larkin made the sign of the cross. He had seen many horrible sights in his fifteen years of serving his fellow Irish immigrants, but this was the worst yet.

Jack O'Grady was still in his tightly closed pine box set on two chairs. The O'Grady children were all dead, tumbled together into the beds they shared, their flesh black with rot even though it was winter and they couldn't have been gone but a day. Little Catherine O'Grady lay dead in her mother's lap, her face as smooth and innocent as a china doll's. Her features were only starting to darken, so the little girl must not have been dead long. Maureen herself was in a rocking chair by the cold hearth, as if she had tried to comfort the dying child, and never had the strength to move again.

A smell of death and decaying human flesh filled the house. The neighbor who had gone for the priest stumbled outside and vomited.

Father Larkin crossed himself again. "What in the name of God has happened here?" he asked the corpse of Maureen O'Grady. She stared back with vacant eyes, her flesh waxen and black, like something from a nightmare.

Larkin had been at the house just the day before to give O'Grady his Last Rites. How could the rest of the family have died so quickly? He had seen much illness and death as a priest in Swampoodle, but never anything that killed so quickly.

The sight of the ravaged bodies struck a chord of fear in him, and Father Larkin began to pray in earnest, something he had not done in years.

He mumbled the words under his breath as he walked the streets of Swampoodle: "Our Father, who art in heaven, hallowed be thy name...."

* * *

Charles Wilson received word from Verville about the epidemic in Swampoodle. Sally had learned about it from a friend's Irish maid.

There was no explanation of Verville's hand in it, only that a newspaper article about it would help their plan. Before Wilson so much as set pencil to paper, Verville had told him exactly what to write.

That did not stop Wilson from playing the part of reporter and paying a visit to Swampoodle to see the havoc there with his own eyes. He had no trouble finding the Irish neighborhood, even though he had never been there before. He just walked until the streets became narrow and trash-strewn. The air was filled with the sour smell of boiling cabbage. People lounging in front of the houses spoke with thick brogues or else in Irish. Hard-looking immigrants watched him with suspicion and muttered to each other in their harsh, guttural language. Wilson couldn't understand a word. It had never occurred to him that he might not be able to communicate with the immigrants who lived here and spoke among themselves in Irish. Was this still his city?

He was nervous, wondering if this was such a good idea, after all, and fought the urge to look over his shoulder. He could feel the eyes of the men boring into his back as he walked deeper into the neighborhood.

There was a priest, standing by the doorway of a hovel. At first, Wilson was taken aback by the fact that the man was wearing a long black cassock, almost like a dress. It seemed incredibly foreign. The priest was a thin and pale man, but somehow imposing, with serious eyes and a hooked nose, and a good six feet tall. Wilson started toward him, because a priest would have some sort of education and might be able to talk to him, unlike the rest of the Irish.

As he moved toward the priest, two men emerged from the doorway carrying a body. Wilson gasped. At first, he thought they were carrying a black man, then realized it was, in fact, one of their own countrymen. The face was dark, putrid, like something rotting. Even the man's hands and bare feet were black.

"My God," he heard himself gasp. The priest gave him a harsh look. Then two more men emerged carrying another blackened body.

Wilson realized with a growing horror that up and down the street, there was a row of bodies in front of each hovel. A horse-drawn cart was making its way slowly down the street and bodies were being stacked upon it like cordwood. Men, women, children. Pretty soon, the cart was going to be full, and judging by the number of bodies on the street, they were going to need another cart. Maybe two. It was like something from history, Wilson decided, like a scene from the Middle Ages when the Black Death had struck some provincial village.

Black Death? It couldn't be ... not in Washington.

He fought the urge to flee and instead placed himself in front of the priest. This was for the Cause, he told himself. He had no doubt now that this was somehow Verville's work.

"Who are you?" the priest demanded. Wilson noticed the man's eyes were pale, watery, the eyes of someone who had lost his way.

"Charles Wilson with *The Sunday Chronicle*." What should he call him? Reverend? Sir? He settled on "Father." Isn't that what these papists called their priests? "I came out to do a story about the epidemic, Father."

"I'm Patrick Larkin," the priest said. "What would you like to know?"

"Everything."

"Come with me," Larkin said. "Let's get off this street before we catch our deaths ourselves of this Rebel Fever."

"Rebel Fever?" Wilson was stunned to hear the name put to it.

"That's what everyone's calling it," the priest said. "You see, the Rebels brought it here, to help them win the war."

131

Every nerve in Charles Wilson's body came alive at once. "Where did you hear that?"

"That's the talk," the priest said. "The fever started with a man who worked in one of the hospitals, Jack O'Grady, and he caught it there from a Confederate patient."

In spite of the grisly scenes they passed in the street, Wilson had to force himself to suppress a smile. He knew at once that Jefferson Verville's plot had been sprung, and now it was time for him to play his own role in it.

"Tell me more," he said.

Chapter 17

Caldwell was making his evening rounds at the hospital. It was a gray winter evening, miserable outside, the ground still coated from yesterday's ice storm. The ward at Armory Square was almost cozy by comparison, even if the stoves had turned cherry red in their efforts to keep the winter cold at bay. It occurred to Caldwell that the man he had hired to see to the stoves, Jack O'Grady, hadn't been at work in two days.

It irritated him that the big Irishman had abandoned the job Caldwell had given O'Grady out of charity. The pay wasn't much, but he knew O'Grady had a family to feed and his wounds at Bull Run had left him in no condition to work as a laborer. But here it was, two days gone, and no sign of O'Grady. That was gratitude for you.

Still, the two former slaves who handled odd jobs around the hospital did a good job feeding the stoves. The biggest problem without O'Grady to oversee them was that an inordinate amount of coal disappeared. Caldwell was reluctant to make an issue of it, because he could only assume the two men were taking it to keep their own families warm.

Caldwell sighed and bent to look closely at the stump of an amputation. The soldier was a lanky fellow, curly-haired, no more than twenty years old. His right hand, too, was heavily bandaged. Caldwell had stopped by the cot because the young man appeared pale and feverish. Not a good sign at all.

"How are you feeling this evening?" Caldwell asked.

"I'm burning up with a fever, sir."

"I can see that. Let me take a look at that arm."

Dutifully, the boy held out the stump. His arm was gone from just above the elbow.

"How were you wounded?" he asked.

"Well, we charged 'em and a bullet hit me in the arm before I had hardly taken a step," the soldier said. "Another bullet clipped my hand as I was kneeling there holding my arm. Them bullets was thick, let me tell you, they was comin' down like raindrops in a thunderstorm. The sawbones – I mean to say, the doctor – at the field hospital had to take the arm off, but he just cleaned up my hand here. At least it was my left arm. I reckon I can still plow with one good arm."

Caldwell grunted. What a stupid, stupid war. Farmboys mangling each other over causes they didn't really understand. He bent down and took a close look at the stump. The arm had been amputated by the flap method, whereby a long piece of skin had been left to sew over the raw end of the bone and severed tissue. This flap did not look terribly healthy. The skin was a deep red, almost like a bruise, and it should have been healing better at this point. He leaned close and sniffed, caught a whiff of that rotting meat smell that indicated gangrene. *Damn.* Not good at all. It was likely the surgeon at the field hospital had left chips of bone or some other kind of debris inside the flap when he had folded it over and sewed up the whole affair. That was what had turned the wound bad.

If the wound had been more recent, Caldwell might have simply pulled back the flap of skin, cleaned out the wound, and sewed it up again. But gangrene had set in.

Almost as an afterthought, he took the boy's bandaged hand and unwrapped it. Now he remembered removing the field dressing and re-bandaging the hand when the soldier had first arrived. He almost recoiled at what he saw as he removed the wrappings. Black flesh, hopelessly gangrene. Red streaks from the spreading infection ran under the skin toward the elbow.

Not for the first time, Caldwell thought that God must be a cruel bastard.

"I'm sorry, son, but I have to take more of your arm," Caldwell said. He was careful to look at the hand, unable to meet the boy's feverish eyes. "Also, your right hand has turned bad. It must come off."

"No," the boy said quietly. "Please don't do that. Not my hand, too. I'll be a cripple. Hell, doctor, I won't even be able to feed myself."

"If I don't do it, you'll die," Caldwell said matter-of-factly.

"That might be better," the soldier said.

Caldwell ignored the comment. "Gangrene has set in. We ought to operate right now, as a matter of fact."

Slowly, the boy nodded. Caldwell thought he saw tears in his eyes and hurried off to find Mae O'Keefe and an orderly. Let the boy cry in peace, he thought.

He asked Mae to help because for some reason, he didn't want Louisa to assist him with this surgery. There was something too brutal and cruel about it that he didn't want her to witness.

There had been cases where surgeons had to keep cutting away at an arm or leg because the infection continued to progress. Say a man lost a foot, but gangrene set in, and then you had to amputate just below the knee. Then the wound turned bad again and you amputated at the thigh. Whittling away at a man one little piece at a time. After a while, you ran out of places to cut, and the patient died anyway.

A cruel war, Caldwell thought. A cruel God.

They amputated the boy's hand and more of his arm. Asleep under the chloroform, his face looked almost peaceful. When they were finished, Caldwell wiped off his bone saw and put it away, hung up his bloody apron, and found the whiskey bottle hidden in the bottom of his sea chest. He had gone several days without drinking, but if there was ever a reason to start again, the heartbreaking operation on the young soldier was about as good as any. He felt bad about it, as if he were betraying Louisa. But then, he hadn't made her any promises.

He took the bottle and locked himself in his office. He was just about to take a long drink when he heard Flynn's booming voice outside the door.

"Doctor! We need you out here." The door rattled on its hinges as Flynn gave it a healthy shake. "Open up."

Reluctantly, Caldwell jammed the cork back in the bottle and stowed the whiskey in his desk behind some papers, where Louisa wouldn't find it without a hard search. She's as bad as a wife, he thought with a twinge. Trying to keep me sober. On the other hand, what would he ever do without her? Without Louisa, Caldwell was convinced he would be as lost as that boy who now had no hands.

He unlocked the door and flung it open. "What the hell is so important that you have to interrupt me while I'm working?" Caldwell demanded.

"Drinking is more like it," Flynn said, giving him a hard look. "The best thing you could do for yourself is to pour that damn whiskey on the ground outside."

"Mind your own business, Flynn," Caldwell snapped. He was in a mood to be mad at the world. "Now what the hell do you want?"

The two men stood there glaring at each other. Finally, Flynn broke the silence. "I just thought you might like to know that there's a newspaper reporter here to see you."

"A newspaper reporter? I don't understand." Caldwell had never spoken with a reporter in his life and didn't know what one could possibly want from him.

"He has some questions about the Rebel Fever, as they're calling it in Swampoodle."

"Swampoodle?" It made no sense. Rebel Fever – a good nickname, considering Verville was behind it – was something that had struck at the hospital, and nowhere else. How could a reporter know about it?

Flynn read his mind. "It seems there's an epidemic of plague there at the moment. Several families have died. According to this reporter, it all started in the home of one Jack O'Grady, who used to work here stoking the stoves. You knew this O'Grady?"

"Oh my God," Caldwell said. "Poor O'Grady. If it's spreading that fast, it must be the pneumonic form of plague."

"What about this reporter?"

"Send him in."

* * *

Charles Wilson had quite a story for the front page of *The Sunday Chronicle*, and now it was just a matter of getting it in print. The War Department would not be happy about a story that might cause a public panic. With the war had come the power to shut down newspapers that spread hysteria or were critical of the government. More than one newspaper editor had found himself in prison for printing news the Lincoln administration did not like.

But Wilson had to get this story out. Panic was part of Verville's plan, and pinning the blame for the epidemic squarely on Major William Caldwell – which was what Wilson planned to do – would plant a false trail that left Verville free to operate.

His editor would never allow a story to be published that might get them all arrested and the newspaper shut down. To get it past the old man, he would rely on two things, a bottle of whiskey and the fact that the office would be empty except for the typesetter.

Although it might have helped further the plans he and his Confederate colleagues had made, it was also a matter of professional pride that no other reporters had found out yet about the Rebel Fever sweeping through the Swampoodle neighborhood. So far, he counted about two dozen of the Irish immigrants in Swampoodle who had succumbed to the plague. If the plague spread beyond the Irish neighborhood, there was no telling how many would die.

The whole city would then resemble Swampoodle, where bodies lay outside the ramshackle houses. Blackened flesh. Grown men murmuring prayers in the streets. Women wailing over the dead. Keening, the Irish called it, an otherworldly noise to send shivers up your spine. Like most newspapermen, Wilson was a cynic by nature, but now that he had seen its potential to cripple the Yankee capital, even he had to admit that Verville's plan was brilliant.

From a reporter's perspective, too, the doctor at Armory Square Hospital,

Major William Caldwell, had actually been quite helpful. It was interesting to meet the man whom Verville professed to hate so much. The doctor had told him everything, including some story about plague-infested rats being released in the hospital by a Confederate agent. If Wilson hadn't known better, he would have thought that part of the story was far-fetched. Well, Wilson would take care of that in his story.

He hurried back to the *Chronicle* office. Most everyone had gone home for the night, but Reese Winslow the typesetter was still there, putting the final touches on the next day's edition. Wilson found a pot of coffee still on the stove. The stuff had been bubbling in a tin pot for hours and was black as printer's ink and thick as molasses, but he dumped in more sugar and poured himself a mug.

Wilson went over to the press area and looked over Winslow's shoulder as he worked. Each page of the newspaper was set as a separate plate, and the individual letters of every word had to be picked out of a tray to Winslow's left. Then, Winslow set the type onto the chase, each tiny letter upside down and backwards. He worked from handwritten sheets to his right on which the newspaper's articles were written. A blank spacer went between each word. Letter by letter, the man filled out each line of type, then moved on to the next line in the column. There were a total of eight columns across the front of the page. When he was finished, the typesetter would lock all the type onto the chase and set it aside, ready to go on the press. It was painstaking work, and not for the first time Wilson was glad he was a reporter and not responsible for making certain all these tiny letters ended up as they were supposed to on the page.

"Working late?" Winslow asked without looking up.

"I have a good story. Save me some room on the front page. Two columns ought to do it."

"I don't know," Winslow said, jerking his chin at a sheaf of papers that comprised the text for the front page stories he was to typeset. "The editor didn't say anything about it."

"I don't suppose he did," Wilson said, then took a deep breath. If you were going to tell a lie, you might as well tell a big one. "I saw him on the way over tonight and he said to tell you to put my story on the front."

Winslow shrugged. "I'll have to pull something out."

Wilson tried to remember the stories the other reporters had been working on that week. "He said to put mine in instead of that Christmas story."

"He did?"

"Yes. So just save me some space while I write it."

Wilson was fully aware that he was breaking all the rules. In fact, there was a chance he could get both himself and Winslow fired over it. Only the editor made the decision as to what went on the front page – or anywhere else in the paper, for that matter.

However, the time had come for him to serve the Cause. His article about the Rebel Fever would be on the front page and the Union's spycatchers would soon turn all their attention to Major Caldwell. Verville would be left alone by the Union spycatchers.

Tonight had to be the night. If Wilson waited, he knew it would be another week before the story came out. He took off his coat, sat down, and drank a big gulp of the viscous coffee. It nearly gagged him. Winslow laughed. "That's left over from this morning."

"That makes it even better." Wilson really didn't care. For some reason, coffee always made him write better, especially late at night. Soon, the only sounds in the office were the scratch of his pencil across paper and old Winslow humming to himself as he carefully set the type.

What Winslow didn't know was that Wilson had taken steps to ensure the editor would not make his usual late-night visit to the newspaper office. Wilson had left a bottle of whiskey on the editor's desk with an anonymous note of thanks. The bottle had been amply dosed with laudanum by Verville. By his customary second glass of evening whiskey, the editor of *The Sunday Chronicle* would be fast asleep in his chair by the fire.

Chapter 18

"My, aren't you doing well!" Louisa cried aloud with genuine pleasure and admiration in her voice as she watched a young soldier navigate the long rows of cots on crutches.

"Next thing you know I'll be dancing a waltz," replied Joseph Carpenter, beaming.

Louisa found there were certain soldiers she began to know better than most. The majority of the time, she simply made her rounds at the hospital, seeing to her duties and exchanging nothing more than a few words with the patients. Many of them were gruff men, laborers and farmers, and while they were kind and treated her with unfailing respect, Louisa had little in common with them.

Joseph Carpenter wasn't like that, however. He was the only son of a couple from New Haven, Connecticut, where his father taught history at Yale. Although Connecticut was a relatively small state geographically, it wasn't so small that Louisa had known him or his family before the war. Besides, she would be the first to admit that she had hardly been a socialite.

He was much younger than Louisa, just twenty-two years old, but he had a maturity far beyond his years. The war had done that to a lot of young men, turning them quickly from boys into adults. Lieutenant Carpenter was far from dour, however, because of a good sense of humor and a quick laugh. There were times when Louisa almost thought of him as a younger brother, and he brought out her mothering qualities.

"Here, let me help you," Louisa said as he returned to his cot. "I don't want you falling."

"After what I've been through, Miss Webster, that would be the least of my worries."

"You're not quite healed, you know. Almost, but if you fall it could be a real setback."

"You just can't stand the thought of me going home, can you?" he joked.

"If you keep talking like that we'll put you on the next train to Connecticut."

Their exchange brought laughter from the soldiers in some of the nearby

139

cots. No matter where you went in this hospital there was always an audience. Smiling, Louisa helped him from the crutches back into bed. He was stubborn about it, though, a typical man, taking her shoulders to steady himself but refusing to let her assist him any more than that. Finally, by degrees, he lowered himself back to his cot.

Lieutenant Carpenter had made remarkable progress since coming to the hospital three months ago. He had been shot through both hips, and the bullet had left a path of torn tissue and shattered bone. It was a difficult wound because all that could be done for him was to hope and pray. Even Caldwell had taken one look at it, turned away, and shook his head. In most of the other similar wounds he had seen, infection almost always proved fatal.

The ensuing fever was bad and lasted for three weeks. When it broke, the lieutenant was weak but cheerful. The young man proved them all wrong. He began to get better.

It was still a painstaking process. At first, he wasn't even able to sit up. Then he was able to perch on the edge of the cot. Eventually he stood and tried a few teetering steps. After nearly six months he was getting around the hospital on crutches.

"You'll tire yourself out," she admonished him now. The young man looked more pale than usual. Louisa suspected he was always in pain, but he never admitted it.

"You're the nurse," he said, smiling.

Louisa left him, moved on to another cot, and another. There was no shortage of soldiers needing attention.

She had heard the news, of course, about the Rebel Fever being loose among the Irish immigrants living in Washington City. Poor Jack O'Grady, she thought, he had brought it home to his family and killed them all. There was little to do other than to order a quarantine of the families that were already sick. Caldwell was in his office with Flynn, probably drinking whiskey.

She turned at the sound of footsteps behind her. It was one of the medical orderlies.

"It's Lieutenant Carpenter," he said. "He's bleeding real bad."

"How can that be?"

"See for yourself, ma'am."

Louisa was puzzled, for the simple reason that aside from the neat entrance and exit holes the miniè bullet had made, Lieutenant Carpenter had no external wounds. How could he be bleeding? She had just left him.

However, as she came closer, there was no mistaking the slick, wet sheen of blood on his blankets. His entire lower half was soaked in blood. He was sitting up in his cot, staring straight ahead.

Quickly, Louisa pulled back the blanket. The wool was heavy with blood. Beneath the blanket, the entire mattress was sopping.

"It's coming from here," he said, lifting his nightshirt enough to expose the exit wound from the bullet high up on his hip. Blood was spurting from the wound, an impossible amount of it, and Louisa instinctively took a bandage and pressed hard until the flow of blood stopped.

"Fetch Doctor Caldwell," she said to the orderly. With a tremor of anger, she hoped he and Flynn hadn't gotten too drunk yet. If only he would stop drinking so much! She knew she might as well hope to visit the moon one day. "He's in his office."

"Yes, ma'am."

There was nothing to do but wait, and Louisa sat on the edge of Lieutenant Carpenter's cot, holding in his blood. Even without the doctor, they both knew what had happened. The churning bullet had left shattered bone in its wake six months ago, and some splinter of bone must have nicked a blood vessel within his hip.

Caldwell came hurrying toward the cot. Louisa could tell with one quick glance that he was sober. Thank God. If there was anyone who could help the young lieutenant, it was him.

Expertly, Caldwell took over the holding of the bandage against Carpenter's hip. With the fingertips of his right hand, he massaged the hip, kneading the knobs of bone, trying to diagnose the problem. He released the bandage, watched the rush of blood for a moment, and quickly replaced the cloth.

Lieutenant Carpenter sat quietly. It was clear from Caldwell's unhappy face that the news was not good.

"Well?" Louisa asked.

Caldwell shook his head. He suddenly looked old, very old, and he stared into Louisa's face without quite focusing on it. He was standing beside Lieutenant Carpenter's cot, so the young officer could hear him, although the explanation was for Louisa's benefit. "I'm afraid there's nothing I can do," he said. "There must still be a sharp edge of bone in there that's cut a deep artery and it's impossible to reach. There's no hope of ligating it. Lieutenant Carpenter can be given some extra time to write a letter home or the like, so long as someone keeps pressure on the wound."

At a loss for what else to say, Caldwell quickly walked away.

"It's not fair," Louisa said. She felt herself on the verge of tears. "All this time getting better, and now this. It just isn't fair."

"Life's not fair," the lieutenant said. "War isn't fair."

"I'll have one of the orderlies hold the bandage while I fetch some paper and a pencil. You'll want to write a letter home, of course."

The lieutenant shook his head. "No, I sent a letter yesterday. A happy note. That's the one I want them to read."

"Is there anyone else you want to write?" Louisa heard a desperate edge in her voice. She was pressing the bandage harder than was really necessary. "Surely there's someone you want to write."

"You've all been very kind these last six months," he said. "I thank you for that."

"Lieutenant—"

"You can let go now," he said.

Louisa's hand seemed to have a will of its own. It was frozen in place. "I can't," she said helplessly.

"Pull your hand away, Miss Webster. Please."

Louisa still couldn't move. Mae O'Keefe appeared, looking less stricken than the rest of them. After all, she had seen a lot of suffering in her life and this was simply one more bitter episode. At a nod from Lieutenant Carpenter, she gently took Louisa's hand and pulled it away. The blood splashed out onto the cot in a bright gush. Louisa felt the world spin. Mae put a strong arm around her shoulders and led her away. She remembered that the human body contains roughly six quarts of blood. One by one, they were running out of young Lieutenant Carpenter.

"Oh God," she said.

Mae took her to the kitchen. "Have a cup of beef tea, dearie," she said.

"I'm all right, Mae, thank you." What Louisa really wanted was to be alone. "You must be busy. Those soldiers need you a lot more than I do."

Mae moved on, her stout peasant's body looking as if it could carry all the burdens in the world.

Louisa allowed herself to cry. It was a rare luxury in a place with so many horrors as an Army hospital. The tears came and came, as if once they were started they would not stop, like a floodgate being opened. This reminded her of Lieutenant Carpenter's blood running out and she cried even harder.

Caldwell found her among the pots and pans in the kitchen and held her.

"Louisa," he said. "I'm so sorry. There was nothing we could do for him."

"It's not right."

"I know," he said, gently reaching for her to offer some comfort. She sobbed even harder and took his arms in her hands to pull them even more tightly around her.

"This war is terrible," she said. "I wish it would end."

"Some day," he said. "It can't go on forever."

* * *

In the early days of the war, many Northern newspapers had unwittingly served as the eyes and ears of the enemy by reporting news the Confederate high command put to good use. Their correspondents sent stories by telegraph that far outpaced the way news had traveled in earlier days, thus allowing information about troop movements and strengths to fall into enemy hands. Ten years ago, the fastest that news could travel was by horse or locomotive. News now traveled with electric speed thanks to the telegraph.

The secretary of war quickly put a stop to this situation by requiring that all outgoing news stories be approved by the official United States government censor. As grand as that position might sound, the censor was in fact located up a flight of dingy stairs at the National Hotel, where he sat in his office with the tools of his trade: glue pots, pencils, scissors and black ink. Newspaper correspondents had to present their stories to him for approval like boys turning in a report to a self-important schoolmaster. He often chopped their stories into a jumble of nonsense, but the reporters didn't have much choice. Breaking the wartime law of censorship meant jail. When this potentate wasn't in his office, a reporter on deadline had to hunt him up in the bars and dance halls in order to get his signature of approval before a story could be sent over the telegraph wire.

Exempted from this system, however, were the Washington newspapers such as *The Sunday Chronicle*. The War Department was mainly concerned about information that went singing out across the telegraph lines, so what was printed in Washington did not require prior approval of the censor. At the same time, that did not give the Washington papers free rein to publish whatever they wished. Any sensitive military information that appeared in print could earn the editor a trip to prison.

Charles Wilson had been well aware of that fact as he labored by lamplight last night over his story for the next day's edition of the *Chronicle*. However, he wasn't overly concerned. He was writing about an epidemic in an immigrant neighborhood. It was Major William Caldwell, painted as the mastermind behind this epidemic by Wilson's story, who would find himself in trouble.

"You're sure this is all right?" the typesetter asked again once Wilson had handed him the finished sheets on which he had scrawled the story in pencil.

"Right on the front page," he said. "The old man said so. He'll be in later to proof the pages. He'll see it then."

"All right," replied the typesetter, and bent to his task, searching for the tiny blocks of type.

Wilson thought with satisfaction that he had done his part. It was now very early Sunday morning. The whole city would know about the Rebel Fever.

There would be panic.

Caldwell would be hunted down and jailed. The blame would be pinned on him. Verville would be free to carry out his plot.

Then the beginning of the end for the Union would start.

* * *

The Sunday Chronicle
TERRIBLE EPIDEMIC!

———

BUBONIC PLAGUE STRIKES CAPITAL

———

REBEL PLOT

———

SCORES FEARED DEAD FROM FEVER

———

Sunday, Dec. 19, 1862, Washington City – A devious Rebel plot to bring a disease not seen since the Dark Ages has struck terror in the heart of Washington City. Dozens of Irish immigrants in the Swampoodle district are feared dead from what has come to be called Rebel Fever.

The epidemic is actually bubonic plague, or the Black Death as this scourge was known in Europe, where it struck down much of the population in medieval times. In most cases the disease proves fatal within a matter of hours, so that a man who has contracted plague is dead by supper time.

The first cases of the disease were found at Armory Square Hospital, where three men have succumbed to this Rebel Fever, said Major William Caldwell, chief surgeon and director of the hospital. He speculated that the disease in Swampoodle was carried forth by an Irishman who worked at the hospital. The man then passed the disease on to his family and neighbors, all of whom have died.

However, sources in the War Department say Dr. Caldwell may have instigated this devilish plague himself. They cite the fact that Caldwell is a native Virginian, and despite the fact that he wears a Union uniform, his true loyalties may lie elsewhere.

"The North is getting what it deserves for the ungentlemanly misery it has inflicted on the Southern states," Caldwell said. "This is only the beginning of Confederate vengeance."

In fact, there has been speculation on the part of a highly placed official that the appearance of the plague in Washington City is actually part of a larger plot. He said many more cases will be seen unless the perpetrator of this sinister plan is brought to justice by government authorities.

* * *

Secretary of War Edwin M. Stanton's naked and rubbery upper lip quivered with rage as he threw the newspaper down on his desk. He and Colonel Lafayette Baker, chief of the United States Secret Service, were alone in Stanton's office.

"Arrest them!" Stanton shouted. "Arrest the fool who wrote this article, arrest the editor of this so-called newspaper, and most of all arrest this surgeon who comes to me hawking rumors about Confederate plots and then turns out to be the very traitor he was warning me against! Damn him!"

"Do you think he's actually a Confederate, like the article says?" Baker asked. "You can't believe half of what you read in these damn newspapers, sir."

"Who knows or cares? Put this Major Caldwell in prison. This is the same surgeon who came here to inform me of this so-called plot and I told him to drop the matter. If nothing else, you would think an officer would know better than to let himself become excited by these wild imaginings, because that's all this plague must be, wild imaginings, I tell you!"

"My men were watching another man, a Southerner named Jefferson Verville," Baker said. "The man is a doctor, and we thought he might have something to do with this plot. He's been associating with some known Southern sympathizers. He's even been to see one of the more notorious waterfront smugglers. We're not sure why."

Stanton paused in his tirade long enough to ask, "What makes you think this Verville is suspicious?"

"Well, sir, we've seen him come and go from the home of a known Confederate sympathizer named Sally Pemberton. Last Thursday, two of my agents were killed while following him. We don't know that this Verville did it, but he hasn't been seen since."

"For God's sakes, Colonel. Who cares about that other man? This newspaper article has just delivered this fool Major Caldwell to you on a platter. What more do you want? Arrest him!"

"Yes, sir. He'll be locked away in the Old Capitol by noon," Baker pledged.

"I will not tolerate this, I tell you! If nothing else, he's going to create a panic."

"Yes, sir."

It was already Monday morning, and *The Sunday Chronicle* had been on the street for more than a day. In that time the front page story about the Rebel Fever had become the talk of the town. Already, there were reports that some families were preparing to leave the city.

"This is why we have an official censor," Stanton went on. He was by nature a man given to emotional extremes, even if he rarely gave voice to them. However, this was one of those times when Stanton's temper was revealed as if the doors of a furnace had been thrown open. The newspaper article had sent him into a roaring rage.

Needless to say, the Monday morning public session had not gone well. As usual, Stanton had held court, hearing entreaties from civilians and soldiers alike in his public fashion, but very few had their requests granted that morning. Stanton was too incensed by the newspaper article to concentrate or to be very sympathetic to those seeking his ear.

"I want guards posted around this immigrant neighborhood," Stanton went on. "Put soldiers at all the streets into Swampoodle. No one must leave. If there is any truth to this newspaper article, I don't want this so-called Rebel Fever to spread."

"Yes, sir. It will be done at once."

Standing just a few feet from the secretary of war's desk, Captain C.J. Wilkerson listened to the tirade with an impassive face. As soon as Stanton had calmed down enough to move on to other matters at hand, Wilkerson slipped out the door. He made no excuses. He would have to think of something later to explain his sudden disappearance.

As he started down the hall, he realized his heart was pounding. His only thought was that he had to warn Major Caldwell. For the doctor or Tom Flynn to be captured now would be disastrous. Wilkerson knew well enough what would happen to them because he had seen Stanton's orders carried out before. Caldwell would be locked deep within the Old Capitol Prison. It was possible he might be released within a few weeks if friends made the right inquiries and bribes, but by then it would be too late. If Flynn was caught, well, it would be a hangman's rope for him.

To his own ears, Wilkerson's boots sounded unnaturally loud in the corridor. He forced himself not to hurry. Whatever happened now, he could not be noticed, or else he would be sharing a cell with the doctor. When he finally reached the stairs, he nearly leapt down them.

He reached the street. Damn. A file of soldiers was already starting in the general direction of the hospital. He counted a captain and six men with bayonets fixed on their muskets. With the soldiers was a man wearing civilian clothes who could only be one of Colonel Baker's detectives. To his surprise, he saw Baker himself join them.

Stanton's orders were always quickly obeyed. In his mind, Wilkerson pictured how the arrest would be carried out: two men to watch the back, the rest making a swift entrance to the hospital. Caldwell and Flynn wouldn't stand a chance, especially with Baker himself there to carry it out.

On the street, the pedestrian traffic swirled around him as people went about their daily routine. As he stood there with his heart pounding, his breath coming fast, he felt angry at these people for being so calm. What the hell was he going to do? Several seconds went by and he blocked the sidewalk as passersby had to push past him. To his horror, he watched the detail sent to arrest the doctor disappear around a corner.

Think. Alone, on foot, it was possible he *might* outrun the patrol. Might. But there really wasn't any other choice. Wilkerson sucked in a breath and began to dash down the street.

He couldn't take the same route as Baker's squad. He ran straight on past the point where the soldiers had turned. Then he darted down an alley and came out on the street right behind the soldiers. He continued on across the street into another alley. He would have to take a parallel course.

Wilkerson quickly realized the long hours as an adjutant in the War Department had made him soft. His lungs felt as if they were on fire and his legs ached. The tailored wool uniform and expensive boots were made for strutting around an office or riding a horse, anything but running. He slipped sideways in a patch of slick mud, caught himself painfully on his hands and knees, then started running again, his immaculate uniform now streaked with mud.

He emerged near the open fields surrounding the unfinished Washington Monument. Armory Square Hospital was within sight, and he sprinted the final distance. The soldiers would be coming out of the street behind him at any moment. He just hoped he would be too far away for them to recognize.

Wilkerson dashed through the door, crying breathlessly, "Caldwell! Caldwell!"

The doctor straightened up from a cot where he was talking to a patient and hurried toward him. His gray eyes fixed on Wilkerson as if he were a madman. "What is it?" he asked.

"They're coming for you," he panted, trying to keep his voice low so that the wounded soldiers nearby wouldn't hear him. Several of the wounded stared at him curiously. "Stanton has sent soldiers to arrest you. They're right behind me."

"What on earth are you talking about?"

"He read the article in *The Sunday Chronicle*," Wilkerson explained. "He wants you imprisoned for causing a public panic, or some such nonsense."

"But half of what's in that article is a lie!" Caldwell protested indignantly. "Surely he can't believe I'm loyal to Virginia."

Flynn had spotted the commotion and was now standing at Caldwell's side. He took the doctor by the arm. "We have to go, Major. Right now."

"But—"

Flynn half pushed him, half dragged him toward the back door. They plunged out into the cold with the doctor still wearing a bloody apron.

Now that he had warned Caldwell and Flynn, there was no place else for Wilkerson to go. He was far too winded to make a run for it.

Nurse Webster approached and looked alarmed at Wilkerson's breathless and muddy appearance. "What's wrong?" she asked. "Why did Mr. Flynn and Major Caldwell leave in such a hurry?"

The front door of the hospital was opening. There was no time to explain. "Just tell them he's not here," he said.

Wilkerson slid into an empty cot, wrapped himself in a blanket, and turned his face to the pillow. It smelled musty from the old straw inside and also had the oily scent of the previous patient's hair.

Boots sounded on the hospital's wooden floor as the soldiers swept in. Nervously, Wilkerson listened as the footsteps approached to within a few feet of his cot and stopped. Maybe he had been seen, after all. Then he realized Louisa was probably still standing near him. He just prayed one of the patients wouldn't point him out, thinking he was a fugitive of some sort. If that happened, he knew there would be no escape – nor any chance at explanations. It would be a quick trip to the Old Capitol Prison.

"Where's Major Caldwell?" Baker's gruff voice demanded.

"He left," he heard Louisa say. "Why, is something wrong?"

Baker moved closer, until he was standing beside the cot. Wilkerson held his breath.

"Where did he go?" he heard Baker demand.

"To the apothecary for some supplies. We were out of laudanum."

"I thought the Army supplied that."

"When they have it. We can't always wait that long for medicines, so the doctor buys a bottle or two to tide us over. He pays for it out of his own pocket, of course."

Baker wasn't interested in Caldwell's philanthropy. "Where is the apothecary?"

"Well, there are two or three where he buys supplies. I'm not sure which one he went to, or maybe more than one."

"We'll wait here then until he returns," Baker announced.

As he lay tightly curled under the scratchy wool blanket, Wilkerson felt his heart sink. He couldn't afford to be gone from the War Department for too long. It might look suspicious.

"He's not coming right back," Louisa said, lying smoothly. "The doctor had business at the Willard Hotel first. He was meeting someone in the hotel bar to discuss something."

"Who?" Baker almost spat the word in his excitement.

"Why, another newspaper reporter, I believe. Evidently, Major Caldwell wanted to set straight all the lies that had been printed about him still being loyal to Virginia."

That was all Baker needed to hear. He moved away from the cot and Wilkerson let his breath out.

"All right," Baker said, and began issuing orders to his men. "Two of you will stay here in case the doctor returns. If he does, you're to arrest him and bring him back to the War Department. The rest of us will go to the Willard and try to find the doctor there."

Damn. He was going to be stuck hiding in this cot for hours. Wilkerson listened as the boots tramped away. A curious murmur filled the hospital as rumors were whispered among the patients. Why would soldiers from the War Department be looking for Dr. Caldwell? Mostly, the murmurs were defensive. These wounded men thought a great deal of their chief surgeon. He heard one or two whisper, "Who's that under the blanket?" If that kept up, it was only a matter of time before the guards left behind would find him.

"You can come out now," he heard Louisa's voice beside the cot. "The two guards are in the kitchen. Mae O'Keefe is giving them beef tea."

Wilkerson sat up. "Thank God," he said. "You tell an excellent story, Miss Webster."

"Hurry," she said. In the kitchen, they could hear the two soldiers from the War Department laughing. "There isn't much time."

"If Colonel Baker comes back, don't try to send him off on any more wild goose chases," Wilkerson said. "He'll be mad enough as it is."

"What about the doctor?" she asked. "Will he be all right? I can't understand why they want to arrest him."

"The article in the newspaper made the secretary of war very unhappy. For the time being, the doctor is going to have to stay as far as possible from this hospital unless he wants to end up in a prison cell. He's landed himself in the middle of something very dangerous."

"But his patients–"

Wilkerson shook his head.

"They're now your patients."

Any second now, the two soldiers would be coming out of the kitchen. "You'd better go," Louisa said.

"Good luck," Wilkerson said.

He felt odd saying it. Wouldn't he be the one needing the luck? Wilkerson slipped out the door and hurried toward the War Department, praying that Caldwell would have enough sense to stay far, far away from Armory Square Hospital for the time being.

Chapter 19

"You'd best take off that apron," Flynn warned Caldwell. "You look like you just ran out of a hospital – unless you try to pass for a butcher."

Caldwell glanced down at the canvas apron, which was spotted with dried blood. "I see what you mean."

He untied the apron and jammed it into a pile of rubbish in an alley, then rejoined Flynn on the street.

"Now what?" Caldwell asked. He was freezing, having run out of the hospital without so much as his coat. They had just escaped the squad sent to arrest him.

"We'll have to find a place to stay," Flynn said. "We can't be wandering around the street, especially in this weather, and we can't go back to the hospital."

"But my patients–"

"There's nothing you can do about that," Flynn said. "The moment you show yourself back at the hospital you'll be arrested and spend the rest of the war deep inside the Old Capitol Prison. I'm sure you don't want that."

"Not really."

"Good. Then come with me."

Flynn started off at a quick pace and Caldwell had to scramble to keep up. He realized how happy he was to be moving, to be doing something. Sitting around the hospital waiting for something to happen wasn't Flynn's style at all, but he hadn't had much choice. He had spent some time, too, at the tavern, but mostly the MacCraes hadn't been around and he had found himself in the surly presence of Harry, whose bruises from the fight were still healing. Consequently, Flynn preferred to pass his time at the hospital.

Verville had melted into the city, disappearing from sight, and unless he showed himself again or unless Flynn was able to track him down through the MacCrae brothers, there really wasn't much else he could do. He was just glad Wilkerson had shown up in time to warn them. It must have been risky for the young officer to do. Flynn decided he must have misjudged Wilkerson and the lad had more sand than he had thought.

"I still can't believe the secretary of war would issue a direct order to have us arrested," Caldwell said.

"Not us, just you. He doesn't know who I am, and doesn't much care. All he knows is that there's an Army doctor causing panic by spreading rumors about something called Rebel Fever that's supposedly going to kill every man, woman and child in the city so the Confederates can march right in and occupy Washington. For all he knows, it might even be your idea."

"That newspaper reporter made it all up about me being loyal to the South. Verville is trying to start an epidemic, not me. I never thought anyone would take that newspaper article seriously."

"Well, if the War Department is having as hard a time finding Verville as we are, I guess they might decide to make do with locking you away."

"Damn Verville," Caldwell nearly spat. "Why the hell couldn't he have just stayed in Richmond? All he's done so far is set a few plague-ridden rats loose, and look at all the trouble he's caused."

"I have a feeling he's just getting started," Flynn said. "He's waiting for something – probably more rats. But as to this plot being published in the newspaper, of course Stanton isn't going to be happy. He has enough to worry about without some doctor getting the city in an uproar."

"Stanton ought to be helping us, not trying to put us in prison."

Flynn wondered how the doctor could be so naïve. "As far as he's concerned, you've already done more damage than any Rebel saboteurs. How do you think it makes him look, you coming out with this wild scheme about the Rebels starting an epidemic? Even being accused of masterminding the scheme? I'll tell you what – it makes Stanton look like he can't do his job, which, among other things, is to protect Washington City from Confederate plots. You made him look bad. Never make your boss look bad. He won't be happy."

"I see."

Flynn wasn't so sure the doctor did, but it no longer mattered.

"Where are we going?" Caldwell asked.

"To see some friends of mine," he said.

Flynn led the doctor to the waterfront, where they stopped in front of the MacCrae brothers' tavern. Caldwell stood staring up at the sign and decrepit building, looking dismayed.

"What is this place?"

"A place of friendship and fellowship," Flynn said. "Just don't look anyone in the eye if you don't want to fight him."

They went inside. After the cold winter streets, the tavern was like a warm, dark cave that smelled of tobacco smoke, spilled whiskey and wet wool. The place would not fill up until evening, when the dock workers arrived to drink their pay.

"Is the boss in?" Flynn asked Harry, who was polishing glasses behind the bar.

"He's having his breakfast." Harry jerked his chin at the inner door.

"That's your problem, Harry, always leading with your chin," Flynn said.

Harry glared at him. Flynn led the doctor to the tavern's inner sanctum. James MacCrae sat at a table under a single lantern. He was hard at work on a plate heaped high with fried eggs, bacon and bread. A huge, steaming mug of coffee was at his fingertips, and beside that was a shot glass filled with whiskey. He was reading a copy of *The Sunday Chronicle*.

"Good morning, Mr. MacCrae," Flynn said, trying to judge the man's temperament. If there was one thing he had learned quickly enough about the MacCrae brothers, it was that they were a moody bunch.

"Mullins." Flynn felt Caldwell look at him with a questioning glance, but he ignored it. MacCrae went on, talking around a mouthful of food, "Look at this story in the newspaper about a Confederate agent using rats to start an epidemic. Bubonic plague, of all things. Now that would be bad for business, having everybody in the city die off." He laughed.

"It's probably just rumors. You can't trust the damn newspapers."

"That's true. Who's your friend?"

"An old companion who's down on his luck. He's an Army doctor, so I thought he might be helpful to you. He can handle things quiet-like when you need it."

"A doctor, you say?" MacCrae looked thoughtful as he used a fingernail to work something loose from between his teeth. "You know, Doc, my foot has been bothering me. Take a look at it."

"Certainly," Caldwell said. "I can come back sometime–"

"Right now is as good a time as any," MacCrae said. He shoved his chair back and threw his right foot up on the table beside his plate of food, then worked the laces loose on his shoe. He took off the shoe and sock to reveal a foot as white and stubby as a boiled potato.

Caldwell studied the foot with professional interest. "What seems to be the trouble?"

"It pains me at times to walk on it. It's as if there's a hot coal in my shoe."

Caldwell went up close and peered at the foot from all angles. "There's the problem," he said. "You, sir, have a plantar's wart on the sole of your foot. It would in fact feel like a hot coal in your shoe. I'll come back sometime and excise it for you – just have a sharp knife for me, a bit of whiskey, and some bandages. It won't trouble you again."

MacCrae looked please as he slipped on his sock and tied his shoe. He went back to shoveling food in his mouth. "What can I do for you, Mullins?"

"The doctor and I need a place to stay. I was turned out of my room."

MacCrae laughed. "How did you manage that?"

"I took a girl home with me, and the old landlady there didn't much like that."

MacCrae laughed. "Won't the Army put up the doctor here?"

"I'm between assignments," Caldwell explained.

MacCrae nodded, then sang out, "Billy!" When the boy appeared, he said, "Take these two gentleman to Miss Paula's house, lad. She won't much care who you bring home, Mullins, believe me."

"Thank you, Mr. MacCrae."

MacCrae laughed. "Hell, it's the least I can do for the man who's going to beat the Kraut for me. You won't even have to pay."

"Surely she'll want something," Caldwell said.

"I own the house, Doc. That woman runs it for me. I suppose I can let someone stay for free in my own house, can't I?"

"Why, of course," Caldwell agreed.

"Good." MacCrae bent back to his plate by way of dismissal. He was noisily chewing bacon and slurping coffee as they followed the boy out.

"I wouldn't have guessed a man like that owned a boarding house," Caldwell said.

"What, Miss Paula's?" Flynn laughed. "That's no boarding house, Doc. That's a whorehouse."

* * *

Among the Washington City whorehouses, Miss Paula's was nothing fancy. It catered to the rough crowd that worked the docks along with sailors and even wagon drivers whose arrival in the city was marked by a jingle of coins in their pockets.

"I only got one room," announced Paula herself, a large, rough woman with brimstone eyes. There was nothing soft and feminine about the whorehouse madame.

"You don't snore, do you?" Flynn asked Caldwell.

"What?"

"We'll take it, and gladly," Flynn said to Paula.

"You called him 'Doc'," she said, and squinted at Caldwell in the dim light. "You really a doctor?"

"A surgeon, actually."

"Well, I got some girls that could use some doctoring."

"You just tell Doc here which ones," Flynn said, and winked. "He'll fix them right up and get them back to work."

"You're that new prizefighter for them MacCraes, ain't you?" Paula asked.

"Aye, that's me," Flynn said.

"Well, I got a word for you," Paula said. "That Kraut fighter everybody's talkin' about? Beat the hell out of him and you can have as many of the girls you want for free. He's a mean one, come in here once and raised hell."

"Well, lass, that's what I aim to do – beat hell out of the Kraut. We'll see about the girls. I'll let the doctor see to 'em first. I like a clean woman."

Paula snorted. "Hell, we'll see what kind of shape you're in after the fight. If you ain't too beat up I might just take you myself."

"I'll be looking forward to it, that I will."

Some kind of ruckus started down the hall as women's voices grew shrill and there was a flutter of undergarments. Paula bore down on the girls like a warship, and Flynn dragged Caldwell inside the room and shut the door. There was a lantern burning and in the dim light they could see it was a dismal room. The walls were cracked and chunks of plaster were missing in places. Crumpled papers and scraps of cloth littered the corners. A foul odor of vinegar and sweat hung in the air, even though the unheated room was chilly.

"Och, the woman wants to jump me bones," Flynn said. "Can you imagine? It's enough to make a man want to join the priesthood."

"Never mind that," Caldwell said. He had turned to face Flynn and was glaring at him. "You have some explaining to do."

"Aye?"

"Don't play the boggy Irishman with me, Flynn, or should I say Mullins?"

"I couldn't go telling the man my real name, now could I?"

"What's this about fighting someone named the Kraut? That woman out there seemed to think you were going to lose to him."

"She also thought I was going to hop into bed with her, so it just goes to show how much she knows."

"Goddamnit, Flynn, tell me what's going on!"

Flynn sighed. He had tried to keep as much as possible from Caldwell, and with good reason. Although he knew he could trust Caldwell, he wasn't so sure what the doctor would say if he were ever arrested and brought to the Old Capitol prison. Some of the methods used by the secretary of war's henchmen in extracting the truth would not have been out of place in a medieval torture chamber. Under those circumstances, Flynn had to assume the doctor would talk. Any man would, and the less Caldwell knew about his whereabouts in the city, the better. Flynn wanted to make it as hard as possible for the Yankee spycatchers to find him and put a rope around his neck.

"All right, then, here's what's going on," Flynn said. "And for God's sakes, don't tell anyone. Not a soul. Not even Louisa."

"Come on, Flynn. You know Louisa—"

"Not even her," Flynn snapped. "If you think Stanton and his gang wouldn't torture a woman to learn something, think again."

Caldwell sat down on the edge of the filthy and rumpled bed. "I never thought the secretary of war would be so ruthless," he said.

"It's not so much Stanton who's ruthless as the people who work under him. Lafayette Baker, for one," Flynn explained, naming the head of the United States Secret Service. "Of course, there is a war on, and wars aren't won by being kind and gentle."

"I suppose you're right," Caldwell said. "Now, why don't you tell me what you've been up to these last few days?"

Flynn told him about the MacCraes, the fact that they were some of the leading Potomac River smugglers, and about prizefighting for them. He had to raise his voice slightly to be heard over the noise a man and woman were making in the room next door.

When Flynn was through, Caldwell sat for a minute, digesting what he had just heard. "You really think all this is going to lead you to Verville?"

"So far, it's the best plan we have. The bastard has disappeared, and Washington City is big enough that if you don't want to be found, you probably won't be, if you know what you're doing. Our only hope is that the MacCraes will lead us to him."

"Meanwhile, you're willing to get yourself killed fighting somebody named The Kraut."

"Who knows? Maybe he's the one who should worry."

Caldwell shook his head. "You're crazy, Flynn. You know that, don't you?"

"Sometimes it pays to be a little crazy. Besides, I really don't have much choice. If we don't find Verville and stop him, I might never be able to go home again."

"Would that be so bad? I've never felt any loyalty to any particular place, just to the Army."

"Sure, and I'm glad the United States Army is so loyal to you, making you hide out because it wants to arrest you and throw you in prison."

"It's not a happy situation," Caldwell said.

He knew Caldwell himself was a Virginia man who had sided with the

Union. Still, that didn't make you a Yankee by heart. All Flynn knew was that he wanted to be able to return home to Richmond, and catching Verville was the best way to do it.

"If we don't catch him, we might not have to worry about it for long," Flynn said. "The Rebel Fever he's planning to set loose will kill us along with everyone else."

* * *

When Charles Wilson arrived Monday afternoon at the offices of *The Sunday Chronicle*, he was surprised to find a squad of soldiers and detectives waiting for him.

A tall plainclothes detective took him firmly by the arm, as if the reporter might try to run away. Never mind the fact that there were several armed soldiers in the room with wicked-looking bayonets on the ends of their rifles.

"My name is Colonel Lafayette Baker," he said. "I am the chief of the United States Secret Service. You're under arrest, and I'm closing down this newspaper."

The soldiers had already made a shambles of the *Chronicle*'s office. In the back room where the presses were, trays of type had been overturned and scattered on the floor. Drawers in the editorial office had been pulled out and the papers strewn around the room. Bundles of the latest issue of the *Chronicle* had been stacked in a wagon in the street.

"We're going to burn them," Colonel Baker explained when he saw Wilson's puzzled look.

The editor of the *Chronicle* sat slumped in a chair, looking extremely dismal. He gave Wilson a doleful glare, like a father might give a son who had betrayed him. A soldier stood beside the editor's chair, ready to bayonet the old man if he made a run for it.

"You're under arrest," Baker told Wilson, in case he hadn't grasped the obvious.

"What's the charge?" Wilson demanded.

Baker fixed Wilson with a cold smile as he answered, "Treason, instigating a public panic, printing seditious lies harmful to the United States of America, and anything else I can think of."

"What?" Wilson could hardly believe his ears. "That's ridiculous."

"The secretary of war doesn't think so," Baker said. "And his opinion counts more than yours. Let's go."

A soldier helped the editor out of his chair. "I should have come back to check the galleys," he was muttering. "I should have checked. Wilson, how could you do this to me?"

Wilson wanted to explain it had nothing to do with him or anyone else. It was all about serving the Confederacy. Of course, he couldn't breathe a word of that, or else they would all hang. "Don't worry. They won't be able to hold us for long."

Baker laughed cruelly. "You don't even know where you're going, do you? Old Capitol Prison. If you're lucky, Stanton will let you out when the war is over."

Wilson gulped, his legs suddenly refused to work, and one of Baker's detectives shoved him roughly out the door.

"Is that your evidence?" Wilson asked as they passed the wagon loaded with *Chronicles*.

"We don't need evidence," the detective said. "We're going to burn these newspapers the first chance we get."

Wilson didn't know what else to say as he shuffled out the door alongside his editor. The old man seemed on the verge of tears as the soldiers guided them toward a carriage waiting outside.

"Take a deep breath," the detective said as Wilson prepared to climb inside the carriage. "That's the last fresh air you're going to get for a long, long time."

* * *

Stanton made it clear that there was to be no more newspaper coverage given to the outbreak of plague in the Irish neighborhood. The official government censor was aroused from his usual lackadaisical manner and warned that no one was to send any details of *The Sunday Chronicle* story over the telegraph wire. There could be no stopping the mail, of course, but by the time copies of the newspaper reached New York or Philadelphia, the incident would be old news. Interest would have moved on to other topics and the epidemic would have run its course by then.

A few people had left the city in fear, but most residents were merely keeping a weather eye open. The secretary of war would make sure there was no more news about this Rebel Fever. The North really couldn't afford a panic situation fueled by what people read in the newspapers. Stanton made sure there were no secrets about what had become of *The Sunday Chronicle*'s editor and reporter. He wanted to send a message that the Old Capitol prison was big enough to hold any number of journalists.

Stanton had effectively muzzled the press, but he still wasn't done. The same afternoon that the editor and reporter had been locked away, he summoned Colonel Baker to his private office.

"I want you to find this doctor, the one who got away this morning from the hospital."

"Yes, sir."

"Find him and arrest him. There's a cell reserved in his name at the Old Capitol. You have your methods, of course, but an Army doctor can't be too hard to find in this city."

"I'll find him, sir." Baker smiled. "You can count on that."

* * *

"They've arrested Charles Wilson," Sally announced.

"Damn. Do you think he'll talk?"

Sally shrugged her lovely shoulders. "It's hard to say. He's a weak man, and I've heard stories of what they do to prisoners in there. And if he does talk–"

"The whole plan is ruined," Verville said. "This isn't a good situation. He managed to get that dog Lafayette Baker off our trail and put him onto Caldwell instead, but if he tells the truth in prison.... Well, he just can't."

Verville paced the floor of the hotel room. He rarely left the hotel anymore. He knew it wouldn't be long before the Russian ship arrived and set his plans in motion. Until then, he tried to stay off the streets as much as possible. Until the article in *The Sunday Chronicle* had come out, he had to assume that the same Colonel Baker who had set the two spies on his trail was still out there looking for him, and very possibly bent on revenge for killing the two men. As if that wasn't enough, apparently Caldwell was caught up with another group that had gone searching for him. The last thing Verville needed was some chance meeting on the street with any of the people looking for him. If anyone saw him now it could spell disaster for his grand plan, and Verville wasn't about to risk everything for the sake of some fresh air.

"We could make certain Charlie Wilson doesn't talk," Sally finally said.

"What do you mean?" Verville asked. "He's locked inside that damned Old Capitol Prison. There's no way we'd ever be able to get him out."

"We could make sure he never gets out."

Verville stared at her. Sally's green eyes were cold and calculating. He suddenly had no doubt what she meant to do.

"Kill him?"

"There's no other way."

"How?"

"There are guards who can be bribed. I know of one or two of them."

Her resourcefulness never failed to surprise him. "Do it," he said.

Sally smiled. "Would you order me killed, too, if you thought I was going to betray our plot?"

"There's only one answer to that," he said. "Don't betray us, and you'll never find out."

She laughed at that. Then an altogether different look came into her green eyes as she came up close to him. The smell of her perfume filled his nostrils. "I hate to leave you all alone—"

"I'm fine," he said coldly. "Go, and see that you aren't followed."

Sally shrugged, and with a pang of anger he realized she had merely been toying with him. She put her bonnet back on and left. As he watched the door close behind her, he wondered, would he in fact have to kill her?

Yes.

And soon.

But not yet.

With Sally gone, the room felt strangely empty and quiet. Her perfume lingered. Verville shook his head and sat down. Most of the time now, he lounged in his chair with the shades drawn against the weak December sunshine, dosing himself with laudanum. He allowed himself up to a wineglass full of the stuff daily, although he knew it was a dangerous amount. Several hours each afternoon passed for him in a kind of dreamy languor. However, his afternoons spent dozing meant that he had a hard time sleeping at night. The hours after midnight were filled with strange waking dreams as he drifted in a state between full consciousness and sleep.

He did rouse himself long enough each morning to dress and go out for the newspaper. Back in his room, he carefully locked the door and sat down to read the paper. He glanced at the front page and moved on to the maritime report. This very morning, he had finally seen the notice he was looking for:

The Russian frigate Rynda *has entered Chesapeake Bay, rounding Cape Henry on Sunday morning. She is just back from a mission to China and will resupply during the winter months at Washington before returning to sea in the Czar's service.*

Verville grinned. From Cape Henry to the mouth of the Potomac River the *Rynda* would have to sail about seventy-five miles. Depending on when she was sighted Sunday, that would put the ship in the Potomac sometime Tuesday or even late Monday. There, the ship would anchor and await Verville, just as he had arranged with Captain Khobotov. He decided that he would arrange with the MacCraes to rendezvous with the Russians to unload his cargo at midnight Wednesday. Coming into port with the cargo was too risky. Too many dock workers and officials had their eyes wide open for smugglers. The ones who didn't go to the authorities would want to be paid off. Verville didn't want any such complications. He had waited too long for the entire plan to be ruined by an overzealous inspector. Even the MacCrae brothers didn't own the waterfront.

And then what? He would have to pay the Russian captain the rest of the money owed for delivering the cargo, a transaction that would cut further into Verville's funds just at the time when he would be needing them most. Not that it could be helped. Khobotov also wanted a share of the profits, and Verville would be happy to oblige. After all, there was nothing aboard but disease, and Verville would be glad to share. Within days, all the Russian sailors would be dead.

He had not shared the news about the Russian ship's arrival with Sally. Some knowledge was better kept a secret. Meanwhile, the time would soon come when he would no longer need her.

It was early, not even lunchtime yet, but Verville pulled the curtains shut against the pale winter light. He counted out thirty drops of laudanum into a wineglass and downed it in one quick swallow. Just a small dose. A bit of celebration. The last few days had been tense, a waiting game, but now the real action was about to begin. Like some seed planted and forgotten, his plot had taken root and was now about to flower.

He lay down on the bed as the opium began to course through him. He needed such large doses now that the laudanum he had just taken created only a mild euphoria, like the first sip of coffee in the morning. Still, it was enough. Verville closed his eyes and drifted in a semi-conscious state, dreaming.

A new nation had been born, the Confederate States of America, and it would prosper.

Above all that reborn land, the red and blue flag of the Confederacy snapped in a magnolia-scented breeze.

Chapter 20

"Tonight we'll try to escape."

"Are you mad?" said Charles Wilson, staring in disbelief at his cell mate in the Old Capitol Prison. "There's no escape from this place."

"I've worked it all out – either we go tonight or not at all." At that, the other prisoner shuffled away.

Wilson had awakened on the floor of the prison feeling cold and hungry. Although there were wooden bunks, like the other prisoners he slept on the floor under a thin blanket. The bunks themselves were just breeding grounds for bed bugs and worse.

The prison was a dreadful place. Located at the corner of First and A Streets, it was a rambling building, with additions that wandered off in several directions. The name "Old Capitol" came from the fact that the building had housed Congress after the British burned Washington during the War of 1812. Later, the building became a boarding house for prominent politicians. Despite its size, the building had never been intended for a prison. Boards were nailed haphazardly over some windows, while iron bars covered others.

It was filthy, with rats scurrying in the dark corners. The December cold crept in through the walls and broken windows. Charles Wilson was given a cell with several other prisoners. One or two were overly friendly, and Wilson avoided speaking with them, especially a fat man who was noticeably cleaner and better fed than the other inmates. It was the fat man who had proposed the escape attempt, and Wilson wasn't sure whether or not to trust him. He had heard how some of the prison inmates were spies or else received preferential treatment for passing on information they gleaned from fellow prisoners.

So far, no one had questioned him at length, a fact for which he was grateful. Already, after just a single day in prison, he was cold, shivering and dejected. Like most men, he liked to think of himself as strong and brave. But one day in prison had taught him he was much weaker than he thought. He worried that he might begin talking about Verville's plot in spite of himself – if only to win better food and a warmer blanket.

Wilson decided if there was a chance to escape, he would take it.

After dinner was brought that night – moldy bread and a thin soup with unidentifiable lumps of gray meat that the veteran inmates advised him not to eat – their jailer forgot to shut the door behind him.

"Come quick," said the fat man, whom Wilson suspected of being an informant. "They've left the door open."

"That's just the door to our room," another inmate said. "We'd never get out of the prison itself."

"We've got to try," Wilson heard himself saying. Even after a short stay in the Old Capitol, he was willing to attempt an escape.

Wilson, the fat man and another inmate ran out. The others stayed behind.

"Come on, this way," said the fat one. They ran down a dim hallway lit only by guttering gas lights and an occasional oil lantern.

Suddenly, the fat inmate ducked into a doorway and disappeared, leaving Wilson and his fellow prisoner alone. They almost ran into one of the prison guards, who had appeared out of nowhere. He had a revolver in his hand.

"What have we here?" the guard demanded, a wicked smile on his lips. His eyes were on Wilson as he seemed to ignore the other man. "Escaped prisoners."

Wilson was panting with fatigue and fright. "The door was open–" he tried to explain.

The guard never gave him a chance. He raised the revolver and shot Wilson at point blank range. Wilson's blood spattered the prisoner next to him. The man screamed. The guard shot him, too, and looked down at the two lifeless bodies.

"Two dead Rebels for the price of one," he said. "Now that's what I call a bargain."

* * *

Death was coming for Father Larkin.

He could feel the sickness building in his body as the fever took hold. Strangely, he realized he did not fear what was to come. He had seen so many others die in the last four days that it was easy to accept his own death. He knew, too, that it would be swift. By evening, he would be a corpse and his soul would have entered the Kingdom of Heaven.

The streets were largely deserted, except for an occasional figure hurrying along with a scarf across his or her face to filter the air. The bodies of whole families lay outside their homes because there was no one left to bury them. The lucky ones had a blanket over them for some measure of dignity, while others had no shroud at all but only their black faces turned to the sky. Pigs and stray dogs sniffed at the dead, then wandered through the open doors of the empty homes, looking for food.

He tried to go home and die in his own bed, outside Swampoodle.

"Come no closer, Father," a soldier with a musket said, lowering the weapon until the bayonet was even with Larkin's chest. "You're not allowed to leave."

"You can't keep us penned up here to die," Larkin protested.

"Get back, or you'll die sooner," said a gruff sergeant, coming up beside the soldier blocking Larkin's path.

"The people here need food," Larkin said. "At least send in some food and water."

"For what?" the sergeant scoffed. "No sense feeding a bunch of corpses – or the likes of you that's about to become corpses."

"May God forgive you," he said.

Larkin lurched away to wander the streets. The quarantine imposed by armed guards affected an area of no more than fifty or sixty houses, but this section of Swampoodle was an enclave of misery in the city. He could understand the need for a quarantine – if this plague spread, the whole city might succumb. Washington would be a graveyard. But the authorities had shown little compassion for the suffering of the dying Irish immigrants.

Not knowing what else to do, Father Larkin found himself in front of the O'Grady house, where the whole epidemic had begun. He was staggering now from the fever. It wouldn't be long.

He took his rosary beads from his pocket, wound the beads in his hand so that they would not slip, even when his fingers grew cold.

Briefly, he pitied himself. He thought with regret of his sins and shortcomings.

And then he began to pray.

* * *

"Well, if it isn't our old friend, Dr. Verville," said James MacCrae, grinning.

"MacCrae." Verville nodded at him. "I have some further business to discuss with you."

"Leave us, boys," James MacCrae said, and there was a noisy scraping of chairs as the other men pushed back from the table and left, scowling at Verville.

Verville knew his plan to spread Rebel Fever might be too ambitious, but he had seen the prize, and that was the destruction not just of Washington but of Philadelphia and New York as well. He would succeed, he *must* succeed.

The Confederacy was depending on him. The leaders might not have the stomach for Verville's measures now but they would thank him later, when the North had lost the war. They would make him a general, a hero of the Confederacy. The Stars and Bars would fly forever above the capitol of every Southern state. Slavery would be preserved. All because he had acted when others faltered or were afraid.

One step at a time, he cautioned himself. He would need help to carry the plague-infested clothing to those northern cities. That was why he was going to see James MacCrae again.

When the last of MacCrae's gang was out the door, MacCrae asked, "Now, what's this about? It had better be important, because I have a lot of business to attend to. We have a big prizefight coming up tomorrow night. An Irishman and a big German nobody's been able to beat. Come if you want."

"I don't enjoy prizefights."

"Then what's so important?"

"I need more help." Verville always thought it best to be direct. "I'm going to be taking some of my cargo to Philadelphia and New York, as well."

"All right," MacCrae shrugged, as if it was no great thing, but his eyes watched Verville warily. "A couple of men ought to do it."

"Of course, we shall be taking the train," Verville said. "It might be necessary for the authorities to look the other way, so that we may bring the cargo aboard."

MacCrae smiled. "Ah. I see."

"Is this something you could arrange?"

"Let's just say that I can arrange just about anything," MacCrae said. "Sit down and we can talk about it."

Verville had been standing several feet away, holding his cane carefully in gloved hands. He sat down, but still kept his grip on the cane. He did not fear MacCrae, but at the same time, Verville knew better than to be careless. You could never let your guard down with a man like MacCrae.

"I assume there are people you can bribe?" Verville asked.

"Of course, of course," MacCrae said. "We'll get to that. Whiskey?"

"No."

MacCrae poured a liberal amount into his own glass.

"We can make the arrangements," MacCrae continued. "It will be expensive, mind you, bribing railroad men. They all have good jobs, families to feed, why should they risk anything, you see? So that makes it expensive."

"Money is not a problem," Verville said, although, in truth, he was already approaching the limits of his funds from Richmond. However, he was not going to let something as inconsequential as money stop him from achieving the South's victory.

"I'm glad you brought that up," MacCrae said. Verville was expecting MacCrae to give him a song and dance about money, but what he proposed next surprised him. "You see, my brother and I have been talking. There's a lot of risk involved in what you're having us do, smuggle in cargo when we don't even know what it is. That's not normally how we do things, and so you can see how it makes us worry a bit. Money is one thing, of course. But what my brother and I would like is to be cut in on a share of the profits from your cargo."

"But there won't be any profit," Verville blurted out, realizing at once that he had spoken too quickly.

MacCrae appeared puzzled. "No profit? Then what's the point of smuggling anything?"

Verville thought quickly. MacCrae had a point about profit, and he would be suspicious if Verville insisted this wasn't the sort of cargo that could be sold. "I see," he finally said. "Being paid is one thing, but you want more."

"Think of the risks we're taking to help you, Verville." MacCrae's eyes twinkled with a greedy light. "It only seems fair."

"How much? Ten percent?"

"Half," MacCrae said. "In addition to what you were already going to pay us."

"That's absurd."

"Who else are you going to get to help you at this point?" MacCrae asked. "You really don't have much choice."

Verville remembered his meeting with the Russian captain, Khobotov, in arranging for him to bring the cargo from the Orient. Like MacCrae, the Russian had been greedy, wanting a share of the cargo. Verville wasn't surprised. It was the nature of men like them to want more than they deserved. They were criminals, after all. Not that it mattered to Verville, so long as they met their end of the bargain. He would be only too happy to give them their share. The Russians would be carrying death itself in their hold, and there was plenty of that to go around. MacCrae was welcome to it.

"I suppose I don't have any choice," Verville said, trying to sound bitter.

"That's the way to look at it," MacCrae said with a self-satisfied air. "You're a doctor, so you know about medicine. Sometimes you have to swallow it no matter how bad it tastes."

Verville stood. "I'll bring the rest of the money Wednesday night. Shall I meet you here?"

MacCrae didn't bother to stand up, although he did raise his whiskey glass in a mock toast to Verville. "See you at midnight sharp."

* * *

No sooner had Verville left the room than Angus MacCrae stepped out of the shadows. In his small, birdlike hand he held a large Colt revolver.

"What's the matter, Angus, don't think I can take care of myself?" his brother asked. His eyes went to the weapon in Angus' hand. "Why the hell are you carrying a gun?"

"I don't trust that Verville. I sent Billy to follow him again. We can at least find out where he's staying now."

"Does it matter?

"Maybe, maybe not. It's just that Verville is too damn smart for his own good – or ours."

"That explains why you thought you might have to shoot him?"

"Don't forget that he almost speared Harry with that sword he keeps in his cane."

"He's just one of those Southern gentlemen with more money than sense." MacCrae took a sip of whiskey.

"You've had enough of that," Angus said.

"Come now, Angus," James MacCrae said. "A couple drinks of whiskey just lubricates my brain."

"Pickles it, you mean. It's not even noontime."

MacCrae put a cork in the whiskey bottle. "Satisfied? Now, what do you think of the arrangement with Verville?"

"I don't like it," Angus said. He walked over to the table and put the pistol down, then sat in the chair Verville had just vacated. "He's not telling us something. He gave in too easy on giving us half the cargo."

"Well, you did hear him say that there wasn't any profit in it."

"Ah, he's just blowing smoke up our arses with that one," Angus said. "It's easy for him to say he's going to pay us double and give us half the profits from the cargo when he doesn't intend to pay it."

"What are you talking about?"

"See what I mean about that goddamn whiskey, James? You're not thinking. Of course Verville says he'll give us whatever we want, that money is no object. Think about it. He doesn't intend to pay us anything else, not beyond the money he already gave us."

James MacCrae was beginning to see it. "The bastard is going to doublecross us."

"Right. I don't know how. It's just him, and he can't be dumb enough to think he's going to get the jump on all of us. He's got something else planned."

"So what do we do?"

"When the bastard shows up tomorrow at midnight, we kill him and go collect his cargo ourselves."

"That's not what we talked about." The brothers' original plan, settled upon after their first meeting with Verville, was that they intended to help Verville collect the cargo, then steal it from him. However, that was beginning to seem too risky. There was no telling if Verville was planning some sort of trap for them. The MacCrae brothers had not thrived in the smuggling business by walking into traps.

"We'll kill him first, James, instead of later," Angus tried to explain it a different way, in case the whiskey really had pickled his brother's brain.

"But how do we know exactly what we're letting ourselves in for? Where do we even find this goddamn ship in the Chesapeake Bay?"

"We beat it out of him first," Angus said, and he smiled. He had a grin that gave even his brother chills. "And then we kill him."

* * *

Mae O'Keefe started to slip past the sentries, but the two men moved to stop her.

Bayonets gleamed on their muskets, so Mae decided she had better do as they said. Ever since the soldiers had come looking for Dr. Caldwell, it was as if the hospital had been transformed into a prison camp. Guards stood at all the doors and they insisted on inspecting everything that entered or left the hospital.

"Off to market, ma'am?" one of the men asked, nodding at the basket on her arm.

"Sure, what else do you think I'm doing?"

The soldier lifted the lid of the basket and peered inside to make sure it was empty. Mae moved on without another word. Being searched was not just an annoyance, it seemed plain silly. What was she going to do, smuggle the doctor past them in a wicker basket?

She didn't know what the doctor could possibly have done to get in so much trouble. There was the business of the newspaper article, of course, but you couldn't believe what the reporter had written. Mae knew Caldwell was an extraordinarily good doctor and had always shown himself to be an honest man. Why anyone would want to arrest him was beyond her understanding.

She left the cluster of hospital buildings and walked on toward the city. She had a list of a few things to buy, mostly requests from the patients for paper and pencils, newspapers, or some delicacy like fresh apples that they were never likely to get from the hospital kitchen. There were also a few small things the hospital itself needed that Louisa Webster had sent her to get. In the doctor's absence, Louisa was nominally in charge of the hospital. Soon enough, however, the Army would be sending another chief surgeon to take over, an event that Mae dreaded. Nobody was as good as Caldwell. He would be very hard to replace.

Mae enjoyed her shopping trips. It was a good excuse to get out of the hospital for some fresh air and a change of scenery. Besides, what could be more pleasurable than spending other people's money? Not that she wasted it. Mae had a peasant's knack for shrewd bargaining and always brought back more than the men expected to get for their money.

She entered one of the open air markets that was always her first stop. She was inspecting the baskets of apples brought in from the Maryland countryside when a voice at her elbow startled her.

"Keep looking at the apples, Mae. Pretend you don't even hear me."

She couldn't help but give a small sideways glance. A big man stood next to her, inspecting apples as well. It was Flynn. He was wearing a different coat and wore a wide-brimmed hat pulled down tightly on his head.

"Is there really a need to sneak about, Mr. Flynn?" she asked. "You're acting like one of those patriots back home in Ireland, all secret-like."

"You were followed here, Mae."

"What on earth are you talkin' about?"

"Don't go staring at him, but there's a fellow over there who came right down the street after you. The one in the long overcoat."

Mae turned just enough to catch a glimpse of the man. "Mother of God, what have we got ourselves into?"

"They want Major Caldwell," Flynn said. "They're thinking you know where he's hiding."

"What should I do?"

"Go shopping and then go back to the hospital. That's all you can do. And when you get there, tell Miss Webster to come see us. We need money, and Major Caldwell needs some decent clothes." Flynn gave her directions to the house where he and Caldwell were staying. "Tell her to be careful and if anyone's following her then she should go back."

"How will she know if she's being followed?"

"It's easy, once you're looking for it."

"This is a crazy business," Mae said.

169

"Aye," he said. "Sometimes the side you're on doesn't seem like the right side at all."

Flynn drifted away, moving on to inspect a bin of turnips. Mae bought her apples and moved on, intensely aware of the man following her. Flynn was right. It was easy to tell once you knew what to look for. Still, she didn't like it, not one bit. She never had any doubts about protecting Flynn and Caldwell. Mae had seen what the Rebel Fever could do, and knew they were only trying to keep it from spreading. What was the War Department doing by trying to arrest Caldwell? The doctor was working to stop the Black Death, not spread it. It didn't make sense.

She decided Flynn was right about something else. Sometimes, it didn't seem like the Union was on the right side at all.

* * *

Aboard the *Rynda*, Captain Vladimir Khobotov walked the quarter-deck with his hands clasped behind his back and watched with satisfaction as his sailors went through the daily routine of running the ship. Most of the men were bundled in wool coats against the knife-edged winter wind that howled across the Atlantic Ocean. Still, the sailors moved easily about the deck, well-accustomed to coiling ropes and a hundred other small chores. After being at sea for nearly a year, the men could very nearly carry out their duties in their sleep.

Of course, the sailors were looking forward to overwintering in the American port. The next few weeks promised to be wild ones filled with whiskey and women, which was all a sailor craved in port. He had already decided to give the entire crew shore leave that first night in Washington City, rather than stagger the leave as he normally did. The men deserved it.

Khobotov, too, was looking forward to their stay in Washington. Once their transaction with Dr. Verville had been completed, he would have plenty of money in his pocket to enjoy the best the Americans had to offer. Then, too, he would be glad to be rid of the cargo. It had brought them nothing but bad luck and even death, and the sooner it was off his ship, the better.

"We should reach the Potomac River by morning, sir," said the first mate, Sergeyevna, as he joined Khobotov at the rail. "We'll be in Washington by nightfall."

"No," Khobotov said, turning his attention to Sergeyevna. He looked as huge and shaggy as a bear next to the thin young first mate. "We won't be going into port directly. We'll anchor the ship overnight in the river."

"Sir?" Sergeyevna was perplexed.

"Our cargo, Mr. Sergeyevna," Khobotov said. "A boat is due to meet us from shore to unload it."

The first mate did not reply. Khobotov was not sure if the young man was disappointed or else reproachful toward the captain for his smuggling activities. Sergeyevna had never seemed to understand a Russian naval captain's prerogative when it came to lining his own pockets. The first mate believed in strictly following the rules. He took his duties to the Czar very seriously.

"Is there a problem, Lieutenant?" Khobotov's deep voice was almost a growl.

"No, sir. You are the captain, and we shall do as you say." The first mate's words were tinged with sarcasm. Abruptly, Sergeyevna turned on his heel and left Khobotov alone at the rail.

Khobotov struggled to control his anger. He would like nothing better than to get his hands around Sergeyevna's thin neck and ... well, it was foolish really. They were far from Russia and the first mate would obey all orders, even if he didn't agree with them. Still, the first mate would bear watching.

Khobotov sighed and continued to observe his sailors go about their routine, although suddenly all the pleasure had gone out of it. He had not seen them before, but he now noticed two or three men shirking their duties, not working nearly as hard as they should, and some of the other sailors moved with a dogged tiredness. He barked at the laggards to get busy.

In a foul mood now, Khobotov decided it would be good to get rid of this damn smuggler's cargo and make some money, then put in to port. They could all use a rest from the sea.

Chapter 21

Louisa's heart was pounding.

She had never done anything like this, never deliberately broken any rules, and she felt now as if her every thought was written plainly on her forehead to give her away.

If she was caught, there was no telling what might happen. Prison? At the very least she would be dismissed from her nursing post.

The new surgeon stopped her outside the kitchen. He was young, completely inexperienced and exceedingly polite since arriving that morning. "Excuse me, Miss Webster. Is there any more iron persulphate?"

"What? Oh, yes," she stammered. "On the shelves near the nurses' room."

"Thank you," he said. He smiled awkwardly and moved on.

Louisa decided that perhaps her deceitful plans were not written on her face, after all. Either that, or the young surgeon was so overwhelmed by his new responsibilities that he hadn't noticed. He was trying hard not to kill any of the patients on his first day and so far he had succeeded, although he had none of Caldwell's skill.

Louisa ducked into the kitchen, out of sight, and sagged into a chair by one of the massive cooking stoves. Another empty chair stood nearby, where a soldier's newly washed uniform had been hung to dry. She hugged herself and basked in the heat thrown off by the stove, letting it seep into her. The hospital ward had a wintry chill that the coal stoves couldn't shake. Her hands were purple from the cold.

What was she going to do?

She had been a bundle of nerves ever since Mae O'Keefe returned from her trip to the market yesterday with the message that Caldwell wanted to see her. As if that wasn't news enough, Louisa was shocked to learn that Mae had been followed by some sort of spy. In her typical way, Mae had been indignant and defiant at the knowledge that spies were following her. For Louisa, the news had been like the touch of ice, making her shiver. It was clear they were in the middle of something sinister and dangerous – and terribly official. It was this last part that frightened Louisa most of all, because the orders to arrest Caldwell and follow his nurses had clearly come from the highest source – the War Department itself. She shuddered to think what might have happened if Lieutenant Wilkerson hadn't risked everything to warn Caldwell that he was about to be arrested.

In the last few hours, everything had turned inside out. Up was down and night was day. Truth was dangerous. And her beloved Union? It could no longer be trusted or believed in.

However, there was one certainty. Louisa was going to see Caldwell and help him any way she could.

But how? Guards stood at all the doors, and from Mae's experience it was clear that spies lurked outside as well. Louisa was well-known at the hospital and if Mae had been followed, there was no chance of her slipping out the door undetected.

Her gaze settled on the uniform on the chair opposite her. The guards and spies would notice her instantly if she was dressed as a woman. But what if she dressed as a man?

Quickly, Louisa gathered up the uniform and hid it as best she could under her shawl. She had to walk some distance to Caldwell's room, but there was no helping that. She reached the room without being seen by anyone.

Once inside, she closed the door and changed into the blue uniform. She had never worn men's clothes before and it was an odd sensation, pulling on the heavy wool pants. She slipped the suspenders over her shoulders. There was a tiny looking glass that Caldwell used for shaving, and Louisa propped it up and inspected herself in the reflection. Fortunately, the uniform was baggy and disguised her figure. She found a pair of his shoes and put them on. That left her hair, which was drawn up in a tight, businesslike bun atop her head. Still, she looked like a woman dressed in man's clothes.

Louisa found a forage cap hanging from a nail and tried it on. The crown was high enough to conceal her bun. She looked at herself again in the mirror.

The transformation was amazing. Louisa the nurse had disappeared. Staring back at her was a young soldier with the smooth, beardless face of a boy. She could hardly believe her eyes and took a step back in fear. What had she done? This was breaking all the military and social rules Louisa had ever known in her life. She was half tempted to give up, to stop herself before this went too far.

She knew that what she was doing was dangerous. If the guards became suspicious and caught her, she might go to prison. If someone followed her, both she and Caldwell might go to prison. What would her respectable family in Connecticut think of that?

Louisa took a deep breath to calm herself. If she was going to do this, she was going to do it right, consequences be damned. She had to think of how to succeed, not what would happen to her if she was caught.

Quickly, she gathered up some things that Caldwell would need. She found his medical kit and tucked it into a pocket. A doctor always needed his tools. She dug a change of linens and his best uniform out of his trunk, along with his good boots. Whatever was to come, it might help if Caldwell looked the part of a proper Union officer. In the bottom of the trunk, wrapped in an oiled cloth, she also found his revolver. This she also slipped into a pocket, not for Caldwell, who probably couldn't shoot someone if his life depended on it, but for herself. There was also some money in a drawer. Louisa stuffed everything into an old carpetbag she found under Caldwell's bed. On an impulse, she grabbed up his sword, too. It banged awkwardly against her legs.

Here goes, she thought, and headed for the door. She kept her head down so there would be less of a chance of someone recognizing her.

Fortunately, the winter day was already passing into dusk. Orderlies were lighting lanterns in the hospital ward. Outside, the sky had taken on a leaden gray color like old ice. The failing light would be a good thing, considering it would make it harder for the guards to get a good look at her face. After all, she might not look as much like a boy as she thought.

She reached the main door. Two soldiers stood just outside on guard duty, bayonets fixed on their rifles. They stamped their feet on the frozen ground to keep warm.

"Where you goin'?" one of the soldiers demanded as Louisa came out. She sensed that the little bit of authority given to him as a guard had gone straight to his head.

"Back to my regiment." She kept her eyes focused on her brogans.

"Where's that?" the soldier asked dubiously.

"Down in Virginia," she said. "I have to catch the steamer that's leaving tonight. I only had a three-day furlough to come up and see my brother."

Too late, Louisa realized a soldier on leave would have a pass, written orders for him to be absent from his regiment. She didn't have any such thing, and she held her breath, waiting for the guard's next question.

"What's in the carpetbag?" he asked.

"Just my brother's things," she said, relieved he hadn't asked for a pass. "He died this afternoon."

"We best have a look in that carpetbag."

"C'mon Ned," the other soldier interrupted. "His brother just died. We're looking for that doctor and Confederate spies. This fellow don't hardly look like neither."

"I said I'll have a look in that bag," the soldier insisted.

"Go ahead," Louisa said. She opened it up and set it on the ground, hanging on to the sword. The other guard shook his head at his partner's zealousness as he poked around inside the carpetbag.

"Your brother was an officer?" the guard asked, noticing the double row of brass buttons, braid and shoulder straps on the uniform in the bag.

"That's right."

"I don't see no blood," he said. "This uniform looks awful clean for one that belonged to a wounded man."

"He wasn't wounded," Louisa said. Her heart was beginning to pound again. She hadn't expected so many questions, so much suspicion. How to satisfy this man? "He died of fever."

"Fever?" The guard was still rooting around in Caldwell's things.

"You know, the one everyone is so worried about. Rebel Fever."

The guard jumped back from the bag as if he had found a snake in there. "Your brother died of Rebel Fever? Shouldn't his things be burned?"

"Well, he wasn't wearing this uniform," Louisa said. "This was his extra one."

Both guards had moved a few feet away. "Go on," the suspicious one said. "Don't want to be late for your steamer, do you?"

Louisa closed up the carpetbag and moved on. The bag was heavy, bumping against her legs, and she wondered if it had been wise to bring it. She would never be able to outrun anyone following her if she was carrying that.

She fought the urge to look behind her as she left the hospital grounds and headed into the city, struggling to carry the heavy carpetbag. Once she did reach the city streets, she put down the bag and looked abruptly behind her into the gathering dark.

Was anyone following her? Several people were behind her on the sidewalk, but no one stopped at the same time she did. Of course they wouldn't, she reminded herself. That would be too obvious. She eyed several men walking along, but they didn't so much as glance at her. That in itself was unusual because a young woman alone on the street always attracted men's attention. Then she realized that to them, she probably appeared to be just another soldier. There were only a few women out, and Louisa didn't think any of them were War Department spies. After all, she had seen no women lurking outside the hospital.

Her heart still fluttering in her chest, Louisa hoisted the bag once more and started down the street.

* * *

Mae watched from a safe distance as Colonel Baker strode through the hospital, looking even more irate than usual. He had been there since five o'clock, and he appeared to grow angrier with each passing minute.

"Where is she?" he demanded.

"Who?" asked the new doctor, who was following in Baker's wake, looking anxiously at his patients. It had become clear to him that the previous surgeon – Caldwell – might be a traitor whom Baker couldn't wait to throw in prison, but there was no question that he had been an uncommonly good doctor. He was quickly finding that running a hospital was no easy task.

"Who?" Baker spun on his heels and glared at the doctor. "Haven't you noticed that your head nurse is missing?"

"In point of fact, Colonel, I had not."

"When was the last time you saw her?"

"About three o'clock, I'd say, when I asked her where to find the iron persulphate."

"And you haven't seen her since?"

"No."

Baker was at a loss. Nurse Webster was not asleep in her room, or anywhere else in the hospital or on the grounds, for that matter. However, no one had seen her leave. In disgust, he stomped away from the doctor and went to find the old Irishwoman. He had seen her kind before in the Irish noncommissioned officers in some of the regiments. Nothing got past them, and they always knew more than they let on.

He found Mae carrying a tray of beef tea between the rows of iron cots. She walked carefully, balancing the steaming tin mugs on the tray, trying not to meet his eyes.

"You there," he said, blocking her path. "We're looking for Nurse Webster."

"Did you look in her room, Colonel sir?" Mae said, laying her Irish brogue on as thick as possible. She had found in America that it was better sometimes not to appear too smart when confronted by people like Colonel Baker. Better to have them think you were nothing but a poor, dumb Mick. "Och, the poor creature was all done in. With the doctor gone, there's been twice as much work to do. Dr. Caldwell will be missed around here."

"You have a new doctor now," Baker said harshly, "so get used to him. Now, where's Nurse Webster gone to?"

"If she's not in her room, then I don't know."

From the look on his face, Baker obviously didn't believe her. He continued to stand in the aisle, blocking her path as she held the tray of beef tea.

"I'll ask you again," he said. "Where is she?"

"Sure and I don't know, Colonel sir–"

In a rage, Baker's hand swung out and knocked the tray from Mae's grasp. The tin cups hit the floor with a tremendous clatter, the hot liquid splashing everywhere. Mae moaned and wiped at her face with a rag where some of the spilled broth had scalded her.

"Goddamn you, woman, I won't have your lies–"

"Shut up, you son of a bitch!" someone shouted from the back of the ward. "Leave her alone!"

A low grumbling filled the ward, and several of the less severely wounded men lurched to their feet. They were a piteous sight, a rabble, but they served to make him forget all about Mae.

"I'll have you all arrested!" he shouted. "You're traitors! Every last one of you!"

"Who are you calling traitors?" a wounded man shouted.

"How do you think we ended up in this place?" another called. "Fighting for the Union, that's how! Not terrorizing women!"

There was an angry swell of voices.

Baker, like the hospital patients themselves, knew his threats to arrest them were hollow. He just imagined what Stanton would say if he told the secretary of war he was having all the patients in Armory Square Hospital imprisoned.

Fuming, Baker stormed outside. On the steps were the two guards who had been on duty all afternoon and evening. They had already told him they had not seen Nurse Webster leave the hospital, or any other woman, for that matter.

"You two can't even do something as simple as guard a doorway," the colonel said to the two men who stamped from foot to foot, trying to stay warm. His pride was still smarting after the encounter in the hospital. "It's a disgrace."

"We already told you, sir, we didn't see no woman," one of the guards said. "And all afternoon there was only a few visitors, on account of no one wants to come here because it's where the Rebel Fever started."

"There is no Rebel Fever here," Baker said.

"Well, sir, a soldier who left here this afternoon said his brother had just died of it."

"That's impossible," Baker said. "There haven't been any new cases, if there were even any to start with."

"That's what the soldier said, sir."

"Who was this soldier?" Baker was suddenly curious.

"Just a boy," the guard said. "Not so much as a whisker on his face. He was carrying a carpetbag full of his brother's things. An officer's uniform, some money, a medical kit."

Baker stood absolutely still. "What time was this?"

"About four o'clock, sir. Why? Was it important, sir?"

"You jackasses," Baker said. "That was no boy you stopped. That was Nurse Webster, the woman we're looking for."

Of course! That explained how she had left the hospital without anyone noticing. None of his own plainclothes detectives surrounding the hospital had noticed, either. The sight of a young soldier was too common to warrant a second look. There was no telling where Louisa Webster was by now. It was likely she had gone to bring the uniform and money to Caldwell. Was he still in the city? And if so, how long did he think he could hide out?

He smiled. Louisa Webster would tell him. She would tell him everything. She might have gotten out of the hospital unseen, but she wasn't getting back in.

"Spread the word," he said to the guards. "If that 'soldier' comes back, I want her arrested. Do you think you can manage that?"

"Yes, sir."

"Good."

Baker walked away toward his waiting horse. It was only a matter of time before he caught the nurse, and then Caldwell would be next. The doctor was going to be locked away in Old Capitol Prison for a long time. And who knew? Because he was an officer, with any luck Caldwell could be charged with treason, and then a firing squad would settle the matter once and for all.

That's what became of traitors to the Union.

* * *

When the carriage arrived, Louisa stood for a moment staring at the house. It was three stories tall, ramshackle, and she could hear faint laughter and piano music coming from within. Not at all where she would have expected to find Caldwell. She took a quick look up and down the street, but didn't see anything or anyone suspicious. As far as she could tell, she had not been followed.

"Have a good time, young man," the driver said with a chuckle as he passed down the carpetbag. Louisa paid him and the carriage drove off.

Louisa wasn't sure what the carriage driver had meant. She hauled the heavy carpetbag up to the front door and knocked. A tall, well-dressed black man answered. His eyes narrowed as he looked Louisa up and down.

"You got the money to pay, soldier, an' I'll let you in," he said harshly. "Otherwise, you wastin' yo' time."

"I have money," Louisa replied. Somewhere between the door opening and the doorman's harsh greeting she had realized what sort of place this was.

"Then come on in," the man said, opening the door wider. The expression on his face was still doubtful.

She followed him into the parlor. The furnishings were intended to be elegant; however, everything had a faded, secondhand appearance, as if it had come from the estate sale of a dowager aunt. The tall windows were swathed in red velvet curtains, an expensive carpet covered the floor, and there were several upholstered couches and chairs around the spacious room. Girls sat watching them come in, and the gas light gave their white faces, rouged cheeks and red lips a ghoulish quality. Someone in the next room was playing a piano – badly – and a pair of drunken male voices sang along.

Louisa set her carpetbag down with a thump, not sure of what to do next. Had she really come to the right place?

"Louisa!"

She looked up to see Caldwell striding through the door. He threw his arms out and embraced her.

"I'm so glad you've come," he said, then whispered, "You weren't followed, were you?"

"No," she said. "At least, I don't think so."

"Good. Let's go upstairs."

Caldwell grabbed up the carpetbag and started upstairs. Louisa noticed that none of the girls in the room reacted to what appeared to be a young soldier being addressed as "Louisa" and hugged. But then, she reminded herself, this was a whorehouse. She had come a long, long way from her family's respectable home in Connecticut.

Caldwell led her down one dim hallway after another to a small, cramped room. He shut the door behind them.

"Where's Flynn?" she asked.

"He had a prizefight tonight," Caldwell said. "I didn't want him to fight, but he wouldn't listen. I might go there later to patch him up."

"A prizefight?" Louisa found the idea repugnant. "That's horrible."

"Flynn seems to think it will lead him to Verville. I'm beginning to think he may be right. Our Mr. Flynn is not everything he appears to be."

Louisa looked around the shabby room. Through the walls she could hear the rhythmic squeaking of a bed. She blushed. "How in the world did you end up in this place?"

"That's Flynn's doing as well. As I said, he's resourceful."

"My God, I can't believe I'm actually in a whorehouse."

Caldwell smiled. "You're also dressed as a soldier."

"I needed to do that to get past the guards and make sure I wasn't followed."

"Things are that bad at the hospital? How are the patients?"

"They're fine. There's a new doctor, although he doesn't know much. Hopefully, he won't kill too many of the patients."

"Not as long as you're there to help him, he won't."

"Well, that's just it," she said. "I don't know if I can go back now. Once someone realizes I'm missing, I won't be able to suddenly reappear."

"You think they'll notice?"

Louisa looked hurt. "How long does it usually take before someone notices the head nurse is gone?"

"You're right," he said. "Not long."

"Oh, what are we going to do, William?" Louisa felt the courage that had helped her slip out of the hospital begin to fade. When she thought about their position, all the dangers they faced, the situation seemed hopeless. They were trying to stop an epidemic and yet the whole force of the government seemed arrayed against them. Tears stung her eyes, but she refused to cry. "There are spies and soldiers looking for us all over the city, and if they catch us we'll be going to prison."

Caldwell leaned across and kissed her. "Thank you for coming," he said. "It was very brave."

"Oh." The room seemed to be spinning around Louisa.

"Do you think it was too forward of me, to kiss you like that?"

To Louisa, everything became clear. Any doubts about why she had taken such risks to find him vanished. "Not at all," she said.

He leaned close. "What if I were to kiss you again?"

In answer, she closed her eyes. She felt his lips against her own, hungry, longing.

"My God," she whispered.

Tangled in each other's arms, those were the last words either of them spoke.

* * *

180

"He's dead," Sally said.

"You're sure of it?" Verville asked.

"Yes. He was shot and killed yesterday during an escape attempt."

"Good," he said, noticing that she appeared not to have any regrets about the fate of Charles Wilson, despite the fact that the man had shared tea with them in this very house. "Excellent."

They were in Sally's parlor. The cold winter dusk outside had quickly changed to night. The heavy curtains were pulled shut to keep out drafts and the coal stove was throwing off a great deal of heat. A single candle provided the only light.

He had carried a huge washtub into the parlor for her and Sally had heated water on the cookstove in the kitchen to fill it. She was now luxuriating in the warm, soapy water, smoothing over her arms and legs with a washcloth. From time to time, Sally sipped from a wineglass on a nearby table. She had taken to adding a few drops of Verville's laudanum to the wine, and the combination of alcohol and opium made her very relaxed.

Verville sat in a chair beside the stove, transfixed by the sight of her. This was exactly as he had feared, he thought. Her power over him was beginning to take hold.

He wasn't overly concerned. After all, the Russian ship was due tomorrow at midnight. Once it arrived, he and Sally would be very busy.

"I'm saving a whole crate of clothes and bedding for the secondhand shops here in the city," he said, trying to get his mind off her naked body in the washtub just a few feet away. "You'll have to distribute most of them yourself because I'll be on the train to Philadelphia and New York with the other crates. Just make sure you don't touch any of the clothing. Let the shopkeepers handle it."

"We've gone over this several times," Sally said. "I understand the plan by now."

"All right," he snapped. "But there's no room for error. Tell me again what you're going to do."

Sally sighed. "I'll sell some of the clothing to as many different shops as I can, but not all of it to one shop. The idea is to spread the plague-ridden clothes around the city."

"And the valise of shirts?"

"That goes directly to the White House as a present for President Lincoln."

"Good," he said. "Very good."

He was nervous about leaving such an important part of their plan to Sally, but he didn't have much choice. He couldn't do it all himself. He would be in those other Northern cities doing the very same thing. The plague would spread like wildfire.

"I must be careful that I'm not followed," she went on, reciting the plan Verville had drilled into her. "If I am, I'm simply to abandon the clothing in the Murder Bay neighborhood, where all the whores and drunks will snatch it up."

"But only if you're followed," he said.

"That's the part I'm worried about," Sally acknowledged, working the washcloth along the underside of one arm. She paused to take a sip from her wineglass. "You know, the house is watched sometimes."

Verville felt himself suddenly grow cold all over, despite the fact that he was sitting beside the coal stove. "You never told me that," he said.

"Well, they've been watching this house almost since the war started," Sally said. "I never made any secret of my sympathies, and so they've been watching me. I thought you knew."

"I didn't." Verville felt like a fool. It was true he had never asked, and he had never noticed anyone watching the house. He struggled to keep his voice under control. "You should have told me."

"It's not that important, is it? If they really thought I was a spy, like poor Rose Greenhow, or that you were, they would have arrested us a long time ago."

It had been a mystery to him that Lafayette Baker's men had known to follow him. He wasn't a known agent to the Union Secret Service. However, if Sally's house had been watched this whole time, it made sense. He was lucky that their attention had turned to Caldwell thanks to *The Sunday Chronicle* article.

"Is there anything else you haven't told me?" he asked. "Was there anyone besides you and Wilson who knew about the plan? Did you tell anyone?"

"No one who wasn't on our side."

"What's that supposed to mean?"

"Only that I might have mentioned you to Thomas Conrad. But that's all right. He's on our side."

"You told Conrad I was in the city?" Conrad might have been a Confederate agent, but he hardly shared the same goals as Verville. The famously cautious Conrad had made it clear he would have nothing to do with Verville's plan to spread the plague through Washington City because he found it immoral. Maybe Conrad was the one who had tipped Baker's men to him being in the city.

"He wanted to know where to find you and if you needed any help, so I told him you were staying at the Metropolitan Hotel. I wasn't about to tell him you could be found here most nights. I also told him you were at the waterfront."

"You told him about the MacCrae brothers, too?" Verville couldn't believe she would be so stupid.

"I thought he might be able to help," she said.

Verville slumped in his chair. This was all beginning to make more sense now. It was Caldwell and the big man he was with who had nearly caught him at the Metropolitan Hotel. Had Conrad given him away, thanks to Sally? He might have done just that if the big man was, as Verville had suspected, also a Confederate agent.

"Are you angry with me?" she said. Her words had a dreamy quality and he knew she had been drinking a great deal of the blended wine and opium. He realized she never would have dared to tell him so much if she hadn't been inebriated.

"No, my dear," he lied. "How could I be angry with you? Here, let me scrub your back."

"Oh, that's a wonderful idea."

He took her gentlyby the shoulders. "Lie back," he said. "Just relax."

Sally closed her eyes and sighed. Verville looked down at her and smiled. "Oh, Sally, you very nearly ruined us. You are one very stupid woman."

He shoved down, hard, forcing her head and shoulders under the water. Her hands closed around his wrists, the nails digging into his flesh, trying to free herself, but he held her pinned under the surface with an iron grip. Her legs thrashed, trying to find a purchase, but the slippery tub didn't offer any.

After a minute, her struggling limbs moved less urgently. Bubbles began to float up as her lungs released air. Soon, even those stopped, and the water in the tub was absolutely still.

"Stupid woman," he repeated, finally taking his hands off her shoulders. He dried them on her towel. "It looks like I'll have to do all this by myself. It's better that way, anyhow."

He left the candle burning and slipped out of the house unseen, leaving by the back door where the alley was shrouded in darkness. If the house was still being watched, he didn't want anyone to see him leave. He had taken a room at one of the cheaper hotels, and he managed to reach it without being followed. He would spend the night there and most of the day tomorrow, and then it would be time to meet the Russian ship.

Chapter 22

It was time to fight.

Flynn stood in the center of a rough circle in the cavernous back room of the tavern. Surrounding him was a crowd of men eager to see the fight, greedy eyes glinting at him, all studying Flynn, sizing him up.

The crowd was a blur.

So many eyes stared at him that Flynn couldn't pick out any individual face. They were wondering if he could beat the Kraut. Nobody else had, and there was no sense wasting a bet. No one spoke to him. He might as well have been alone. It had always been like this before a fight, back in the old days.

This time, however, he had so much more riding on the outcome. If he won, the MacCraes would keep him in their employ long enough to lead him to Verville. Losing meant being tossed out on the street, most likely after James MacCrae got in a few punches of his own on Flynn's already battered hide. There would be no tending bar like old Harry, who had been with the MacCraes for many long years.

No, it would be the street for him, turned out of the room at Miss Paula's just when he and Caldwell needed it most, considering the entire United States Secret Service was probably looking for them by now.

Flynn had been in enough prizefights in his time to know just how brutal they were, and to know that winning meant everything. It was a cruel business.

He felt hands on his shoulders, squeezing him. Flynn turned to look into MacCrae's face. His eyes were red with whiskey and excitement.

"You ready to fight, lad?" MacCrae asked.

"Aye," Flynn said.

"There's a lot of money riding on this fight," MacCrae said. "Beat the Kraut, lad. That's all I got to say to you."

Flynn nodded, looking away from MacCrae's piggish face. He reminded himself MacCrae wasn't the reason he was fighting, and neither was the money. For all he knew, the whole outcome of the war might depend on who won tonight's fight.

His thoughts were interrupted by an ear-splitting cheer. All heads were turned toward the doorway. The Kraut had arrived.

Flynn tried to get a look at him, but the crowd was too thick. Somehow, hundreds of men had packed themselves into the room. There was a stirring as the Kraut came toward the ring, with the crowd moving and swaying the way tall grass does when some animal pushes its way through.

Flynn was still straining to get a look when the ring of men parted and the Kraut stepped into the clearing.

"Jesus," he muttered.

The German was big, not only tall, but broad, and heavy through the shoulders. Flynn had expected a large and bulky man, fat from sauerkraut and sausages, but there was not a bit of fat on the German. His muscles were as hard and defined as if they had been chiseled from stone. He had close-cropped yellow hair, bright blue eyes and a square jaw. His face was expressionless as he watched Flynn from the other side of the small ring.

Some of Flynn's doubt must have shown in his face, because, with a shout, bets were suddenly changed and handfuls of money were waved overhead. Even if he had been deaf, he would have known the bets weren't being placed on him.

"Ten dollars on the Kraut!" someone shouted, nearly in Flynn's ear. "He's going to kill the Irishman!"

"I'd have to agree with that," he said under his breath.

This was more than he had bargained for or expected. Most of the prizefighters Flynn had known were tough men, but this fellow looked like Apollo. Someone might be able to beat the German, but Flynn doubted he would be the one to do it.

"Ha!" MacCrae was shouting in his ear. "He's a big bastard, ain't he? Just remember that the bigger they are, the harder they fall. Ha, ha!"

"Start the goddamn fight," Flynn said. "Let's get this over with."

"That's the spirit, man."

Quickly, in the moments before the fight began, Flynn tried to settle on a strategy. With some fighters, it was better to lead them on and tire them out, keep dancing around them while they wore themselves down throwing punches and chasing you around the ring. The Kraut didn't look to be the kind of fighter who tired quickly.

With other fighters, a good strategy was to charge right in swinging, because you were never going to wear them down. You wanted to knock them out as fast as possible.

Which method would work best with this big fellow? Flynn decided he would need some time to find out, provided he lasted that long.

MacCrae climbed a chair so that he could be seen above the crowd. The clamor in the room died away to a murmur as everyone's attention turned to the ring. Some men at the back of the room were standing on crates or even taking turns sitting on each other's shoulders for a better glimpse of the ring. The ring itself had no boundaries or ropes, it was just an empty space in the big room, maybe twenty feet across and roughly circular. MacCrae had put some of his men in charge of making sure the crowd didn't press too tightly, and they worked the edges of the ring, pushing the crowd back. Billy, the urchin of a boy who hung around the tavern, ran out and drew a chalk line in the center of the ring. He gave Flynn a quick smile and darted away again.

Flynn and the German approached the line. The Kraut kept those hard blue eyes on him, boring into Flynn's own. Both men put their right foot forward, just touching the line, and faced each other in a crouch. The German was still staring at him.

"Eyes don't win a fight, lad," Flynn said. "Fists do."

In reply, the Kraut muttered something in his guttural language. Flynn wondered if his opponent could speak a word of English, and for some reason this made him more uneasy than anything else about the German. It made him all the more inhuman.

"Fight!" MacCrae's voice boomed like a gunshot, and the crowd roared around the two prizefighters.

Flynn kept his fists up, waiting for his opponent to make the first move. The two men danced back and forth, taking each other's measure. Despite his size, there was nothing slow about the German, and he looked to be a few years younger than Flynn, none of which was encouraging. The two men were so close that Flynn could smell the light sweat on the other man, a vague stink of cabbage and onion, and he studied the face for some sign of weakness. He noticed the corners of the German's eyes had none of the telltale scars that marked an experienced fighter. Even his nose was perfectly straight.

The Kraut won because he was bigger and stronger, Flynn told himself, not because he was a better fighter.

Flynn threw a jab at that perfect nose. The Kraut parried, struck Flynn in the belly with a left hook that lifted him clear off his feet.

Flynn crashed to the floor.

A wild cheer went up. The German grinned at the crowd, the first time he had shown any emotion. Flynn lay there gasping for breath, feeling as if he had just caught a cannonball in his belly. So much for his theory that the Kraut didn't know how to fight.

Flynn climbed to his feet and put his hands up. "Come on, you big ox," he said. "You didn't beat me yet."

With a grunt, the German lowered his head and came at him. It was like a bull charging, or a bear. There was nowhere for Flynn to go, so he bunched himself up, putting his elbows down low to cover his belly and his fists over his face, turning his shoulder into the rain of fists. Each blow felt like a sledgehammer. He staggered into the wall of men that formed the perimeter of the ring and felt several blows delivered by the spectators thump against his back and kidneys before he was shoved violently back toward the Kraut's punishing fists. Flynn's guard slipped just a fraction and the German delivered a hammer blow to his jaw that knocked him to his knees.

The crowd was booing. Flynn tasted the coppery tang of blood in his mouth and spat. Above all the noise, he could hear MacCrae bellowing, "Fight him, you Mick bastard, fight him!"

Flynn struggled to his feet. The German was on him at once, coming in close again, pummeling Flynn's torso and sliding punches past his raised fists to pound his face. A square blow struck Flynn's chin and the room reeled. He fell to his knees again.

The men watching the fight cursed him in disgust.

"Hell, this is going to be over before it even got started."

"Good thing I put my money on the Kraut!"

Flynn got to his feet again. He didn't want to think about how many times the German had hit him. His mouth was bleeding freely and his ears rang from the crowd and the head blows he had taken.

"Try it again, lad," he said, raising his fists.

The German didn't understand his words, but there was no mistaking Flynn's posture. He waded toward Flynn as before, pressing in close, punching, punching.

Flynn could see that perfect, unbroken nose behind the wall of fists. He let the German come in close, too close, those fists pounding him, then grabbed the man in a bear hug, pinning his arms to his side.

Flynn slammed his forehead into the German's nose.

At once, he released the Kraut and shoved him away. Then Flynn punched him again and again in the nose, short, powerful blows that smashed the man's broken nose even flatter. Blood poured down his face in a sheet.

Flynn hit him in the chin with a right, then a left jab. The German staggered backwards, stopped by the wall of men at the edge of the ring, and hung his head like a very large, angry bull that's about to make a charge. Blood dripped onto his chest. He launched himself at Flynn with a howl of rage.

Flynn planted his feet and swung with a killing blow that landed square

187

on the German's chin. The big man sat down suddenly and shook his head to clear it. In spite of himself, Flynn was impressed. He thought he had hit the German hard enough to knock out an ox. The Kraut struggled back to his feet.

After that, the German wasn't eager to wade right in. He circled Flynn cautiously, feinting, throwing an occasional punch that Flynn easily blocked.

The mood of the crowd had changed considerably. Where minutes before they had been ready to give up on Flynn in disgust, they now cheered him. A new round of wagering had begun, now that it looked as if the Kraut wasn't such a sure winner.

Still, the fight wasn't over. Hurt or not, the Kraut was still a formidable opponent. And Flynn was in pain, too, from the punishment he had taken earlier. It had been a long time since he had been in a prizefight, he realized, and he wasn't as young as he used to be.

The Kraut came at him again with the same rage as before. Flynn tried to beat him back and hold his ground, but the Kraut charged in and hit him with a left hook that took Flynn's breath away. Another punch found his jaw and Flynn staggered. Once again, he was trying to protect his face and body as the Kraut's fists rained down with telling effect.

There was nowhere to escape. Flynn felt himself pressed up against the ring again and the men there tried to push him back. He fell awkwardly toward the Kraut and the two men grappled with each other. The German was so strong Flynn felt himself being pushed back, his feet unable to get any traction on the worn floorboards.

When all else fails, Flynn thought, fight dirty. He leaned into the German close enough to whisper into his ear, "My turn now, Herr Kraut." Then Flynn sank his teeth into the German's earlobe.

As the man winced, Flynn reached up and ground the broken nose under the heel of his palm. The pain was enough to make the big German drop his guard, and Flynn hit him so hard the German staggered.

He pressed the attack, throwing punch after punch, the German trying to dodge out of the way but Flynn's fists either cracked against bone or thunked against flesh every time. The Kraut swung back in defense, catching Flynn a glancing blow along his cheekbone, but the punch threw the other man off balance. Flynn saw his opening and swung again, putting the whole power of his heavy shoulders into the blow. He struck the Kraut with all the force of a swinging ax, lifting him so high off the ground that only his toes touched, and he went over backwards.

The crowd went wild, screaming drunkenly with blood lust as the Kraut hit the floorboards. But he wasn't finished. Somehow, he managed to get on his hands and knees, then half stand, half crouch as he got to his feet.

Flynn was waiting for him. As the German turned a face toward him that held all the savagery of some beast gone mad, snarling like a rabid dog, Flynn struck. The fist cracked against the Kraut's jaw and the angry light in his eyes winked out. He slumped to the warehouse floor, knocked out cold.

The cheer that followed nearly lifted the roof off.

All at once, the crowd surged around Flynn and obliterated the ring where the two men had fought. A group of rowdies tried to lift him to their shoulders, but half dropped him when they realized what a ponderous weight he was. He was sweating profusely and bleeding freely from a deep cut above one eye. Somewhere in all the swirling men he caught a glimpse of MacCrae's laughing face. Then another face stood out, a dour and disapproving one, alone in a sea of grins and laughter.

"My God," Caldwell said, shoving his way to Flynn's side. He looked horrified. "What have you done to yourself?"

"I did win the fight, you know," Flynn said. "Aren't you supposed to congratulate me?"

"I saw the fight," Caldwell said. "You're damn lucky to be alive, if you ask me. That other fellow might have killed you."

Flynn noticed a smallish young soldier who seemed to be staying close to Caldwell's side. The soldier had boyish good looks, a face that was almost pretty. Flynn stared. There was something very familiar about the soldier.

"Louisa?"

"Not so loud," Caldwell warned. "Yes, it's who you think it is. Now, let's find someplace where I can patch you up and I'll explain everything."

There was a smaller room off the main warehouse where Flynn had fought the German – who, Flynn noticed with satisfaction, had yet to stir as the crowd stepped around and over him. Flynn felt a twinge at the thought that it could just as easily have been him out cold on the floor. They managed to work their way through the crowd and entered the room where Flynn had stashed his coat and shirt in preparation for the fight. There was a lantern on the table, its dirty globe providing only a feeble glow, but Caldwell adjusted the wick until it gave a reasonable amount of light.

"Let's fix you up," Caldwell said. "You might have won that fight, but your friend there still managed to beat the hell out of you."

Flynn snorted, and noted that Caldwell must be right, because even that small bit of movement hurt. "He's no friend of mine."

"Louisa – Louis, I mean – would you please hold this lantern close to his face here so I can see what I'm doing?"

Louisa hurried to do as Caldwell requested, and with a quick glance at the doorway to make sure they were truly alone in the room, Flynn said, "Sure, and you're a pretty lad, Louis. You look a great deal like a nurse I used to know at Armory Square Hospital."

"I don't think you'd find that nurse there tonight," Louisa answered with a mischievous grin. "I understand she had to dress up like a soldier in order to get out of that hospital, considering there were guards at all the doors waiting for Dr. Caldwell – or you – to reappear."

"That bad, is it?"

"Yes. It seems the good doctor upset some very powerful people by claiming in that newspaper article that this outbreak of bubonic plague in the Irish neighborhood was the result of a Confederate plot."

"Very interesting." Flynn jerked his head away as Caldwell probed the deep cut above his eyes. "Jesus! You're hurting me worse than the bastard who gave it to me."

"It's a deep cut, Flynn. It's not going to close up on its own anytime soon and you'll have one hell of a scar. You'd better hold still while I sew it up."

"All right, then, but make the stitches small. I've got to stay handsome for the ladies."

"It's going to take more than a few stitches to do that," Caldwell said, then set about preparing to stitch up Flynn's face. From the small surgeon's kit Louisa had smuggled out of the hospital, he selected a small needle, every bit like a sewing needle except that it was curved and silver-plated so that blood wouldn't corrode it. Then he unwound a length of silk thread from a tiny spool and threaded it through the needle's eye.

"Damn," he muttered, straining to see in the dim lantern light. "My eyes aren't what they used to be."

"Let me try," Louisa said, and, taking the needle from Caldwell, she deftly threaded it and handed it back.

"Now, hold still," Caldwell said, and he began to work, pushing the needle through the flesh and pulling the silk thread through.

Flynn winced. "Damnit, man! That hurts."

"It's your own fault for getting hit so much."

"Normally, Doctor, I'd tell you to go to hell, but I won't do that seeing as to how you're occupied sticking a needle in my flesh."

"Well, Flynn, I reckon that proves you're not a complete idiot." Caldwell continued to sew, with Louisa holding the lantern close so that he could see what he was doing. He was just pulling the last stitch taut when MacCrae walked in.

Chapter 23

James MacCrae was grinning from ear to ear and his cheeks had an alcoholic glow. Several other men tumbled into the room behind him, all of them hooting and cheering Flynn, waving bottles of whiskey. Angus MacCrae drifted in, too, and hung back quietly in the shadows, watching everything with his quick, feral eyes. He and Flynn nodded at each other.

"By God, lad, you showed that German!" James MacCrae roared, and he might have slapped Flynn on the back if the Caldwell hadn't been busy putting the last stitch in the cut above Flynn's eye.

MacCrae recognized the doctor and nodded at him, then narrowed his eyes and gave Louisa a curious look before turning his attention back to Flynn. He was too excited to pay much notice to a young soldier helping the doctor. "That was one hell of a fight. By God, it was! Still, I thought it was a close thing there a few times."

"Aye, that it was," Flynn said, allowing the shadow of a grin to play over his lips. "It was a close thing, indeed. I'm glad in the end it's him on the floor out there and not me. He's a strong fighter, that's for sure."

"Well, you showed him," MacCrae said with a laugh. "The bigger they are, the harder they fall."

"I'm just thankful the big bastard didn't know the first thing about fighting dirty," Flynn said, laying his Irish accent on thick for MacCrae's benefit. "Once I bit his ear, that was the end of him."

"I knew you could fight," MacCrae said, filling the room with one of his belly laughs. "I knew it the minute you walked in here." He approached the table where Caldwell had spread his medical kit and tossed a thick roll of paper bills there.

"I reckon that's my share of the winnings tonight," Flynn said, glancing at the money. "What sort of percentage are you giving me?"

MacCrae laughed again, but when he spoke his voice had an edge to it. "There are no percentages for you, lad. You win fights, and I give you money. You'll get what I see fit to give you. It's the same for any prizefighter. You ought to know that, because you've done it before."

Flynn shrugged. "Aye," he said, sounding bitter. The truth was, of course, that the money meant nothing to him. He hadn't signed on as a fighter to win money, but to get closer to Verville. Reminding himself of that now, he pressed the point home with MacCrae.

"The money is nice, Mr. MacCrae, but I'd like something a little steadier to keep me going between fights," Flynn said.

"Ah," MacCrae said. He cast a quick, cautious glance at the doctor and the young soldier helping him, but both appeared to be absorbed in their work of dabbing at the cuts and scraps on the Irishman's face and upper body. Then he looked at Flynn shrewdly. "Have you got mouths to feed at home, Mullins, a wife and children I don't know about?"

"No, Mr. MacCrae," Flynn said. "Just myself. But I want something to keep me going between fights."

"Fine, then, come by tomorrow about midnight," MacCrae said with a wink. "We'll have a bit of work to do then, if you're up to it."

"I'll be here," Flynn said, knowing that what MacCrae was offering was no less than an opportunity to take part in a smuggling operation. With any luck, it might be the one that would lead him to Verville.

"Fine, lad, I'll see you then," MacCrae said, and he started for the door. He nodded to the doctor. "Fix him up good now."

Caldwell grunted in reply as he finished cleaning Flynn's wounds. MacCrae, followed by his silent brother, quickly left the room to join the high-spirited and drunken crowd outside that was celebrating Flynn's victory. The few men who had come in with the MacCraes also left, leaving only Flynn, Caldwell, Louisa and the MacCraes' errand boy, Billy, in the room. The lad was eyeing some cheese and dry sausage Flynn had bought earlier in the day to eat after the fight, knowing it would be too late later on to find any place selling food, and he wasn't eager to sample the fare at the tavern or back at Miss Paula's. He saw the boy's hungry eyes. "Eat up, lad," he said. "You need this more than I do."

Gratefully, the boy retreated to a corner and set about gnawing at the meat and cheese. Flynn noticed for the first time that the boy was rail thin, and wondered if the MacCraes ever bothered to feed him.

Caldwell was busy washing and wrapping Flynn's skinned knuckles with a strip of linen. "I don't like this," he said. "First getting involved in a prizefight, then promising to help these thugs with a smuggling operation. I don't see how it will ever help us find Verville."

"We'll find him, all right," Flynn said, although, as the aches from the fight began to settle into his bones, he, too, was beginning to wonder if they were any closer to catching him.

The boy spoke up. "Verville? Are you talking about that doctor fellow from down South?"

"Aye," Flynn said, lifting one eyebrow as he looked at the boy. "What do you know of him?"

"Well, if you're looking for him, I know where he is."

"And how is that, lad?"

"Why, I done followed him after he come to see Mr. MacCrae."

The boy now had the complete attention of the three adults in the room, a fact that was not lost on him. The food suddenly forgotten, he listened intently as Flynn asked, "Where was he staying, lad?"

"I'll tell you for ten dollars," the boy blurted out.

Flynn smiled. The boy had spunk. But what boy wouldn't who managed to survive around the likes of the MacCraes? "I have a whole pile of money here, lad, and all you want is ten dollars?"

"If I asked for more, you might get mad and whip it out of me, and not give me any money," the boy said. "Ten dollars seems fair."

"Ah, you're a smart lad," Flynn said. Pulling himself away from Caldwell's hands, he dug into the depths of his trouser pocket and produced the twenty-dollar gold coin he had won from James MacCrae the day of his initial bout with the tavern's barkeeper, Harry. He tossed it to Billy, who snatched it from the air with the lightning-fast reflexes of a boy used to picking pockets and dodging the drunken blows of James MacCrae. "There's twenty dollars, in gold no less, not this paper money. Now, where can we find this fellow Verville?"

"At the National Hotel," the boy said, still staring in wonder at the gold coin in his palm. "I followed him there myself."

Having provided the information, the boy scampered out of the room with the gold coin clutched in one fist and a bit of cheese in the other. Flynn smiled from between his bruised lips. "You see, all you have to do is ask."

"What are we waiting for?" Louisa asked. "Let's go get him."

Flynn groaned. "Give me a minute there, Louis. In case you haven't noticed, I just got the hell beat out of me."

Louisa reddened at Flynn's language.

"Pardon me, Louis," he said. "I didn't think an old soldier like you would be so delicate."

"It doesn't matter," she said. "I've heard far worse here tonight and at Miss Paula's, believe me."

"I agree with Louis here," Caldwell said. "We don't want to waste any time. For all we know, he might be moving from hotel to hotel every day. We should go get him right now."

"Get who?" asked a voice from the doorway. They looked up in surprise to find C.J. Wilkerson standing there. The captain wore the same immaculate uniform that he did in the War Department, and the blue cloth and brass buttons stood out sharply against the tavern's ramshackle backdrop.

"Wilkerson!" Flynn said gruffly, without making much effort to hide his dislike for the dapper Union officer. There was something oily about Wilkerson, but Flynn tried to give him the benefit of the doubt. They had few enough friends in Washington as it was. "Where in the hell did you come from? If you came to see the prizefight, you're too late."

"Well, I was too late to see the fight," Wilkerson said. "I understand I would have won some money if I had bet on you."

"Damn right you would have," Flynn said. "But I don't suppose you're much of a betting man."

"You might be surprised." Wilkerson stepped into the room, but was brought up short at the sight of the soldier at Caldwell's side. "Is that who I think it is?"

"It was the only way out of the hospital," Louisa said, gesturing at the uniform she wore. "The guards posted there wouldn't have let me leave, or, at the very least, they would have had me followed. Dressed like this, nobody even gave me a second look."

"That's brilliant," Wilkerson said. "It also explains why Lafayette Baker is in such an uproar. They said at the hospital that you slipped out. The patients were having quite a laugh over it, but the guards didn't think it was funny, not after Colonel Baker got through with them."

"How did you know where to find us?" Flynn asked.

"I asked the Irish nurse, Mae O'Keefe," Wilkerson explained. "She told me about the so-called boarding house where you were supposed to be. When I didn't find you there, the woman who runs the place told me to come here."

"That would have been Miss Paula herself," Flynn said. "Fine woman."

"If you like them built like Juno. Anyhow, here I am."

"Well, Captain, you're just in time. We know where Verville is, and as soon as the doctor finishes fussing over me, we're going to go get him. Verville is slippery as an eel, and we don't want him to get away this time. You can help us, because we'll need another hand."

"What about me?" Louisa asked.

"But you're a woman," Flynn said.

Louisa gave a short laugh and tugged at the blue tunic she wore. "Not anymore, I'm not. In the dark, Verville wouldn't be able to tell the difference, anyway."

"That's just what I'm afraid of, Louisa," Caldwell said. "I don't think you should come."

"I'm coming with you, and that's the end of it," Louisa said, turning to the doctor. "Besides, what else am I going to do? I can't go back to the hospital, not with it still being guarded, and there's no way I'm going back to that whorehouse alone."

Flynn shrugged. "All right, I suppose you might as well come with us. We can use all the help we can get."

As soon as Caldwell finished patching him up, Flynn got to his feet and put on his shirt and coat. He was just reaching for his hat when Billy burst into the room.

"You best run, and quick," the boy said breathlessly. "There's soldiers come to arrest you."

"How can that be?" Louisa gasped. "No one followed us."

"Aye, but they might have followed him," Flynn said, glaring malevolently at Wilkerson. "That is, if he didn't lead them here himself."

"I swear to you, I had no idea!" Wilkerson said. "They must have seen me talking with the nurse and become suspicious enough to have a detective follow me. Damn it all."

"Let's worry later about how it happened," Caldwell said. "All that matters now it that we need to get out of here right away. There's not another second to lose."

Flynn chanced a look outside into the main hall. It was still crowded with revelers who were celebrating his victory drunkenly, bottles of whiskey clutched in their hands. No wonder the MacCraes were so eager to stage fights at their tavern. It was likely most of the men there were spending most of their winnings on whiskey. He looked more closely at the crowd, and noticed a few blue uniforms standing out among the dull grays and browns of the workmen's coats. Less than half a dozen, that he could see. There might be plainclothes detectives, too, but Flynn couldn't pick any out.

He spotted Lafayette Baker himself prowling through the crowd, looking for Wilkerson or Caldwell. At the sight of Baker, Flynn felt a cold tingling along his spine. The man had a reputation for ruthlessness and Flynn had no desire to be captured by the likes of Baker.

Flynn was certain Baker and his men would be less likely to recognize him. After all, it was Caldwell who had spoken during the meeting with Stanton at the War Department to let the secretary know about the Confederate plot to spread bubonic plague in the city and it was Caldwell again who had been named as a source in *The Sunday Chronicle* article. It was Caldwell they wanted, whom they knew by name and sight, and it would be no more than a minute before Baker and his men made their way across the crowded floor to the room that now hid Caldwell.

He ducked back inside. "Colonel Baker and his men are right outside," he said. "They'll have the front of the building blocked off and probably all the other exits, too. Any ideas?"

Wilkerson stepped forward. "I could try to distract them, or maybe bluff my way through the guards at the doors. The rest of you might be able to get away."

"Don't be a fool, Captain," Caldwell snapped. "If you were followed here, it means they think you're one of us now. If they catch you, you'll be going to prison – or worse. Besides, I doubt you could buy the rest of us enough time to get away, anyhow."

"What do we do?" Louisa asked. "They'll find us any second now."

For once, Flynn was stumped. He had no more idea than the rest of them how to escape, and each moment they wasted made getting away from Baker's men less likely.

"I know a way," said Billy. Flynn had forgotten him, but the boy had stayed in the room after delivering his warning.

"How?"

"There's a secret way out that Angus MacCrae done made for him and his brother," the boy said. "Mr. Angus always says you never know when you'll need to give someone the slip."

"Where is this secret way out?" Flynn demanded. In his mind's eye, he imagined Baker and his men right outside the door, waiting to burst in.

"Follow me," the boy said. "Best bring the lantern."

He darted out the door into the main room, where the fight had taken place. Flynn looked at his companions and shrugged. If anyone thought it was odd that they were trusting their fate to a mere boy, no one said anything.

Fortunately for them, the main hall was still crowded with spectators. Flynn grabbed the lantern from its hook above the table and moved into the room, the others following behind him. He had a glimpse of Baker's uniformed men moving through the crowd and he expected at any moment to hear a shout of alarm from one of the soldiers. After being battered by the Kraut, he was in no condition to run or fight, so he said a silent prayer as he followed the boy along the wall to another door. The boy pushed it open, and the four adults following him hustled inside. Flynn locked the door behind them.

"What is this place?" Flynn asked, looking around at the desk, chairs and ledger books lining the walls.

"It's Mr. MacCrae's office," the boy said. "Now, watch this."

He pulled back a rug that covered the board floor. There, cut into the floor itself, was a trap door. A latch handle had been neatly inset so that it was flush with the surface of the boards. The boy's small fingers quickly worked it free. Flynn helped him pull up the heavy door to reveal a ladder leading down into darkness.

"Dark as a cave down there," Flynn said, getting a whiff of dank cellar air. It smelled of dampness and must. "Where does it go?"

"You climb the ladder down to the cellar," the boy said. "On the far wall are some empty shelves. You push those out of the way and there's a passage between this cellar and the cellar of the building next door. Then you climb the stairs and find the back door. Nobody will be watching the building next door."

Flynn nodded. "Major, grab a candle off the desk there. Wilkerson, you got any lucifers on you?"

The captain produced some matches, which he used to light the candle. Louisa was peering dubiously down into the cellar hole. "I'm not going in there," she announced.

"We don't have much choice, Louisa," Caldwell said.

"I'd rather take my chances with Colonel Baker and his men."

"No, you wouldn't," Flynn said. "You're coming with us if I have to throw you over my shoulder and carry you."

Louisa might have argued further, but there was a knock at the door. Whoever it was waited a moment for a reply, then, hearing nothing, began to pound on the door.

"No time to lose," Flynn whispered urgently. "Someone might have seen us come in. Down the ladder we go. Of course, as soon as Baker's men get the door open they'll see the carpet out of place and notice the trap door. We won't have much time."

"I'll stay behind and cover it up," the boy said. "No one will ever know."

"What will you say when they open the door?"

The boy smiled. "I'll tell them I was sleeping." He yawned dramatically. "Now, who wouldn't believe that?"

"All right," Flynn said. He had to wonder if they could trust the boy or not, but there wasn't time not to. The pounding at the door had grown more urgent, and someone was fiddling with the lock. Baker's men would have it open in seconds.

Flynn, holding the lantern, climbed down the ladder first, quickly followed by Caldwell, Louisa and Wilkerson with the candle. Overhead, the boy was struggling with the heavy trapdoor, and Flynn climbed partway back up to help him lower it in place. They could hear the grating sound of the latch being slid back.

"Let's hope we can trust that boy," Caldwell said. "For all we know, he's

197

outsmarted us all and trapped us here in the cellar for Baker's men, hoping to get some kind of reward out of them."

"Well, if that's the case, it's too late to do anything about it," Flynn said. "We're caught as surely as pigs in a slaughterhouse."

He lifted the candle high and swept it in a circle to light the cellar. The place was long unused, full of cobwebs and damp. Something scampered out of the reach of the light and Louisa gasped.

"Quiet," Flynn cautioned. "You'll have us all caught."

"What was that?" Louisa whispered nervously.

"Probably a rat," Flynn said. "Have you ever known a cellar in the city that didn't have a few?"

Overhead, the floor rang with the sound of boots. Hiding in the cellar was like being inside a muffled drum. They could just make out a harsh, demanding voice that must certainly be Baker's, followed by the boy's voice in answer. It was impossible to make out the words, to know if the boy had betrayed them or covered their tracks.

They quickly explored the cellar, looking for the way out. The lantern and candle cast weird lights that seemed to make the cobwebs dance. Finally, the flickering candlelight fell upon a shelf along one wall. Like the rest of the cellar, the shelves, too, had the look of being long unused. Flynn found it doubtful that they masked some kind of doorway, and began to wonder if the boy really had led them into a trap, after all. He could still hear voices overhead.

"Come on," he said. "This way."

The cobwebs surrounding the shelves were so thick with dust that they resembled an old woman's dingy lace. Flynn brushed them aside with the back of his hand and grabbed hold of the shelves. They were heavy, damn heavy, and his battered body protested.

"Let me give you a hand," Wilkerson said. He gave his candle to Louisa and threw his shoulder against the shelves. At first, nothing happened.

"The boy tricked us!" Wilkerson said. "He trapped us down here like a bunch of fools."

"Try it again," Caldwell said. "Push the shelves toward the opposite wall this time."

Flynn and Wilkerson made another attempt, pushing in another direction. The shelves slid to one side easily this time, revealing a dark passageway in the cellar wall. It was just high enough for a small man to walk through. Flynn had to stoop as he swung the lantern into the passageway. The tunnel was only about six feet long, and it ended at what appeared to be a boarded-up wall.

"Come on, Wilkerson," Flynn said. "Leave your candle with Louis there and bring your shoulder."

Flynn and the captain quickly pushed an old cabinet out of the way and stepped into the cellar of the house next to the tavern. "Well, looks like the lad was right about this getaway route," he said.

"Let's close up the entrances again in case Baker and his men do figure out we went down into the cellar hole," Wilkerson said.

"Good idea," Flynn agreed. They re-entered the tunnel to close it off at one end with the old shelves, then came back out and shoved the cabinet back into place. Anyone following them into the cellar would think that they had disappeared — if they had ever been there at all. Caldwell and Louisa were already halfway up the stairs, and he and Wilkerson followed. The stairs led to an unlocked door, which they opened to find themselves standing in the empty kitchen of the house.

Flynn looked out the window. Next door, he could see uniformed guards standing around the entrance of the tavern. "Let's try the back," he said, and they went through the house to a door at the back. It opened onto a narrow space between the next house rather than on the alley itself. There were more guards at the back of the tavern, but their view of the back door that Flynn and the others stepped through was hidden by the bulk of the house.

"Quietly now," Flynn whispered. The guards were only a few feet away.

It was almost pitch black in the alley and to keep from attracting attention to themselves they had extinguished their lights and left them behind. They groped their away along as quietly as they could, although it wasn't easy because the alley was littered with debris. Behind Flynn, Wilkerson's foot kicked a bottle and it made a noise that sounded loud as a gunshot in the stillness.

"Who's there?" called one of the soldiers guarding the back of the tavern. The iron heelplates of his shoes rang on the cobblestones as he walked toward them.

Flynn and the others held themselves very still as the soldier stood there, listening. They heard one of the other soldiers say, "It's probably just a cat."

"I reckon," said the first man. His voice sounded like it was just a few feet from where they were hidden. Flynn held his breath. Finally, the soldier muttered something in disgust and moved away.

"Come on," Flynn whispered, and he and the others felt their way as quietly as they could down the alley until they came to the outlet at a lighted street. No soldiers were in sight.

"That was close," Caldwell said.

"Aye, it was," Flynn agreed. "Now let's see if our luck holds and we can find Verville where the boy said he would be. We don't have a minute to lose."

Chapter 24

"Keep your eyes open and stay together," Flynn warned as they hurried from the tavern. "We may have left Baker and his men behind, but there's still plenty to worry about at night on these streets."

"Are we going to get Verville now?"

"Yes, and there's not a moment to lose. The sooner we catch Verville and put an end to this mad scheme of his, the better."

"Besides, if we catch Verville we'll have some proof of his plans, and we may get the Union Secret Service off our backs," Caldwell pointed out.

The truth was, Caldwell was still puzzled at how they had suddenly become fugitives through the simple action of trying to do their duty. For all his cynicism, Caldwell had always placed great faith in the Army and the institution of government. To find all that turned against him now was confusing and disturbing. He noticed that Flynn appeared to take it all in stride.

The hotel where Verville was staying was located on Pennsylvania Avenue and was popular with Southerners. It was also a place where Caldwell could not have afforded to stay. Billy, the boy from the tavern, had even known which room Verville was staying in. That was useful, considering he might not be registered under his own name.

"Do you think he'll know we're coming?" Caldwell asked.

"How would he?"

"He seemed to know at the Metropolitan Hotel," he pointed out.

"Aye," Flynn said. "Something spooked him. He got lucky that time, but I doubt he can escape from us twice."

As soon as they reached the hotel, Flynn described his plan to capture Verville. "The doctor and I will go in the front door," he said. "Wilkerson, you and Louisa watch the back. I'm sure there's a door that opens onto the alley, and if we spook him he might try to escape that way."

"I'll stop him if he tries that," Wilkerson said boastfully. "You can count on that."

"See that you do," Flynn said. "And make sure no harm comes to Louisa here while you're at it."

"I can take care of myself," Louisa said, hands on hip. In her soldier's uniform she looked to be all business.

"I'm sure you can," Flynn said. Secretly, he was glad Louisa was wearing the uniform. If Verville did see them, he would think he was taking on two men, not just a man and woman.

"Besides, I have a pistol," she said, patting her pocket.

"God save us," Flynn said. "Don't go shooting anybody by accident."

Caldwell didn't appear concerned about the pistol, but moved toward Louisa and took her gently by the wrists. "Verville is a bad character, Louisa," he said. "You don't have to do this. Wait right here until it's over."

"No," she said stubbornly. "I'm going to help."

"Be careful, Louisa," Caldwell said. "I don't want anything happening to you."

"All right then," Flynn said. He smiled one of his unsettling grins. "Let's go catch ourselves a Confederate spy."

* * *

Most of the news Verville read in *The Washington Star* was pure drivel, but he had bought the newspaper to check ship arrivals and was pleased to see the *Rynda* listed. She was due in Washington City tomorrow night, the paper reported, having been sighted passing Cape Henry at the entrance to Chesapeake Bay. He circled the ship's name with a pencil.

Good. As long as the Russian ship remained on schedule, everything would go as planned with the MacCrae brothers and their crew of smugglers.

Still, he had an uneasy feeling about the MacCraes. He wasn't quite sure he could trust them, but at this point he didn't have much choice. It was too late to make other arrangements – and how could be sure that the next bunch wouldn't be worse than the MacCraes? He would simply have to take care when it came time to deal with them tomorrow night.

Then came the knock at the door.

He did not answer. No one knew he was here; with Sally and Charlie Wilson dead he had no friends in the city. He was expecting no one. The only one who could have found him was someone with no good reason to find him.

Was it Caldwell or someone else? Had Lafayette Baker found out who killed his two spies? Caldwell alone he could have handled, but he was sure the doctor would not have come by himself.

Verville realized he was trapped.

Desperately, he looked around the room. The only door opened on the hallway. That left the window.

Verville went to it, looked out. He had already propped it open despite the chilly winter air, because the room had been too stuffy when he sat to smoke a cigar. He eased it open a few more inches and leaned out. The alley below was four floors down and hidden in darkness. Too far to jump. But the window was his only hope of escape.

He cursed himself for not thinking this through before, but he had not thought it possible that someone would find him. Except for a narrow ledge that ran along the bases of the windows, the wall was too sheer to allow any kind of grip.

A knock again, more urgent this time. Whoever it was would be pounding at the door next, trying the lock. Then it would be only a matter of minutes. The door was not very thick.

Verville shoved his cane through his suspenders to leave his hands free, then propelled himself out the window. Not to jump – that would be suicide. But he stood, backwards, aware of the black nothingness behind him, and his hands groped for a hold overhead. He found something, a joint in the brick that allowed his fingertips some purchase. Precariously, standing on one foot, he managed to shut the window with his boot.

He hoped that the closed window would confound whoever pursued him. With luck, they would think he had disappeared into thin air.

His heart hammered in his throat. Calm, he ordered himself. Be calm.

He moved his feet sideways, inching them along the brick. The ledge was no more than three or four inches wide, merely a decorative feature of the building itself, but it was just enough to give his feet some purchase. Overhead, he worked his fingers along the seam of brick, pressing so hard that he could feel the mortar gathering under his fingernails.

He hugged the wall itself with his chest and belly. He did not look down or even think about how high up he was, knowing that to do so would make him dizzy. He knew that to even consider logically what he was doing would be fatal. He didn't need to think, only to act. The cold wind bit at him viciously, gnawing at his very bones like some kind of starved animal, but he ignored it.

It was perhaps eight feet from his window to the next, and he reached it and kept going, knowing from the sounds he had heard earlier that night that someone was asleep in that room. He had heard the noises of them getting ready for bed, the creak of bedsprings, mumbled prayers. He crept past the window, unseen by the room's occupant.

Just beyond the window, the seam of mortar into which he had jammed his fingers all but disappeared.

He cursed and sought for another handhold in the brick, but now the mortar was almost flush with the face of the brick, leaving nothing to grasp onto. To make matters worse, his fingers were growing stiff with the cold. The ledge for his feet was still there, but there was no longer any grip for his hands.

If he fell, he would die.

* * *

Flynn charged the door.

It crashed open and he tumbled inside the room. He had his hands out in front of him, ready for anything, expecting Verville to have a gun or knife. What he saw was a still-burning oil lamp, an open copy of a newspaper, but no sign of Verville.

"Where the hell is he?" he shouted, heart pounding.

"He's not here," Caldwell said, coming through the doorway where the door now hung on its hinges like a flag on a listless day. "He must have heard us coming."

"Impossible!"

"There's always the window."

Flynn crossed the room in three long strides and flung up the sash. He leaned out, saw nothing but a sheer wall that disappeared into shadow.

"The street is so far down I can't even see it in the darkness," he said. "I'm beginning to wonder if this goddamn Verville is even human, or if he changed himself into a bat and flew away into the night."

"He's human, all right," Caldwell said, reaching for a small blue bottle on the table beside the bed. There was also a glass containing a sticky, black residue.

"What's that?"

"Laudanum," Caldwell said.

"Drugged or not, the bastard still got away from us. I want to know when his luck is going to change."

"Not tonight."

They spent several minutes making a quick search of the room but found nothing useful.

"We'd better check downstairs," Flynn said. "He only got out just ahead of us, from the looks of it. That means he'll be heading for the front door – or the back."

Caldwell looked worried. "What about Louisa?"

"Come on," Flynn said. "There's not a minute to lose."

* * *

He must not fall.

Verville felt himself swaying and pressed desperately against the wall, hoping the mere friction of his body might hold him against the bricks. His only choices were to go back to the room that held the sleeping man – who would surely wake up and shout in alarm – or else move on, hoping that the next room was empty.

He tried hard not to think about the fall that awaited him if he lost his balance. His plans couldn't end like that, broken on the pavement below. The future of the Confederacy depended upon him, and if he failed now, there was no one else to carry his plans forward.

It must not end like this.

Other men might have prayed, beseeched the help of the Almighty, but even in his fear Verville scoffed at that notion. His God did not reward weakness.

He heard a window open, then close after a moment. So, they were in his room. The darkness had hidden him. Besides, no one would have believed he could make it so far on the tiny ledge.

With new confidence, he spread his hands as wide as he could, trying to take advantage of every bit of the rough surface. Even his cheek was pressed against the wall. Inch by inch, he moved on. He slid one foot along the ledge, then the other. He could almost touch the frame of the next window. He warned himself not to hurry. Any slip or mistake now would be fatal. The window was dark, which was a good sign. He reached the glass and peered inside, but the stars didn't provide enough light to tell if anyone lay sleeping inside.

It was a chance he would have to take. He had tempted fate enough by crossing those last few feet of wall, and he dared not try to reach the next room.

Still, he had to get inside. Opening one of the hotel's heavy windows from outside while balancing on a four-inch-wide ledge several stories above the ground was no easy task. He hung suspended for a moment, unsure of what to do. He could take the chance that someone might be sleeping inside and tap on the glass to awaken them. Just as quickly as he had thought of it, he dismissed the idea. Anyone who awakened to see him silhouetted against the night-time sky would think the Devil himself had come for them.

Verville remembered his cane. It was the only tool he had. Carefully, he pulled it from where it was safely tucked under his suspenders and used the tip to probe the base of the window, searching for some slight gap into which he could wedge the tip. He found a slight purchase and shoved. The window raised maybe an inch, just enough for him to get a toe of his shoe under. Balancing precariously on one leg, he raised his foot, and with it, the window. Breathing a sigh of relief, he slipped into the room, pulled the window shut behind him.

Empty.

He opened the door a crack, then peered into the hallway. Nobody there. His pursuers were still in his room. Quickly, Verville slipped out and ran silently down the carpeted hallway to the stairs.

* * *

Louisa was just starting to wonder if they were wasting their time when the rear entrance of the hotel opened and a man came hurrying out. He was tall and dressed in black. She squinted in the dim light to try to make out the man's features.

He walked quickly toward where she and Wilkerson stood, blocking the way toward the street. The man turned his head slightly and she got a good look at his face. The sight of it made her blood run cold. There was a glint in his eyes, a gleam of madness. Although she had never seen Verville before, there was no doubt it must be him.

"Captain," she whispered nervously. "It's Verville."

"Are you sure?" Wilkerson asked. He didn't sound so brave anymore, not like he had been earlier that night. "How do you know?"

"There's no time. He's coming—"

Verville, if it really was him, was upon them. Louisa stepped forward to block his path. He started to dodge around her, but Louisa moved with him.

"Out of my way!" he snarled, and flung an open fist at Louisa, as if to swat her away. She managed to duck, but the blow knocked her hat off. At first she was indignant. How dare he strike a woman! She had forgotten she was still wearing a soldier's uniform. She realized her face was in full view, awash with light from the gas lamp near the back door, and Verville stared at her.

"You," he said. "You're the nurse from the hospital!"

Before Louisa could answer, the alley echoed with a howl as Wilkerson came out of the shadows and launched himself at Verville.

Verville's eyes seemed riveted on Louisa. At the last instant, he pivoted like a bullfighter and his cane flashed down. The heavy boar's head grip struck Wilkerson in the side of the head. He collapsed in a heap on the cobblestone floor of the alley. Verville raised his cane as if to finish

Wilkerson off, and it gave Louisa enough time to remember the pistol in her pocket. She pulled it out and leveled the weapon at Verville.

"Put that cane down or I'll shoot."

Verville smiled. Even in the dim light, Louisa could see his lips curl into a nasty grin. "What? How could a nurse shoot someone?" Still, he lowered the cane, but did not drop it.

"I will shoot if I must." Louisa struggled to hold the heavy pistol steady.

"Where's Caldwell?" he asked.

"He's on his way."

"Are you certain of that?" His teeth flashed in a grin again, superior, confident, like a wolf smiling at a sheep. Louisa's heart skipped a beat. "Right now, he's up in my hotel room, scratching his head and wondering where I went. It's going to take him some time to get here, and if you want me to stay until then, you're going to have to shoot me, I fear."

He took a step toward her.

"No–"

Wilkerson groaned, and Louisa glanced at him. It was all Verville needed. He swooped forward and snatched at the pistol, yanking it toward the sky. Louisa pulled the trigger, but the hammer swung down with an empty click.

Louisa gasped in surprise. Laughing, Verville tugged the pistol from her hands, glanced at it, and tossed it aside. "It's not even loaded, you dumb Yankee bitch." He gripped her firmly by the arm. "Let's get going. And don't even think about screaming, because if you do make a sound, my dear, I'm going to break your neck."

Louisa had no choice but to hurry alongside Verville as he plunged through the night, holding tightly to her arm. She struggled to keep up, gasping for breath more from fear than exertion, as the hotel – and any hope of rescue – fell farther and farther behind.

* * *

"Where's Louisa?"

Flynn and Caldwell found Wilkerson on his hands and knees, shaking his head groggily. Even in the dim light streaks of blood gleamed wetly on the captain's face. Louisa was nowhere to be seen.

"What happened?" Flynn demanded, grabbing Wilkerson roughly by the shoulder. "Where did Louisa go?"

"God, I still see stars," Wilkerson muttered. "He hit me with a cane."

"You'll live," Flynn said, helping him to his feet. "Now, where's Louisa?"

207

"He took her," Wilkerson said.

"What?"

"She had a pistol and tried to stop him, but he took her by the arm and dragged her away."

"My God."

Caldwell made a strangled sound, then reached for a pistol on the ground near his feet. "She must have found this in my trunk. I didn't realize that was the pistol she had. I've never even loaded the thing."

"Which way did they go?"

Wilkerson pointed vaguely into the darkness. "That way," he said. "I think."

"Come on," Flynn said. "Maybe we can still catch them."

They ran down the alley, out into the street, leaving Wilkerson to nurse his own wounds. A few people were visible in the dim gaslights, but there was no sign of Verville and Louisa. The night was very dark and cold, and people hurried by with their faces hunched into their collars. Verville could have ducked down any alley and been swallowed up by the blackness.

"Louisa!" Caldwell shouted, his voice high-pitched and brittle with desperation. "Louisa!"

Flynn sprinted for some distance down the street, praying he was going in the right direction and hoping to overtake Verville and Louisa. The wind was bitter, sapping his strength, and after a while he gave up and bent over double, gasping, struggling to catch his breath. His body ached after the prizefight earlier that night, and knocking down the hotel room door had done something to his shoulder. The cold seemed to be scalding his throat as he sucked in lungfuls of air. Caldwell came running up behind him.

"It's no use," Flynn panted. "Damn! I knew I couldn't count on Wilkerson. He's a fool and a coward."

"It's not his fault, Flynn," Caldwell said. "I should have stayed with Louisa and sent Wilkerson with you."

"But I thought for sure we would catch Verville in his room. I never dreamed that the man would run out on us again. The man's the very devil, I tell you."

"What do we do now?" Caldwell asked. With Louisa gone, swallowed up in the night by Verville, he was suddenly as helpless as a child.

"Go back to the hotel," Flynn said. "We'll collect Wilkerson and go have a look at Verville's room. Maybe there's some clue that will tell us where he's gone, or what he's planning."

Together, they slowly walked back the way they had run. Flynn found himself staring into the faces of the oncoming pedestrians, hoping for a glimpse of Verville. But it was no use. Verville was gone, and Louisa with him.

Chapter 25

Verville's hotel room was as bare and orderly as an operating chamber. Flynn searched it a second time, looking for clues, but there wasn't much of anything in the room beyond some spare clothes and the half-empty bottle of opiate on the bedside table.

"Damn him," Flynn muttered. "First he disappears into the night, and then he doesn't leave anything useful behind."

"He knows his business," Wilkerson pointed out. "He's obviously had some experience as a spy, or else he's a very careful man."

"I'd say it's a little of both," Flynn said. "He's done some secret work for Richmond, but I think by nature he's a slippery man. After all, what kind of person would even dream up a scheme like his?"

Caldwell said nothing, just stared idly at the carpet. He shuffled across the room as if in a dream and sat on the bed. "I can't believe she's gone," he said. "I don't want to think about what that bastard is going to do to her."

"Don't worry, we'll find her," Flynn said, although he wasn't so sure they would do so anytime soon. Any man who disappeared into thin air out of a fourth-floor hotel room without leaving the slightest clue behind could not be underestimated. Still, he had to say something to comfort Caldwell.

There was a noise at the door of someone clearing his throat loudly, and Flynn looked up to find a hotel clerk standing there. The man was well-dressed and prim, and was staring at the broken door, plainly aghast.

"What has happened?" he managed to stammer.

"My friend here had too much to drink and lost his key," Flynn said, nodding at Caldwell, who in his dejected state looked as if he might have been drinking. "He broke the door down."

"I'm afraid he can't do that," the clerk said.

"Well," Flynn pointed out. "He already did."

"He'll have to pay."

"Of course," Flynn said. "In the morning, when he's sober. We're very sorry for the trouble."

"I don't know–"

Flynn stood and walked over to the clerk. He towered over the man, who looked up in shock at Flynn's face, which was badly battered and bruised from the prizefight. "You're not going to give us trouble, are you now?" Flynn said, his voice menacing.

"Oh, you can pay in the morning," the clerk hurried to say. "It's all right."

Once the clerk had retreated, along with a curious guest or two who lingered in the hall, Flynn set the door of the room back into place. The bottom hinge had pulled free and splintered the frame when Flynn broke it open, but he was still able to pull the door shut.

"Do you really plan to pay for the damages in the morning?" Wilkerson asked.

"Why not?" Flynn asked. "We'll be spending the night here, I suppose. It's as good a place as any. After all, we can't go back to Miss Paula's, not now that Baker's men know where we were staying, and we can't go back to the hospital, either."

"I suppose you're right."

"Come on, let's take this place apart," Flynn said. "Dump out all the drawers, look under the mattress. There must be a clue here somewhere. Something he forgot, or else hid and didn't have time to take with him."

Flynn set Caldwell to searching under the bed, just to get the man doing something. After several minutes, it was Wilkerson, however, who gave a triumphant shout.

"What is it?"

"The newspaper," he said excitedly, flapping it at Flynn. "Verville circled one of the ships."

"The *Rynda*," Flynn said. "It says here that it's a Russian ship. What in the world does that have to do with Verville?"

"Where is the ship coming from?" Caldwell asked. Both Flynn and Wilkerson turned to look at him. He had been silent so long that they had almost forgotten he was in the room.

"China," Flynn said, checking the newspaper again. "It's a Russian warship coming from China and it's due in port tomorrow."

"My God," Caldwell said. "If there's one part of the world where the plague is endemic, it's China. That's how he's bringing the plague to Washington. He's smuggling it in."

Flynn smiled. "And we'll be there to stop him, thanks to the MacCrae brothers. They asked me to give them a hand tomorrow night, and that can only mean one thing."

"You think they're meeting the Russian ship?"

"What else?" Flynn said. "If Verville can be stopped, we'll be the ones to do it."

211

"What about Louisa?" Caldwell asked.

"We'll find her," Flynn found himself saying, although he wasn't as confident as he sounded. Washington had been transformed by the war into a large city, and if Verville wanted to stay hidden until tomorrow night, it would be very hard to find him – and Louisa. He could be staying in any one of a hundred hotels and boarding houses under an assumed name. After all, they never would have found him at the National without the boy's help. "Verville may be a madman, but he's no fool. He'll try to use her as a tool against us when the times comes, but we'll be ready."

* * *

Verville hailed one of the few hired carriages that was still out on the street so late. By chancing a peek through the curtains Louisa could see that they were moving back toward the center of the city. It was where the President's house, Treasury Department, War Department and other government offices were located.

"Where are you taking me?" she asked.

"Well, we need a place to spend the night, my dear. I'm afraid I was rather rudely chased from my last hotel by your friends. We'll be staying in a rather more elegant hotel. I believe you'll be happy with it. After all, we may as well enjoy ourselves. There's no telling what tomorrow will bring."

"I'm not staying anywhere with you," Louisa said.

"Oh, but you will, Miss Webster. You'll see."

"How do you know my name?"

"I know everything about Caldwell's hospital, including the name of his chief nurse."

Louisa shivered, and it wasn't entirely from the winter cold. She stared at the man across from her, getting a good look at him for the first time. A swaying lantern lit the inside of the carriage, and the flickering light made his face demonic. His eyes were deep-set, hidden in shadow, but to Louisa they seemed to glint with a light all their own. Was that truly a gleam of madness?

"What are you?" she demanded, suddenly angry. "Some kind of madman?"

Verville laughed. The noise in the cramped carriage made Louisa's flesh break out in goosebumps. "Ah! You have spirit, Miss Webster! I admire that in a woman. To answer your question, no, I'm no more mad than you were to leave whatever home you had and come to work in the hospital. I believe in what I'm doing, in my cause. There is, after all, a war being fought, and the South will have victory. I ask you, how can it be madness to serve a cause one believes in?"

"But to kill innocent people, to set the plague loose–"

Verville shrugged. "Who is truly innocent, Miss Webster? Maybe the smallest babe. In war, there are no innocents, only enemies."

Louisa made a sound of disgust. "You, sir, are a horrid man."

"And you, my dear, are my prisoner."

They rode for several minutes in silence. Finally, Verville seemed to notice that she was wearing a soldier's uniform. "Why are you dressed like that?" he asked.

"It was the only way I could get out of the hospital," she replied. "Colonel Baker has it under guard."

"Ah, yes, Colonel Baker." Even in the gloom, Louisa could see a look of pure hatred sweep over him before he could compose himself again. "You outsmarted him. Good for you. That makes two of us. But those clothes simply won't do at all. Not for what I have in mind."

"What might that be?" Louisa asked.

"All in good time. Now, where can we find you some proper clothes? I trust you have some back at the hospital?"

"Yes, but we can't go there. It's still guarded–"

Verville cut her off. "We'll see what we can do."

When the carriage arrived, it was evident from the soldiers at the doors that Lafayette Baker's men were still watching the hospital carefully. However, they didn't pay much attention to the carriage driver, whom Verville sent in with a message for Mae O'Keefe to give the man some of Louisa's clothes. It was done in just a few minutes, with the guards merely glancing into the package the driver carried out. Verville waited outside the carriage while Louisa put on a dress. Mae had picked out one of Louisa's better outfits, but had not included a hoop. That was just as well. Since becoming a nurse and not wearing one, Louisa had already decided she might never wear one again. What was the point? It just got in the way.

Verville rapped on the carriage door. "All done in there?"

"Yes," Louisa said, wondering if she should have used the time in an attempt to escape. That would have been pointless, she knew, because Verville probably would have caught her with ease.

"You see," he said, climbing back into the carriage, "I'm a true Southern gentleman."

"Why?" Louisa asked, incredulous. "Because you let me dress alone? You seem to have forgotten that you kidnapped me."

"You're a prisoner of war, Miss Webster. There is a difference."

"Well," she said, smoothing the fabric of the dress over her knees. "I'm not in a position to argue."

"There is one thing I would like to know," Verville said as the carriage rolled on. "How did you know where I was staying?"

"The boy at the tavern told us," she said. "Of course, Mr. Flynn has been looking for you for days."

"Flynn?" Verville asked. "I'm afraid I don't know anyone named Flynn."

"He's a Confederate agent," Louisa said. "He came up from Richmond to find you."

"I see."

Verville seemed to withdraw into himself, and Louisa wondered if she had said too much. She had assumed he would know who was looking for him. He sat quietly, the tip of his cane between the toes of his well-polished shoes, tapping rhythmically on the floor of the carriage, his mind evidently lost in thought.

Louisa's own thoughts were racing. Desperately, she wondered if she had any hope of escape. There was a chance the carriage might stop somewhere on the streets and she could open the door on her side and leap down. Just as quickly, she dismissed the idea. She knew she didn't have much chance of outrunning Verville. She might also be able to jump out and start screaming to attract attention, but it was now getting very late and the streets were largely deserted. It was likely she would be wasting her breath. Besides, she was determined to be dignified, if at all possible.

The carriage swung onto Pennsylvania Avenue. Puzzled, Louisa asked, "Are you finally going to tell me where we're going?"

"To the Willard Hotel, Miss Webster. As I said before, your friends rather rudely evicted me from my old room, so we must have accommodations somewhere. That is, unless you prefer sleeping on the street?"

"No, I suppose not."

Louisa felt a glimmer of hope. The Willard Hotel was always busy. There was no way Verville was getting her through the lobby doors without her screaming for help.

Verville stopped tapping his cane and instead moved his feet closer together to brace the tip. His gloved hands had been resting atop the heavy silver boar's head at the head of the cane, but he now began turning the boar's head, unscrewing it. The head of the cane came away, revealing a hollow compartment that contained a cylindrical glass vial of clear liquid. Verville removed the vial and held it up for Louisa to see.

"This, my dear, is chloroform. You know something about it, I'm sure, from your duties as a nurse."

"Of course."

"I'm sure your Major Caldwell has told you that I'm a doctor by vocation. A good doctor never travels without some of the tools of his trade, and I've found that this cane makes an excellent place to carry this vial. It fits perfectly inside this cushioned space here, protected from any blows. It's really quite clever."

Puzzled, Louisa watched as he uncapped the vial and shook some of the chloroform onto a handkerchief. A shiver of fear went through her as she realized what Verville intended to do.

He smiled, and Louisa was reminded of the smile she had seen some surgeons use when they were explaining to a soldier that his arm or leg must be sawn off. Now, even if she had wanted to scream, Louisa didn't have the breath to do so.

"Of course, I realize you won't go willingly into the hotel," he explained. "I'll have to carry you upstairs, explaining you've had some sort of fit."

"No–"

He lunged at her, caught her. She tried to fight back, to squirm out from under him, but he was amazingly strong.

Then, just as she sucked in her breath to scream, the handkerchief closed over her face. Verville had timed it perfectly. Instead of air, she inhaled the chloroform fumes. That was the last thing Louisa remembered before the world went dark.

* * *

Flynn decided Louisa must be dead, but he kept that thought to himself. Since first light, he and the others had been scouring the city, searching for Verville and Louisa. They had made inquiries at a score of hotels, asking if anyone had seen a tall man dressed in black arrive late at night with a young soldier. So far, the answer had been negative. No one could remember, and most of the night shift had already gone off duty. Of course, Verville knew better than to check in under his real name. That was why he had managed to elude them so long up until last night.

There were only the three of them to search the city. The fact that they were being sought themselves by members of Lafayette Baker's secret police didn't make matters any easier. Three times that morning, Flynn had to drag Caldwell out of sight because he spotted one of Baker's watchers. Sometimes they were uniformed soldiers posted in a doorway, other times they were civilians with a vaguely disreputable air who appeared to be all too alert to the passersby. It was Caldwell they would recognize. If Baker was worth a pinch of salt as a detective, he had found the tintype in the doctor's room made at the beginning of the war that showed Caldwell in uniform. Passed among his watchers, it would be all they needed to identify the doctor.

Wilkerson, too, would be known to them. The War Department adjutant was now as much a fugitive as the doctor. Still, he had insisted on helping to search for Louisa. He had gone off by himself to try some of the city's outlying areas.

Only Flynn remained anonymous. There was no likeness of him to pass around, and it was doubtful any of Baker's men knew what he looked like. Still, he knew it wouldn't take them long to catch on and begin looking for a large man with bruises on his face. If any of them were captured, the game was up. Verville would be free to carry out his plan, and the plague would be set free in the United States capital.

Sometime in midafternoon, Flynn and Caldwell trooped back to the room they had taken over since Verville had hastily abandoned it. They couldn't even return to the tavern in full daylight because Baker would have watchers there, too. Exhausted, Flynn flung himself on the bed. Caldwell slumped into a chair and poured himself a large whiskey from the bottle Verville had left behind.

"Easy on that whiskey," Flynn cautioned. "We still have a night's work ahead of us."

"What's the use?" Caldwell nearly spat out the words, then took a long drink. He suddenly flung the empty glass against the wall, where it shattered. "She's gone. I hate to think what that monster Verville has done to her. That bastard murdered my wife, and now he's going to kill Louisa. You don't know what that's like, Flynn, to see two women you love harmed by the same man. Goddamn him."

"We don't know what he's done with her," Flynn said, amazed at Caldwell's sudden rage. "So the best we can do right now is hope for the best. Getting drunk won't solve anything. If the worst has happened, there will be plenty of time for drinking later."

"All right," Caldwell said. He contemplated the bottle. "I don't need the damn stuff, anyhow."

He had just finished putting the bottle down when there was a knock at the door. Flynn got up to let Wilkerson in.

"Anything?" Flynn asked.

Wilkerson shook his head. "No sign of them anywhere. Nobody saw a civilian and a soldier come in late last night."

"And nobody saw you?"

"You mean from the Secret Service? I don't think so. At least, I hope not."

"You'd better hope not," Flynn growled. "Because if any of Lafayette Baker's men saw you, it's likely they followed you here. Which means we can look forward to being arrested at any moment. And you had just better hope that Baker's men get to you before I do."

"You seem convinced that I'm somehow a traitor."

"That's enough, you two," Caldwell interrupted "We have enough enemies as it is without us fighting among ourselves. And in case you haven't noticed, we still haven't found Verville – or Louisa."

"You're right," Flynn said, nodding. "Look, it's getting late. I suggest we get something to eat, and then we try to get some rest. I'm supposed to meet the MacCraes at midnight – and all three of us will be going. If this is the night the MacCraes are supposed to meet the Russian ship, then Verville will be there, too. And in all likelihood, he'll lead us right to Louisa."

Flynn sent Wilkerson down to the hotel kitchen to see if they would send up three plates of food.

"I hope you're right about tonight," Caldwell said, and he settled again into the chair. Flynn noticed that the doctor looked exhausted. His skin had taken on a gray color and there were bags under his eyes. Louisa's disappearance at Verville's hands had been especially hard on him.

"I'm going to ask you something, Doc, and you can tell me to go to hell if you want to. Is there something between you and Louisa?"

"Between us?" Caldwell appeared surprised at the question. "How could we work together that long and not have some sort of relationship?"

"I'm not talking about doctor and nurse," Flynn said. "I'm talking about man and woman."

"Well, Flynn, I believe this is the part where I tell you to go to hell."

Flynn gave a short laugh. "I take that to mean 'yes'."

"Frankly, I don't know what I would do without her." Caldwell's voice began to crack. "She means the world to me, Flynn, and that bastard Verville'd better not harm her."

"He won't," Flynn said. They both knew it was a lie, but Flynn said it anyway, hoping it would make Caldwell feel better.

"Promise me one thing, Flynn. If something happens to me, promise you'll make him pay."

Flynn was staring at the ceiling, his thoughts already on what would happen tonight. "Oh, you'll be able to do that yourself. Just you wait and see."

Chapter 26

"Frightened?" Verville asked, pointing a pistol at Louisa, who sat shivering on the carriage seat across from him.

"No, I'm not frightened," she said. "I'm cold."

"It's going to get a lot colder where we're going," he said.

"Where might that be?"

"You'll find out soon enough."

They rode on in silence. Darkness had fallen once again on the city and the night air had a damp chill that clung to wool cloaks and bare flesh alike. Louisa continued to shiver.

He had considered chloroforming her again to leave the hotel and decided against it. Carrying her up the hotel stairs unconscious last night had been one thing, but carrying her down again in the same state might have raised suspicions. Besides, he wanted her wide awake on her feet tonight, not groggy.

It had been risky, Verville knew, to take her captive. He should have left her behind in the alley, or else killed her. However, at the time he had thought she might prove to be valuable. It was only a question of how, and he had finally struck upon an idea, remembering his last meeting with the Russian captain, Khobotov. He was a lusty man fond of bragging about his whoring.

Why not give Louisa Webster to the Russian? Khobotov could keep her imprisoned on his ship and do what he would with her. Verville would present her as a bonus for delivering the cargo on time. It wasn't that he was generous so much as he was being practical. After he paid off the MacCrae brothers for their help in smuggling the cargo ashore, there would be only just enough money to pay Khobotov the second half of his fee. If Khobotov tried to extort more money, as Verville knew he would, Louisa might be enough to satisfy him.

He noticed Louisa couldn't take her eyes off the pistol still carelessly pointed in her direction.

"This epidemic you're planning, you can't go through with it," she suddenly blurted. "I know where we must be going tonight. We're going to

218

get whatever it is you need to set the bubonic plague loose in the city. That's it, isn't it?"

"You're very observant, Miss Webster," Verville said. "Yes, that's what we're doing tonight."

"I think you're insane," she said. "No country or cause is worth the price."

"My country is worth it," Verville said. His tone was icy, in spite of himself. He had known, of course, that few people agreed with his plan. Still, they had to be struck by the brilliance of it. He had treated Louisa well, doing nothing to compromise her honor in the hotel room, and had hoped she might be somewhat more appreciative, to see things from his viewpoint, at least. He was glad, now, that he planned to hand her over to Khobotov. If the captain didn't want her, then maybe his crew would. If nothing else, Verville would make sure she was pitched into the icy black waters of the Potomac. "You had better save your strength. You're going to need it tonight, one way or another."

They rode in silence to the doors of the tavern. Louisa recognized the place at once.

"So, they're the ones who are going to help you? The owners of this tavern?"

"Once again, Miss Webster, you stun me with your powers of observation." He smiled. "Such a smart woman. Now, I would advise you to remain silent from here on out. The men I'll be dealing with tonight do not share my gentlemanly view of women as creatures to be set on a pedestal and admired."

"How do they see women, then?"

"Really, Miss Webster, you don't need me to answer that, do you? Now, don't forget I have this pistol." He showed her the derringer, then slipped it into his coat pocket, where he kept his hand on it. "If you cry out or try to escape, I won't hesitate to shoot."

They climbed down from the carriage. Verville paid the driver and the iron-rimmed wheels clattered away over the cobblestones. It was a cold, crisp night and nothing else was stirring, so the sound seemed to carry a long way. The tavern itself was lit only by a few lanterns and the flickering light from the fireplace. Only a few gruff, sullen men were gathered around the tables, and they looked up expectantly as Verville and Louisa entered. James and Angus MacCrae were waiting at the bar. It was clear from James' red face and easy grin that the whiskey glass at his elbow had not gone untended, thanks to Harry behind the bar. Angus had no glass, and his face was expressionless as he watched them come in.

"You're early," James MacCrae said, studying Louisa with curiosity. "Not that it matters. I reckon now is as good a time as any."

"Yes," Verville agreed. He was uneasy, feeling the eyes of the men in the dimly lit tavern upon him. He still had the hidden pistol in his pocket trained on Louisa, his cane in his other hand.

"I see you brought some help of your own," MacCrae said, nodding at Louisa. "I didn't know there was a woman involved."

"She's part of my business transaction tonight," Verville said. "A little something extra for the ship we're meeting."

"Aye," MacCrae said in a husky, all-knowing voice, leering at Louisa. He laughed. "Something to sweeten the deal. Ha! I can see that, that I can."

"Is everything ready?" Verville asked. "If so, I think we should get going. There's much to do tonight."

He noticed the MacCrae brothers glance at each other. "Aye, it's all ready," James said. "One of the Russian officers is already with some of our men down at the boats. He's going to guide us to where the Russian ship is anchored."

Angus spoke for the first time. "Everything is ready, but we have some last-minute business to discuss, Dr. Verville. Something we need to settle before we get down to the night's work."

"Fine."

"Harry here can take your lady friend into the back room while we talk, or she can stay here."

"She stays with me."

Angus nodded, then turned to the room filled with men. "All right, lads, get down to the boats. We'll meet you within the hour and we push off at midnight sharp. This gentleman you see here will tell us what to do."

The room soon filled with the sound of chairs scraping away from the tables and the low mumbling and laughter of the men. Verville counted twelve smugglers. They filed out the tavern door in groups of two and three, leaving just him, Louisa, Harry and the MacCraes in the tavern.

"Let's get down to it," James said. He sat up straighter on his stool, and suddenly he looked far more sober than he had just a moment ago. Beside him, Angus had slipped off his own stool and was waiting expectantly, tense as a tomcat about to pounce.

"Is there a problem?" Verville asked. He had expected there might be, that the brothers might try something at the last moment. His hand curled around the pistol in the pocket of his overcoat.

"Not a problem, Dr. Verville, but an opportunity. That cargo we're supposed to take off that Russian ship. You still haven't told us what it is."

"Does it matter?" Verville asked, tightening his grip on the pistol in his pocket. "All you and your men have to do is help me get it off the ship and bring it ashore."

"We're taking risks, Dr. Verville. It seems to me that what you're paying isn't enough for the dangers involved, especially since we don't really know what the cargo might be."

"Opium, that's what it is," Angus said, speaking up for the first time. "The newspaper says there's a Russian warship arriving in the city from China. There's only one sort of cargo worth all this trouble."

"Dangerous work, smuggling," James said. "Hardly worth the amount you've paid us, considering what that opium is worth. You haven't been entirely honest with us. How were we supposed to know what was aboard that ship?"

"Devious, is what it is," Angus hissed. He had appeared, menacing, at Verville's elbow. Verville couldn't recall seeing the man move. "We ought to kill him now, brother, for lying to us, trying to cheat us out of our due. Let's kill him and this strumpet he's brought."

Louisa gulped.

"Not yet, Angus," James said hurriedly. "If killing is what they need, fine. But maybe the doctor here will see the wisdom of the way things are in the world and offer us a percentage of his profits off that Russian ship."

"I don't know," Angus said icily. "I'm for killing him and the woman."

"Half the profits, Verville," James said. "What do you say? Otherwise I let my brother here have you, and we'll take your cargo for our own. Think quickly now, both for your sake – and the woman's."

Verville considered playing along, acting frightened, and agreeing to pay them any percentage they wanted. After all, if the MacCraes wanted a percentage of that cargo of death and disease, they were welcome to it.

However, some part of Verville refused to give in. It was his pride. He would not give these brothers the satisfaction of thinking he was afraid.

Also, there was a more practical matter. The crates they would be smuggling ashore for the most part held plague-infested clothing, not opium. Although the brothers might be feigning outrage now, there was no doubt their anger would be very real if they opened one of the crates while out on the Potomac and discovered it did not hold a fortune in raw opium, but only clothes instead. They might dump his precious cargo into the river, and him along with it.

Verville laughed. "Do you take me for a fool? The woman means nothing to me, and besides that, you won't get any of the cargo from the Russians without me. It's a warship, remember, and I doubt your men are much of a match for a Russian frigate." In his pocket, he cocked both hammers of the twin-barreled derringer.

"What's your answer then, laddie?" James MacCrae's face had grown even more red. "Think careful now, because my brother and I have had enough of your goddamn arrogant Southern foolishness."

"The only foolishness I've heard tonight is your own, MacCrae," Verville said. "You and your brother think you can cheat me out of my cargo by threatening me, but you're both fools. We've already made a deal and you'll abide it, or damn you both!"

James MacCrae lunged at him, but Verville was ready. In the pocket of his coat, he fired both barrels of the derringer in rapid succession. The pistol was not powerful, but fired from point-blank range it knocked MacCrae backward into the bar. He stared down in surprise at the two small, neat holes in his chest. The bullets had gone clean through him, leaving gaping wounds in his back. In shock and horror, his legs began to fail and he slid slowly down the front of the bar, leaving a smear of gore behind him.

That left Angus MacCrae and Harry. They both went for him at once, Harry's thick arms grabbing at him from behind the bar and Angus charging at him. Harry managed to get a grip on his shoulders and began pulling him backwards over the bar, which worked to Verville's advantage. He braced himself against the bar and kicked out at Angus, both feet off the ground. His boots caught the smaller man in the chest and sent him crashing into the chairs and tables on the tavern floor.

The sudden kick broke Harry's grip and Verville shrugged free. He had dropped his cane and he reached to pick it up as Harry came out from behind the bar with a club he used for keeping order in the tavern.

"You'll pay now," Harry growled. "See if you don't."

Harry swung the club in a killing blow at Verville's head, but he managed to knock it aside with his cane so that the club glanced off his shoulder. Verville grunted in pain, but stepped back out of Harry's reach. He took the head of the cane in his right hand and unsheathed the sword concealed inside. The blade slithered free and glittered savagely in the dim light.

"Remember this?" Verville asked.

"That pigsticker don't scare me. You're a dead man." Harry roared and came at him, swinging the club.

For all his years as a fighter, Harry was still big and clumsy. Verville stepped neatly aside, dodging the club as it whistled past his head, and drove the blade into the other man's belly. It sank deep, right to the hilt, and Harry screamed.

Verville needed both hands to pull the sword free. He swung around, the blade dripping blood, to face Angus MacCrae. The man was calmly watching from the shadows of the tavern and he stepped forward with a revolver in his hand.

"Harry didn't learn his lesson about that sword of yours, but neither did you," Angus said. "I believe my brother pulled a gun on you last time and settled the matter. A bullet beats a blade any day. Now put that thing away."

"You're not going to shoot me?"

"Who's going to meet that Russian ship if I kill you?" Angus asked. "No, business is business. James was my brother, but he could be a fool when he lost his temper like he did just now. I might kill you later for James' sake, or I might not. It depends what happens tonight. At any rate, I'd say your whole cargo is forfeit to me."

Verville decided he had better just play along. "I suppose I don't have much choice."

"No, you don't."

Verville wiped the blade on Harry's shirt to clean it, then sheathed it inside the cane. "May I keep it?" he asked Angus, holding up the cane.

The other man shrugged. "Why not? You won't have much chance to use it aboard the boat, and if you try it, one of my men will split your head with an oar before you can get the blade clear."

"Fair enough," Verville said. He felt suprisingly calm, looking down at the two bodies on the floor, but death had never bothered him. Maybe that came from being an Army doctor all those years, and seeing so much of it. Rivulets of blood were now staining the worn boards of the tavern floor. "What about them?"

"I'll have this mess cleaned up later. Right now, we've got to get down to the boats. It's almost midnight and my men will be wondering where we are."

Louisa had stood off to one side during the brief fight, too frozen with fear to even think of escape. She stared in horror at the two dead men. What kind of man would watch his brother be brutally killed, then go on about his business as if nothing had happened? This smuggler must have a heart of stone. She did not protest when Verville took her by the elbow and guided her toward the door.

* * *

The tavern was strangely dark and silent as the carriage carrying Flynn, Caldwell and Wilkerson rolled up outside.

"You two wait in the carriage," Flynn said. "The MacCraes will be expecting me, but it's better if you stay hidden. Once I'm inside, have the driver stop the carriage out of sight around the corner and wait until we leave for the wharves. You can follow us then – just keep a good distance."

"All right," Wilkerson said. He already had his pistol out. "But if anything happens in the tavern, give a shout."

"Put that thing away until you need it," Flynn told him. "You might go accidentally shooting the doctor."

Glaring, Wilkerson slipped the weapon back into his coat pocket. All three of them were tense and beginning to grate on each other's nerves. It had been a long and exhausting day, first searching desperately for Louisa while trying not to be found in turn by Baker's men, then giving up the search and trying to sleep in the cramped hotel room after what had been a largely sleepless night.

Caldwell eyed Flynn grimly. "You sure you know what you're doing? These MacCraes seem like bad people to cross, and Verville is the devil himself."

Flynn winked. "Aye, but it's me they've got to watch out for."

He got out and told the driver to wait. Looking again at the tavern, it seemed awfully dark. If the MacCraes were already gone, there would be no point in hanging around the tavern.

"Are we late?" Flynn whispered.

Caldwell took out his pocket watch and read it by the light from the carriage lanterns. "It's just half past eleven. I thought you said MacCrae told you to be here at midnight?"

"He did. Which is why I'm wondering why it's so quiet." Flynn took out his LeMat revolver. There was something ominously still about the tavern that he didn't like. Something was very wrong, indeed.

Inside, all was dark. He tried the door but it was locked. He rapped on the door, hard, but no one answered.

"I don't understand," Caldwell said, leaning out the carriage door. "Where is everyone?"

"To hell if I know," Flynn replied, then banged the door until it rattled in its frame. "Damnation. I can't believe we've missed them."

Flynn went back and took down a lantern from the carriage, then walked to a window. The glass was grimy, but it allowed enough light inside for Flynn to see at once that the tavern was deserted. He looked closer, noticing that the chairs and tables were in disarray, some having been knocked over. Some kind of scuffle had taken place. He looked again and saw the bodies on the tavern floor. Two of them. Neither was that of a woman, thank God. He thought he recognized Harry, the ex-prizefighter, as being one of them. The other body was clearly that of James MacCrae.

"What is it?" Caldwell asked.

"James MacCrae and one of his men are dead in here."

"What happened?"

"I don't know, but whatever it was, it can't be good."

"Louisa–" Caldwell left the thought unfinished.

"I don't know, Doctor. I don't know." Flynn realized he was nearly shouting at the doctor and lowered his voice. "The best we can hope for now is to catch them at the wharves."

"Someone's coming," Wilkerson warned in a strained voice.

There was a clatter of hooves far up the street. Horses coming at a trot. The riders were still out of sight beyond a curve in the street, but their shapes were backlit and magnified by the gas streetlamps so that their giant-sized shadows flickered over the storefronts and in the fog that had begun to creep off the Potomac.

"Maybe it's the smugglers coming back," Caldwell said.

"Not goddamn likely," Flynn replied, swinging into the carriage. "It must be Colonel Baker and some of his men. Let's go!"

The carriage had no hope of outrunning mounted men. Instead, the driver moved off at an unhurried pace, so that the carriage was already in motion by the time the riders came into view. At first, they ignored the carriage and rode right up to the tavern. Peering from the carriage, Flynn could see drawn guns and the flash of a sword blade. He counted a half dozen soldiers.

"Baker's men, sure enough," Flynn said. "The question is, did they come after us, the MacCraes, or Verville?"

"I don't know who they came after," Wilkerson said. "But it looks like we'll do."

The soldiers had discovered that the tavern was empty. It was hard to say whether or not they noticed the bodies, because they had no lights with them, and so might not have been able to see inside. Their attention now turned to the carriage, which was being driven away at an unhurried pace.

"Here they come."

"Damn," Caldwell said. "If Baker catches us, we'll never find Louisa."

The carriage turned a corner. "Everybody out," Flynn said. "Let's jump and head for the wharves on foot. With any luck, Baker and his men will keep following the carriage."

Flynn flung the door open, and the driver, seeing their intentions, slowed down. All three men jumped to the cobblestoned street. Flynn waved a roll of bills at the driver, then tossed it up to him. The man's white teeth flashed in his dark face, and the carriage rolled on. Flynn and the others ducked into an alley. Less than a minute later, Baker and his men clattered past on the trail of the carriage.

"Let's go," Flynn said. "Maybe we can still catch MacCrae at the wharves."

Chapter 27

MacCrae's men were waiting at the wharves. Verville counted three boats, and he saw two empty wagons at the waterfront, ready for their return with the cargo.

"We have to be back before dawn," Angus explained, nodding at the wagons. "I've bribed the captain in charge of the soldiers guarding the wharves, and he's given us until first light. After that there are no guarantees. That means no foolishness tonight, Verville. We get to this Russian ship, load the cargo, and get back to shore. We'll have just enough time if all goes well – and if it doesn't, you'll be the first to go overboard. You and your lady friend here."

"Believe me, I want the cargo just as badly as you do," Verville replied.

"Good," Angus said. He still carried his pistol and kept it trained on Verville. "That settles it. Into the boat now, and if you try anything foolish you're going straight to the bottom."

They clambered into the boat. It was a sleek wooden skiff, maybe twenty feet in length, with four men manning the oars. Verville and Louisa worked their way forward to the bow and Angus MacCrae sat in the stern.

The Russian officer who was to serve as their guide also sat in the bow. Even in the semi-darkness, Verville was able to recognize Lieutenant Nikolay Sergeyevna, whom he had met nearly a year ago when making his arrangements with Khobotov. Sergeyevna was bundled deep into a heavy wool sea coat, and he looked particularly morose.

"Lieutenant," Verville said. "Is there a problem?"

"No," Sergeyevna said stiffly. "My captain has ordered me to guide your boats to our ship, and that is what I shall do."

Verville suddenly realized he had not considered all the details. "How will we find the ship in the dark?"

"I can guide us using some of the lights and landmarks visible from shore, and the rest I shall leave to my compass. When we are close, I will ask your men to light a lantern, and the ship will fire a flare in answer."

Around them, the smugglers were settling in at their oars. "Cast off," MacCrae ordered. He sniffed at the air. "Damn, but I swear I can smell a fog rolling in. That's the last thing we need tonight."

It took just seconds for his men to untie the skiffs and set to their oars. The night was still and damp, not so much as a breeze disturbed the air, and the bow slid silently across the black surface of the Potomac. Louisa shivered beside him.

Verville knew that before the night was through he would have to kill Angus MacCrae. Certainly, MacCrae was planning to do the same to him, and was likely only waiting until they got the valuable cargo off the Russian ship and safely into the landing boats. After that, MacCrae would have no need of him. Besides, MacCrae would be wanting revenge for his brother's death. He might be acting as if it mattered nothing to him, but a man would have to be cold-hearted indeed to have no reaction to his own brother's death.

It would be a stealthy game they played tonight, each man planning to kill the other and waiting for the right moment. Verville knew he must not lose. The fate of the Confederacy depended upon the outcome of tonight's work. Too much hung in the balance to allow a smuggler's greed to ruin his plans.

Carefully, so as not to attract any attention, Verville balanced his cane across his knees. MacCrae had made the mistake of allowing him to keep it. With a pistol in his hand, MacCrae probably did not consider the cane or the sword it concealed to be much of a threat.

Verville turned the boar's head handle until it was locked securely in place. There were two small catches the head was now aligned with. He pulled the handle hard against them, straight out, and there was a metallic click as the spring-loaded mechanism within was set. MacCrae's men were all busy working their oars, so nobody paid any attention to him as he reached down and unscrewed the brass cap that covered the tip of the cane. The end of the cane now resembled the dark muzzle of a pistol. He kept the cane across his knees, waiting for when the time was right.

"Do you have a pistol with you, Lieutenant?" Verville asked quietly, the creak of oars in their locks and the splash and gurgle of water under the boat masking his voice from MacCrae.

"Yes, I do," Sergeyevna said. "Why?"

"Keep your hand upon it," Verville said. "You'll be needing it before the night is through."

They settled into an uneasy silence as the skiff slipped across the dark river toward the waiting Russian ship.

* * *

"It's too late," Caldwell said. "They're already gone."

As swiftly and silently as possible, the three men had reached the wharves. There was no sign of Verville or the smugglers. The boats carrying them might only have been a few yards off shore, but the night was so dark the smugglers' skiffs would have been swallowed up in the blackness.

"Damn," Flynn said. "Are you much of a swimmer, Wilkerson?"

Nearby, the Potomac River lapped at the waterfront pilings. What they could see of the river's surface appeared black and forbiddingly cold. It had been warmer than usual the last two nights, otherwise there would have been ice on the river. The warmer air and cold water was the perfect combination for a winter fog.

"You can't be serious about swimming out there," Wilkerson said nervously, staring at the river. "We'll drown."

"Don't be a fool, we can't swim after them. But I sure as hell hate to think we've lost them. Once Verville has his cargo ashore, there will be no stopping him. He could land anywhere."

"Louisa's with them, too, I'm sure of it," Caldwell said. "There's no telling what Verville might do to her if we don't find them."

Flynn looked up and down the waterfront. There were no sentries in sight. The only military presence appeared to be an ironclad warship tied up to the dock. The vessel was one of the small ships used to patrol the Potomac and there appeared to be some activity on board. Aside from the ironclad, several large workboats also were tied up to the wharves, but they were far too big for the three of them to handle.

"We could take one of those skiffs," Caldwell said, pointing out several of the smaller craft tied up alongside the larger boats. "They can't be that far ahead of us."

"I'm not about to try," Flynn said. "None of us knows the first thing about boats, and as soon as we got a few feet from shore we wouldn't even be able to tell where we were. That is, unless Wilkerson here knows more about boats than he's letting on."

"I'm not a sailor," Wilkerson protested.

"Then we're out of luck. I know you're concerned about Louisa," Flynn said. "But to go out on that river on a winter's night would be suicide."

"There may be another way," Caldwell said.

"What might that be?"

"There's someone on board that gunboat down there," he said, tugging his uniform back into some kind of order as the three of them sized up the activity on the ironclad. "I am an officer in the United States Army, and that, I believe, is a military vessel. Just follow me."

* * *

"Show a lantern," ordered Lieutenant Sergeyevna. He was peering into the darkness, although it was impossible to see a thing. MacCrae was right about the fog; it was beginning to gather in wisps across the surface of the river.

"Do as he says, boys," MacCrae said. "There's a fog coming, and we want to fetch this cargo and be off the river before it gets thick."

One of the lanterns the smugglers carried was unshuttered and a man held it high. In answer, a rocket shot into the sky, lighting the river with a hazy glow until it hit the water and snuffed out. The smugglers' skiffs were still half a mile from the Russian ship and the men pulled hard on the oars. They had neither seen nor heard any other vessels on the river, so the smugglers kept their lantern held high and the Russian ship answered from time to time with another rocket. After twenty hard minutes at the oars they were alongside. The lieutenant shouted something to the waiting ship's crew in Russian, and a booming voice answered. Verville knew it must be Khobotov. The American smugglers worked their oars expertly and the skiffs coasted silently alongside the huge Russian ship.

Verville saw his chance. As Angus MacCrae stood in the stern to direct his men, he was silhouetted against the lights from the Russian vessel. Verville raised the cane and aimed for MacCrae's chest. There was just enough of a swell on the river to make the boat dip up and down, and holding his aim steady wasn't easy, not even at that short distance. At the last instant, MacCrae saw him and started to shout something – a curse, a warning – when Verville depressed the hidden trigger that fired the weapon.

There was a blinding flash and a sharp crack as the disguised pistol went off. The ball struck MacCrae squarely in the chest, knocking him off his feet. He landed in the river with a splash and sank. Several of his men scrambled toward the stern and reached into the water, practically diving in after MacCrae. But it was too late. He sank like a stone, dead before he hit the water, and there was no hope of finding him in the night-time murk.

When it became apparent that MacCrae was gone, the remaining smugglers turned their attention on Verville. "You bastard!" one of the men in Verville's boat howled before launching himself at Verville.

The lieutenant raised the pistol Verville had warned him to keep handy and the attacker came no closer. However, several of the smugglers were armed, and the cold air resounded with the click of pistol hammers being cocked and the hiss of knives being drawn from their sheaths. Above them, anxious Russian shouts came from the ship.

"Listen, all of you!" Verville shouted. "I'll use my dying breath to tell this warship to blow us all out of the water. MacCrae is dead, but if the rest of you want to live you had better put your weapons away. Better yet, you'll find yourselves well-paid for tonight's work. Lieutenant, tell your shipmates what I just said."

Keeping his pistol trained on the angry smugglers, Sergeyevna called up to the ship in Russian. There were shouts in reply and overhead came the sound of the Russian sailors cocking their own small arms and aiming them down into the skiffs. The smugglers' boats were too close for the Russian ship to depress any of its big guns low enough to fire at the skiffs, but from their vantage point the sailors would still be shooting fish in a barrel with their pistols and navy carbines.

The smugglers could see at once that Verville had the upper hand. Grumbling, they put away their pistols and knives. They had no particular loyalty to MacCrae, and if Verville got them back to shore with money in their pockets, it was all the same to them.

Sergeyevna gave the orders, first in Russian, and then in English. The sailors aboard the *Rynda* put away their weapons, too, and tossed down several lines and unrolled a rope ladder.

"Make the skiffs fast to the lines," Sergeyevna said. "Half of you men wait in the boats and the rest come aboard to help with the cargo."

Within minutes, the orders were obeyed. Verville found himself standing before Khobotov, who seemed even larger than he remembered. The Russian captain was wrapped in an enormous sea cloak and he greeted Verville with a bear hug as if they were long-lost brothers. He appeared to be amused by the scene he had witnessed in the boats.

"Do you Americans ever get along or are you always shooting each other?" he asked with a laugh.

"The man I shot was a traitor," Verville said. "Traitors deserve to die."

"I couldn't agree more," Khobotov said. He looked past Verville to Louisa, who was being helped over the side of the ship by Lieutenant Sergeyevna. The captain's eyes lit up hungrily. "What have we here?"

Louisa started to speak, but Verville slapped her into silence. The lieutenant started toward Verville but Khobotov stopped him with a wave of his hand. He laughed.

"A feisty one," he said.

"You like her?" Verville asked. "Then she's yours."

"Oh, Doctor," Khobotov said. "You are most kind. Bring her along to my cabin, Lieutenant. And you come, too, Doctor. We can finish our arrangements there."

Khobotov's quarters were surprisingly neat, but they smelled of stale saltwater and were cramped for such a big man. "Your cargo is ready to be unloaded, Dr. Verville. It hasn't been touched during our voyage and you may inspect it if you wish."

"That won't be necessary." It was Verville's turn to smile. "Had you opened it, you would all be dead."

Sergeyevna looked unhappily at his captain, but Khobotov ignored him. "Well, I believe it is now up to you to complete your half of the bargain, Dr. Verville."

Verville placed a sack of gold coins on the table. "There's the rest of the money, as we agreed."

Khobotov picked up the sack and felt the heft of it in his paw of a hand. "But I must tell you, Dr. Verville, that this cargo has been difficult. It has made the men uneasy during the entire voyage, which is some distance, I can tell you. I'm afraid the price of our arrangement has gone up."

Verville had expected as much. "That's why I brought you the woman."

Khobotov considered. He looked Louisa up and down. "I see. And what does this woman think of this – or do you Confederates trade in white slaves, as well?"

Louisa tried to stammer some response, but she was clearly too shaken to speak. Verville cut her off. "It's not up to her, Captain. She's yours now. Keep her in your cabin, as a play thing. No one will be the wiser. Besides, if you don't want her, I'll toss her into the river."

Khobotov reached out and felt a loose strand of Louisa's hair. He sighed. "I should hold out for money, but I'm a sentimental man. I like pretty things. You have a deal. Now, let's get this cargo of your unloaded. There's a fog coming up, and you'll want to get back to shore. Besides that, there's no telling when some damn American Navy vessel is going to show up and make things hot for us."

* * *

The USS *Middletown* was an ironclad river gunboat. She carried twelve guns, all neatly hidden now behind their iron shutters. Her dual smokestacks still belched sparks and fumes into the night sky, so she was under steam although the twin armored paddlewheels at her stern were silent. Overall, the *Middletown* was a little more than one hundred feet long. She hardly looked like a boat at all, but more closely resembled a metal trough turned upside down and floated upon the river.

For all her ugliness, the *Middletown* had a tremendous advantage over the more graceful sailing vessels moored at the waterfront, which was that cannonballs bounced harmlessly off her and she had no masts or rigging vulnerable to an enemy's broadsides. Her twin paddlewheels also made her very fast.

A plank had been laid from the dock to the gunboat's deck, and Caldwell marched fearlessly aboard. Flynn and Wilkerson followed. They were stopped by a sentry armed with a short carbine.

"What's your business here, sir?" the sentry asked courteously, noting that two of the visitors were officers.

"We need to see your captain, right away."

The sentry seemed unsure what to do, until a man wearing a naval officer's uniform stepped into the lantern light. "I'm in command of the river squadron here, including this vessel. My name's Captain Mason. What can I do for you?"

"I'm Major Caldwell, and this is Agent Flynn of the Secret Service," Caldwell lied. Flynn thought he sounded very authoritative. "This is Captain Wilkerson from the War Department. We need your ship."

Flynn was sure the captain would have them all tossed overboard. Instead, the man scratched his head and squinted at them in the dim light. "You're from the War Department? Why the hell do you need my ship?"

"To catch a Confederate agent who is trying to smuggle contraband ashore. We were about to arrest him but he was one step ahead of us and put out on the river."

Mason seemed curious, if not convinced. "How long ago?" he asked.

"Maybe twenty, thirty minutes ahead of us."

"Hell, we'll never find them now, not at night, on the river," Captain Mason said. "Good night, gentlemen." He turned to go.

At that moment, far out on the river, a single rocket suddenly arced into the sky.

"Sir–" the sentry began.

"I see it," Mason snapped. He stood for a moment, watching the rocket arc down and wink out. "Looks like your spy is meeting a ship out there. Why don't we go take a look, after all? Come aboard, gentlemen."

Flynn was impressed by how quickly the gunboat got underway. The plank they had used to board the vessel was pulled in, the mooring lines untied, smoke roared from the stacks as the engines were stoked. Sailors ran about the deck performing a hundred small chores. It was all a mystery to Flynn, who was a landlubber through and through.

Captain Mason laughed as he watched the newcomers dodge the busy sailors. "Not used to boats, are you? Army men! Ha! Best thing to do is stay out of the way and let my boys do their job."

Within minutes, the *Middletown* was steaming away from the pier. Caldwell nudged Flynn's shoulder and pointed toward shore.

"Look who just showed up," he said. "We're getting underway just in time."

Several horses were dancing skittishly along the wharf. One of the men was yelling something at the *Middletown*, but the churning steam engine and paddlewheels drowned out the noise. None of the crew noticed the horsemen on shore and the gunboat was quickly leaving the wharf behind to be swallowed up by the night.

"Colonel Baker's men figured out where to find us, after all," Flynn said. "Well, at least we have a head start on them."

"We'll have to come back to shore sometime," Caldwell said.

"By then we'll have proof that you're not a traitor to the Union."

Another rocket lit the sky far out on the Potomac. At the helm, Captain Mason set a course to chase after it. The gunboat's bow cut through the river with impressive speed. It was hard to see the wake, however, because a layer of fog was building along the river's surface. Already the fog swirled and eddied across the deck. Although there was hardly any wind, the night air was bitterly cold, damp and raw.

"We'll never find them if this fog settles in," Caldwell said.

"I believe that's just what our captain is thinking," Flynn said. "He seems to be moving ahead under full steam."

Mason called to them from the wheelhouse, which sat nearly amidships near the twin smokestacks. It was an ugly rectangular box, heavily armored, with several small windows that allowed Mason a full view of the ship's deck. The bow itself was hidden by the sloping angle of the elevated deck.

"Get out of the wind," he said, welcoming them inside. "No sense freezing yourselves. There's coffee, too, if you want it."

"Captain, I can't thank you enough," Caldwell said. "If you hadn't agreed to help us, this bastard would be getting away."

Mason laughed. "Maybe I'm the one who ought to thank you, Major. It can be awful dull duty patrolling the river. As long as these fools keep firing rockets, we shouldn't have any trouble finding them. Any idea what kind of ship this spy of yours was going to meet?"

Flynn and Caldwell looked at each other. They both knew they had to tell Mason the truth, but that it might change his enthusiasm in a hurry.

"We'll be coming up on a Russian warship," Flynn finally said.

Captain Mason stared for several long moments. Then he smiled. "Really?" he said. "A Russian warship? In that case I had better order the men to open the gunports. We don't want to get caught with our britches down around our ankles, do we?"

"You mean there might be a fight?" Wilkerson asked nervously.

"Only if we're lucky," the captain said.

Chapter 28

Aboard the *Rynda*, the first sign of trouble came when the lookout shouted a warning in Russian.

"What's wrong?" Verville asked.

"He's spotted the lights of another vessel headed our way," Khobotov explained. He shrugged his massive shoulders. "It could be anything. Nothing to worry about."

"It might be a Federal patrol boat, sir," Sergeyevna said.

"How close are we to having my boats loaded?" Verville didn't like this situation at all. He knew the smugglers' chances of returning to shore undetected weren't good if a Union vessel was sniffing around on the river after them.

"We'll need another half hour," Sergeyevna said. "Nothing was on deck. Your crates were all stored in the hold in case we should be stopped by an American vessel."

On the quarter-deck now with the ship's officers and Louisa, whom Khobotov had insisted on escorting around the ship, Verville could see the lights of the approaching vessel. It was on a course headed right for them. There would not be enough time to finish loading his precious crates.

"You'll have to fight them off," Verville said. "You could blow their ship right out of the water."

"Are you mad?" Sergeyevna said. "We can't attack an American ship."

Khobotov was laughing, a sound that carried to all corners of the *Rynda*'s deck and seemed to calm the anxious crew, even the smugglers, who were working frantically to fill the skiffs with Verville's cargo. "I appreciate your confidence in our fighting abilities, Doctor, but Lieutenant Sergeyevna is right. We're not about to fire on a United States vessel. At least, not yet, anyway." His voiced boomed across the deck, spouting orders in Russian.

The *Rynda*'s were a well-trained veteran crew to a man and they jumped to see that their captain's orders were carried out. There were several thuds and trundling noises as the gun ports were opened and the heavy guns moved into position.

"My God, he's not going to fire on that other boat, is he?" Louisa asked.

"You heard the captain," Verville warned. "Keep your mouth shut, Miss Webster."

Lights were extinguished and lanterns shuttered. The ship was enveloped in darkness. All loading of the crates had to stop, to keep anyone from tumbling down a ladder. The ship moved downriver, toward a bank of fog that was rolling in from the Chesapeake Bay. The fog billowed upward like the sheer face of a cliff, blotting out the stars above it. Directly over the *Rynda*, a few faint stars were still visible.

"Quiet now!" Khobotov warned the smugglers in English. "So much as a whisper will carry across the water on such a still night. When that patrol boat gets here, all she's going to find in the spot where we were is dark water."

Despite the *Rynda*'s evasive action, the other vessel drew closer. They could clearly hear her churning through the river. Khobotov lifted a telescope to his eye. He looked for a long moment, cursed, then handed the telescope to Sergeyevna. After the first lieutenant had taken a look, the two ship's officers quickly conversed in Russian. Sergeyevna nodded, then hurried off, shouting orders. The ship began to turn, positioning itself so that the *Rynda*'s full broadside would be aimed at the oncoming vessel.

"It's a Union gunboat," Khobotov said. "They must have seen the flares and gotten lucky finding us in the darkness. Lucky or not, if they think I'm going to surrender my ship without a fight, they're making a mistake."

"You can't fire on them," Louisa protested.

Khobotov laughed. "I can't? My dear, you are going to learn many things from me." He leered at her. "But first you are going to learn how a Russian sailor fights."

He gave several orders to his officers, who took their places near the deck guns. The gunboat steamed closer. Aboard the *Rynda*, there was a stillness as if the crew was holding its breath.

Khobotov gave a shout, and the night erupted in fire and smoke. Aboard the gunboat, the Russian sailors could hear wounded Americans screaming in agony. One of the gunboat's cannons flashed, but the shot whined harmlessly past. Then the *Rynda* slipped silently into the wall of fog and disappeared from sight.

* * *

"Damn that son-of-a-bitch!" Captain Mason was howling mad. "How dare he fire on me!"

"They're heading right into the fog, sir," one of the officers in the wheelhouse called. "We'll never find them in that mess."

"Should we go after them, sir?" asked the helmsman.

"No, not yet. Let's see how badly we're hurt first." Mason turned to Caldwell. "That's a Russian ship, you say?"

"Yes."

"Russian or not, damn them! I'll make sure they're on the bottom of the river before the night is through."

The broadside from the Russian ship, fired at such close range, would have been sufficient to sink a wooden vessel the size of the *Middletown*. However, the shot had simply bounced off the iron sides. The worst structural damage occurred when a ball struck one of the ship's smokestacks, knocking it slightly askew.

While the ship had escaped with little damage, its crew wasn't as lucky. The Russian broadside was much crueler to human flesh and the crew was taken by surprise. Blood spread in a crimson sheet near the bow, where a ball had severed a sailor's legs. Another sailor screamed, flopping on deck, where a shard of iron had cut him down like a mower's scythe.

My God, Caldwell thought. It's Antietam all over again.

For a moment, he froze. This wasn't like hospital work. Even on the winter air, the smell of fresh, wet blood was heavy and sickening. He took a deep breath. This was going to be a night when more than one man faced his worst fears, and he would be no exception. The slaughter at Antietam had overwhelmed him. Tonight, he would see if he was able to overcome that old horror.

"I'd better go help the wounded," he announced. "You have medical supplies aboard?"

Captain Mason looked at him in surprise. "You're a doctor?"

"As a matter of fact, I am."

"Of all things, a doctor working for the War Department. Well, there's a small surgery below." Mason surveyed the carnage the broadside had caused. "Damn those bastards!"

Caldwell turned to Wilkerson. "Get below and find whatever supplies you can. We'll need bandages and any tourniquets they have. Don't worry about the rest of it. I'll work on the men below."

Wilkerson hurried away.

Caldwell motioned for Flynn to follow him out to the deck, where the doctor crouched beside the man who had lost his legs. Several sailors stood frozen in place as they stared at their wounded shipmate, shocked by the butchery and the blood that had begun to stain the deck. After all, these were men used to patrol duty, not fighting sea battles.

Wreckage and human carnage were a familiar sight to Caldwell, even if, deep down, he knew he was just as frightened as the men around him. None of that fear showed now as he took command of the wounded.

He unbuckled his sword belt and tossed it to Flynn. "Put this silly thing to use and cut me a length of rope. About two feet ought to do it."

Flynn unsheathed the sword, took the hilt by two hands, and began chopping at some loose lines on the deck. He tossed a section of rope to the doctor.

"You, sailor, are about to bleed to death," Caldwell said, marching up to a man with a gash on his arm. "Sit down now, and put your head above your arm and keep it there. That's it."

With deft movements, Caldwell tied a tourniquet between the gash and the man's shoulder. The flow of blood lessened considerably. "That will do for now. Keep that arm up in the air unless you want to die. Some of you others help him below until I can finish up here."

Caldwell glanced at the man with the severed legs, but there was nothing he could do there. Already, the life had drained out of him, making the deck slippery with blood.

Quickly, he moved on to a young sailor pinned beneath the leaning smokestack. He had guessed that this boy was already dead or soon would be, because the weight pressing down on him was nothing short of tremendous.

Wilkerson came running up with the supplies.

"He can't breathe," Wilkerson pointed out.

"That's obvious," Caldwell snapped.

Caldwell crouched beside the boy and felt over his body. "His throat is crushed," he said calmly. "The first thing we have to do is get this damn stovepipe off him. Flynn, can we move this thing?"

"We can sure as hell try."

Flynn squatted, put his hands under the leaning smokestack, and heaved. At first, nothing happened. Then Flynn adjusted his grip and heaved again. A low, animal growl rumbled from somewhere deep in his chest and the veins stood out like taut ropes on his neck. Slowly, the smokestack shifted just a fraction of an inch.

"I'll be damned," an amazed sailor remarked.

"Lend a hand!" Caldwell barked. "What the hell's the matter with you?"

Quickly, men jumped forward to push against the smokestack while others helped Caldwell drag the boy free. The sailor flopped on the deck like a fish on a river bank, struggling to breathe as his hands clawed at his crushed windpipe.

"Look out!"

With a groan of rending iron, the smokestack settled at an even more pronounced angle. Only the guy wires holding it in place kept the entire smokestack from toppling over. Still, smoke poured from the top and also from the gap that had developed where the stack met the deck.

"Flynn, hand me back my sword for a moment."

Caldwell produced his medical "housewife" from a deep pocket of his uniform coat. The small leather satchel was lined with velvet, with several wicked-looking instruments held in place with straps and loops. He selected a small scalpel and laid it atop the open case, ready for use. Using the tip of a probe, he worked loose a strand of wire from the sword's grip and unwound it. Then, taking a pencil stub from another pocket, he wound the wire tightly around it, then slipped the pencil out to reveal a tube made from the neatly coiled wire.

"What are you doing?" Wilkerson asked.

"Hold him," Caldwell said by way of explanation. "There's not much time."

As several hands gripped the sailor, Caldwell tilted the sailor's chin back to fully reveal his crushed throat, and with his left hand he covered the man's eyes. He picked up the scalpel in his right hand, poised it over the white skin, calculating, then quickly made a deep incision. No sooner was the cut made than he had inserted the metal tubing.

Air rushed into the sailor's lungs. After a few moments, a healthy pink flush began to return to overtake the blue color of his face.

"That's it," Caldwell said. "Feels better to breathe, doesn't it? Your lungs know just what to do. You'll be fine now, lad. We'll get you to a hospital, where we can take care of that crushed throat, and then you'll be good enough to go home, I dare say."

"That's amazing," Flynn said. "That man would have died otherwise. Wherever did you learn that?"

"Out West a trooper took an arrow in the throat. I made him a new breathing hole lower down with a penknife and a bit of wire off a sword grip, and that lasted him until the arrow wound healed."

"I'll be damned."

"Well, that's the worst of it," Caldwell said. "I'll go below and see what I can do for the others."

He went below and found the surgery. It was cramped and poorly lit, but it would suffice. Several of the wounded were waiting for him there. Caldwell found an apron and set to work. It wasn't long before one of the gunboat's boys appeared with a pot of coffee and a bottle of whiskey.

"The captain sent these, sir, thinking you might need them."

Caldwell smiled and reached for the coffeepot. "My compliments to Captain Mason. Give the whiskey to the wounded. They need it more than I do."

* * *

The *Middletown* floated blindly in the fog, feeling its way along the dark Potomac.

"I know these waters better than the reflection of my own face in the mirror," Captain Mason muttered to Flynn as the two men stood side by side in the wheelhouse. Only the dim light from a shuttered lantern lit the space. Mason had ordered the rest of the ship's lights extinguished so that the Russian captain wouldn't spot them coming. The only sound came from the thrum of the engine and splash of the paddlewheel inside its armored casing, but that couldn't be helped. "But in this damn fog I might as well have my eyes shut."

"If it's any consolation, Captain, remember that the Russians are just as blind as we are."

Mason grunted. "Let's just hope we don't run aground in this mess, or worse yet, run down some other vessel."

"Are you sure you don't want to show a light?"

"And have those bastards rake us again? Not a chance."

"They must not have any lights, either."

"That Russian captain is no fool. He knows he's hurt us with that broadside, but he knows his ship is no match for an ironclad. He'll try to run. Unless, of course, he actually intends to try and sink us. They can throw a lot of iron at us, and you never know when he might get a lucky hit."

"So what do we do?" Flynn was the first to admit he was no mariner.

"Ever hunt bear?"

"Can't say as I have," Flynn said.

"I used to when I was a boy. The last thing you want to do is wound a bear and then have to go into the woods after him. You know why? Because you can't see him until the last instant. And by that time, that bear will be charging you." Captain Mason grinned. "We're the bear."

Flynn grinned back. "I like the way you think, Captain. I do, indeed."

He had hardly finished speaking when two shots rang out nearby on the deck.

"What the hell was that?"

Mason ordered another officer to take the helm, and the captain ran

241

outside with Flynn. Most of the sailors were below, manning the guns, but they found Wilkerson sprawled on deck with a smoking pistol in his hand.

"Wilkerson, what the hell is going on?"

"I'm sorry," he sputtered. "I fell."

"What are you doing roaming the deck with a revolver in your hand?" Flynn asked, helping Wilkerson to his feet.

"I thought I saw something ahead in the fog and I thought it was the other ship," he said. "I must have tripped in the darkness and the gun went off."

"You're not going to sink a warship with a pistol," Mason said. "Besides that, you're damn lucky you didn't fall overboard. We'd never find you on a night like this. Now put that gun away before you make any more noise with it and tell the Russians where we are – if you haven't already done that."

* * *

Aboard the *Rynda*, the sound of the pistol shots was heard as clearly as twin thunderclaps. As he stood on the quarter-deck with Verville and Louisa, Khobotov quietly gave the order to swing the ship around.

"We're going to drift right toward them," Khobotov said. "Then we'll give these Americans another broadside. We'll show them how real sailors fight."

"Can you sink them?" Verville asked.

"We'll know the answer shortly, Doctor, won't we?"

Now, they could now hear the gunboat's churning engines cut through the river. The *Rynda* itself was silent, ghostly. As the two men stood peering toward the sound of the Union gunboat, Louisa slipped toward the lantern mounted near the wheel. Like the rest of the lights on deck, it, too, was shuttered.

She uncovered the lantern, filling the foggy air with a bright halo of light.

Immediately, there were shouts from the Union gunboat. Any hope of ambushing the other vessel had vanished.

"Damn you!" Khobotov shouted. He crossed the distance to her in two quick steps and slapped her, knocking her to the deck. "What the hell have you done?"

Even if he had expected an answer, Khobotov never would have heard it. The *Middletown* fired its four port guns in a deafening volley. Shot whistled through the rigging and pounded the oak sides of the *Rynda*. The Russian ship fired its own broadside, but the shot only glanced off the gunboat's iron plating. The gunboat fired again and the Russian ship lurched underfoot.

"Captain, this is madness!" cried Lieutenant Sergeyevna. "This is an act of war against the United States."

Khobotov ignored him and turned to Verville. "Lock this bitch you've brought aboard my ship in my cabin where she can't cause any more trouble," he said.

Verville pulled Louisa up and half-carried, half-dragged her toward Khobotov's cabin. Around them, the deck had been transformed into a scene from hell. Some of the *Middletown*'s guns had been loaded with canisters of grapeshot, which had mauled the Russian crew as effectively as a giant shotgun. The deck ran with blood like a charnel house and wounded men cried out in agony. Still, the sailors fought on, running their heavy guns in and out, firing and reloading. Answering fire came steadily from the Union vessel, which had fewer guns but was bringing them to bear with telling effect.

They reached the Russian captain's quarters. "You stay in here," Verville warned as he shoved her inside. "After Khobotov has fought these Yankees off or lost them again in the fog, there will be plenty of time to deal with you."

He locked the door and rushed back toward where he had left Khobotov. Verville was amazed at the carnage. He noticed, too, that the ship was listing a few degrees. Had the gunboat damaged her that badly?

"You must strike the colors, sir," Sergeyevna was saying. "They're going to sink us."

"What's happening?" Verville demanded. "Half of my cargo is still down in the hold. You can't surrender."

"I'm afraid my first officer is right," Khobotov said. "We could fire at that ironclad all night and not sink her while she took her time cutting us to pieces."

He gave the order to cease fire and strike the flag.

"You can't surrender!" Verville shouted. "What about my cargo?"

"Your damn cargo has hung over us like a pall this whole voyage," Sergeyevna said. "It's your fault this is happening."

"The last of the boxes must be brought up," Verville insisted. "If I can get them into the skiffs, I can still get to shore."

"Captain," Sergeyevna protested. "This man has brought this on us!"

"No, Lieutenant, I have," Khobotov said. He turned to face Verville. "If any of your smugglers are still alive, you're welcome to try to get your cargo off. You'll have a few minutes yet, and your skiffs are out of sight on the opposite side of the ship. Do what you must."

Verville hurried away. The firing had stopped between the two ships, but

243

the silence left by the big guns was filled by the screaming of the wounded aboard the *Rynda*. An officer on the gunboat hailed the Russian ship and indicated that the Union vessel would be sending over a boarding party.

"As you wish," Khobotov shouted back in English. "We surrender."

Chapter 29

"Damn," Captain Mason said as his crew prepared to lower the boats that would bring them across to the *Rynda*. "I haven't got enough men for this."

"The Russians don't know how many you have aboard," Flynn said. "Send twenty men. That will look respectable."

"I don't know," Mason said. "Twenty men isn't much of a boarding party. There must be one hundred men in that crew, at least. If they decide to fight, there's no way we can stop them."

"Just keep your guns trained on them," Flynn said. "If they give us any trouble, fire away. That will remind them why they struck their colors."

"If I send twenty men with you, I'll barely have enough to man the four guns on the port side."

"The Russians won't know that," Flynn said. "Besides, you've damaged their ship and they're in American waters. Russia is very, very far away. What choice do they have but to surrender?"

"All right," Mason finally agreed. He moved off, shouting orders.

Flynn turned to Wilkerson. "Coming?" he asked.

"Wouldn't miss it for the world," the captain said. He had his revolver ready in his hand.

"Just don't shoot yourself in the foot," said Flynn, who was still holding Caldwell's old cavalry saber. It wasn't as dull as the doctor had claimed, and while it would have been a clumsy weapon in another man's hand, to Flynn it felt light as a hickory switch. "You damn near got us sunk before, when you slipped and your revolver went off."

They went down the steeply pitched side of the *Middletown* and crawled aboard one of the two launches that now bobbed on the Potomac. Neither man was comfortable aboard boats, and they gritted their teeth anxiously as Mason's hand-picked men quickly crowded into the launches. Within moments, the crew was rowing steadily toward the Russian ship.

* * *

245

Captain Khobotov watched the Americans approach the wounded *Rynda*. Although he had surrendered the ship, the look on his face was still fierce. This was a disgrace, he knew, allowing a Russian frigate to lose a battle to what was merely a river gunboat. Of course, the rational part of his mind had agreed with Lieutenant Sergeyevna that their only choice was surrender. The tough little ironclad would chew them to pieces in a fight. But as he watched the boarding party approach, a much stronger emotion built in Khobotov's heart. It was pride.

The American boats were just bumping against the *Rynda* when Khobotov bellowed across the deck, taking his crew by surprise. "Fight!" he roared, holding his own cutlass high. The lights on deck reflected in the steel and he waved the gleaming blade like a torch. "No surrender! We fight!"

Moments later, the Union sailors swarmed over the side. They were well-armed with swords and pistols, but vastly outnumbered by the Russian crew. Only the fact that the Russian sailors had dejectedly been preparing for surrender kept the Americans from instantly being overwhelmed. Within moments the *Rynda*'s deck was in turmoil with fighting men.

"Kill them!" Roaring like a bear, Khobotov charged toward the Americans, swinging his heavy cutlass. His men saw him and threw themselves into the fight. Those without weapons grabbed anything handy to use as a club. One sailor even fell upon the boarders with nothing more than a mop.

Khobotov confronted an American sailor who was dwarfed by the big captain. Still roaring, Khobotov cut the man down and jumped toward his next victim. He slashed at a man wearing an officer's uniform, but was surprised when his blade was halted in mid-strike with a jolt of ringing steel. Khobotov found himself staring at an American just as big as he was, armed with a wicked-looking cavalry saber. He disentangled his blade and swung at the man, who parried the blow and whipped his own sword at the captain. Khobotov dodged aside, cursed, and thrust again at the big American.

All around them similar battles were being fought man to man. A Russian sailor howled in agony as an American rammed a sword between his ribs. Screaming for revenge, a Russian sailor swung the heavy swabber from one of the *Rynda*'s deck guns and split the American sailor's head. The deck, already slippery with gore after the *Middletown* had raked the Russian ship with grapeshot, began to run with fresh blood.

Khobotov and Flynn were locked in a duel all their own. Sword combat for any length of time is exhausting, but both men were big enough to handle the heavy swords with ease and their blades clashed and parried as the other fighting swirled around them. Finally, Khobotov slipped in the blood, throwing him off balance. A gentleman might have waited for him to recover to fight gamely on. But not Flynn. He drove the saber with all his might into the Russian captain's belly. Khobotov stared in amazement at the sword buried up to the hilt in his body. Then Flynn dragged it free, the blade making a horrible wet sucking sound. Khobotov staggered backwards and fell.

Nearby, Lieutenant Sergeyevna witnessed the captain's death. He was fighting savagely because his ship and his comrades were under attack. But with Khobotov's death, he was next in command. Briefly, he looked around at the pandemonium on deck and thought, *This is madness.* There was no question they could defeat the badly outnumbered boarders, but then the guns of the ironclad barely one hundred feet away would make short work of the *Rynda*. If they escaped the ironclad, they were still deep in American waters. With the heavy federal blockade patrols, they would never reach the open seas.

His mind made up, Sergeyevna dropped his sword and climbed several feet up the rope ladder on the mainmast so that he could be seen by all on deck. Then he shouted first in Russian, then in English, "Stop fighting! Men of the *Rynda*, put down your weapons!"

The American officers took up the cry. The fighting died out as quickly as it had begun. Some of the exhausted sailors on both sides threw themselves down on the crimson-stained deck, gasping for breath.

Flynn looked around for Wilkerson but he was nowhere to be seen. He ran up to Sergeyevna, who was shouting orders in Russian from the ladder. "Where's Verville?" he demanded, hoping the man spoke English.

"He's below, still trying to load his damned cargo," Sergeyevna shouted back. "He's to blame for this disaster."

Sword in hand, Flynn went to find Verville. The Russian ship was large, but there would be no hiding aboard it. He plunged down ladders and through dark gun rooms, shouting, "Verville! Where the hell are you? It's over, give yourself up!"

At the last instant, Flynn saw the bright blade flash toward him in the dim lantern light and tried to twist out of the way. The sword stabbed through his coat and cut down to the bone, glancing off his ribcage. The slicing steel felt like a red-hot flame. The blade darted in again, but Flynn beat it aside with the heavy saber. The thinner sword snapped.

"Verville!" Flynn cried, finding himself face to face with the spy he had hunted so long. Verville was taller than he had imagined, with dark eyes and long dark hair. In the dim light in the ship's belly, he looked deranged, and he was still holding the hilt of his broken cane sword.

"I should have known those cowards in Richmond would send someone to try and stop me," Verville hissed. "It's too late."

"I don't think so. Your cargo of plague is never getting to shore. One of the Russian officers already told me you didn't get it all unloaded."

"Captain Khobotov told you that?"

"The captain? He's dead." Flynn smiled maliciously. "I rammed this sword through his guts. Whoever was next in command had the good sense to surrender."

"That was Lieutenant Sergeyevna," Verville said. "He seems to suffer from some misguided sense of duty. Khobotov just wanted my money. But it doesn't matter now. You're too late."

"What the hell are you talking about? We're in command of this ship now."

"You're forgetting about Captain Wilkerson."

"What?"

"Whose side do you think he was on?" It was Verville's turn to smile, an expression so evil-looking that it made Flynn's skin crawl. "Wilkerson and the smugglers are already gone with what we managed to load into the skiffs. You see, you're much too late."

"Wilkerson?" Flynn was shocked.

"Yes," Verville said, smiling. "He's one of ours – or mine, I should say. You never even guessed, did you?"

"That bastard," Flynn said. He should have trusted his misgivings about Wilkerson.

"I knew you or someone like you would come after me, so I had him take the skiffs. I used myself as a decoy." He glanced down at Flynn's sword wound. It was bleeding freely, but it wasn't life-threatening. "Pity I didn't kill you in the process, although I imagine that hurts quite a bit."

"You bastard."

"Go ahead and kill me now," Verville said, opening his coat to expose his immaculate white shirt. "Run me through with your sword. I'm not afraid to die for my country."

Verville closed his eyes. The look on his face was utterly peaceful.

Flynn leveled the saber, drew it back.

"No," he said, stopping himself. "Not yet. What did you do to Louisa Webster?"

"Caldwell's woman?" Verville laughed. "She's locked in Captain Khobotov's cabin."

Relief swept over Flynn. So, Louisa wasn't dead, after all. But he wasn't through with Verville. Keeping the sword tip near Verville's throat, he took down two lanterns hanging nearby and handed them to the other man. "Lead me to the hold," he said. "I want to see the rest of this cargo of yours."

Verville shrugged. "This way. But it doesn't matter. We got at least half of it off the ship."

"What are you bringing ashore?" Flynn asked. "More rats, like you let loose at the hospital?"

"No, large numbers of rats wouldn't be practical to keep alive on such a long voyage, especially if they had the plague. The cargo is made up of the clothes and blankets of European plague victims in China."

"Clothes? I don't understand."

"The clothing is to be sold in the streets and second-hand shops. That's how the disease will spread."

Now Flynn understood. He had seen how quickly and painfully the plague killed its victims, and he was horrified by Verville's plan. "This is madness," Flynn said.

Verville only laughed.

They were already deep inside the *Rynda*. Khobotov had ordered the cargo loaded into the deepest part of the ship, down in the lower hold with the ballast. That was why it had taken so long to unload the crates. He wouldn't have his own men touch the cargo, but let the smugglers handle the crates. Verville led them to a square hatch into which a ladder descended into the hold.

"The rest of the crates are in there."

Flynn leveled the sword at Verville's chest. "Get down that ladder."

Some of the smirk that constantly played over Verville's lips disappeared. "Why don't you just kill me now?"

"I will if you don't get in that hold."

"What are you going to do, lock me up in there until I can be brought to shore for a proper hanging?"

"Something like that."

"None of that will matter, you realize, once Wilkerson gets that cargo to shore."

Verville started down the ladder. Flynn passed him the extra lantern. He wanted Verville to see everything that was going to happen to him. "See you in hell, you bastard," Flynn said.

Verville was still looking up, puzzled, when Flynn shut the hatch cover and latched it. Too late, Verville must have realized his fate. He banged on the hatch, shouting, but Flynn ignored him. It was just the sort of dark place where Jefferson Verville belonged, he thought.

Flynn climbed back up to the deck. The wounded were already being helped, and he was amazed to see Louisa moving among the prostrate men on deck, carrying bandages and water.

"Louisa!" he cried, running up and taking her by the arms. "You're all right!"

"I was locked in the captain's quarters," Louisa said. "Lieutenant Sergeyevna let me out."

"Caldwell is going to be glad to see you alive and well," Flynn said, smiling. "The man has been worried sick."

"Well," she said. Even in the darkness on deck, Flynn could have sworn she was blushing. "I'll be glad to see him, too. Did you find Verville?"

"Yes. He's the one who's locked up now," Flynn said. "I put him down in the hold."

She noticed his bloody shirt. "You're hurt," she said. "Let me help you."

"It's not as bad as it looks," he said. "I'll be all right. What I really want to do right now is find Wilkerson. Have you seen him?"

"No," said Louisa. "Did he come aboard with you?"

"I'm afraid so."

There was a shout from the *Middletown*, which had drawn up within hailing distance of the *Rynda*. Captain Mason was on deck, calling for Flynn.

"What is it?" he shouted back. "Everything is secure here."

"It looks like one of the smugglers' boats got away," Mason shouted. "I'm going after it. What do you want me to do with it?"

"Blow it out of the water!" Flynn responded. He was sure it must be Wilkerson. If he got to shore with the plague-infested cargo, the Rebel Fever might yet spread through Washington City.

The *Middletown* steamed off. Now that the fog had lifted, the skiff heading toward shore was clearly visible in the starlight. The ironclad quickly gained on it and one of its forward guns fired on the skiff. A splash erupted beside the small boat, but the smugglers aboard kept rowing. Another gun fired, and the wooden craft disappeared in a shower of splinters and water. Wilkerson and the cargo of plague sank to the bottom of the river.

Within minutes, the *Middletown* had drawn up once more alongside the Russian vessel, which was beginning to list. The ironclad's guns had holed the *Rynda* below the waterline.

Flynn found Sergeyevna. "Lieutenant, we need to get everyone off this ship. Give the orders and come with me."

They climbed into the skiff the smugglers had not taken. "Why did they leave this one?" Flynn asked Sergeyevna.

"They probably only had enough men for one boat. This one is loaded with crates of raw opium. The other cargo is what Verville really wanted," he said.

"Well, it's at the bottom of the Potomac now, thank God."

They took several of the less severely wounded Americans with them and crossed the open water between the wooden ship and the ironclad. Louisa also went with them.

Caldwell was on deck, ready to help the next influx of wounded, when he saw Louisa. He swept her into his arms. "My God," he said, his voice cracking. "I thought you were gone."

"Oh, William," Louisa said, holding him. "I thought I would never see you again."

"Did he.... Did Verville hurt you?"

"No," she said. "I was just so much baggage to him. He traded me to the Russian captain for helping him smuggle the cargo."

"That bastard," Caldwell said. He studied Louisa's face. "You must be exhausted. You should go lie down. The captain already offered the use of his cabin."

"No," she said resolutely. "I'm a nurse. I'm going to help the wounded."

Caldwell smiled. "Well, I'm a doctor. A doctor always needs a good nurse."

He and Louisa held each other a moment longer. Then Louisa turned to Flynn and asked, "Did you ever find Captain Wilkerson?"

"He's dead," Flynn said. "He was trying to get away with the cargo of plague."

"What?"

"Our friend Wilkerson was part of the conspiracy. Verville told me everything."

As Louisa and Caldwell stared at him in disbelief, Flynn told them what had happened and how Verville intended to spread the plague.

"He fooled us all," Caldwell said when Flynn was finished.

"Verville was even more clever than we thought. He was manipulating us the whole time, making sure the Secret Service pursued you and not him."

Caldwell shook his head in disbelief, then turned his attention to the wounded. More launches were on the way, carrying Russian sailors toward the *Middletown*.

Captain Mason watched them coming. "What the hell are they doing, trying to board us?"

"No," Flynn said. "I told Lieutenant Sergeyevna here to bring his men aboard."

"Why?"

Flynn gestured around him at the carnage on deck. "How do you intend to explain all of this?"

"That's not my job," Mason said. "You're from the War Department–"

Flynn shook his head. "No, I'm not. None of us are."

"What are you talking about?"

"It doesn't matter, Captain. All that's important is that the cargo aboard that ship will never reach shore now. There was a Confederate spy on board who was trying to start an epidemic with clothes and blankets from bubonic plague victims. We're telling the truth about that."

"Then I suppose it was worth it," Mason said.

"But how are you going to explain a sea battle between a United States ship and one of her European allies?"

"I don't know," Captain Mason said, clearly overwhelmed. "I thought I would just explain what happened in the regular course of duty–"

"No one would believe you," Flynn said. "Smuggled cargo? That was reason to start a war with Russia?"

"You tricked me," Mason said angrily.

"There's a way out of this," Flynn said. He looked at Sergeyevna. "You understand what I'm talking about?"

Sergeyevna nodded. "Sink it."

Mason stared. "What?"

"Yes," Flynn said. "Sink it. She's already taking on water and you can hurry the end before someone else comes along and we have more explaining to do."

"I don't know–"

"You see, there was a fire aboard and you went to investigate. Your men and the Russian crew were hurt during the explosion–"

Sergeyevna was nodding. "Yes, the powder magazine exploded. That explains all the noise and injuries. Captain Khobotov was killed in the blast. You took on the survivors and the *Rynda* sank."

Mason nodded slowly. "I see. None of the crew speaks English, I take it?"

"No one whose story will matter," Sergeyevna said.

Flynn smiled. "Good. It's all settled then. I'm leaving now."

"Why?"

"Maybe Dr. Caldwell can explain it to you. I'll take one of the skiffs and head to the Virginia shore."

"The Confederates will snatch you up," Mason warned.

"That's the idea," Flynn said.

He went down the side of the ironclad again, to the partially loaded smugglers' skiff they had rowed over from the *Rynda*. The crates were filled with raw opium, worth a fortune for medicinal purposes in the Confederacy.

He would make a fortune – and then some. Flynn took the oars. He would have been the first to admit he was no seaman, but the night was now clear and he could see the Virginia shore. The wound Verville had given him was minor enough, and he doubted he would have any trouble rowing across.

From high up on deck, Caldwell and Louisa saw him in the skiff. They didn't try to stop him. There would be explanations enough for all aboard without a Confederate agent involving himself in the mix. He raised his hand in farewell. Caldwell and Louisa waved back, standing side by side.

Flynn leaned into the oars and the skiff slid across the water. He quickly left the *Middletown* behind. They were lucky, he thought, that Wilkerson hadn't made it any farther with his cargo of plague before the ironclad caught up to him. Flynn shook his head, amazed that Wilkerson had fooled them. He must have been one of Verville's conspirators all along. He had even managed to hoodwink the United States Secretary of War. The South had lost a valuable spy, even if Wilkerson had been as twisted as Verville if he thought the only way to victory was through unleashing the plague on the Union.

Wilkerson had helped pin the blame for the Rebel Fever conspiracy squarely on Caldwell. He had helped the doctor and Flynn stay a jump ahead of Lafayette Baker's men, thus keeping Baker on Caldwell's trail. Verville had been able to carry out his plot without any interference because the United States Secret Service was pursuing the wrong man.

In the distance, the ironclad's guns boomed again and again. The dark hulk of the *Rynda* settled lower into the water, carrying its remaining cargo of plague deep into the Potomac. He thought of Jefferson Verville trapped in the hold as the cold river water swirled around him. Verville was drowning with all his twisted dreams.

Flynn smiled and rowed toward Virginia.

* * *

Colonel Lafayette Baker and his men were waiting at the wharf when the *Middletown* steamed in after midnight. Baker stormed aboard, worked up into a fury because his quarry had escaped him earlier that night, making a fool out of him in front of his men.

"You!" he shouted, pointing out Caldwell on the deck, where he was tending the wounded. "You're under arrest! You'll hang for this, I can promise you."

Secret Service men swarmed toward the doctor.

Captain Mason stepped forward to block their path. "You're not arresting anyone," Mason said.

Baker's voice held a dangerous note. "Captain, I'm warning you not to interfere—"

"Or what?" Mason demanded.

Baker appeared to look around the deck of the gunboat for the first time. He and his men were surrounded by sailors whose faces were black with gunpowder. The whites of their eyes stood out in an otherworldly manner. Some of their uniforms were coated with gore or splashed by blood. Their hands were on the revolvers stuck in their belts or else on the cutlasses that gleamed in the starlight. Everywhere the gunboat showed the marks of battle in the battered armored walls of the wheelhouse and the glistening stains of blood on the deck. The captured Russian sailors stood in a group nearby under heavy guard. Wounded littered the deck, wrapped in blankets against the Potomac's wintry chill.

"My God," Baker said, clearly appalled. The fire seemed to go out of him. "Are those Confederate sailors you've captured? We heard guns in the distance, out on the river. What the hell happened?"

"Those are Russians," Captain Mason said. He had decided to tell Baker the truth. The man could tell the public some other story if he liked. "We sank their ship."

"What the hell are you talking about?"

"It's been quite a night." Captain Mason pointed to Caldwell and smiled. "You see, this man here just saved the Union."

Epilogue

WASHINGTON CITY, JANUARY 1863

Church bells rang on New Year's Day and the city's population of free blacks and former slaves alike rejoiced. President Abraham Lincoln had signed the emancipation proclamation, freeing the slaves.

For Caldwell and Louisa Webster, it was simply another day of work. They had given most of the other staff members the day off and made the rounds of the hospital themselves. Caldwell examined the soldiers' wounds and Louisa worked beside him, bathing feverish foreheads and handing out tin mugs of beef tea.

"The proclamation is one more nail in the coffin of the Confederacy," Louisa remarked, standing briefly by an open doorway to listen to the ringing bells. The day was cold and crisp; the breeze felt refreshing compared to the close air of the hospital. "It's one more sign that the Union cause is more moral than that of the South."

"All I know is that I chose the right side," Caldwell said, joining her in the doorway. "Virginia is my home, but the United States is my country."

Under different circumstances the two of them might have been heroes, having worked to stop Jefferson Verville's evil plot to spread bubonic plague throughout the Union. Even the outbreak of pneumonic plague in Swampoodle had been contained. In the wake of the battle at Fredericksburg and the controversy over the emancipation proclamation, the death of a score of poor Irish immigrants had received little attention.

Of course, the real story behind Jefferson Verville's plot could never be made public. Caldwell and Louisa had been sent back to work in the hospital, anonymous once again, on the run from Lafayette Baker and the Secret Service no longer.

The official story remained the one that Flynn and Lieutenant Sergeyevna had agreed upon aboard the *Middletown*. The newspapers reported that the Russian *Rynda* had caught fire in the Potomac. There was an explosion. The survivors had been plucked from the sinking ship by the *Middletown*'s crew.

"I'm so glad it's all over," Louisa said, lingering with Caldwell in the doorway.

"It won't truly be over until the Union wins the war," Caldwell said. "That's the day I'm waiting for."

"In that case, Dr. Caldwell, I believe I shall wait with you."

Smiling, Caldwell reached for her hand, and they stood in the open doorway, listening to the ringing bells.

*

Printed in the United States
1382900004B/127-129

9 781413 70005